DIANNA

PRAISE FOR THE *NEW YORK TIMES* BESTSELLING BELADOR SERIES:

RISE OF THE GRYPHON

"...It's been a very long time since I've felt this passionate about getting the next installment in a series. Even J. K. Rowling's Harry Potter books. It's a story you don't want to end and when it does, you can't help but scream out 'No! NO THEY DID NOT JUST DO THIS TO ME!! NO!!!!'" ~~Bryonna Nobles, Demons, Dreams and Dragon Wings

"...shocking developments and a whopper of an ending... and I may have exclaimed aloud more than once...Bottom line: I really kind of loved it." ~~Jen, Amazon Top 500 Reviewer

"I want more Feenix. I loved this book so much...If you have not read this series, once again, what are you waiting for?" ~~Barb, The Reading Cafe

"..fantastic continuation of the Belador series. The action starts on page one and blows you away to the very end." ~~Fresh Fiction

THE CURSE

"The Beladors series is beloved and intricate. It's surprising that such a diverse and incredible world has only three books out." ~~Jessie Potts, USA Today, Happy Ever After

"The precarious action and genuine emotion in THE CURSE will continuously leave the reader breathless...a mesmerizing urban fantasy story overflowing with heartfelt emotions and dramatically life-altering incidents." ~~Amelia Richards, Single Titles

"If you're looking for a series with an epic scope and intricate, bold characters, look no further than the Belador series...This new addition provides all the action and intrigue that readers have come to expect...a series to be savored by urban fantasy and paranormal romance fans alike." ~~Bridget, The Romance Reviews

ALTERANT

"There are SO many things in this series that I want to learn more about; there's no way I could list them all... have me on tenterhooks waiting for the third BELADOR book. As Evalle would say, 'Bring it on.'" ~~Lily, Romance Junkies Reviews

"An incredible heart-jolting roller-coaster ride...An action-packed adventure with an engrossing story line and characters you will grow to love." ~~ Mother/Gamer/Writer

"An intriguing series that has plenty of fascinating characters to ponder." ~~ Night Owl Reviews

BLOOD TRINITY

"BLOOD TRINITY is an ingenious urban fantasy with imaginative magical scenarios, characters who grab your every thought and more than a few unpredictable turns ...The paranormal action is instantaneous, while perilous suspense continuously escalates to grand proportions before the tension-filled and satisfying conclusion. The meticulous storyline of Book One in the Belador series will enthrall you during every compellingly entertaining scene." ~~Amelia Richard, Single Titles

"BLOOD TRINITY is a fantastic start to a new Urban Fantasy series. The VIPER organization and the world built ... are intriguing, but the characters populating that world are irresistible. I am finding it difficult to wait for the next book to find out what happens next in their lives." ~~Diana Trodahl, Fresh Fiction

"BLOOD TRINITY is without a doubt one of the best books I've read this year... a tale that shows just how awesome urban fantasy really can be, particularly as the genre is flooded with so many choices. If you love urban fantasy, don't miss out on BLOOD TRINITY. I can't wait to read the second book! Brilliantly done and highly recommended." ~~ Debbie, CK2s Kwips & Kritiques

DEMON STORM

BOOK FIVE
IN THE
THE BELADOR SERIES

NEW YORK TIMES BESTSELLING AUTHOR

DIANNA LOVE

Cover Design and Interior format by The Killion Group
http://thekilliongroupinc.com

DEDICATION

This book is for Karl – there would be no books without you.
Thanks for all of your love and support

ACKNOWLEDGEMENTS

This book – and series – is very special to me. Many of you know that I created the Belador urban fantasy series years ago and released the first novella called MIDNIGHT KISS GOODBYE in the anthology DEAD AFTER DARK, then I went on to co-author the first four books with #1 NYT bestseller Sherrilyn Kenyon. After taking stock of both of our schedules (Sherri is really busy with movies and television shows coming out on her series – woot!!), we decided I should continue these books on my own since I know the series inside and out, and because giving readers the stories they want is priority one both of us. So, thank you, Sherrilyn, for being an amazing friend and for always putting the readers first. Love ya!

Cassondra M is with me every step of the way on all my books. She's the first and last read, with other editors and beta readers in between. She also keeps me sane and on track as both my assistant and is my intrepid traveling companion. She has an incredibly sharp eye when it comes to story and continuity. Joyce Ann McLaughlin is always ready to be an early reader, which is so valuable, but it means she sees the book while it still has a few bumps to smooth out. She catches things that help me hand over the best book I can. Sharon Griffiths is another beta reader who brings an enthusiastic approach to the stories, giving me valuable feedback and supporting me in many ways. Thank you, Steve Doyle, for reading in the middle of whatever is happening and catching little things that mean so much. There is no perfect book, but due to the diligence of these early readers and editing, I'm able to catch errors large and small before the book gets to you. Any mistakes are on me, because at the end of the day, it's my job to hand you the best story I can.

I want to give a shout out to Barb Liebman of TheReadingCafé.com and Amelia Richards of Singletitles.com who give their time to read manuscript copies in advance of the release and share reviews that readers have come to trust. Kim Killion worked her magic with the cover once again (really love this one Kim!) and Jennifer Jakes takes my pile of pages and hands them back all perfectly formatted and ready to roll - thank you both! USA Today bestseller Mary Buckham is not just a dear friend, but she's always ready to kick around ideas when I'm brainstorming a new story - much appreciation. Also, thank you to my amazing STREET TEAM!! It has been such a joy to have you in my life and to share my days with you. Thank you for all the wonderful messages and the endless ways you support me. My goal is to meet you all in person at some point (any reader who'd like to join my street team is welcome – Dianna Love Street Team)

This special thank you is for Lauren M. I'm a better writer because of my years with you. I hope you enjoy this book, because as you know – my goal is to make every book better than the last and the last one with you was a bit epic. Thank you for your constant support of my writing and your continued friendship.

Last, but never least, thank you to my incredible husband, Karl, who does so much to allow me the ability to write these stories. My journey would mean nothing without you by my side.

CHAPTER 1

Storm moved silently through the obsidian night, staying within striking distance of Nadina, the witch doctor who dared to threaten Evalle.

Nadina had made a huge mistake.

Not that Evalle Kincaid wasn't deadly in her own right as one of the Beladors who protected humans from dangerous preternatural predators. She was.

But Evalle was also the woman Storm had taken to mate.

He just hadn't told her yet.

Small detail, because he knew Evalle loved him. He hadn't intended to ever care for anyone again, not after Nadina had killed his father. But Evalle had stolen his heart.

No one, not even a witch doctor with Nadina's powers, was going to harm the woman he loved.

Nadina performed black majik for entertainment as much as for the power she gained from the victim's fear and pain. He would not allow that to happen to Evalle.

Two questions kept drumming his skull.

Where was Nadina leading him? What was her game tonight?

She'd snuck into his house, threatened Evalle then run, knowing he'd follow.

That witch doctor had a reason for everything she did.

Storm couldn't allow her to lead him into a trap. At twenty-eight, he was far more powerful than when he'd escaped her years ago, but she had surprised him with her own improved powers.

Cool October air stole through Inman Park, a historic section of Atlanta where very little moved at one in the morning on a Tuesday. East of downtown, the area sprawled in a jumble of old neighborhoods and industrial properties. Much of it was being reclaimed, and even the warehouses were being renovated as eclectic neighborhood residences.

Sirens whined downtown, too far away for human ears to pick up, but Storm heard every tiny noise. Like the scuff of Nadina's shoes when she stopped quickly on the asphalt a hundred feet ahead of him.

Pausing in the shadow of a scraggly water oak, he sniffed at the smoky licorice scent spiraling in her wake. It was the smell often associated with practicing witchcraft on demons.

The witch doctor wasn't trying to hide her path. Her power reached out, calling to his. Taunting him.

Claws shot from Storm's fingers and muscles rolled beneath his skin as his animal chomped to be freed. He gritted his teeth and forced his jaguar back under control.

Bad sign.

That involuntary flash of change had happened twice in the last half hour.

The longer he chased the woman and the closer he drew to his prey, the more difficult it became to hold back the call of his tainted blood.

Tainted because it was hers. He'd inherited the dark blood from Nadina. His mother. Storm felt his lip curl into a sneer. *Mother* was too good a word for the evil bitch. The Ashaninka witch doctor had trapped Storm's Navajo shaman father with a spell while his father had been in South America giving aid to reclusive natives.

Storm wouldn't hold Nadina's evil against the innocent Ashaninka tribe. You couldn't blame an entire race for one narcissistic psychopath.

But she would pay for all she'd cost Storm.

Just as soon as he had his animal settled down so he could take another step without shifting.

He stood beneath the tree limbs, shuddering against the battle stirring between his demon blood and the humanity he'd inherited from his shaman father, who'd also passed him the genetics of a Skinwalker. He had to pull himself under control before he confronted her or she'd gain the upper hand. She'd been a powerful witch all those years ago when she used majik to seduce his father for the sole purpose of breeding a demon.

A half Spiritwalker, half Skinwalker who shifted into a black jaguar. Then she'd forced the Skinwalker genes Storm carried to actually manifest–by stealing his soul. Mix in the dark blood passed down to him from Nadina's ancestor Sinaa–a child of jaguars–and Storm struggled against the constant threat of losing his grip on humanity.

If Storm gave in at any point and allowed the animal to control his shifting rather than *him* controlling *it*, Nadina would have her demon.

She'd almost succeeded once, back when she'd first tricked him with twisted words and taken possession of his soul. She'd acted as his sponsor, forcing him into brutal beast fights where he'd be forced to shift in order to survive. He'd struggled to control the shifting every minute back then, but the moment had come when he'd snapped. He won a bloody battle, then he tore through a crowd of mixed deadly predators and their dark-arts sponsors just to escape that bitch.

Storm had enjoyed freedom for all of a day until word of his father's death had reached him. He'd had to face Nadina again to bury his father.

He'd been too young to realize just how dangerous she was or that she'd also taken his father's soul.

His father's deep voice had whispered through Storm's mind as he'd stood at the grave of the only real parent he'd ever known. "Be true to your Navajo blood. Hold onto your human side. Never allow the demon to rule even once or you'll be lost forever. Do not trust Nadina, for she killed me and will tear your heart from your chest just to make you watch the last time it beats. Run, my son. Run as far as you can."

Nadina had disappeared from the burial site before Storm could turn his rage on her.

But he'd taken his father's advice to heart and vanished, hiding in the deepest parts of the Amazon jungle where he spent every waking minute working on his skills, growing stronger. He studied the light arts–and the dark–from Santeria babalaos, priests of the Santeria path. He studied every form of black majik he could find, and once he could travel outside

South America, he even learned kala jadoo, an art he would normally never touch.

All because he had one goal.

To know his enemy and grow stronger than she was.

Until recently, Storm wouldn't have cared if he lived or died as long as he made Nadina pay up, then choked her until she gasped her last breath.

But now he had Evalle's safety to consider first.

Nadina would die painfully if she touched Evalle.

Wind swirled past his face and he picked up a new scent. Something old that smelled of decay. He had no time to spare for whatever unnatural being crept through the city at this hour unless it was connected to Nadina.

As long as it wasn't another of the witch doctor's tricks, he'd leave the creature to VIPER agents–Beladors and other supernatural warriors who kept such beings from preying on humans. Those humans were unaware of the deadly things that prowled the night, or of the guardians who held them at bay.

Nadina's scent continued to burn strong on each inhale Storm drew. Clouds cleared and moonlight dusted an old brick building at an intersection up ahead.

Ignoring everything but stalking his prey, Storm continued the hunt, searching far ahead of him in the dimly lit streets.

A blur slashed across his field of vision, moving toward one of the large windows on the street side of the brick structure.

A tall window swung open and the blur disappeared through the opening, then the window closed. Nadina was leading him where she wanted him to be. If she hadn't been, he wouldn't have seen her at all.

Fine. One place was as good as another for her to set her trap, and for him to evade it. With no humans present to witness his nonhuman speed, Storm took off running toward the building. Just as he passed two tall evergreens at the street corner, he felt power coil and snap at him.

He whirled away, but not fast enough to dodge a chain that slapped across the back of his neck.

Shoving his hands up to his chin, he spread his fingers to stop it from wrapping his neck.

Razor sharp metal thorns jutting out along the chain slashed his skin. Pain seared his hands, but he spun away from his attacker and the chain fell away.

The foul smell of decay overpowered Nadina's licorice scent.

A seven-foot tall demon stared down at Storm, with red eyes glaring bright as two warning beacons in the night.

No coincidence that the creature was here in this spot. It had to be Nadina's, because he couldn't place this demon as any particular type. What had she traded to end up with *this* one?

Storm didn't know and didn't really care. He had to kill it quickly or risk losing Nadina.

Moss-green hair stuck out in a scattered mohawk that arced over the demon's oversized head and turned into a rattail falling past a sharp shoulder. Claws as long as Storm's fingers curved on the hand holding the end of the chain, and sores covered the gray skin clinging to its bony body.

Storm caught a familiar smell mixed with the putrid decay. Not just alongside it, but *part* of it. The demon stank of Nadina's scent.

An *anaye*? Had Nadina *created* this thing?

The demon opened his wide jaws and released a gurgling snarl.

If this was a test, Storm had no time for it. His body shook with the drive to shift into his jaguar and get that extra burst of power.

Wouldn't Nadina love that?

Yep, this had to be her abomination.

The anaye stomped forward, slinging the jagged chain around and around. Power sizzled along the metal this time.

Ah hell. That was not good.

Winding the metal whip faster, the demon released it.

Storm dove beneath the spinning links that would slice his head if they made contact. The chain whistled as it passed overhead, close enough for Storm to feel the wind created by the spinning weapon.

The demon had been ready for Storm's defensive move and lifted a foot to crush his head.

Staring up at a four-toed foot the size of a garbage can lid, Storm shoved both hands up to grab it. The damn demon felt like it weighed as much as a car.

He wouldn't be able to hold that downward force for long. His muscles were shaking already. Searching all around for something he could use to knock this hulk off his feet, Storm's gaze latched onto the chain.

If Nadina had also created those deadly links, that weapon would answer to Storm. He called out a chant, ancient words rolling with power he directed at the metal.

The demon was too busy trying to break Storm's arms to notice the chain silently snaking through the tall weeds.

Dark blood boiled inside Storm just from interacting with Nadina's majik, a connection he'd fought his whole life, but he had no other choice at the moment. He forced his beast to stay inside and held that control in an iron grip.

To the chain, he shouted, *"Huelga para matar!"* Strike to kill!

Coiling behind the anaye, the razor links shot up in the air and struck the demon in the throat then wrapped itself around and around.

The demon stumbled backwards.

With the pressure against Storm's arms finally gone, he rolled away and shoved up to his feet.

Storm couldn't leave this demon free to walk the streets of Atlanta. He uttered a command and the chain tightened, cutting through the anaye's neck. The severed head fell to the ground. In the next three seconds, the head and body shriveled until it became liquid. A wide maw opened up in the earth and sucked in demon liquid as if pulling it through a straw. Storm whispered a last order and the chain slinked over the edge, falling into the bottomless void.

The ground closed up and weeds crawled back through the surface, leaving the spot as if it had never been disturbed.

Was that the best Nadina had to throw at Storm?

If so, then she'd severely underestimated his power. Had she watched her little demon show, expecting Storm to give in to his dark blood and shift?

Not today, bitch.

If the point of this exercise had been to force his jaguar out of hiding, that demon had barely challenged him.

But now there was no reason to continue playing hide and seek with her.

Storm crossed his arms and spoke in a quiet tone. "We can play these games all night or you can face me, Nadina. You wanted me to come to you. Here I am."

The windows on the building opened on their own and Nadina's voice drifted out to him. "You have surprised me with your abilities, but you will need more than majik tricks to protect Evalle. You will have to accept your destiny to become one with the black jaguar."

Or I could just kill you and forfeit my soul.

If it was only Storm's soul at risk and he'd never met Evalle, he'd make the sacrifice without hesitation, but then his father's spirit would wander endlessly between two worlds.

And Storm had promised to return to Evalle.

Climbing through that window meant potentially breaking that promise. But walking away meant far worse–leaving Evalle at risk. It was time to end this here and now.

With no choice left, Storm dropped to his haunches and prepared to leap.

CHAPTER 2

Storm barely touched the metal frame on his way through the window of the two-story brick building. He landed inside on the concrete floor as lightly in human form as he would've as a jaguar. He allowed his senses to take stock of the dark surroundings, but his natural night vision took over.

His nose picked up traces of a tinny smell where oil had been heated when metal ground against metal, the sweat of men laboring and pesticides sprayed along the edges.

A machine shop of some sort.

Nadina had cloaked her scent when she'd hidden inside Storm's house, but she couldn't manage it while on the run. Her nauseating licorice smell hung on the still air, turning sharp and bitter with emotion. His empathic senses caught something unexpected.

Not fear, but ... anxiety.

He still had to be extra careful not to rush into a trap.

He'd underestimated her once when he'd been too young to know better.

That had cost him dearly. Even now, after years of preparing to face her again, she'd surprised him by slipping inside his home undetected and had enjoyed informing him that Evalle had been snatched from beneath his nose by the Medb.

That damned Medb priestess, Kizira, had teleported Evalle away from his bedroom six hours ago without him realizing it. He'd been in the kitchen making coffee. Evalle was still missing while Storm raced around hunting Nadina's worthless hide.

Had Evalle escaped the Medb? Was she at Treoir, a Belador

island hidden in another realm? Was she alive?

Of course she was alive.

His heart continued to beat, didn't it? He'd know if anything had happened to his mate.

Still, worry over Evalle ate at him, pushed him to turn his back on Nadina and search for the woman he loved. But logic raised its head. Storm had used his majik to embed an emerald chakra stone into Evalle's chest that would alert him if she returned to this world. He hadn't felt a pull from the stone since Evalle had disappeared from his house. Between the emerald and his mate bond with Evalle, he had to believe that she was still in another realm, but alive.

If Storm lost Nadina at this point, she might get to Evalle before he did, and Nadina would take pleasure in hurting Evalle.

That narrowed his decision back to the one choice in front of him.

Deal with Nadina once and for all.

Moving silent as a gentle wind, Storm walked deeper into the building. His blood churned with the witch doctor so close, and the beast inside clawed at his control, pushing to get out.

He used his majik to meld with the shadowy interior. A dim fluorescent lamp in the ceiling at the far end of the long building flickered on and off at random intervals.

"You said no more games, Storm. Make yourself known."

He continued in the direction of Nadina's voice as it echoed against the two-story walls. Steel i-beams shot up both sides and across the ceiling that towered over the open area running the length of the building.

Pigeons cooed in the rafters.

The building was old, but appeared to be in occasional use based on the forklift parked at one end and equipment for metal fabrication positioned in rows along each side.

"Do not test my patience, Storm."

As if he cared.

Between the scent stinging his nostrils and the sound of her voice, he had to be within twenty feet of her, but she'd also cloaked her body from view.

He stopped. "I'm here. Show yourself."

A small glow erupted above an extended feminine hand. Nadina continued bringing the glow to life until it expanded past Storm and illuminated the center of the shop.

Nadina smiled and her beauty would bring a room of men to a standstill, but it was literally skin deep. Eyes so dark brown they looked black watched him with the intensity of someone prepared for fight or flight. Lush hair fell around her shoulders in a black mantle, striking against the blood-red blouse and black pants that clung to her body. If a sculptor had created the perfect mold for a female form, he broke it after forming Nadina.

Just as perfect and heartless as a Greek statue.

She was nothing compared to the woman Storm loved.

Evalle was lean and tough, loyal and protective. She had exotic green eyes he could fall into and never hope to be saved. The most desirable woman he'd ever met, bar none.

And she was his to protect from this kind of evil.

"You are ready to talk now, yes?" Nadina asked in a voice spiced with her Latin heritage.

"What would we talk about, Nadina?" he asked, letting his disgust pour through his words. "The way you tricked my father into marrying you only to breed a powerful demon? Or maybe we should talk about how I outwitted you and escaped?"

The only sign of hitting his target dead on was the narrowing of her eyes that glared bright yellow for a fleeting moment before turning black again. "You were a difficult child. I should have suffered through two births, then I would have been assured of one who would not disappoint me."

She was put out that she failed to plan for a second child as a spare?

Storm shuddered at the thought. One more person he'd have to shield from her. "I want the souls back. Both of them. That little display outside should have made it clear that I'm not going to be your demon. If you don't return the souls and give me an oath that you will leave Evalle alone, I will kill you where you stand. If I don't kill you here, I'll hunt you to the end of your days and make you suffer before you die."

"See? This proves you are mine." She grinned, thrilled at

his threats.

The woman was mental.

Bat shit crazy, and now loaded with power from an underworld ruler.

"You cannot deny your blood, Storm. You may fight it all you want, but you are a demon deep inside."

He refused to accept that and would never have allowed himself to mate with Evalle if he'd doubted his humanity.

Before he met his mate, he'd been convinced that the demon part of him held the power, but Evalle had brought everything good inside him to the surface. For her, he would never allow the demonic blood that flowed through his veins to rule him.

He warned Nadina, "I'm not making an empty threat. There was a time when I wouldn't have allowed you to live no matter what, but ... things have changed. If you force me to end this, I will and you won't like it."

Releasing a hiss of air sizzling with irritation, she said, "You will not kill me."

"Let's add schizo to psychopathic." Storm took a step toward her.

Nadina raised a hand in defense. On a human woman, that would be a weak obstacle, but Nadina controlled a wicked amount of power she could wield with one finger. "If you kill me, we both lose. I need you to help me pay off a debt."

"You what?" That was ... hell, he had no words for how she could possibly think he'd help her do anything. He studied her long enough that she started to fidget. "What happened to you Nadina? Did all that power cook your brain?"

"This is not a joke."

Crossing his arms, he shook his head. "I am not doing anything for you except sparing your life *if* you give me what I want right now. The offer is good for this minute. No more."

"You are not listening, my black demon."

Storm speared her with all the hatred in his heart. "I don't know what delusional world you live in, but I have *never* been anything of yours except the mistake you birthed. If I could wipe any trace of you from my blood, I would. You're wasting the one chance to save your life, because when I'm out of patience, one of us is not walking out of here alive."

"You are the delusional one if you think to kill me."

He snorted. "And why is that?"

"If I do not return to Hanhau, everyone will bear the brunt of his displeasure, including your Evalle."

Storm's blood chilled. "What are you talking about?"

"Hanhau. We have an arrangement."

"Yeah, yeah. I haven't forgotten your boast back at my house that you're now aligned with him. Why should that matter to me?"

"Because your father's soul and yours are no longer mine to return to you. Not while Hanhau is my master. If I do not deliver what he demands, he will order me to call Evalle to him."

Storm's voice rose with each word. "You made a *pact* with a demon ruler for what? That plastic beauty of yours? Are you crazy?" He grabbed his head. "What am I saying? Of course, you're insane."

Her perfect face distorted, twisting with fury. "Do not call me loco. I had no choice. I did not need him for this." She pointed at her face. "I learned the secrets of maintaining my youth before I grew breasts. A Macumba witch captured me to trade to Hanhau for demons."

Macumba was the Brazilian practice of Candomble, basically Voodoo, Latin style.

If not for how this would complicate his life, Storm would be chuckling over the irony of Nadina getting to experience being possessed by someone stronger. But right now all Storm cared about was how to terminate any threat to Evalle and regain two souls.

Couldn't Evalle get a break without everyone making her a target?

Storm's empathic senses would catch a lie the second it left someone's lips and nothing Nadina said so far had lit up his bullshit meter. He'd received that gift through his Navajo genetics. But along with the ability to determine if someone was lying to him, Storm suffered a painful backlash if *he* tried to lie.

If Nadina were any other witch doctor than one he shared blood with, he wouldn't have the shadow of doubt hovering over his thoughts. She'd managed to successfully twist the truth when he was younger, but his majik and powers had matured since then.

He powered up his empathic perception and pressed her. "I want straight answers. No playing with words, Nadina." When she inclined her head in reply, he continued. "A Macumba witch captured you, yes or no?"

"Yes."

"Then the witch traded you to Hanhau for how many demons?"

"Three."

Truth, so far. "So Hanhau now holds full control over you and all you possess, yes or no?"

"Yes."

No sizzle on his skin to warn him of a lie. By all that was holy, was he actually considering doing this? "If I help you then you will release my father's soul, return my soul and swear a blood oath not to harm or go anywhere near Evalle. Got that?"

"Yes, I will give you my oath that if I leave Mitnal with all my possessions, I will grant what you wish." Mitnal was the underworld ruled by Hanhau.

Still nothing that indicated she was lying. "Why should I believe you when this could be a trap?" When she rolled her eyes, he asked, "*Is* this a trap?"

"Of course it's a trap."

"Nadina, you strain my patience."

"Am I allowed to speak freely now?"

He growled something that could be construed as yes.

"If I wanted to kill you, I could have done it days ago when you were weakened by my Langua up in the mountains, *si*?"

Storm had gone to the mountains to track a suspicious witch after meeting her at a secret beast fight. He'd happened upon Nadina and her Langua, a human-looking pet Nadina had created using necromancy. The Langua had passed a deadly infection to Storm when he'd fought the creature. He'd wondered then why Nadina hadn't stayed around to take advantage of his weakened state once he destroyed the Langua and escaped.

Nadina arched a sculpted eyebrow at him. "You see, I am telling the truth. I have never wanted to kill you, but I admit that I want you back and could have captured you then if not for my deal with Hanhau."

Everything she said sounded logical. Why did his gut keep yelling at him that it was all a lie? "If I consider helping you, and that's a big if, what do you need?"

"For you to travel to Mitnal with me."

He scoffed, "I can't just stroll into Mitnal."

She drew herself up with a regal move. "No, you must be invited by Hanhau or enter accompanied by one of his ... how do you say–" She stared off, thinking.

"Minions?" Storm supplied, then added, "Slaves, bitches, groupies–"

"Representatives!" Nadina snapped. "You can enter with me."

"You think Hanhau is going to let me just go walking into his domain as your guest?"

"Actually, he is expecting you. He *sent* me here to find you."

This just got better and better. "Why?"

Her arrogance came back, blanketing her words. "He is building an army of demons–"

"Why?"

"Do not interrupt me," she ordered as if Storm were *her* minion.

"Why?" he repeated with a sharper edge.

She harrumphed. "Hanhau does not share all his plans with me, only that he is building an army and needs one such as you to turn his demons into more powerful killers." She waved her hand around. "You know. Like general of army."

Storm scratched his chin. *Now we're getting to the truth.* "Why would he think I was the one to lead his army?"

Her dainty shrug did nothing to appease his anger, but it did jack up his suspicions. She took her time, but finally admitted, "I had no choice but to tell him of the blood that runs through your veins and that you had been bred for power."

Like a prize bull in a ranch full of killers. "You threw me out as a sacrifice to save your own butt."

"What did you want me to do when it was that or be left to suffer Hanhau's disgusting whims?"

"I certainly never expect you to do anything honorable."

She crossed her arms and sighed. "Fine. I admit that I might have been a bit unfair to you."

A bit unfair? Storm's jaw throbbed from grinding his teeth so hard. "How does he know about Evalle?"

The drama bitch rolled her eyes. "Because I had to convince him that I could bring you back with me or he would not have allowed me to leave. Without Evalle, there would be no way to motivate you."

She had a point. "Does he know what Evalle is?"

"Yes, and not because I told him," she was quick to clarify. "He already knew Evalle was an Alterant thing and with the Beladors."

Storm didn't waste his breath straightening out Nadina, but Evalle was not an Alterant *thing*. Being part Belador and part unknown classified her as an Alterant, but in her heart she was Belador all the way. She'd fight to the death to protect the tribe of powerful warriors whose gifts had been passed down through their blood from two thousand years ago. She was the epitome of honor and all woman.

She was not a damned *thing*.

"What does Hanhau want with Evalle?"

"Nothing. He said turning an Alterant into a demon would be too much trouble and drain his energy to the point he could not trust Evalle to be in Mitnal with her ties to the Beladors. But he would order me to call her to me and send enough demons to kill her if I could not talk you into coming of your own free will."

"If either of you touches her, I would first rip *you* into too many pieces to identify without a DNA test and then I'd find Hanhau next and show him a demon like he's never seen." Only for Evalle would Storm walk into the equivalent of the bowels of hell. "So I just show up and tell Hanhau I'm his new demon wrangler?"

"No." Nadina made a testy sound. "Hanhau will say nothing to you, but he will question me and I will tell him you have come to train his demons."

Was that rusty hinges on a trap being set that Storm heard squealing in his brain? "Then what's the plan? Because I won't stay."

"If you convince him that you accept his terms and ask for an invitation, he will allow me to open the bolthole from this side. Once we are there, we make him comfortable until he lets down his guard. All we have to do is find a way to sneak out without drawing his attention. I have studied him for weaknesses that can be exploited and—"

"Exploiting a weakness sounds familiar," Storm snapped, jabbing at a wound by reminding himself of how she'd duped his father.

"I find your humor irritating. I am trying to show that I know how we can escape."

"I wasn't being funny. And you'll give your oath?"

"Yes, yes, yes. How many times do I have to say yes?"

"Until I'm convinced this is not a trap."

"I already told you it is, because he sent me here to capture you!" She huffed out a breath. "I have told you the truth about Hanhau expecting you and wanting you to lead his demons. If I had not convinced Hanhau that I could deliver you, he would have captured Evalle first to use as bait. That would have been far easier, but it would not solve my problem. I have never been in this position and will not be again, plus I did not wish to give you up for all of this. But I find some goals must be forsaken in the interest of survival."

Yeah, she'd thought once she captured Storm that he'd give in and turn into her own personal four-legged killing machine? What a selfless bitch to give that up. "What about Hanhau? Won't he come hunt you down when we escape?"

"You do not understand the rules of Mitnal. You must ask to enter, but not to leave. If you enter *without* asking, you will regret it once Hanhau has his hands on you. But, if you escape Mitnal on your own, Hanhau will not hunt for you, because his power would not be as strong beyond the limits of Mitnal."

"He'd just let someone go?" Storm hadn't caught any hint of a lie in that, but he had a hard time believing a demonic ruler would be so cavalier about an escapee.

Nadina lifted her chin at the challenge to her words.

"Hanhau does not want to return a runaway to his world who will create problems with his demons by showing them how to escape. Besides, he knows that once a demon has belonged to him, that demon will not be fit to live among humans. The death and destruction an escaped demon wreaks in the natural world is enough to appease him."

"What about his hold over you and your possessions?"

"All deals with Hanhau end the minute I am free of Mitnal by escaping, because my agreement with him was bonded in Mitnal. If I manage to escape on my own, I break my tie to Hanhau. If that happens, I am free and my possessions once again belong to me as long as I remain in the mortal realm or some place other than Mitnal."

The guy must have a league of attorney demons to keep up with the fine print in contracts like that one.

Again, nothing Nadina said touched off Storm's internal lie detector. But if he did this, he couldn't stay in Mitnal very long. To do so would risk Storm involuntarily shifting and turning fully into a demon that would very likely rival any Hanhau currently owned.

Storm asked, "How long will it take to get in and out?"

"We will enter the minute you request passage into Mitnal and, if we are able to escape, we can do so and be back in this world in less than a day."

"How long is a day in Mitnal?" Storm had concerns over staying for even a few hours.

Nadina explained, "There is no way to tell time in Mitnal, but you will know a day has passed here in the mortal world when Hanhau shuts down to regenerate his powers. That is only for what feels like ten minutes. He shares his power with his demons, which constantly depletes him. Then he has to draw new power from Mitnal itself. That short break is the only time he is in a weakened state. If I open the bolthole from this side, then I can lead us back out the same point, but I cannot get past the demon gatekeepers while Hanhau is resting. Not alone."

Storm ran through all she'd said and still had a sick feeling this was a bad idea. What was he missing? "What if I want a day to think on this?"

"Then do not blame me for what happens. I have no control over Hanhau or his whims. If I return empty-handed, he may decide to kill me. Then you will lose all chance of regaining any souls or protecting Evalle. He will send the demons for her. If she is as deadly as her reputation, then she may be fine, but even so you will never see your soul."

Why didn't I kill this bitch back when I figured out how to escape her years ago?

Because he was determined to prove to himself that even though he'd been bred for demonhood that blood would not govern who he was.

The first step in proving that to himself had been walking away from killing Nadina in cold blood. But once he'd spent enough time training on his own while researching the majik she used, and once he convinced himself he would never succumb to the darkness in his blood, Storm had gone after her to regain two souls. That search had led him here to Atlanta, to VIPER, and to Evalle.

And now that plan had just flown out the window on flapping wings.

Nadina made a grinding noise in her throat. "If you kill me, Hanhau holds your souls forever. If Hanhau kills me, you will have to free the souls from an entity far more powerful than I am."

Thanks, but he'd figured that one out on his own. Deal with her or battle the ruler of an underworld demon army. Allowing Nadina to live had been a huge miscalculation on Storm's part. Who knew he'd come to regret an honorable decision?

He should have killed her first, *then* set his moral barometer. "How many demons does Hanhau currently rule?"

"Over a thousand."

"That's not a big enough army?" What did Hanhau have in mind?

"He desires one five times as large."

"What's his target?"

She thought for a moment and said, "I told you, he does not tell me his plans, but I heard him yelling once about someone called Sen who slums with mortals. Do you know who that is?"

Unfortunately, yes.

Sen was liaison between VIPER agents in the Atlanta headquarters and their ruling body of deities known as the Tribunal. It was rumored that a majority of deities were aligned with the coalition, meaning VIPER controlled the greatest supernatural power base presently tasked with watching over the mortal world.

Sen had been a bastard to Evalle the entire time Storm had been with VIPER, so he'd hand Sen over without a moment of guilt, but Storm couldn't allow Hanhau anywhere near Evalle. Was Hanhau after *only* Sen? Or was he after VIPER headquarters in Atlanta? If Evalle survived going back to the Medb, which Storm believed she would without a doubt, then she would stand with her Beladors to protect VIPER against anything.

Even a legion of demons.

Nadina arched and yelled out, "I'm almost done!"

"Who are you talking to?"

She panted out several breaths and had her hand on her lower back. "Hanhau. He is tired of waiting. Before you walked into the building, I called out to Hanhau and told him you were coming. He is out of patience and I am out of time. You must go now or not at all."

This was screwed nine ways, but bringing Hanhau into the mix had just upped the game. Storm said, "Give me your blood oath now."

"We don't have time."

"Then I'm not going." He'd put himself between Evalle and every demon Hanhau turned loose if that was what it took to protect her.

Nadina grumbled, "You must be quick or he will pull me away before it is done." She produced a knife and said, "Find something to burn."

Storm glanced around, found a drum with garbage and pulled out a long wood shaving. He stepped back over to Nadina. "I assume you can light this with your powers."

He could, too, but he wasn't showing her any of his cards.

"Of course." She sliced her palm and allowed her blood to drip onto the wood.

Storm sliced his palm, dripping blood to comingle with hers

and started the oath. "I, Storm of the Ashaninka, agree to aid you in escaping Mitnal, but only if you uphold your agreement to return my soul, my father's soul and swear to never harm or even speak to Evalle. You also agree to never come near me again or touch anything that is mine."

"Anything? How am I supposed to know if something belongs to you, Storm?"

"By staying a million miles away from me and mine. Give your oath word for word the way I stated mine."

Nadina spoke through lips pulled tight in anger. "I, Nadina, witch doctor of the Ashaninka who worship Koriošpíri, daughter of the powerful Spiritwalker Sinaa, agree to return Storm of Ashaninka's soul and his father's soul upon the moment that I leave Mitnal with Storm and have control of those souls. Once we escape together, I also swear to never harm or even speak to Evalle, plus I agree to never go near Storm again or touch anything that is his."

He hesitated, hoping he hadn't missed something. Storm released the wood shaving that remained suspended between them. "Burn it."

The wood burst into flames, Nadina's deadly black majik burning a licorice smell through the air. The only black magic more deadly than hers was Noirre. He hoped his nostrils weren't permanently coated from her majik miasma.

His heart pounded a fast staccato. He was going to enter the demon realm. But with a little luck, this would end his journey to release his father's soul so that his father could cross over to his final resting place in the afterlife. And it would allow Storm to feel whole again.

To know that he would be the man who deserved Evalle.

And above all, this would eliminate a threat that would otherwise haunt his and Evalle's future.

Nadina arched again, feet off the floor. She cried out, "Storm is ready. Speak to him, my master."

Her feet hit the floor and she heaved one breath after another, holding her arms around herself. Even Storm was convinced that she'd suffered in that moment.

A smooth voice that deserved to be on the radio asked, "*You are the demon Storm?*"

Storm shot a warning look at Nadina who gave him a just-play-along look. He answered, "I'm Storm."

"You wish to enter Mitnal?"

Not really, but Storm replied, "Yes." He gritted his teeth against the sharp jab of pain from lying.

"Why?"

Before Storm could send another death glare her way, Nadina wound her hands in the motion of keep talking. Staying as close to the truth as he could, Storm said, "I understand you want someone to train your demons."

"And you wish to do that?"

"No," Storm told him in all sincerity, because every minute in Mitnal put him at risk of losing what grip he had on humanity. He hoped he really could last one day there.

Power lashed through the air from one side of the brick building to the other, striking steel I-beams and leaving burn holes in its wake.

Nadina covered her face with her hands and trembled, looking like someone expecting to die.

Storm continued. "I don't want to do it, but I will since I understand you're threatening Evalle. I figure we can either do battle or work something out."

"Wise decision as you would lose a battle."

Not necessarily, but even Storm had to admit that until he had a chance to size up Hanhau he had no idea exactly what he was going up against. "How long do you expect me to stay?"

Every word had Nadina's shoulders hunching against possible retaliation.

Hanhau said, *"You may leave Mitnal when I release my army. Very soon."*

"What's very soon in your world?"

"Time has no relevance to a demon."

A vague answer when Storm needed specifics. He pressed on. "And you'd trust me to lead that army?"

"I trust no one, but I do know that once you leave here by my order that you will follow my orders without question."

The confidence in Hanhau's voice gave Storm a moment of hesitation. But he could gut out anything the demon ruler hit him with for one day after having survived what Nadina put

Storm through as a young man. He'd walked away from that with his humanity in spite of having no soul.

He could make it through this.

Hanhau's voice didn't rise in sound but it filled out with power. *"Decide, Storm of the Ashaninka."*

That decision had been made the minute Evalle was put at risk. "I request entrance into Mitnal."

"I grant that request," Hanhau answered. "Open the bolthole on your side, Nadina."

When she dropped her hands from her face, her skin had blanched. She lifted her arms, chanting as she moved her hands apart, palms facing. Light exploded between her palms and grew into an arch. In the next moment, the glowing arch moved from her palms to the concrete floor.

She chanted and continued lowering her hands to her sides, then quieted long enough to say, "Follow me."

When she walked through the arch, Storm followed her through the bolthole into Mitnal.

Cold rushed across his skin, peppering sharp stings that felt like ice picks striking him. He'd expected as much upon entering the underworld of the cold, but hadn't expected his body to go icy on the outside and hot as a stoked blaze on the inside. Sweat dripping from his chin hit his chest and froze. Within two steps, he entered a hall of gleaming black stone that flickered with light from hundreds of candles.

A thousand pairs of red eyes turned to the new arrivals.

Demons lounged on surfaces cut into the walls of the massive chamber. Bodies were in all shapes from bulls to serpents to others that were mere skeletons with skin. The smell of despair and hate wound through the air, clinging to Storm's skin. The energy of the demons crawled over him, seeping into him to test his blood.

He allowed his own energy to pulse through his body and shoved it out hard to back off any inquiries. Several demons howled. *Don't like getting your fingers slapped with an invisible ruler, huh?*

He kept following Nadina through the hordes of demons until she stopped and bowed low. That was something Storm had never expected to see.

She hissed at him. "Bow."

"No. Not part of the deal."

Bright orange-red light flared in front of them, illuminating a throne of skulls. Not carved to look like skulls, but empty-eyed bone ghosts staring out at nothing.

Perched on that was a being with arms and legs that gave the impression of human and male.

Storm had heard of Hanhau's owl-shaped head, but this hideous manifestation insulted the beauty of owls. The demon ruler had skin that looked like it was made of bone. It was whiter than snow and smooth as polished alabaster, all except his face, where black, orange and red jagged lines radiated from his eyes to his ears and chin. Spikes of yellow and blood-red hair tufted between two pointy ears. Thick wads of hair fell to his shoulders, past his arms and to his waist in different lengths, braided thick as two of Storm's fingers. One horn shot straight up from his forehead. His eyes were nothing but flickering flames. A necklace of bones rough-cut into circles swung from his neck.

Not just circles. Those were eye sockets.

When Hanhau opened his mouth to speak, fire raged at the back of his throat. "You have asked to enter my domain, Storm of the Ashaninka, and I have granted it. To remain here, you must state your intentions for coming to Mitnal."

"That's not what—" Nadina started to argue and her lips disappeared from her face. She turned wild eyes on Storm.

Storm shook his head at her, careful to sound more demon than human in front of Hanhau when he told Nadina, "Sympathy is the last thing to expect after striking a deal with someone more evil than you are."

Cold hatred shoved the wildness from her eyes.

Storm ignored her to concentrate on how best to answer Hanhau. "I thought we discussed that before I came through the bolthole."

"That was to allow you to enter. To remain, you must state your intentions. If you came here with ulterior motives, you will regret it."

Nadina's eyes rounded large, begging him to allow her to speak.

Standing with arms crossed and legs apart, Storm said, "I came here to train your demons."

That lie caused no physical pain, but Storm ignored the oddity for now and focused on the threat he faced.

Hanhau sat forward. His horns erupted into flames.

What was wrong? Storm had given the demon ruler what he wanted, according to Nadina.

Hanhau's lips twisted into a smile, then his mouth burst open with belly-deep laughter. His demons howled and chortled with him. Hanhau clapped his hands, "I am much pleased, Nadina."

Storm swung his head to Nadina, whose lips had returned and were now smirking at him.

No, this couldn't be happening.

He fought to bring words up from his throat.

She had no trouble speaking. "I told you I would have you as my demon, but I'm willing to share you with my master, Hanhau. You and I will not be leaving together so that oath is of no use, but I found it entertaining." She laughed, a brittle, evil sound that died just before she tossed his own words back at him. "Sympathy is the last thing to expect after striking a deal with someone more evil than you are."

His world was crashing in on itself, but Storm couldn't hear it above the screaming inside his head.

CHAPTER 3

Standing here was going to kill her.

Or someone else if this didn't move along soon.

Evalle shifted her feet, tired of standing in place waiting, waiting, waiting.

Enough already.

She had to find Storm for any hope of tracking down Brina. The longer the Belador warrior queen was missing from Treoir Castle, the longer all the Beladors back in Atlanta, and the rest of the mortal world, were at risk of annihilation.

Treoir Castle stood, as powerful looking as it had been the first time Evalle visited this island hidden in a mist above the Irish Sea. The structure might still be strong but without a Treoir descendant physically inside the beautiful building, Belador warriors had no powers. As it was, only an empty-eyed, holographic effigy of Brina, the last living Treoir, remained. She'd been attacked with black majik dust.

Not just any run-of-the-mill black majik, but Noirre.

Hundreds of warriors standing around Evalle on the lawn leading up to the castle shifted their feet, anxiously waiting for their goddess Macha to speak.

Sooner than later would be nice, but this deity moved at her own pace.

Evalle had already mouthed off once and survived that. Twice in one lifetime would be pushing her paper-thin luck.

Not that she had any issue with spending the last six hours here to help deal with their dead. Helping to prepare each body to be sent back to families for proper burial had broken her heart. But those fallen had known the jeopardy of accepting the duties and risks that came with being a Belador warrior. Beladors were a race of beings living in the mortal world, but who were far more than regular mortal humans. They were born under the PRIN star and had inherited powers passed down through the blood from ancestors two thousand years ago.

Those ancestors had been bloodthirsty killers who would have enjoyed the carnage from the battle fought mere hours ago here on Treoir against the Medb coven of warlocks and witches, but in today's world things were different. Modern day Beladors upheld a vow to act with honor or face possible death, with their entire families subject to the same punishment.

Macha meant it when she swore that her Beladors would never take a life dishonorably again.

But every warrior standing here–and those back home in the mortal world–wanted retribution for the bloodbath Treoir had just suffered at the hands of the Medb.

And for the attack on their warrior queen, Brina.

This place no longer reminded Evalle of a fairytale world. Not the kind with happy endings, anyway. The Medb had declared war with their attack, and Beladors all over the world were suffering the loss of everything from kinetic powers to telepathy.

Their greatest enemy, the Medb, had changed the Belador power base in one day.

Evalle would find a way to save Brina, but she couldn't do it without Storm, who should be at his house waiting for Evalle to return, but no. According to the note he'd left for her, he'd gone after that blasted South American witch doctor.

If that miserable witch doctor harmed one hair on Storm, Evalle would ...

Power surged inside her and cartilage shoved the skin up her arms in advance of her shifting.

She froze, cutting her eyes around to see if anyone had noticed. Thankfully, these warriors were more focused on receiving orders and making someone pay for violating the Belador stronghold than on her.

They might not even care if she shifted into a gryphon again after she'd saved lives in that form during the battle, but *no one* shifted into an altered state while on Treoir without Macha's permission. Not unless they wanted to tick off an already enraged goddess, which was why Evalle needed to get a grip on her anxiety over Storm before Macha zapped her with enough energy to light up North America.

"What's the holdup?"

Evalle jumped at the deep voice right behind her then turned, wishing *she* had the power to zap Tristan. "What are you doing in human form without getting Macha's okay?"

"You didn't say anything about needing her rubber stamp to shift *back* to human form. Why would she be pissed off about that?"

He had a point, but it would have been nice if he'd waited until Macha made up her mind how she was going to deal with the gryphons since they had not been accepted into Macha's pantheon yet.

It was a question of if, not when, at the moment.

Was it too much to ask Tristan not to draw Macha's attention until Evalle had a chance to ask the goddess where she stood on gryphons, since they carried half Belador and half Medb blood in their veins? Just like Evalle, Tristan and the other gryphons had started out as Alterants, then evolved into powerful flying creatures, a race with no clear status as of yet.

Several warriors had turned her way to listen, which wouldn't take much with their sensitive hearing, unless that Belador power was also out of order. Evalle would speak to Tristan telepathically, but Macha might consider it rude if she stepped out onto the front steps in the midst of their speaking mind to mind.

Who knew with a goddess who created her own version of Miss Manners' rules as she went?

Evalle angled her head for Tristan to follow her and stepped away from the crowd until they were beneath the sprawling arms of an oak tree. She kept her voice down to protect her conversation. "Didn't we agree that you'd wait for me to come tell you and the other gryphons what's going on?"

"I am waiting. I just choose to do it in this form."

Tristan will be the death of me. He'd come close to causing

Evalle's demise more than once.

His blonde hair spiked in that messy way that men got away with, and the amused blue eyes stared down at her, but only because he had five inches on her five-foot-ten height. He clearly waited for Evalle's volley. She wasn't going to ask where Tristan had come up with a clean pair of jeans that fit him snug enough to raise the pulse of any female Belador warrior in the crowd. Any woman except Evalle, who had vacillated between wanting to strangle Tristan and thank him for his help when the Medb attacked Treoir.

It would be easy for many Beladors to blame Tristan since word had circulated that he'd joined the Medb, when in truth, he'd been captured and compelled to act.

He'd gone along with Evalle's plan when they left, and he'd fought for the Beladors once Kizira, the Medb priestess leading the attack, had died in battle, freeing everyone she'd compelled.

Thinking of the battle, Evalle reminded him, "You *will* need Macha's approval to become a gryphon again."

Tristan gave a careless shrug. "If she wants my help, she'll have to let me do what I need to watch over the island."

"When are you going to make my life easier?"

He stopped checking out the crowd and castle to drop a glare at Evalle that came loaded with hostility. "When are you going to make *my* life easier? I've got six other gryphons and two Rías to keep pacified while everyone's standing here waiting for an edict from Macha. I have yet to hear any atta boys coming from O'goddess for all we've done."

"She said thank you."

"I say thank you to someone who brings me coffee. I expect a little more for putting our lives on the line for this bunch after the Beladors had a shoot-to-kill order on us until just now."

"That was technically an order from the Tribunal," Evalle said, trying to stem the fit of anger building up in the man beside her.

"The Beladors didn't hesitate to *follow* that order, did they?" Tristan challenged, then cut his gaze hard at the handful of warriors who were angling their bodies to catch Tristan and Evalle's conversation. "Did you?" Tristan challenged in their direction.

The warriors swung back around, but not before Evalle caught embarrassment on their faces. Tristan had a point, but alienating the Beladors was not going to be productive.

"Tristan." She said it softly, imploring him to back off the attitude.

He scrubbed his face with one hand then crossed his arms, but when he spoke it was in a civil tone. "All I'm saying is we're keeping this place protected better than any Belador can right now with their powers jacked up, and we still aren't a recognized race with rights. We're just Macha's Treoir pets."

"Give her a chance to—"

Tristan lifted a hand, cutting her off. "I get that everyone is in turmoil over Brina, but I'm out of patience."

"Getting on Macha's nerves right now might be a dangerous mistake."

"Really? She didn't torch you when you defied her about leaving Treoir to hunt for Storm. We all heard you tell her 'I dare to piss off the entire fucking universe if that's what it takes to get him back.'"

"That's different."

"Why?"

"Because the only person I put at risk with that was me, not the rest of the gryphons. She knows I handed off leading the gryphons to you."

"Whatever." He muttered something then his gaze zeroed in on her with curiosity. "Speaking of that loser jaguar, why'd you risk getting turned into a crispy snack to go after him?"

Because Storm is worth more to me than you can ever understand.

Telling Tristan that would just encourage him to continue haranguing her about something that was none of his business. Instead, she'd give him something to think about. "Funny you say that, because Storm asked me why I'd risk my life and fragile standing with the Beladors to help a backstabbing bastard who walked away from me when I stood between him and a black ops team. *His* words, of course. And, why would I continue to stick my neck out to trust you after you took me to meet with a guy who turned out to be a Medb plant and why—"

"I got it, E-*valle*. Give me a break."

No. Tristan started this. She added, "*And* Storm has come for me every time I've been in a jam. Every. Time. Don't ever think I won't turn this world upside down for him."

"Must be nice," Tristan muttered.

"What?"

He stared off, taking a slow breath. "To have someone you love that much."

She felt Tristan's despair with her empathic senses, reminding her of the loneliness he'd suffered while locked away in the jungle in a spelled cage. It was during times like this that she often overlooked how much of a jerk he could be.

He was right. It was nice to know she was going home to someone who loved her, which she was doing just as soon as she returned to Atlanta.

She changed the subject and told Tristan, "Work with me so all of us can have lives. We're at the closest point all Alterants have ever been to that happening. Macha has proof that we're not a threat to Brina, which was her major concern about Alterants."

Thinking on that reminded Evalle that Tristan had been given a Medb concoction that had resulted in his being able to teleport at times. He could only take one person at a time and had to rest to regain his powers when he did, but...

"Hey, Tristan, can you still teleport?"

"Short distances inside the Treoir boundaries, but I can't get out."

"You tried?"

"Of course I tried," he scowled at her. "Don't give me that look. I wasn't abandoning my group, just checking out my resources."

In a way, Evalle wished he'd been successful, because now she was stuck with only the goddess to teleport her back to Atlanta, and Macha had a memory longer than eternity.

She would not soon forget Evalle's words only hours ago.

But speaking her mind had felt good. Evalle was sick and tired of being told who she could or could not protect. Ultimately, she was going to give Macha what the goddess wanted by bringing a powerful Skinwalker/shaman to Treoir who could track pretty much any majik.

Storm would have enjoyed watching Evalle stand up to the Celtic goddess.

It had been a beautiful moment for all of the fifteen seconds it took for Evalle to realize she'd just verbally bitch slapped the only person here who could teleport her back to Atlanta–to the mortal world.

Even so, she didn't regret it and wouldn't retract her words. They'd come from a heart that ached to be back in Storm's arms. She missed him with every breath.

Storm *had* constantly put himself in danger for the sole reason of protecting her or helping her with some deadly, impossible task.

Because of him, and only him, she finally knew what it was to care for a man instead of fearing his touch. Storm was her world and her future. She would not sit quietly and wait for him to come to her while he might be fighting that crazy witch doctor.

"Beladors!" Macha said, drawing attention to where she floated above the steps that led up to two massive doors carved with triquetras, a triangle-shaped Belador symbol. Macha might look to be in her late twenties, but she'd been around since life had taken hold on this planet. She normally showed up in a sparkling gown made of some impossible material, but today she wore a dark blue top and pants that swirled with a gauzy effect.

Her hair usually moved all over the place and changed colors faster than a chameleon crossing a rainbow, but now it was cinnamon red, and floated with a quiet calm around her face and shoulders as Macha spoke, "I am proud of the way you fought the Medb, and grieve with you for our fallen."

Tristan muttered, "Incoming."

The sound of large wings flapping in the air preceded six gryphons on approach to land. Warriors stepped back, opening up a clearing for the ten-to-twelve-foot tall creatures with thirty-foot wingspans that settled as smoothly as a flock of geese on a lake. But these were no birds. They each had an eagle's grand profile from head to shoulders, then a lion's body that flowed to the long tail. A few of them had golden feathers on their heads.

Evalle looked around then whispered to Tristan. "Where are your two Rías buddies?"

"They didn't want to come since they aren't in human form and their beast form isn't *pretty* like gryphons," Tristan said with his usual dry sarcasm. "So they're hiding nearby ... to scope out the Belador women before they're allowed to shift back to men."

Evalle smiled. She'd met the two Rías when Tristan took her to the Maze of Death, a bunch of tunnels beneath Atlanta that harbored Civil War ghosts. With the exception of having normal human eyes where Evalle's were bright green, Rías shifted into monsters similar to Evalle's original beast form—the one she'd had before she evolved into a gryphon—and they were definitely not an attractive sight.

The gryphons *were* pretty, magnificent even, and she was one of them. In fact, she was now their leader, the strongest in the pack.

Or she would be when she came back from finding Storm. Tristan had better do his job as leader while she was gone to the mortal world.

Turning back to Macha, Evalle noted the indecision that seemed to hang in the air.

What had the goddess hesitating?

Macha finally came to some decision and said, "We welcome the gryphons who defended our island and remain to watch over Treoir. Now that we know what an Alterant is, or at least what one becomes, I will finalize the petition to have Alterants recognized as a race with rights. Every Alterant who swears fealty to me and the Beladors will from that point forward belong to my pantheon."

Chills raced along Evalle's skin.

How long had she waited to hear those words? To be accepted as a true Belador and no longer be persecuted for the unknown part of her blood?

She turned to Tristan, whose jaw was slack with disbelief, then he snapped his mouth shut.

She held her breath to see if he would forgive the Beladors for their transgressions against him when he'd been caged like an animal. Or would he snub Macha's offer? Brina may have been the one who actually locked Tristan away for five years inside that cage in a South American jungle, but Brina took no action without either Macha's blessing or direction.

Would any of that matter to Tristan?

Macha stood perfectly still and Evalle realized the goddess waited for a sign from the gryphons.

The Belador warriors turned en masse to stare at Tristan, Evalle and the gryphons.

Technically, Evalle was already a Belador, but she bowed her head and prayed that Tristan would not start mouthing off.

Out of the corner of her eye, she saw him slowly lower his head, then six gryphons dropped their upper bodies and dipped their heads, wings spread in a breathtaking display of colors and acknowledgment.

Evalle's eyes were swimming but she wasn't about to put on a waterworks display, not even one with happy tears.

She was a warrior.

No, she was a *Belador* warrior, equal to everyone here.

Macha's voice rang out. "Your fealty is accepted, gryphons and Rías, and your service in continuing to guard Treoir is appreciated."

Standing upright again to face her goddess, Evalle searched for Tzader and Quinn. She found them standing off to the side, both rigid with arms crossed.

Not a happy face between them.

They were her two closest friends. The two people who knew more than anything what this meant to Evalle.

What was wrong? Why weren't they winking at her and smiling? What could have those two so upset?

Oh, besides the love of Quinn's life stepping between him and death to suffer being gutted, only to die in his arms? Or Tzader racing into the castle to protect Brina, only to have the ward almost kill him—correction, it *did* kill him—and come back to life to find nothing but her holographic image left?

Tzader had never told Evalle, but she'd seen enough to suspect that Brina was far more to Tzader than just the warrior queen of the Beladors.

Yeah, her two best friends were suffering. Celebrating on

her part could sit on the back burner until their worlds were better.

That wouldn't happen for Tzader until they found Brina.

As for Quinn, Evalle had no idea how to console someone for the kind of loss he'd suffered. There would be no consoling *her* if Storm had died in her arms. She couldn't even think about that without her heart having spasms.

Macha was going on about how they would stand strong in the face of the damage the Medb had done to their tribe. They would return Brina to the castle and, moving forward, that changes would be made to insure her safety and protect the Belador power base.

Got it, Macha. Can you move this along a little faster?

Macha paused and her gaze tracked to Evalle.

Oh, hell. She couldn't have heard that thought, could she?

Irritating Macha *again* before teleporting was a good way to end up flung back to Atlanta like a ragdoll thrown through a wood chipper, and Evalle didn't need encouragement to toss her cookies even on a smooth ride.

She teleported about as well as Macha accepted criticism.

Not a pretty scene.

"Now we face an even greater battle," Macha went on, talking about what came next. "Many of you suffer intermittent or non-existent powers as do other Beladors across the world. Preternatural criminals are attacking Beladors, which means the word about our power base being weak is traveling quickly."

There had never been a plan for ending up with only an empty-eyed hologram of Brina inside the castle. It had happened when a Belador traitor had tossed deadly Noirre majik dust on Brina.

Macha wrapped it up by saying, "Maistir Tzader Burke of North America will decide who stays here and who returns to the mortal world."

Maybe Evalle could hitch a teleportation ride back with a group without having to draw Macha's attention to her specifically.

When Macha disappeared and the crowd began to disperse, Evalle turned to Tristan. She was ready to go, but had to make sure she didn't come back to fallout from him irritating Macha.

The gryphons flocked on the lawn, a herd of giants whose bodies would glisten beneath the sun back home. Evalle wouldn't mind some sunshine, but none shone in the sky above Treoir.

In Atlanta, she'd lived in the dark, because the sun would burn the flesh from her body. But that had changed when she morphed all the way into a gryphon.

Please tell me this is a permanent change and I will never be relegated to living in the dark again.

Evalle decided to take a positive tack and compliment Tristan on his good behavior to set the right tone for discussing what he had to do. She smiled to sell it. "Thank you for accepting Macha's offer. She might not deserve forgiveness, but the Beladors deserve to have all of us in the tribe. And now Alterants evolved into gryphons and any other Alterants still out there can have a life."

"I'm not stupid, Evalle. The Medb know we betrayed them during the battle and VIPER won't allow us to survive without a pantheon. It was a win-win. For now."

She did not like the sound of those last two words. So much for being subtle. "Don't screw this up, Tristan. You have your sister and your two friends to keep safe."

"I'm not doing anything, so don't get your panties in a wad. When can we leave Treoir?"

"I don't know yet."

"I'm not staying here, or in gryphon form, forever. Flying's a gas until you do it over and over and over again. I'm ready for some down time and so are the rest of them."

She couldn't argue with that. "Let me find out from Tzader who is going to be point person here and get them set up to work with you until I get back with Storm."

"You get R and R time while we're stuck playing air patrol. What's fair in that?"

Just when she was feeling friendly toward Tristan he had to push her pissivity button. "If you're going to be a dickhead, I'll let *you* negotiate your terms for remaining here, but keep in mind the mortal world is now a battleground for anyone supernatural, especially anyone with Belador blood. Staying here is a pretty sweet deal, but I'm sure I can convince Macha to send you back where you can't shift at will without VIPER yanking you in to face a Tribunal trial for exposing paranormal activity to humans."

She snapped her fingers. "Oh, and you'll have a target on your back from the Medb in addition to any other preternatural predators."

Tristan cocked his head, looking at her as if he found something fascinating. "I had no idea that Storm found crazy women a turn on."

Evalle tossed her hands up in the air and walked away to the sound of Tristan calling her back. She flipped him off and his words ground into a deep chuckle. Jerk.

When she found Tzader and Quinn, they faced each other, talking in low voices. Harsh sounds rumbled. Quinn's jaw was rigid and his lips pulled tight and flat when he said, "Find someone else. Not my problem."

Tzader growled back, "What? You're just going to go off and hide again? Great. Just when we need leadership you disappear. I don't have that luxury."

"Leadership? You're the damned leader, not me."

"I'm *ordering* you to go back and fill in as Maistir," Tzader said, shoving a blast of fury at Quinn.

"You can only order me if I remain in the tribe."

Tzader snarled, "You'd turn your back when the tribe needs you most?"

"Me?" Quinn laughed, but the sound was dark and grim. "I'm not the Maistir who intends to sit here and wait for someone who's probably not even alive any more."

Evalle sucked in a breath. Quinn had never been cruel.

"Brina *is* alive," Tzader said, as if anyone trying to convince him otherwise would be a deadly mistake. The sentient blades hanging on each side of his hips hissed and snarled, ready to attack. "And you will do your duty or you'll *wish* you had."

And Tzader had never threatened any member of the tribe, especially one of his two best friends. He wouldn't unleash those blades on Quinn, right?

CHAPTER 4

Evalle's hair stood on end.

She'd never heard Quinn and Tzader go at each other this way, sounding as if one of them was close to grabbing the other's throat. They were facing each other and leaned in, looking like two bulls ready to charge.

She stepped up with her hands between them. "Hey, you two. What's going on?"

"Shut up," Quinn snapped without looking her way.

"Don't fucking talk to her that way," Tzader warned, shocking Evalle with the unexpected curse.

"Thank you, Tzader," she said, glad that one of them had control of his emotions.

Then Tzader snarled just as lividly when he ordered her, "Get out of here, Evalle."

Nope. No control on his part either. She pushed closer. "No. You two stop this ... whatever is going on between you, and calm down."

They both swung feral glares at her.

She had to be in a time warp. What happened to Tzader and Quinn, and who were these two asswipes?

Crossing her arms, she glared right back and let them have it. "I will kick both of your butts if you give me any more lip. What the devil is going on?"

Tzader looked away and muttered, "Dealing with a dickhead."

Quinn shot back, "And here I thought that was the definition of an inconsiderate prick." But Quinn stretched his neck then told Evalle, "Sorry I snapped at you."

"Apology accepted."

"But I am not qualified to lead anyone. Plus, is it too damned much to ask for time to mourn *my* loss? Or should I say *losses* since Lanna's gone, too, only with no hologram to indicate she was ever here?" Quinn swung a heated look back at Tzader.

So that's where Quinn had been when she'd lost track of him and Tzader earlier. They'd been looking at the Brina hologram that showed nothing of Lanna, the young woman who had been wrapped against Brina. Only the threads of Noirre majik covered a hollow shape where they'd stood before they'd both vanished.

Quinn had lost the woman he'd loved and his teenage cousin in one ugly act from a Belador traitor.

Still, something was severely off with Quinn and Tzader.

Evalle opened up her recently discovered empathic senses that were getting better with practice. Quinn was literally bleeding pain over losing Kizira, the Medb priestess he'd secretly loved who had died in his arms during the battle. Tzader was a roaring hot mess of anger and worry with Brina missing and no idea what her fate was at this moment.

Even so, this made no sense.

Tzader and Quinn had always been *her* two rocks to depend on. She could handle having one of them emotionally crippled right now, but not both.

Neither could the Beladors. But both men had lost women they loved. If there was any decency in the world, Evalle would at least be able to bring Lanna and Brina back.

She spoke gently to Quinn. "I do believe we'll get Lanna back and I know that there is no such thing as a right amount of time to mourn what you've lost." She paused to glance at Tzader, who had the decency to look embarrassed over his harsh words. Then she continued, "But if Trey manages the warriors back home for a day, could you fill in after that for a little while so that Tzader can handle interaction between Macha and the gryphons?"

When nothing came out of Quinn's mouth, Evalle added, "If you could, it would allow me time to find Storm and bring him here to help us bring back Brina and Lanna."

Quinn stared at her with hollow eyes rimmed in a misery she'd never seen on his face before, but he nodded, "I can do that."

"Thank you." Then Evalle turned to Tzader, and if the pain in his gaze had a sound it would be an animal howling. Not knowing where Brina was had to be torture. "Tzader, will you be okay here while I go back to Atlanta to find Storm?"

He swallowed and the hard movement of his throat looked painful, but he nodded. "We'll be fine."

Quinn wouldn't look at Tzader when he said, "I'll need to be teleported *with* Kizira's body."

Oh, boy. Wait until Macha was asked to do that.

Evalle jumped in. "I'll go with him. Maybe you can send a group of us at one time, Tzader."

"I'll handle it." Tzader strode off, shoulders hunched against the world, looking as alone as he must feel. Watching the grief of the two men she loved as brothers was squeezing her heart. Her chest should be bleeding from how much it hurt.

Evalle put her hand on Quinn's arm. "I'm so sorry about Kizira."

"You don't have to keep apologizing. Her death wasn't your fault. At least you tried to free her from the Medb."

"She tried to help me too. She was instrumental in helping me get our people out when it came time to escape TÅμr Medb. I will do anything I can to help you through this, Quinn. I wish I had words to ease your loss, but I know nothing can make this better. I miss her too." That drew his attention sharply to Evalle's face. She nodded. "I never thought I could even like a Medb priestess, much less care for her, but I got to know the real Kizira and see glimpses of the woman you fell in love with."

A tear ran down the side of his face.

Evalle pushed words past the vise squeezing her chest. "It hurts me to see you like this and know that you ended up losing her after she told me she only wanted peace and to be with you. Do you want me to stay with you for a few days?" That would delay helping Tzader, but Evalle had bought him time to wait here for Brina's return, which she knew was the only reason he refused to leave.

She could do no less for Quinn.

Quinn shook his head. "No, but I'll go to Atlanta for only one week. No more."

One week might not be enough time. "I don't know how long it's going to take to track down Storm, then I have to bring him here for any hope of finding Brina."

"I'm sorry, Evalle, but I'm pushing the limits just to stay in Atlanta for a day, much less a week. I ... can't control my anger, or my mind. I almost dove into Tzader's head a moment ago to lash back at him."

Her mouth fell open. "You would never–"

"Evidently I would, and I'm not proud of that. It may be our powers corrupting that's causing it. I'm battling right now to keep from striking out at anyone and everyone. I don't want you near me after today." He walked away toward nothing, just ambling.

How could she leave two of the most powerful Beladors who were closer than brothers, or had been, to get through this without someone watching over both of them?

She needed to keep them safe from each other.

What would Quinn do once she left him in Atlanta in what was reported just an hour ago to be a hotbed of preternatural aggression right now?

The best way she could help was by tracking down Storm as soon as she could, which would soothe Tzader and free him up to run North America.

Once that happened, Evalle could then focus on Quinn.

Wouldn't it be nice if Storm was waiting for her at his house?

Tzader's voice came into her mind, sounding like a bad connection. *Come ... castle now ... Brina.*

Evalle took off at a run and put her body into overdrive to cross two hundred yards and reach the castle in seconds. She flew up the steps and through the entrance that two Belador guards held open for her.

No one was in the lobby.

She raced toward the sunroom where Brina had been before she vanished.

Please let there be a real person standing in place of that empty hologram.

Evalle sucked in air, winded as she neared the sunroom. She'd always packed more power than the average warrior due to her mixed blood, but even she had noticed a slight change in her power level with Brina gone.

What about the other gryphons? Tristan in particular.

Was the corrupted Belador power the only reason Tristan hadn't been able to teleport out of Treoir?

"Do not touch her!" Macha shouted and the entire castle shuddered.

Evalle slid to a stop at the door to the sunroom then walked in cautiously. Tzader, Macha and an old druid blocked Evalle's view of all but the head of Brina's translucent image.

Nope. Brina had not returned yet.

Tzader stared at the floor ... or was he looking at the bottom of the hologram?

The old druid in a dark green robe stood next to him, mumbling something in Gaelic, then said, "That canna happen."

"How do you know?" Macha demanded, hair flicking wildly with her emotions. "That's Noirre majik. Anything can happen. Just back away and do not touch that nasty majik again."

The white-haired druid had a matching snowy beard that hung to the middle of his chest. A dark gray cap drooped off one side of his head, sort of an oversized, limp beret. He backed away and should have been bowing and speaking softly, trying to appease the goddess, not shouting, "We're losin' her. I had a vision. Just as I have told ya, this calls for someone who *can* wield black majik!"

"There will be no black majik ever brought in here again! Do you hear me?"

Evalle was pretty sure someone in another universe had heard Macha.

The druid's robe whipped around his legs and he fisted his hand, shaking it at Macha. Was he powerful enough to do that and survive? He opened his mouth to shout something else.

Macha whipped her hand at the old guy and poof. He was gone.

Guess that answered the question of who had the most

power, not that there'd been one.

Then the goddess rounded on Evalle. "What do you want?"

Crud. *Everyone* had a bad case of nasty temper today.

Evalle quickly assessed that Macha didn't realize Tzader had sent Evalle a telepathic call and Tzader was staring at the bottom of the hologram by Macha.

Now would be a good time to diffuse some of this anger.

Evalle owed the goddess a thank you. "On behalf of the gryphons and the two Rías, I want to extend our appreciation for processing the petition for our race and welcoming our group into the Beladors."

"I suppose you're welcome," Macha replied, just as surly as before. "Keep in mind that as their leader, you are responsible for any infraction."

And here we go again. But it wasn't as though Evalle hadn't expected some strings attached. "I understand."

"If that is all, you are dismissed."

Tzader shook his head as if he'd been in a fog and told Macha, "I asked Evalle to come up. She can help us."

"What do you expect a gryphon to do that a three-thousand-year-old druid can't?"

Anger flared in Tzader's face. "Evalle told you she'll bring Storm back."

"A Skinwalker in league with a witch doctor? Didn't I just say no black majik? Evidently I need to be more concise. No one with any hint of black majik is coming in here."

"He is *not* involved with the witch doctor," Evalle argued louder than she probably should have.

Macha swung around, hair billowing and eyes sizzling with anger when she faced Evalle. "You must have a death wish to dare raise your voice to me."

Tzader's eyes flared with fury that Evalle had rarely witnessed in all the time she'd known him.

What was wrong with him?

Whatever it was also affected Macha and Quinn.

Evalle didn't want to end up zapped away to who knew where like the druid, and she had to keep Macha's attention away from Tzader, who looked seconds away from going postal. "I didn't mean to raise my voice to you, goddess. Please forgive me. I'm just as upset about Brina as anyone else and failed to control my volume." That sounded so much better than telling Macha she could bite Evalle's boot, which would be her last words. "All I'm saying is that Storm is not in *league* with the witch doctor. She is his enemy."

Tzader's words were taut with stress, but he managed not to sound aggressive when he addressed Macha. "Storm has proven to be exceptional in tracking preternaturals for VIPER. It's more than his Navajo skills. He has majik as well. We don't know how long Brina has left."

Evalle stepped past Macha to take a look at Brina's image. It reminded her of the bastard child of an ethereal image and a glass ornament made of pink and yellow translucent crystal. All that wrapped in dark threads woven with black majik.

She asked, "Did that druid have an idea of how long she can stay in this form?"

Macha answered her with no small amount of exasperation. "Garwyli has no idea about black majik. He kept yelling something about four days, but he can't actually know."

Tzader's head came up sharply at that. "Four days?"

"He has nothing to base that on beyond laying his hands on the Noirre," Macha argued. "It might have infected his mind for all we know."

Inclined to heed the ravings of a druid that old, Evalle pointed out, "But what if Garwyli is right about how long Brina has left? We can't risk running late bringing her back. And Brina," Evalle added to remind the goddess that two lives were at stake.

"I'm well aware of what is required, but we can't be reckless and put the Beladors at any more of a power deficit." The goddess spoke with a terse tone obviously meant to hide her fears, but anxiety hid beneath her words. "Our warriors are losing their powers in different degrees everywhere. The German Maistir is dead and our warriors are vulnerable to attacks from any enterprising nonhuman. Our enemies are quick to take advantage of what they see as a wounded tribe."

Macha paused, staring at the vacant-eyed hologram. "Brina is in this situation due to Medb witches and a traitor that managed to infiltrate this castle with Noirre majik. I can't trust

someone who possesses black majik skill not to take advantage
of the Noirre majik already in place and destroy this hologram.
As long as it is here in the castle, the Beladors have some use
of their powers. If I allow someone to destroy it, every Belador
would face extermination as powerless humans." Macha
pinned her gaze on Evalle. "I will allow your Skinwalker
entrance if you can swear that he will not bring dark majik into
this castle."

Evalle had no idea for sure where Storm's majik originated,
but she trusted him to bring no harm to Brina or the castle. She
opened her mouth to speak, but Tzader cut her off with a
booming decree.

"*I* swear on my immortality."

Evalle sucked in a breath at that.

Tzader spoke in her mind. *Would Storm practice black
majik?*

No. Her quick answer came straight from the heart.

*Then I trust your judgment and, if I can't get Brina back,
immortality means nothing to me.*

She had nothing to say that would change his mind.

Tzader told Macha, "The sooner you send Evalle back, the
sooner we'll be able to determine whether Storm can help us."

Macha appeared to be considering Tzader's vow and was
clearly not happy about him speaking up, but she addressed
Evalle. "Very well. Have Trey contact Tzader once you've
located the Skinwalker. If I'm convinced that he's acceptable,
I'll teleport him to Treoir. When you're ready to teleport back
to Atlanta, envision where you wish to arrive."

"What about VIPER? Will there be any fallout from me
entering the beast games?" Evalle quickly added, "Which I did
for the benefit of the Beladors."

Specifically, she wanted to make sure Sen didn't snatch her
out of thin air and drop her in a Tribunal meeting to be judged
after all she'd gone through to protect her tribe.

"VIPER will be informed that you were compelled by the
Medb to go with Kizira to TÅµr Medb, then compelled to join
the battle."

That wasn't exactly how it all went down, but if Macha was
willing to sell that through, then Evalle wouldn't argue since

Kizira–and probably the Medb queen, Flaevynn–were both dead. It wasn't as if someone could counter Macha's explanation.

With that, Macha lifted her arms and disappeared in a whirl of spinning air sparkling with blue and silver.

Evalle didn't want to consider the consequences of Macha not finding Storm acceptable. She waited to think about where she wanted to land, because that had sounded as if she'd be whisked away the second she pictured the location in her mind.

Handy, if she didn't get snatched away before she was ready.

She needed to take care of one more thing before she left and turned to Tzader. "Tristan will be responsible to you for managing the gryphons and Rías while I'm gone. They need to take a break from their gryphon form and return to their human bodies, but they won't all do that at the same time."

Tzader nodded, his gaze returning to Brina. "What the hell?"

Evalle stared at a piece of the hologram the size of a cookie that had broken away. It turned into tiny crystals and blinked out of existence.

Covering his mouth with his hand, Tzader stood there, thinking. Over the next minute, he absorbed what he saw and the result was a heartbreaking expression of misery. When he moved his hand, he said, "Now we know what Garwyli was ranting about. What he saw in his vision."

Losing Brina would be devastating for Tzader. But losing this last part of Brina would sever the only ties Beladors had to the Treoir power base.

CHAPTER 5

"If I wasn't desperate, I wouldn't do this," Evalle mumbled, looking over at Nicole, who was riding shotgun in Nicole's wheelchair-accessible van with only the dash lights illuminating her features. Now that sunlight was not an issue, Evalle had spent the better part of two days driving all over Atlanta in Storm's old Land Cruiser since her Suzuki GSXR was still up north in the mountains at VIPER headquarters. But when she realized she needed the help of her gifted friend, she'd left the SUV back at Storm's house and taken the train to Nicole's so they could drive the van.

She'd wait until Tzader returned to reclaim her motorcycle.

No point in giving Sen any chance of grabbing her when no one was looking.

But in all the time she'd spent traveling around Atlanta, she'd failed to squeeze out a drop of intel on Storm.

"It's okay, Evalle," Nicole said in that soothing voice of hers. "I told you, Red is out of town until tomorrow night. I'm happy to help. In fact, I'd have been hurt if you hadn't asked. This is what friends do for each other."

How could anyone not love Nicole?

At twenty-seven, she was as beautiful on the inside as she was on the outside. Her brunette hair fell softly around her shoulders. Every color looked great against skin a rich cappuccino brown, but today she wore a deep-pink dress that would look awful on Evalle.

Red, Nicole's significant other, was another issue altogether.

Evalle and Red got along like two starving Rottweilers

thrown in a cage with one meaty bone. Red would not be happy about Evalle taking Nicole away from their apartment on the east side of Atlanta, and she'd be even *less* happy that Evalle was taking Nicole to Storm's house just north of downtown. In spite of knowing how powerful a white witch Nicole was, Red always tried to take care of errands away from the apartment just to make Nicole's life easier, so Red did have a nice side. But she didn't like any of this crazy supernatural shit, as she described it, and was always worried that Evalle was putting Nicole at risk.

Evalle admitted, "I appreciate that Red's not around to rip me a new one, but that's not what's bothering me right now. I'm rethinking this whole trip."

"Why?"

"I'm worried about exposing you to that witch doctor even through a vision or whatever you can do at Storm's house to find him. I'll do anything to get a lead on him, but not at the risk of harming you."

Nicole smiled and her eyes sparkled. "Stop fretting over me. I won't allow any dark majik to pull me in."

"Thycle!" Feenix exclaimed from behind Nicole's seat.

Evalle smiled into the rear view mirror at her little gargoyle. "What is it, baby?"

Nicole twisted in her seat and put her hand out. "Let me see."

Evalle's two-foot tall gargoyle flapped his gray, batlike wings. They felt like soft leather when you touched them. When he finished depositing something into Nicole's hand, he raised his head. Orange eyes the size of tangerines and a toothy grin smiled back at Evalle in the mirror. "Make thycle."

Nicole brought her hand around and Feenix had smushed the glob of Play-Doh she'd given him into something that *might* be a motorcycle since it had two lug nuts for wheels.

Beaming a smile at him, Evalle said, "Beautiful, baby."

When Nicole passed it back to him, Feenix plucked the two lug nuts with his fat little four-finger hands and shoved them in his mouth, crunching.

Evidently it was an edible cycle. "Your bike won't go far without tires," she reminded him.

Feenix's eyes drooped as he tried to figure that one out, until Evalle reached down to the stash Nicole kept for him in the van and tossed two more lug nuts toward the back seat. Feenix flapped his wings, flying up to catch them, then floated back down, squishing his clay again and chortling happy noises.

"Don't eat the clay, okay?" Evalle said, not sure if she'd gotten through to him until he made a pfft sound.

"No eat clay. Tathe like glue," Feenix mumbled.

Now Evalle wondered what he'd eaten to taste glue.

She turned up the narrow street to Storm's house, an older home in an area known as midtown, where a large number of houses had been built in the early 1900s with wide front porches and tiny garages, if any. When she reached the house, she parked in the driveway behind the Land Cruiser.

Evalle had left it in the exact spot where it'd been when she first checked Storm's house almost two days ago.

She'd known then that he wasn't in the house or he'd have come out the minute she stepped onto his property. He would be watching for her. If he were in Atlanta, he'd have called her by now.

Or emailed or texted. Something.

Wasn't this emerald he'd stuck on her chest supposed to be some kind of homing device for him or her? He'd used majik to stick it permanently on her chest before she entered the beast games, saying he could find her that way.

So where was he that he couldn't get in touch with her some way?

As Nicole prepared to exit the van in her wheelchair, she asked, "You said both notes were found here, so you feel pretty certain Storm did not get yours?"

"Yep. Tzader said the one I left in the bedroom was faced down. I remember wanting to flip it over, but that was the moment when Kizira teleported in and snatched me before I could say a word to Storm."

"That sucks."

"I wanted to strangle her at the time, but she was only doing what the Medb queen had compelled her to do. Poor Kizira tried to help me at every turn."

"I'm sorry for you and Quinn."

Evalle hadn't mentioned anything to Nicole before now about Quinn and Kizira, but Evalle had never dealt with someone close to her going through this kind of loss. She was worried about Quinn disappearing and never seeing him again. Nicole was the one person, other than Tzader or Quinn, who Evalle could trust with secrets.

Nicole sat up and took a long look at the house. "Has anyone besides Tzader been in there?"

"Not that I know of. I didn't go inside after you warned me to leave everything as undisturbed as possible in case I needed help." The kind of help a witch with a few extra abilities could give Evalle, but staying away from the one place she could feel closest to Storm had been difficult.

Evalle came around and backed Nicole's wheelchair out of the van, then pushed it over to a side entrance into the kitchen where no one would see her use kinetics to lift Nicole and her chair up through the open door. It took a little more effort than it normally would, but at least her kinetics were still working. Once inside, Evalle stared at the full pot of coffee. Tzader told her that when he'd first walked in, the coffee smelled like it had been freshly made.

Nicole said, "The witch doctor was in here unless Storm allows someone else with dark majik in his home."

"Why do you say that?"

"I can feel hate lingering in the air. His and another person's, but the second one is so filled with malice that it reeks of a dark presence." Nicole sniffed. "Licorice. Smells like someone cooked it on a grill."

"That would be the witch doctor he's been hunting, because he smelled that at the beast games last week."

"Or perhaps she was hunting *him*," Nicole murmured as she wheeled herself forward. "Did you bring the notes with you?"

"Yes." When Evalle had taken a couple of thirty-minute naps so she wouldn't fall on her face, she'd slept with the two pieces of paper. Tzader had given her the notes as soon as the battle ended in Treoir. He'd come to Storm's house searching for Evalle, and evidently he'd arrived right after she'd been teleported away and Storm had left to hunt for the witch doctor.

What had happened to make Storm do that on the heels of Evalle leaving?

She didn't know and she was afraid to let go of the two notes, her one tiny connection to Storm.

When Nicole reached the center of the living room, she angled her head back and forth, then looked over where a rug woven in the geometric Navajo pattern covered a spot directly in front of the fireplace. "He comes here to be with ... someone."

"We've, uh, spent some time out here." Could Nicole tell what they'd been up to the last time Evalle was here? That had started out in the living room and ended up in the bedroom.

"No, someone else."

"What?" Evalle's stomach dropped at that. No way would Storm have been here with another woman.

Unless maybe it had been before Evalle started coming here. But even that thought nauseated her.

"Evalle," Nicole called out softly. "I'm not talking a human or someone that Storm was intimate with, but an ethereal being."

Had she been that obvious? "Oh, sure, I know."

Nicole wheeled around and rolled over to her, taking Evalle's hand. "I also feel his love for you here everywhere. When you were here, his happiness permeated the air and the walls. I'm not sure he's ever been really happy until meeting you because of how strong his emotions had to be to imprint on a structure. It is clear he loves you, so no matter what we find, you must not doubt him or that you are ..."

When Nicole paused, Evalle said, "I am what?"

"Special. Very special to him." But Nicole looked away, embarrassed over something.

Special was nice, but Evalle felt certain that Nicole had wanted to say more. Nicole had never held back anything before. Why now?

Evalle let it go in favor of focusing on their task. "What can you figure out by being in here?"

"You told me Storm has a spirit guide. That's probably who I'm sensing in this room and over here close to the fireplace. I'm going to try to reach that spirit and see if she has met with

Storm."

"Whoa, hold everything, Nicole. Storm hasn't told me everything about growing up in South America, but that's where this witch doctor came from and Storm was forced to fight in beast games down there. I have no idea what else went on so there's no guarantee the spirit hanging around here is friendly."

"No, this is a being of the light." Nicole's wheelchair sat in the middle of the rug now. "I have a sense of comfort in this area near the fireplace. I believe this might be one place that he meets with his spirit guide."

Evalle glanced around, feeling twitchy at the idea of a spirit visiting while she and Storm had been naked in his house. She dealt with ghouls all the time downtown. They were Nightstalkers who would trade their intel on preternaturals and humans for a handshake with someone like Evalle. The brief connection with a powerful being gave the ghoul ten minutes of corporeal form that most of them used to guzzle as much cheap wine or rot-gut whiskey as they could find.

And if every Nightstalker she'd searched for, including her favorite one, hadn't been hiding from preternaturals stalking the city, she might have gotten a sliver of intel.

But meeting with ghouls downtown was business, where having a spirit here in Storm's house was too close to home.

Literally.

"What's wrong, Evalle?"

"Do you think the spirit just popped in and out of here at will?"

"No. With Storm being Navajo, I believe he and the spirit might have a bond that allows them to communicate with each other when needed. The spirit would not enter uninvited."

Nicole had answered Evalle's unspoken question, which meant Nicole knew exactly what Evalle was actually asking. Life around preternaturals and psychic witches meant there were few secrets some days.

"Why don't you light some candles and give me some time to see what I can figure out," Nicole requested.

Evalle doubted that Nicole needed the candles so much as Nicole knew that Evalle had to do something to be of use.

Once the candles were lit, Evalle sat out of the way on the sofa, determined not to fidget. But two minutes later Nicole was still staring into the barren fireplace. Evalle lost her battle with impatience and stood up.

Nicole spun around, surprised.

Evalle held her hands up. "Sorry. I have to do something."

"There's nothing you can do to help me, except remain very quiet."

"I can do a better job of that out of here." Evalle strode down the hallway, slowing when she reached the bedroom and stepping into it without turning the lights on. The bed was still rumpled from the most amazing night of her life.

She walked over and lifted the pillow to her face, inhaling deeply. His scent sparked the memory of being touched and held. Of Storm hovering over her, hunger burning in his eyes as he slid inside her.

Her knees gave way and she dropped to the floor, kneeling next to the bed where she laid her head down, clutching the pillow. Forty hours since she left Treoir and not a word from him or any sign that he was alive.

Tzader had to be frantic, which Evalle could appreciate since she was no longer as confident as she'd been when she arrived in Atlanta.

Where are you, Storm?

She closed her eyes, as exhausted from worry as she was from being on her feet for so long without rest. She wanted to be near Storm so much that his face finally filled her mind's eye. He was smiling, then he kissed her the way a man did when he wanted a woman to know she belonged to him. Evalle hugged him to her, loving the feel of his long fingers on her skin. She whispered, "I miss you." His hands turned cold on her skin and she pulled back to see his face.

His eyes were open, but not seeing.

His body was a bluish-gray color and it floated in a haze that made her skin pebble with chill. His eyes continued to stare straight ahead at nothing. So deathly still. Then his lips moved with sounds too low for her to hear them. She moved toward him, swimming through the air.

Swimming? That's what it felt like.

When she got within an inch of his lips, he said, "I am not coming back."

"No!" She reached for him and he drifted backwards out of her reach. He turned yellow eyes on her. *"Go!"*

She jerked awake, searching the room.

"Hello?" Nicole called from the living room. "Where are you?"

Evalle pushed up on shaky knees and dropped the pillow on Storm's bed. The nightmare had been so real.

"Evalle?"   Wheels rolled toward the bedroom. Nicole appeared in the open doorway. "Are you okay? You're pale."

"I'm fine. Battle nap. Was I out long?"

"Maybe a half hour."

Evalle walked toward Nicole who turned around and led the way back to the living room. On the way, Nicole said, "I'm sorry, but I haven't been able to reach his spirit guide or anyone else."

Over two days were gone. Brina might only have one more. Two at the most.

Evalle asked, "What else can I do?"

Nicole didn't answer right away, maneuvering her chair back in front of the fireplace while Evalle stopped to lean against the wall. When Nicole turned back to her, she suggested, "I can use something of Storm's and try to find him through astral travel."

"No! You're not doing that out of body thing where a witch or something worse might grab you and never let you come back." In that moment, Evalle finally admitted the one thing she'd been avoiding.

Storm might be somewhere he couldn't escape.

Leaning back in her chair, Nicole sighed. "I have another idea, but you aren't going to like my suggestion."

"Then I'll get over it. I have to find Storm." Yes, Brina was important and so was her Belador tribe, but Evalle couldn't face a world without Storm.

"It might be difficult—"

Someone knocked at the front door.

"I don't care, Nicole. Whatever it takes," Evalle said on her way to the door. She checked the peephole to see a familiar head of blonde hair.

"Are you kidding me?" she muttered, opening the door to find petite, curvy Adrianna there. Adrianna Lafontaine, a Sterling witch who had nursed Storm back to health while Evalle had been locked away in a VIPER prison.

The Sterling name belonged to a dynasty of witches who practiced black majik.

Does my day not suck enough? "What do you want, Adrianna?"

"It's not what I want, but what you require."

"Then thanks for coming by, but I don't need anything you're pedaling."

"Evalle?" Nicole called from behind her.

"Yes?"

"You know that suggestion I was talking about?"

"Yes."

"It's standing in front of you."

Nicole wanted Evalle to ask for Adrianna's help to find Storm? *Oh, hell no.*

CHAPTER 6

Does my father wander through a morbid realm like this, forever searching for a resting place he'll never find without his soul?

Storm had backed into a recessed area in the cavernous Mitnal. He'd found a spot where no demon could sneak up on him. He shook with the constant assault of icy film on his skin and a heat roaring inside his body. Hanhau kept his demons perpetually on the edge of violence so that when he pointed one at a target, the demon needed no encouragement to unleash all that pent up fury.

I can't let Nadina and Hanhau win. I will not allow my jaguar to shift at will. I will not become a demon.

Storm had repeated that mantra over and over, but he was no fool. If he didn't escape soon, his body would give in to the cursed witch doctor blood that had battled his honorable Navajo ancestry his whole life.

His father had traveled to South America with the sole purpose of helping the reclusive Ashaninka tribe hold on to its heritage in the face of corporate mining and farming operations threatening every inch it owned. His father had lost faith in his own people back in North America, specifically his immediate family who'd traded their heritage for money. Storm never doubted his father's love for his Navajo people. But after years spent fighting changes that he believed would destroy all he held dear, his father had packed up and gone in search of places he could make a difference.

His father once told him, "I grew tired of fighting my own people and decided I needed to take a break and come back with a fresh outlook, so I went far away to South America and what I found rejuvenated me. The Ashaninka are kind people with no champion. I decided to be theirs."

But a witch doctor had stolen even that from his kind father.

A swirl of energy disturbed Storm's moment of peaceful memories.

He should have clear night vision in this dark due to his Skinwalker traits, but he stared out at pitch black.

His jaguar would be able to see in here.

Storm shook off the tempting thought.

Maybe Hanhau thought to drive him from his hole. Not happening. This was the best place to avoid fighting. That didn't mean he had any way to prevent the threat that was currently slithering toward him.

He opened his empathic senses. Ah, now he recognized the smell and feel of the menace approaching him.

The same demon that had paused nearby a while back, then crept up close until Storm had growled in warning, sending the demon fleeing.

His growl alone hadn't actually accomplished that feat.

In that same moment, Storm had begun to change, because his control had fractured. When he put the brakes on his change, he'd stopped as a half-formed jaguar, half-human that had been scary enough to make a demon think twice about attacking.

Shifting into a jaguar here was nothing like in the mortal world. Normally, his jaguar weighed two hundred and fifty pounds. When he'd started changing here, he could tell his animal was going to be much larger and a far more dangerous beast.

His shifting involuntarily in Mitnal would be the final victory for Nadina. Once Storm grew into a full-fledged demon, right down to the glowing red eyes, it wouldn't take long for his dark blood to claim any ounce of humanity he had left.

Then there would be no going back.

Nadina would be thrilled to return to Mitnal to find him that way. She'd left to insure Storm wouldn't try to force her to escape with him since their blood oath worked only if they left together.

There was no way she'd risk being around him until she was sure he'd lost all touch with being a human.

He'd be lying to himself if he didn't accept that turning into a demon was inevitable, but every time Evalle's face came into his mind he redoubled his effort to not give in, telling himself, *I can do it for her. I can do anything for her.* But with no soul to begin with, he was left with few tools to fight Nadina's blood that coursed through him. Once he spent enough time in Mitnal, all his best intentions to battle the shift would fall beneath an onslaught of demonic drive.

Storm had watched Hanhau turn a new arrival into a demon in minutes.

His best guess had him closing in on two days in this place, and the only reason Storm had made it this far was because he hadn't been forced to battle yet. Hanhau was crafty, waiting for Storm to admit defeat and roll over, because that would take far less of Hanhau's energy than forcing the change.

Or he *had* been waiting.

The demon crouching closer outside his den now indicated time was up. When the demon moved another step forward, Storm's jaw yanked down and widened to allow for fangs.

He curled his fingers tight and forced the shift back until his face felt right again.

But when he opened his hands, the claws curling from his fingers had dug into the palms and fur covered his forearms.

I will not shift if I have to fight him.

Storm's body quivered so hard he had to clench his teeth to keep from banging his jaws together. The ice filming his skin dropped another ten degrees and the fire burning inside him threatened to consume his body from the inside out. All due to the blood pushing him to break out his animal so that he could meet the threat and make the kill. It was all about fighting to the death. Not allowing any demon to defeat him. Ever. Storm would rip this one into a hundred pieces then lap up his blood like cream. He would–

No! I will not shift.

The demon was moving with intent now. His glowing red eyes pierced the darkness fifty feet away.

So Hanhau had run out of patience and wanted to see if Storm was as powerful as Nadina had sold him to be.

Power rushed through Mitnal, throwing light across the room, lifting demons to their feet. They howled and screamed for blood, turning in his direction.

Was Hanhau unleashing all of them on him?

Had Nadina's partner changed his mind and decided Storm was too much trouble?

When the closest demon rushed forward to attack, Storm was on his feet, hands raised to battle.

CHAPTER 7

"I am not interested in any help from a Sterling witch," Evalle told Nicole over her shoulder while she and Adrianna, the

in question, still faced each other at the door to Storm's house.

"Please allow her to enter, Evalle. Are you really willing to quit this easily on finding Storm?"

Nicole didn't pull punches when things got serious, which Evalle loved about her even though she hated that Nicole was right.

That didn't make accepting Adrianna's help any easier. Evalle stepped back and held the door open. "Come in."

Once Adrianna had stepped inside, Evalle closed the door and turned to Nicole. "So explain why I need ... her?" She angled her head at Adrianna who stepped over to the nearest upholstered chair and perched on it, looking perfect as usual. Her maker had packed a lot of body into just a couple inches over five feet tall, and carved it up to force men to salivate.

Smoky blue eyes watched everything and her red lips looked as though they wanted to smile, but never quite reached that point.

"Please have a seat," Nicole said to Evalle. With her wheelchair backed up to the dormant fireplace, Nicole showed far better manners than Evalle by asking Adrianna, "Would you like something to drink?"

"Thank you, but no."

"Then I assume you're here because you heard that Storm is missing and want to help."

"I'm here because I spent three weeks playing nurse and I can't collect on that debt unless he returns."

Evalle had just dropped onto the sofa as far as she could get from Adrianna, but that comment spiked her blood pressure. "That's only because Storm's spirit advisor grabbed the first skirt she could find while I was locked beneath VIPER headquarters."

Adrianna shrugged. "Still, I was there and he owes me."

Steamed at Adrianna, Evalle glanced over to find Nicole smiling. What the hell?

Nicole rolled her eyes. "There is nothing going on between Storm and Adrianna. To think so would insult Storm."

Yet again, Nicole made a valid point, but it failed to dilute Evalle's anger at seeing Adrianna in Storm's house and listening to her point out how Storm owed her for nursing him back to health.

"I assure you I made no moves on Storm," Adrianna said. "Nor did I try to sway his interest from you."

"And you expect me to believe that?" Evalle challenged.

"Of course. If I had wanted him, you would not have had a chance."

Evalle stood up and calmly asked, "Is that your favorite outfit?"

Adrianna shifted her confused gaze to look down at her short black skirt, matching jacket and pink blouse. "Why?"

"Because that's what they're going to bury you in."

"Okay, you two," Nicole interjected. "Retract your claws and let's get back to the business of finding Storm." Nicole turned to Adrianna, "Please don't antagonize Evalle. This is going to be difficult enough."

Adrianna smirked, but held her tongue.

Evalle hadn't had real sleep in days and knew she was overreacting, but she was done with being patient. "What is going to be difficult enough?"

Using a voice that would soothe a gang war, Nicole said, "To trust Adrianna to help us find a connection to Storm."

"You have to be joking. What can she do?"

"Did you not just say that Storm's spirit guide contacted Adrianna when he was injured?"

"Yes." *Did they have to keep bringing that up?*

"Then Adrianna may be able to accomplish what I've failed to do since we arrived. She may be able to contact his spirit guide, who may know where Storm is."

That was perfectly logical and something Evalle should have figured out if her head hadn't been shoved up somewhere she couldn't see daylight. Humble pie was her least favorite dessert, but she'd eat it if that meant any lead at this point. Turning to the dark witch, Evalle gave herself points for ignoring Adrianna's quirk of a smile and asked, "Would you help us contact Storm's spirit guide?"

"Why, yes I will." Adrianna stood and asked Nicole, "Do you want to be a part of this?"

"I appreciate the offer to include me, but I have to decline."

Adrianna tipped her head in acknowledgment.

"You're not going to do this?" Evalle asked Nicole.

"I'm in conversation with Rowan's coven and can't mingle my gifts with that of a dark witch or I could end up sanctioned, not to mention being shunned. Rowan is lobbying for me to join because she feels it's important. I have never participated in any dark arts, even for a good reason. For me to participate now would reflect badly on Rowan and would go against my beliefs."

Rowan was the sister-in-law of Trey McCree, the most powerful Belador telepath Evalle had met. Rowan was also Evalle's friend. *I just asked Nicole to do the equivalent of my turning my back on the Beladors.* "I'm sorry, Nicole. I wasn't thinking."

"I know and I would be in the same frame of mind if I was worried over finding my mate."

Storm wasn't Evalle's *mate*, but she got Nicole's point.

After waiting for Nicole to wheel over to the far side of the room, Adrianna pointed at the rug in front of the fireplace and told Evalle, "You should sit there."

"Why?"

"If you're going to argue the whole time, this will not work. You must be very still and allow the spirit guide to either come here to speak with you or take you to her world."

"To her world, as in the dead world?"

That drew a pained sigh from Adrianna. She looked over at Nicole who said, "I am placing a protection spell around me to prevent any contact with my skin. I can't be involved, but I will not allow anything to happen to you, Evalle. You're going to have to work with Adrianna if you want to meet with Storm's spirit guide, who has no reason to come here when Storm is not present, nor any reason to harm you."

Evalle stared up at the ceiling fan turning slowly and took a couple of deep breaths. Why was it so hard to pull her head out of her nether regions where Adrianna was concerned?

Storm would go through far worse for her. When she lowered her head to face Adrianna, she said, "I'm ready." Then she sat down on the rug.

Adrianna said, "Close your eyes and push everything away. When I begin whispering, envision somewhere that is quiet and makes you feel safe. That is where his spirit guide will be."

Evalle closed her eyes and started hunting visually for a place that was quiet and safe feeling. Something generic and quick. She was in a hurry to talk to the spirit and get moving. That's how she dealt with Nightstalkers. Offer her deal and give them one chance to shake that minute or not at all. They always took it.

She stared at the darkness behind her eyelids. No spirit was appearing.

"Relax," Adrianna's voice was a soft whisper around her. "Let go a little. Don't try to force it."

Easier said than done. What sort of setting would look inviting to a spirit? Ocean? Mountains? Forest?

Evalle slowed her breathing and tried to relax her shoulders as she pictured each of those places.

Adrianna's whispering filled the air circling her ears, riding a tide of highs and lows until it mushed into a chant that Evalle didn't recognize.

Actually, she didn't care where the spirit chose to meet. This place was as good as any.

She felt sleepy and needed rest. She should just lie back on this soft grass and stretch out for a while. The thick leaves on the branches overhead offered shade from the warm sun that she could finally appreciate.

"So *you* are the one he has chosen."Evalle blinked her eyes open at the censure in this woman's voice. A Native American female faced her. Mid thirties and attractive in a simple way. "Who are you?"

"Kai. Storm's spirit guide. Whom did you expect to find here?"

Evalle admitted, "You, but I'm a little off balance. Where am I?"

"In my realm. We do not have long to speak, so you should choose your questions with more care."

Evalle's pulse raced.

She was really talking to Storm's spirit guide, who had sharp cheeks and warm brown eyes. Storm had said Kai died in her thirties, but that had been twelve hundred years ago. Licking her dry lips, Evalle chose her next question more carefully. "Do you know where Storm is?"

"I know where he is not."

This might be more difficult than Evalle had thought. "Is he with that witch doctor?"

"He left to follow her and I believe he found her."

"Do you know where he found her?"

"At the last place she stopped."

This could take a while if Kai kept answering in circles. Did that drive Storm crazy when he met with Kai? Back to the point in all this. Before Evalle could continue twenty questions, Kai said, "I believe Storm is no longer in your world."

"No! He can't be dead." Evalle hurt from head to toe at the possibility.

Thunder rumbled overhead and the sun disappeared behind dark clouds. *Now I'm going to get drenched in the spirit world?* She started to ask Kai what that was all about until she took in the spirit guide's dark frown. Was the weather here in direct relation to her mood?

Lanna had that same ability in the mortal world, and Lanna was an unknown entity.

Time for another slice of humble pie, evidently. "I didn't mean to yell at you, Kai. I just refuse to believe Storm is dead."

Bam, the weather cleared up. Kai had a calm face again. "I do not believe he is dead either."

"But you said—"

"You can talk or you can listen. Which will it be?"

This Kai was tough, even when she was being nice. "I'll listen."

"I do not feel Storm's spirit in your world, but neither have I seen his spirit pass by on the way to a final resting place. That means he is somewhere else."

"Okay, I'm still listening. Where?"

"I don't know, but he has been gone too long to be somewhere from which he can return on his own. Especially if it is somewhere the witch doctor led him. If so, there is only one person he cares about enough to go through whatever it will take to return, and that is you."

Evalle grinned. *Take that, Adrianna.*

"But," Kai continued. "He carries the blood of the witch doctor as well as that of our ancestors. He has fought a valiant battle for many years to avoid going over to her world. If he is there now, he has been tricked or captured. Either way, he will not want you to follow him."

"I don't care. I am going to find him and I will bring him back, no matter who I have to fight."Kai nodded. "As it should be from one of your standing."

Wait, what had Kai meant by that? *What standing?* Evalle didn't get a chance to ask before Kai continued.

"I can only tell you that this witch doctor led him to a building that had machines, and then I lost track of him. I could not follow his essence once he left this plane, but the witch doctor disappeared at the same time. So I believe he is in her domain."

"Do you think I can find him where he disappeared around machines?"

"No. I would not waste time searching the last place where they traveled."

Evalle opened her mouth to ask how that was any help in finding him, but Kai wasn't through explaining things. "The witch doctor possesses the souls of Storm and his father."

Evalle frowned. What did that mean, exactly? She didn't have time to ask. Kai spoke faster now, obviously trying to get the information out while she could.

"I doubt that you know what you're up against with the witch doctor. She holds his soul and owns his life, neither of which she will release to anyone as long as she lives."

"Guess I'll just have to take that decision out of her hands," Evalle said, not joking a bit.

Kai's soft features turned sad. "You must allow Storm to regain his soul and free his father from wandering between worlds. Storm believes that the one who kills the witch doctor before that happens will gain her possessions. It's critical to him that he be the one to take back the souls. You must be careful not to interfere with Storm's chance to regain something he believes is necessary to have a life with you."

Air backed up on Evalle's next breath at those words. A normal life with Storm would be all she'd ever want. Had he said something to Kai about wanting one with Evalle?

Kai began to fade.

Oh no. "Stop, Kai. Please. I need to find the witch doctor. Where do I start?"

"Use resources in your world and your connection to him."

"You mean this emerald in my chest?"

Kai wavered out of view then came back into focus just long enough to say, "No, your connection as his mate." Then she was gone.

Mate? Did she mean like ...

Evalle couldn't come up with any other definition for mate except the one that meant being bonded as a couple.

"Where are you going? I want to know what you meant about ... " Evalle stopped shouting when Storm's living room came back into view.

"Meant about what?" Adrianna asked with genuine curiosity in her voice.

Evalle was not about to admit that she didn't know what Storm's spirit guide had meant about being his mate or that the witch doctor possessed Storm's soul. Not to the Sterling witch.

Covering her outburst, Evalle said, "About finding Storm. Kai said she thinks he followed the witch doctor to another realm."

"Kai?" Nicole asked, wheeling back into the conversation circle.

"His spirit guide," Evalle explained. "Oh, and Kai also said that Storm would *only* return for me."

"Then you are the only person who can locate him," Adrianna was quick to point out.

Evalle nodded, "Exactly."

Nicole looked worried. That couldn't be a good sign. She asked, "You do realize if the witch doctor is in another realm, it's the kind that might require a dark guide."

"No, it *will* require a dark guide," Adrianna corrected.

Evalle nodded. "Storm told me the witch doctor is pure evil. He wouldn't even speak the woman's name." This was no time for being vague or testing the waters. Evalle pushed up to stand and asked Adrianna point blank, "Can you lead me to Storm?"

"Possibly. For the right price."

"What's your price?"

"If I get you to Storm, plus help you figure out how to free him, then you and he will both fulfill his debt to me."

"Done. What is it you need?"

"I'm not telling anyone until you're both ready and neither of you is right now." Adrianna folded her hands in front of her, always so prim and proper. "If you don't go for him soon, Evalle, you may not have a reason to go for him at all."

The skin along Evalle's necked chilled at that warning. "What makes you say that?"

"I first heard about this witch doctor the week Storm was injured. A Nightstalker tried to trade with me for information on a woman from South America who was in the city hunting a Skinwalker who could shift into a jaguar."

"Did you tell Storm?" Evalle asked.

"Yes, but I haven't spoken to him since then, well, not in private–"

And you're not going to if I can do anything about it.

"–but I've heard more since then."

Realization hit Evalle at the same moment Nicole narrowed her eyes at Adrianna, but Evalle was first to speak. "You've been trading for information on Storm?"

"Not exactly, but you may view it that way."

"And you expect me to trust you to guide me into some dark

realm."

Adrianna lifted a delicate eyebrow. "No, I don't expect you to do anything. Storm is depending on you, not me."

"Point taken." With little sleep and no sign of Storm in the mortal world, Evalle was getting testy. No point in taking it out on everyone around her. "What did you find out about Storm and this South American woman? Was it the witch doctor?"

Adrianna dipped her head in acknowledgement. "You're asking the correct questions. Yes, the woman asking about him is the witch doctor, a dark witch of the highest caliber."

"Or lowest, depending on your world view," Evalle muttered.

Ignoring her, Adrianna continued. "If this woman has either captured Storm or tricked him into another realm, somewhere Kai can't find his spirit, then I'm guessing it's for one reason. To take control of him."

"No one controls Storm," Evalle argued.

"Not in the state of mind he was when you last saw him, but if he's turned into Nadina's slave, the game changes significantly."

"Nadina? That's the witch doctor?"

Adrianna nodded. "Now you can be glad for the research I've done."

Evalle had to admit that she was thankful for any intel right now.

According to Kai, Storm did not have his soul. Would that make him even more vulnerable to this Nadina? Evalle had to sit down. She felt light headed with so many possibilities and none of them good.

For once, Adrianna's voice held a compassion that Evalle had never heard. "I know you don't want to trust me, but the more you can tell me the better chance I have of figuring out just where he went. The longer we take, the less chance of getting him back."

No. I will not lose him now that I've found the man I want to spend forever with. Even his spirit guide believed Evalle was Storm's mate. Evalle sat up straight, shifting into battle mode. She could keep trading insults with Adrianna or she could step out on a limb and offer trust in exchange for help–two things she'd learned to give and accept because of having Storm in her life.

Decision made, she said, "What I'm about to tell both of you is Storm's personal business, but it is relevant to what's going on. I don't want to risk a mishap because I didn't share everything."

Nicole offered her a smile of understanding, because Nicole knew how hard this was for her.

Evalle explained what Kai had told her about the witch doctor stealing Storm's and his father's souls. When she finished, Adrianna's dainty face took on a hard expression. "Needing to get his father's soul back adds another obstacle, but there is a way to regain his soul and free his father's."

"How? I'll do it."

Adrianna said, "First you have to be sure this witch doctor hasn't traded the souls for something else."

"Okay, then what?"

"You kill her, which passes possession of those souls from her to you."

Evalle shook her head, thinking out loud. "That's a problem, because Kai warned me not to screw up Storm's chance to have his soul returned. If I ended up with the souls, I have no idea how to return them to the rightful owners and I don't want to own Storm's."

"There is a danger in owning souls, but you can't overlook that as a potential solution," Adrianna added with plenty of warning. "Besides, a being as powerful as Nadina has few vulnerabilities unless you're a deity, so killing her is not as simple as you think, but none of this will matter unless you can locate Storm and the witch doctor."

"Which one can we locate the quickest?"

"Storm, because of your connection to him, but you'll have to trust me to help you reach him."

Trust a Sterling witch. Locate Storm. Make the witch doctor hand over his soul and his father's.

All in less than twenty-four hours or Brina would just disintegrate and that was assuming the witch doctor didn't vaporize Evalle first.

Evalle asked, "Trust you to do what?"

Adrianna said, "It will be easier to show you."
I knew you were going to say that.

CHAPTER 8

Evalle parked Storm's sport utility close to Grady Hospital.
She'd named her favorite Nightstalker after the place because
he usually hung out here. Nicole had been a sweetheart to keep
Feenix for her and, if Evalle was being entirely fair, Adrianna
had done her a favor by following them to Nicole's apartment
and giving Evalle a ride back to Storm's house.

Adrianna must really want that debt paid.

If the Sterling witch helped Evalle find Storm, Evalle would
more than do her part to repay Adrianna.

Evalle checked her watch. Thirty-two minutes until meeting
Adrianna. Just enough time to hunt down a cranky ghoul.

Snagging her backpack from the passenger seat, she hooked
her arms through the straps as she headed out to find Grady. He
should be near the narrow stretch of road between the hospital
and an eight-foot-tall right-of-way barrier that did little to
diffuse noise from the heavily traveled interstate that ran
through Atlanta's downtown. This *should be* Grady's usual
haunting ground, but he'd recently expanded his territory.

He also took corporeal form on occasion without requiring
the handshake with a powerful being.

That would be Evalle's fault, and a favor she'd granted that
might one day come back to bite her, but she had too many
jaws after her butt right now to spend time worrying over that
one.

She raced along the quiet back street abutting the hospital,
hissing, *"Grady!"* every three steps.

He hadn't been here earlier, but she'd only done a half-assed
search since all the Nightstalkers had vanished, gone into

hiding from predators stalking the city. Getting to Storm's house had been priority one at the time.

A movement off to her right yanked her attention sideways. There he was, hovering in the shadows next to a dumpster, talking to someone in a cloak.

A person Evalle didn't recognize.

A cloak? The weather hadn't turned cold yet. Not brisk enough to wear something that appeared to be wool.

She headed for Grady and his suspicious friend, ready to use her VIPER status to inquire as to the stranger's identity.

Nothing confrontational.

That was the plan until the stranger shoved a hand out to shake with Grady.

Evalle caught a hint of rotten limes and the hair rose on her neck. She called, "What's going on, Grady?"

The cloaked stranger turned toward Evalle, face hidden inside the dark hood, then backed up and rushed away. Not the reaction of an innocent person. She reached Grady just as he was scowling up a storm.

He crossed his filmy arms that were covered in the same plaid shirt he'd worn since dying as a homeless person. His baggy pants attested to how thin he'd been when he died. Grumbling like an old bear run out of his cave before he was finished hibernating, Grady told her, "You better have somethin' to make up for that loss."

"Who was that?" She inhaled again, and the rotten lime smell verified her earlier impression. "Medb? You were going to share intel with a Medb?"

"I ain't the only one," he argued.

"That's my enemy."

"I *know* that. That warlock was gonna tell me what's goin' down in town."

This was beyond bizarre.

She grabbed her head and took a second. Getting Grady riled was never helpful. When it came to getting information, he could be tougher than prying a clam open with fingernails, but he had a soft spot for her. Sometimes.

In a calmer voice, she asked, "What's a Medb doing in Atlanta to begin with when they've just attacked Treoir, and what is going down in the city that you think he could tell you about?"

Grady just hovered with his arms crossed and his bottom lip shoved up in stubborn determination.

She dropped a strap off one shoulder and swung the backpack around. When she lifted Old Forrester into view, Grady's eyes flickered with desire, but he tried to hide his interest.

She shook the bottle at him. "I am not going to apologize for stopping that trade. You know better than to deal with a Medb, Grady."

"Things have changed in the last few hours."

That was news, but not enough. "What changed?"

"You cost me a deal. I'm gonna want more than one handshake."

"What? Are you kidding me? I gave you–" She caught herself and lowered her voice. "–more than *two* handshakes at one time." She'd broken the VIPER rule of not shaking hands with a ghoul for more than a minute, because Grady had wanted to be in human form to hear and see his granddaughter's wedding. So Evalle had hidden with him on the balcony of a church and she'd held his hand almost solid time for twenty minutes.

Finally, he lost the glower and hunched his shoulders. "I just haven't been able to stay solid on my own for the last two days and you been gone."

Great. Now she felt guilty. "Then make a deal with me and shake," she said in more gentle tone.

"What you lookin' for?"

Hadn't she just asked him about the Medb and whatever was going on in town? Did ghouls get dementia? "I want to know what is up with the Medb and I need information on a witch doctor."

"Done." He stuck his wrinkled hand out and warm eyes peered at her from a coffee-bean-brown face.

When they connected, the power raced down her arm and vibrated around their hands. Grady's eyes rounded. He said, "What's happened to you?"

Had evolving into a gryphon changed her power? "A lot and

I'll tell you all about it as soon as I have time, but I'm under a time crunch."

When Grady let go of her hand he stood in his human form with gray whiskers and skin dark as a walnut. He wiped a hand over his mouth. "You gonna sweeten the deal or not?"

She handed over the bottle, giving him time to guzzle a good belt of it before moving him along. "What's happening in town?"

He tucked the bottle next to his chest. "Someone turned a bunch of demons loose."

Two would be too many. "What's a bunch?"

"Heard sightings of eight so far."

"Who would have done that?" she pondered out loud.

"Don't know. I ain't seen any myself to know what kind they are or where they might have originated."

"Why did you think that warlock would know anything?"

"Cuz there's Medb all over the city?"

"And VIPER's allowing *that*?" Evalle asked, furious. "Beladors are their largest force." Had everyone in VIPER forgotten that the Medb just attacked Treoir?

She wanted to stomp Sen's butt. The liaison between VIPER agents and the Tribunal had to be the one allowing this.

But that made no sense. Sen hated Evalle, but pissing off the Belador agents would put him in ill favor with the Tribunal. Not even Sen would want to face a Tribunal of two gods and a goddess who would decide his fate.

"You through havin' a hissy fit?" Grady asked.

She rolled her eyes. "Start talking."

He slugged another drink first. "Like I said, someone dumped demons out here and VIPER is in upheaval because the Beladors ain't pullin' their weight." He lifted a hand. "Before you go off on me again, you have to know the Beladors are having power problems, right?"

"Yes," she admitted.

"How come?"

"The Medb attacked Treoir and the Belador traitor was inside with Brina. He tossed some Noirre dust on her then Tzader killed him, but not before Brina vanished, leaving her hologram. The Beladors should have no power, but that hologram must be holding a connection between Brina and Treoir. Apparently the power base is still intact but corrupted." She realized who she was talking to–a Nightstalker social butterfly–and pointed a finger at him. "But you don't need to advertise that."

"Don't be pointin' no finger at me."

With some beings, pointing a finger could be construed as a threat. In Grady's case, it just annoyed him, which was nonproductive. The clock was chewing up minutes, but she had a duty to the Beladors here in Atlanta as well. "Have any of the demons been caught or killed?"

"That's the kicker. I've heard of two different incidents where Medb witches and warlocks have killed the demons and saved a human."

Had the earth dropped off its axis? What was going on? "So now you want me to believe that the Medb have turned into good Samaritans?

He held his arms out. "I don't make this stuff up. They've been turnin' up all over town, not causin' trouble and savin' VIPER's bacon."

Was she just too cynical to accept this at face value? No, it was more a matter of being too realistic to believe thousands of years of deadly behavior could change overnight. There was something way wrong with this picture. What were the Medb up to now? And who was running their show?

Grady pointed at Evalle. "You got big problems. Sen's been on a tear. You need to do somethin' with Quinn."

"Why?" She had a sick feeling this might be about Quinn's lack of control.

"He ain't right. Word is that Sen came in and cleaned up one of Quinn's messes then told Quinn that being actin' Maistir does not give him free rein."

Leave it to Sen to make things worse when the Beladors could use a hand. "What did Quinn do?"

"I heard he caught a troll stalking a human. Grabbed the troll and did some kind of mind control then sent the troll on his way."

"That doesn't sound bad." Quinn hated to take control of a person's mind by force and tried not to be invasive. If the troll went away then Quinn must have thought the troll was no longer a threat.

"That's not the problem. A bit later, Quinn found a Medb warlock hanging around Centennial Park. Word is that Quinn snatched the warlock's mind, left the guy wandering around until he walked out in front of a Marta Bus. When Sen showed up to clean up that mess, he told Quinn if he had to come back again for bullshit, that Quinn could explain it to a Tribunal."

The Medb were playing ambassadors of Atlanta and Quinn had turned into the Terminator. The best way Evalle could help Quinn and all the Beladors was to bring Storm back and hope he could pull off the impossible once again and locate Brina.

Their most powerful Belador druids had tried and failed.

This was the only hope Evalle could offer.

"I need to find a witch doctor named Nadina."

"That nasty thing that brought Langaus into the city?" Grady shivered at the appalling suggestion. "What you want with her?"

"Storm is missing and I think she's behind it."

"That injun let a witch doctor outfox him?"

Trying to correct Grady's politically incorrect terminology would be wasted breath. "Maybe. I just need to know where she is."

He scratched his whiskered chin. "I don't know. Come back a little later and I'll see what I can find out on her."

"I'll be back soon. The longer Brina is missing from Treoir the weaker the tribe gets."

"You too?"

"Not as bad as the pure bloods, but I've noticed a few things."

Trey came into her mind. *Evalle, can you hear me?*

She held up a hand for Grady to wait. She replied to Trey, *Yes, but your voice isn't as strong as usual.*

My telepathic ability is weak but at least it works even if I am the only one capable of reaching anyone else this way. At least I can hear you, which is a nice surprise. I heard from Quinn that we need you to find Storm. I've got everyone we can spare looking for him, too. Have you had any luck?

She wanted to give Tzader and Quinn something positive,

but she didn't want to paint blue skies. *I've found a source who will help me locate Storm and I'm going there next.*

Do you have a cell phone?

No. Mine was trashed in the battle. I'll call you as soon as I have one again. She mentally added that to the endless list. Quinn could get her one if he wasn't busy running herd over the Beladors.

And stripping the minds of Medb warlocks.

That shouldn't bother her because the Medb were a bunch of murderers. Normally. But she didn't like the picture Grady had given her of Quinn.

Trey continued, *I know you're doing what you can, but find me the minute you have Storm. We're losing warriors everywhere.*

Will do, she assured him.

Trey withdrew from her mind.

Her stomach rolled at having even less time. And now there was a hunt for demons going on.

She hooked the backpack in place again and reminded Grady, "Do not shake with the Medb."

"Why not? They got juice."

"You would help them?" She couldn't squash the insult in her voice. He was supposed to be her friend. "They been doin' your job. Maybe they changed."

"Oh, sure, and maybe you'll turn entirely human again and take Sen's place at VIPER."

He sighed. "I'm not takin' sides against you, but I heard that there's new management in the Medb."

"Did you hear specifically that Flaevynn is dead?"

"Naw, but what the hell else would new management mean?" he groused. "Anyhow, about the Medb here in the city. Word is that Sen said he was glad to have the help. Don't you want me to shake with some of 'em and find out what I can from the Medb?"

She had no argument to counter that logic, which should worry her since Grady was being the reasonable one right now. "I guess so."

Grady's voice and expression turned grave. "I don't know what the Medb are doin' here, but it cain't be good."

There was the person who had helped her time and again. "Agreed, so be careful."

Next stop was meeting Adrianna in a secluded place on the edge of the city. The dark witch had said for Evalle to come alone and allow no one to follow her. From anyone else, Evalle would think she was being set up for an ambush.

Evalle had Storm's Land Cruiser in sight when a thought struck her. Dark witches and warlocks of the Medb coven were infiltrating the city.

Would Adrianna know about that?

CHAPTER 9

"I'm not understandin' this place," Brina whispered, staring out at nothing but an endless blue-gray fog. The same thing she'd stared at since opening her eyes hours ago.

Had it been hours?

Felt like forever in this realm, wherever it was, where she and Lanna had regained consciousness.

When Lanna didn't answer her, Brina looked down to where Lanna sat next to her with her legs crossed. "Lanna!"

Blonde curls with black tips bounced when the teenager lifted her head quickly. "What?"

"Were you asleep again?"

"Yes, but not for long."

"Is being in this place causin' you to be drowsy?" What would Brina do if Lanna went to sleep and didn't wake up?

"No." Lanna stood up. All five-foot-two of her. She had to be somewhere around eighteen, though she looked younger at times then acted older just as often. Lanna stretched and looked all around again, mumbling, "Maybe we have died and no one was informed to come get us."

Brina rubbed the chills on her arm. "I don't believe we are dead, but I cannot explain this place."

The fact that Lanna wasn't mouthing off attested to just how frightened the teen was, too. Understandable even for someone with Lanna's power, and Brina had felt that power when they first met in the castle.

Power that might be even more formidable than Brina's, which was saying something. Brina had inherited hers from generations of Treoirs tasked with being an anchor for all

Belador powers. Even so, faced with the unknown, Brina welcomed the company and Lanna had not taken a step away from Brina's side since they opened their eyes to this gloom.

Lanna's exuberance had calmed significantly, another reason to worry over the girl. In spite of the strange hair, she was an attractive one with huge blue eyes filled with experience Brina wouldn't expect in one so young.

Much like me when I was informed of being responsible for all the Beladors four years ago, not long after I'd turned eighteen.

Da and her brothers had died in a battle with the Medb. Not one male Treoir had walked away.

She was the sole living descendant and now she'd left the Beladors vulnerable. Not her fault since, once again, the Medb had gained the upper hand, this time attacking her in her own castle. But she'd left Tzader at risk *and* believing she didn't love him.

That lie had been Macha's doing.

If I get out of here, I'm done with bending to Macha's will. The first thing I intend to do is find Tzader and beg his forgiveness for allowin' Macha to manipulate me.

Enough of worrying over something Brina couldn't change until she returned. *If* she returned. As the Belador warrior queen, it was her duty to protect her tribe. She needed to get busy doing just that.

With nothing here that was of any use, Brina considered what tools she had on hand for finding her way back. She took a hard look at Lanna. "What exactly are you? I felt a fair amount of power pourin' off you when we were attacked."

Lanna heaved a long sigh and answered in her broken English. "I do not know. I have had much power since I was small girl in Transylvania. My family are long line of gypsies and other things they have not shared with me."

Brina couldn't attribute the kind of energy she'd noticed to mere gypsies. "You're Quinn's cousin. He's a Belador. Does he think you might have Belador blood?"

"No. I wish I did then Cousin would not keep trying to send me home. I need to stay here ... I mean in Atlanta near him. I have much trouble at home. Big trouble that follows me, but I must find way to stay in Cousin's country."

Brina smiled. They were stuck in some realm with no idea how to return to the castle and Lanna was worried about staying in Atlanta. "If we find our way back, I'll see what I can do about your stayin' with Quinn."

Lanna's blue eyes lit up. "Thank you. Now I have even more reason to find a way back for us."

As if returnin' to our bodies would not be enough? Brina appreciated Lanna's spirit and that the girl was not wailing away, making her crazy right now. She hated that Lanna was with her, but she was thankful not to be alone with nothing more than her thoughts. "I was thinkin' that we should retrace our steps to when we were attacked."

Lanna waved that off. "If we could do such thing, we would be home now."

There was the smart mouth again. "What I mean, Lanna," Brina said slowly to keep from snapping at her. "Is that we should think back to when we were attacked in the castle and try to figure out what happened. Maybe that will give us an idea how to return."

"Oh. Good idea." Lanna brightened. "We were in sunroom..." Lanna paused. "Why is that called sunroom when it has no windows for sun?"

"All the windows were replaced with stone when my da and brothers died, to limit the ways a threat could enter."

"In that case, you must put windows back when you return."

"Macha would have a fit after my already being attacked."

"But enemy was already inside. Windows stopped nothing, but make room gloomy."

Brina couldn't argue that point.

The Belador traitor had been inside the castle while the Medb coven attacked. She'd been brought low by one of her own. Over two years ago, Horace had blamed Macha for the deaths of his wife and child who were attacked by trolls while he was away battling with the Beladors.

Macha had unleashed a team to hunt down the trolls and make them pay, but that evidently had not been enough for Horace. He'd carried a grudge so deep that he went to the most deadly of the Belador enemies looking for revenge on his own.

Brina had hurt for the old man before she realized what he was doing to them with Noirre majik. But she could not understand such betrayal. No matter her pain, she would never have harmed her tribe. She shuddered to think what the Beladors might be going through right now.

Did they have any powers at all?

Brina could prevent the Medb from being successful if she could just return to her body. "Perhaps I will have windows installed when we are back on Treoir," she told Lanna. "For now, let's keep analyzin'. I was facin' you."

Lanna jumped in. "Yes. Then old man protecting us turned around and started throwing Noirre majik at you. Majik smelled bad, like nasty limes when it turned into threads that could not break. Had to be from Medb."

"It was. We've been huntin' for the traitor over the last two years." That was when the traitor had almost caused the death of … she blanked mentally, losing the rest of that thought.

"Brina? Is that all you remember about the attack?" Lanna asked.

Shaking off the mental hiccup, Brina replayed the last few seconds at Treoir out loud. "When you attacked Horace, he knocked you into me then the threads wrapped around you."

"My skin burned where it touched. Did you feel yourself lose power as threads kept wrapping around?"

Brina said, "Yes."

"Me too. Noirre was killing us. That is why I teleported."

"Is that what you did?"

"Yes. Only way to get out of trap."

Brina rubbed her forehead, thinking. "I was also teleportin' at the same time, but I was leavin' my hologram in place."

"Where were you teleporting?"

"Out to the hallway where I could call Beladors and direct them into the room. Where were you takin' us?"

"Outside where I could find Quinn." Lanna looked guilty all of a sudden. "But I have practiced teleporting only three days. Last time was in two rooms inside Medb tower."

Good goddess, as Quinn would say. The girl could have teleported them into a stone wall or a sword fight. "Do not use your powers here."

"I have to or we will not return."

"Then don't use them without your tellin' me first and gainin' my approval."

Lanna's face fell. "I cannot always wait on that."

"You will. I'll have your word on it."

Finally, Brina hit gold when Lanna's face paled. The young woman must take her word seriously, which only supported Brina's speculation that Lanna was something quite powerful.

"I give my word–"

"Good"

"–unless I think you are in danger again," Lanna quickly clarified.

That was probably as much as anyone would get out of her so Brina accepted that.

Lanna's forehead furrowed with thought. "If we both tried to teleport at same time, then we must find way back using that power."

Sounded logical, but majik sometimes defied logic. "I don't think we should try that until we've run out of ideas because we might end up separated."

"No," Lanna whispered.

"So do you have any other ideas?"

"Yes. I was trying to find way while I slept."

Brina had no clue where Lanna was going with this, but she gave her rein to continue. "Go on."

"I think if we reach someone in their dreams, we can find our way back. We tell them what happened with both teleporting and maybe they have druid or mage who can help us."

"Why would you be thinkin' that we can reach someone in their dreams?"

Heat rushed into Lanna's cheeks. "I met nice boy back home that I wanted to date, but his family was afraid of mine. I searched for him in my dreams ... and finally found him. We would meet there every night and–" Lanna caught herself. "He sent me note telling me he wanted to meet in person. He could not live forever with dreams only, so I know he remembered dreams when he woke up."

Brina made a decision right then that Lanna would be

trained. The girl had gained a great deal on her own by experimenting, but what would she be like with tutoring?

Then again, who would tutor her?

A worry for another time. Brina said, "I understand. How do we make this dream communication work?"

"You believe me." Lanna hadn't asked, but had spoken with awe.

"Of course I believe you. Now start explainin'."

Lanna smiled again, confidence beaming in her face. "When I slept a moment ago, I was trying to reach cousin, but I cannot find his dreams. Maybe he does not sleep while he worries about me. He must have nodded off at one time. I could feel his power so I try to push through to reach his mind, but I was knocked backwards."

"Lanna, you must be very careful with Quinn. I've never known a more powerful Belador mind than his."

"This is true. The few seconds I touch his mind it was bad place. Very angry and ... chaos. I am concerned that if I try cousin again he might accidentally kill me." Lanna added, "If he does, do not blame cousin. He is good man."

"I wouldn't blame him, but don't try that again."

"I do not know how to recognize power of anyone else or I would hunt for Evalle."

"Maybe I can do it," Brina suggested, talking to herself more so than Lanna.

"You must have strong connection," Lanna warned. "Someone who is family or close friend or ..." Lanna's face blushed. "Lover."

Tzader. That was the name she'd been trying to recall a moment ago. How could *his* name slip her mind? If Brina could reach anyone, it would be him, but she wasn't about to admit to Lanna that Tzader had been Brina's one and only lover.

The man she'd planned to marry until Macha forced her to give Tzader a chance at a life without Brina, since he could not enter Treoir at the time, and Brina could not leave.

If she connected to Tzader and he helped bring her back to Treoir, Macha would have to give him anything he asked for.

But would Tzader choose Brina when she'd spent the last

few weeks convincing him that she no longer loved him?

"You are not listening," Lanna admonished.

"What?" Brina hadn't meant to snap at her, but the possibility of Tzader believing that ruse about Brina wanting to move on with her life had her insides twisted up.

"I was saying you must be careful meeting someone in dream realm. There are dangers."

"Such as?"

"Dream travel is much like real life. I allowed this boy to kiss me and he left mark on my neck."

Brina smiled. "Think I can survive a bruise or two, Lanna."

Lanna started shaking her head and warning, "You could enter wrong person's dreams and be captured by a powerful dream merc ... or killed."

"What's a dream merc?"

"Very bad. I have heard their majik works only in dreams, but I have not met one to know for sure. You must be careful."

Just when Brina thought things couldn't get any worse, Lanna shattered that all to pieces. Brina asked, "How can I be tellin' if I've found the right person?"

"When I first figure out how to visit boy back home in my dreams, I went to sleep thinking of secret place we liked to meet. Think of somewhere you were with someone important to you and how much you want him to meet you there."

Brina lifted an eyebrow at her. "How do you know it's a *him*?"

"Your face was very happy when you drifted off. Must be man who means much to you." Moving on, Lanna added, "Very important that you always remember I am here waiting. If you forget, you may not return. I have heard some choose to stay in dreams forever."

Brina cocked her head. "Why?"

Lanna drove her fingers into her hair, concentrating fiercely. "Like ... uhm ... " She pulled her hands down and snapped her fingers. "Like astronaut who gets space sickness and lets go of link to ship so he can stay in stars forever. If you do that, I will not be able to call you back."

"Tell me how to watch for it."

Shrugging, Lanna said, "I do not know all about dreams.

This is not my majik. I only know what little I have heard, but I can feel your power. It is strong. If I stop feeling it as strong, I will try to pull you back."

Try? Brina would have liked a more encouraging word, but Lanna had found a possible way to reach out for help. Some options did not come with guarantees.

"No point in puttin' this off," Brina said, looking down at the mist rolling around their feet.

"Lie down and close your eyes," Lanna instructed. "Relax and think of private place where you went with only this special person, then call out to him. Ask him to join you. That is best way I know to find right person's dreams."

"Understood," Brina said with more confidence than she felt, considering she had no idea how to find Tzader's dreams or how to prevent ending up stuck in dreamland.

CHAPTER 10

Tzader shook off the grogginess that threatened to drag him under and kept pacing around the hologram in Brina's solarium.

"I can relieve you," a male voice called out from the door.

The sound of *that* one's voice sent Tzader's blood pressure boiling over. He swung around to face Allyn, one of Brina's guards who had taken advantage of his ability to be inside the castle when Tzader couldn't.

Allyn was as fit as any other royal guard and pristine in his emerald green and black vest, white long sleeved shirt and black pants. Tzader could see where a woman would find Allyn's face and physique attractive, but Brina wasn't just any woman.

Tzader growled. "Stay out of here."

Allyn stiffened. "I care about her, too."

"You may care about the Belador queen as your *leader*," Tzader enunciated, taking steps toward the door. "But you will not care about Brina in any other capacity. Understood?"

"Ordering me not to have feelings for her is illogical."

"I don't give a damn if it's irrational. Don't ever go near her again."

Allyn should have tucked his tail and backed away quietly from a Belador Maistir, but he was either more confident than he should be or without basic survival instinct. He said, "Have you forgotten that Brina and I are engaged?"

Nope. Not a drop of survival instinct in those genes.

Tzader crossed his arms and took three more steps, placing himself in front of Allyn and barring the doorway. "I have no idea what was discussed when I was not present, but Brina and I have been committed to each other since we were young."

A scoffing noise came out of Allyn. "Do you expect me to believe you've been celibate for the four years that you couldn't walk through the ward on this castle?"

"I don't care what you believe. I only care what Brina believes and she knows the truth. The minute she returns, I intend to straighten out this mess."

Allyn finally showed some proper humility and said, "I see that I've been misinformed, Maistir. If it is as you say and she truly does not care for me then I have made a huge mistake with my words."

You think, dickhead? Tzader had a feeling either he and Brina had been played by Macha or the goddess had confused Brina. For the last few weeks, his Brina had not been herself. She'd tried to convince Tzader that there was no future for them since Tzader was immortal, a gift he'd never asked for, and Brina was stuck inside a castle warded against immortals with the exception of her and Macha.

Macha had convinced him to do the honorable thing and let Brina move on. How could it be honorable to walk away from a bond forged with love? But on recent trips when he'd traveled by hologram to visit Brina, she'd been distant and made similar noises that echoed what Macha had said.

Sure, he'd heard about Brina's *engagement*, but he'd had yet to witness any joy in Brina's eyes over it.

When she returned, he was not leaving until he had the truth with her standing in front of him and staring into his eyes.

Allyn waited to be dismissed.

Tzader struggled not to shove the guard's words back down his throat. Not an acceptable action from one in his position of authority.

But Allyn's words had sounded sincere.

Could Brina really have moved on from what she had with Tzader? Exhaustion pulled at his thoughts, tangling them into a garbled mess of confusion.

"By your leave, Maistir." Allyn dropped his head in a respectful bow, still waiting.

"Granted."

Allyn vanished down the hallway.

Tzader paced the room back and forth twice until he crossed to a recessed sitting area that had been carved into the stone wall and covered with thick cushions. It was going on sixty hours since Brina had vanished. Once he'd delegated security here and in the mortal world, he'd spent the majority of that time sitting or standing in this room watching her hologram as if he could will her back.

When he sat, he sank into the thick cushions and glanced at the hologram for the millionth time.

Her crystal image floated above the floor, missing pieces from her knees down. More had disintegrated while he'd paced the room.

Where were Evalle and Storm?

Didn't she realize how little time Brina had left? Was Evalle more concerned about finding Storm than helping Brina? And what if Storm had no way to track Brina once he got here?

Doesn't anyone give a damn besides me?

Fisting his hand, Tzader drew back to strike the wall and stopped when Brina's face appeared before him. He croaked, "Brina?"

One blink and the image was gone.

Now he was hallucinating from lack of sleep?

He looked at his fist and shook his head. What had gotten into him? First he'd raked poor Quinn over the coals when the guy was gutted, next he been ready to jump Allyn and now he wanted to ram his fist into the wall because Evalle wasn't back yet.

Evalle had to be doing everything within her power to save Brina.

Tzader had never had a reason to doubt her.

He'd never had so short a fuse either.

He leaned his elbows on his knees and held his head in his hands. Exhaustion was eating at his emotions and his mind until he was walking around in a half-comatose state. He could do Brina no good if he lost touch with reality.

Rolling onto his back, he laid an arm across his eyes and let the memory of hiding in this very spot to steal a kiss from Brina bloom in his mind. Life had been so simple back then.

They'd planned out their future, anticipating an entirely different one than they'd been handed.

A groan rolled off his lips. He was so damned tired. Staying awake hadn't brought her back last night. Ripping into everyone who mattered to him sure as hell was not helping.

He had to shut down for a battle nap.

But how could he rest with Brina still gone?

Turning his head, he stared at the hologram.

Another section the size of a silver dollar vanished right before him.

His heart had never hurt like this. He'd thought losing her to another man would be impossible to survive.

He'd been wrong.

Losing her this way would destroy his world. He'd have first hand understanding of the way Quinn suffered. Next time Tzader saw Quinn, he owed his friend better than he'd given him so far.

As Tzader's breathing calmed, the aggression that had been chewing at him backed off. Not entirely gone, but diminished.

With his eyes closed, he pictured his Brina running through the forest and swimming at their special place in the lake on Treoir. She was so pretty. Red hair flying behind her. Laughing.

She used to laugh all the time.

Four years of being locked in the castle had stolen her joy.

He loved to see her smile. Loved the way she kissed him. Just loved her period.

A soft voice whispered, *"Miss me?"*

Tzader jolted at the touch, and sat up straight, coming awake instantly. No one was in the room.

He could swear that had been her voice. The hologram showed no signs of life. In fact, a piece of her index finger blinked out.

Hurt threatened to crush his heart.

He was losing his mind. He dropped back onto the cushions, closed his thoughts to everything except sleep. The sooner he got some shuteye, the sooner he'd be back on duty watching over her form.

Scattered thoughts tumbled through his mind for all of a

minute, then he drifted into a dark vortex of boneless sleep.

"Where are you, Tzader?"

"Brina?"

Cool air swirled around his face and arms. *"Come to me, Tzader."*

Where was she? "I can't find you."

"Remember our tree?"

That simple suggestion was all it took for sunshine to pierce the darkness and beckon him into the light. He strode forward through a field of wildflowers dancing in a gentle wind. When he reached the other side of the field, he entered the forest of trees a hundred feet tall and with trunks too large for him to reach around. Walking beneath the canopy of thick leaves and branches, his shoulders relaxed. He'd missed this place where he and his da had spent hours tracking game.

"Find our tree and you'll find me," whispered close to his ear.

Tzader paused, looking around. That's why he'd come here. Brina was calling him. Not the eighteen-year-old Brina he'd once shown his favorite areas so many years ago. No, the one calling him now had a woman's voice. She should be in the castle. Not out here where danger could find her.

Had the Noirre majik pulled him into its web of deceit?

If it did, Tzader hoped to be sent to Brina, even if it meant being trapped there forever.

He rushed to the tree that stood at the end of a spring-fed lake, as imposing as a centurion watching over their special private area. His blood burned in his veins as he ducked to search beneath sprawling limbs. Branches reached thirty feet from the tree, clothed in wide leaves that had once been a private shelter for their loving. The tips fanned the ground far from the trunk.

But no heart-stopping young woman waited for him.

Tzader felt the pain as sharply as a blade shoved into his chest, slashing his heart into pieces that would never match up again.

Where was Brina?

This was the spot where they'd pledged themselves to each other. A place and time carved into his memories. From that moment on, he'd never wanted another.

"Tzader?"

He shoved up and took a step back at the sound of her so close.

There she was, with her lush red hair spilling down around her, shoulders covered with a silvery-blue, hooded cloak. She looked more like the forest nymph he'd once called her instead of the Belador warrior queen.

Light spilled through tiny gaps in the trees, shifting and moving. Brina faded and came back.

This couldn't be real.

Brina never left the castle.

Wait. Why did she never step out of Treoir Castle?

Something tugged at the back of his mind, trying to tell him this was important. There was a reason she stood out here in the woods alone.

He should ask, but his heart was pounding too loud in his ears for him to hear his own thoughts. His body took over all decision making. The need to touch her was the only thing that mattered.

Brina stared at him with eyes full of disbelief and murmured, "I've missed you, *mo gradh.*" *My love.*

She stayed solid this time.

Real or not, in that moment, his world narrowed down to holding this woman again.

Tzader closed the gap between them, reaching for her.

She lunged into his arms and kissed him with the same reckless abandon that had ended with clothes being shed the last time they were in this spot.

He was onboard with that idea.

His mouth hungered for hers. He kissed the lips that fed his soul and tasted like all his tomorrows. Her hands clutched at him, touching his face, neck and shoulders, begging more from him.

For the first time in too long, nothing would prevent him from meeting that request.

Holding her soothed the bone-deep pain of missing her.

She made a sound in her throat, sexy, hot and demanding.

That was his little warrior who never wanted half measure

in anything. She reached down and ran her hand over his chest and lower until her fingers touched his hard length.

Memories of their last time together flooded him, lighting his skin on fire. She was all he'd ever want.

All any man could ask for.

And she was his.

Brina nipped his lip and licked, murmuring his name over and over. Her fingers gripped his shirt, wrenching it up until he stopped long enough to yank it over his head.

Her mouth was on his, her tongue playful at first then turning serious.

Grasping her hair, he gently tugged her head up and back. He kissed her soft cheeks then her neck, and on down until he had her draped over one arm. He took that moment to stare at her delicate skin, so pale against the dark brown muscles of his arm.

He gave her the words he'd told her that first time they made love. "*Tá mo chroí istigh ionat.*" *My heart is in you.*

Eyes as bright as a spring day and shining with love met his. She answered just as she had before. "*Gráim thú.*" *I love you.*

Then her eyes lit with challenge. "I'm missin' all of ya, Tzader. Not just that sweet tongue of yours."

He yanked the tie loose on her cloak and flipped it away.

The material stalled in the air, stretching out flat then floating to the ground as if ordered to become a blanket.

"Let your arms fall away," he whispered.

Watching him from where she hung with her hair cascading to the mossy ground beneath the tree, she lifted her arms and let them fall slowly.

Her gossamer gown shimmered when she trembled.

He lifted the thin strap at her shoulder and slid the material slowly over the peaked tips of her nipples, taking his time to unveil the pert beauty.

Every muscle in her body was taut, waiting, anticipating.

He lowered his head and took her breast into his mouth, sucking.

She arched and let out a painful cry that picked up volume when he raked his teeth carefully over the hard bud. He moved to her left breast, biting the material and dragging it out of the way. Then he brushed the rough skin of his tongue across her nipple and used his free hand to tease her right one.

Her body strained and quivered under the erotic attack.

It felt like forever since he'd held this treasure.

While he tormented her breast, sucking and nipping, drawing sexy sounds out of her, he eased her dress up and massaged his way north to her wet heat. No panties.

Dear goddess.

One touch and she grabbed her head, calling out, begging him. "Please..."

He'd intended to take his time and turn a deaf ear to her demands to end this torture. But two strokes over the sensitive skin and she bowed, crying out. Power zinged around him, buzzing his skin. He smiled.

Brina had no control over her power when she climaxed.

She was half-dressed so he finished the job, leaving her filmy gown in a pile and lowering her to the cloak. "You are magnificent."

He whispered words he'd held inside for too long. "I missed you. Missed us."

"I refuse to wait ever again," she vowed.

"Never. You are mine and no one will keep you from me." He'd never survive another four years.

Four years? That couldn't be right, could it?

He dug for how long they had been apart and drew a blank.

Brina's chest rose and fell with deep breaths, lifting her sweet breasts each time. The nipples were soft again, looking ignored.

He could remedy that.

But first he wanted another kiss. It was as if he searched for water as a dying man thirsts in the desert and her mouth was a clear spring. Leaning over, he rained kisses from her forehead down her cheeks to her lips. Full, abused lips that he would take care with, but fully planned to abuse some more.

Her hand fluttered down to cup him and he hissed. "Careful, *mo gradh.* I want you so much you'll end this too soon."

She smiled at him. One simple smile and his entire world came into focus. "If it ends too soon, we'll just have to be startin' over then won't we?"

"That's a promise."

"If I can't have you inside me soon, I may have to resort to majik to be gettin' what I want," she warned in her sweet Irish brogue.

Tzader sat back on his knees and unzipped his pants. He must not have been moving fast enough, because they flew away as if snatched by an invisible hand. He gave her a loaded look. "So it's like that, huh?"

"Oh, aye. It's time you finish what you started."

"Demanding *and* beautiful." He scooped her bottom and dragged her to him, lowering his head.

Now he'd get a true taste of her.

He made one slow brush of his tongue through her heat and she clamped her legs tight over his arms. He pointed the fingers on each hand toward her breasts and used his kinetics to play back and forth across the sullen nipples, teasing them back into action.

"Tzader, what are you ..."

Plunging his tongue inside her then stroking the tense flesh ended any conversation. At least he couldn't understand anything intelligible coming out between her moans. When he had her at the very edge of oblivion, he lifted his head, drawing a sound of loss from her.

He said, "Look at me."

She did and said, "Don't make me wait any more."

Stretching forward to cover her, he eased inside her and the look on her face was pure heaven. Chills ran up his chest at the first stroke. He clamped his teeth, determined to hold back.

When had control been so damned hard?

He'd given his pledge of love in the past, but they came out in a primal vow, yanked from within. "I love you, Brina. I always have, always will. Never doubt that."

"I love you more and forever," she proclaimed.

Her body lifted off the cloak, moving up and forward until she faced him and he sat back on his knees. She was using her kinetics to push herself down, driving him deeper on the next stroke. He shuddered against the surge of power he held back, waiting to give her more.

She put her hands on his shoulders and they flexed under

her touch. "Don't hold back. I want all of you."

Her voice was enough to push him over, but he gripped his control with a ruthless will. He moved a hand to touch her, finding that spot where he'd left her teetering. She was panting and moving in rhythm with him.

One well placed stroke and her inner muscles clenched him.

He dove off that edge right beside her.

Power exploded around him, bursting with colors.

He was lost to everything, blinded by the force of his climax and lost in her love.

Time had no meaning. The world shifted and warped, images flashed through his mind, too confusing to grab onto one and hold it still. Darkness smothered him until he opened his eyes.

He floated in ether, lulled by more than being sated. By joining with the other half of his soul. His Brina. No one would ever take her from him.

To try would be to welcome death.

Gradually, the air chilled his skin. He felt a soft cushion beneath him ... not the forest floor.

No warm body touched his. No fine hair fell across his chest. He couldn't draw a breath that didn't burn with painful reality.

He'd feared few things in his life as much as opening his eyes, but only a coward would avoid the truth.

When he turned his head, he blinked and there was Brina's hologram. One hand was now missing.

It had been nothing more than a dream.

"No. Brina."

He covered his eyes with his arm, unwilling to face the truth behind what he'd just glimpsed—a future of being left with nothing more than her memories. The pain of losing her would eventually consume him, leaving nothing but a shell. He'd only thought he knew how Quinn felt.

He'd just opened the door to Quinn's living hell.

CHAPTER 11

"Maybe we should bring Nicole back," Evalle said, wiping her damp palms on her jeans and staring at the altar. Did this really have to happen out here in the woods with sixty-six candles? Creepy, which was saying something considering that she fought demons on a regular basis.

"You don't want to do that to Nicole," Adrianna said as she prepared her ceremony.

"Why? She'd just be here to watch."

The Sterling witch paused from lighting one of the fat red candles spread around the clearing on a piece of property that belonged to someone Adrianna knew in north Atlanta. She explained in the same quiet way someone told a first grader that play time was over. "Allowing Nicole to remain in Storm's living room earlier while I called for Kai was fairly safe since Kai is of the light and Nicole shielded herself, but being anywhere near this ceremony might leave a mark on a white witch that would be easily identified. Nicole would have no way to avoid admitting that she'd been here. You don't want to do that to her."

"No, I don't," Evalle admitted quickly, then suspicion bubbled up through her next question. "But why do you care?"

Adrianna normally maintained an even keel, never showing an emotion or letting on about her thoughts, but her blue eyes flared with insult that boiled through her angry words. "You know, just because I'm a Sterling witch doesn't mean I'm an evil, inconsiderate bitch. I healed your wound when that Medb-influenced ghoul stabbed you when we hunted for the Ngak Stone. I watched over Storm for three weeks and pulled out every trick I knew to keep him alive only to catch a backlash from Sen for being gone so long. Now, I'm helping you locate Storm. So I want to know. What did I ever do to you to deserve all this grief?"

Evalle opened her mouth, then closed it without saying a word. Put that way, she didn't have an answer.

She'd been angry with Adrianna from the first moment the Sterling witch walked into the mission room at VIPER headquarters just because, well, Adrianna was the epitome of female perfection.

Crud. That was rotten.

If Evalle forced herself to admit the truth, Adrianna had never been anything but nice around the teams. But Adrianna stayed on Evalle's bad side because the witch had a habit of smiling at Evalle as though she knew something Evalle didn't, which she did.

Adrianna could probably fill a library with what she knew about men when Evalle couldn't fill a pamphlet.

Storm had never shown any male interest in the witch, but Adrianna was the walking vision of what Evalle would never be.

Graceful, elegant and confident in a room full of men who were ogling her.

Now that Adrianna had called her out, Evalle owed her an honest reply. And hell, maybe an apology.

After months of carrying around this grudge, it now felt unfair and Evalle was tired of spending the energy required to stay angry. "You're right. I should be thanking you for the times you've helped all of us. I'm sorry I haven't exactly shown my appreciation."

Adrianna lifted one eyebrow at the understatement, but allowed it to pass.

Evalle would never be besties with Adrianna, but she could treat her with the same consideration Evalle tried to give everyone. She could treat her like a teammate as a start.

Storm would be all over Evalle for this, because he'd told her that you never touch a dark witch voluntarily, but she extended her hand and said, "Thanks for your help tonight. I would do anything to bring Storm back. When it's time to pay his debt, we'll both be there."

Adrianna stared down at Evalle's hand. The surprise in her gaze gave more weight to the significance of Evalle's offer. Adrianna clasped hands and shook, the entire moment registering strangely in Adrianna's face as if touching–let alone shaking hands–was actually unfamiliar. When she withdrew her hand, she said, "Your offer is accepted and held in great esteem. So let it be spoken, so let it be done."

Things didn't automatically turn chipper after that, but the hostility hovering between them settled to a guarded acceptance.

As long as they were on friendly terms, Evalle wanted to find out where Adrianna stood with the Medb infiltrating the city. "Have you heard about the Medb showing up in Atlanta?"

"Yes."

When Adrianna didn't expound, Evalle said, "Are you on friendly terms with them?"

"No. I don't associate with all dark witches. In fact, I associate with very few."

Fair enough.

Once Adrianna had everything in place, she pointed to the stone slab. "Please take your place."

Evalle eyed the slab that just so happened to already be here on the ground when they showed up. Asking Adrianna if she'd been out here sacrificing chickens would likely put a kink in their tentative ceasefire. "Do I have to lie down?"

"No." Adrianna had that irritating smirk back in her eyes. "That's only for *virginal* sacrifices."

"Very funny." A dark witch comedienne.

Evalle stepped on the smooth stone and it might have been her imagination, but she could feel vibrations coming up from beneath her feet. "Are we on some kind of fault line here?"

"That's the energy you'll need to reach Storm."

"I don't teleport well."

"It's not teleporting. This is more like astral projection. Your body will remain here, but you should be able to speak and see things in another realm. However, you will be able to speak *only* to Storm, because of your connection to him."

Oh, boy. An out-of-body experience, literally. "Can

something in that other realm grab me and keep me there?"

Adrianna tapped her jaw, thinking, then said in a little girl's voice, "You mean like the boogie man?"

And just like that, the ceasefire disintegrated. "You still need our help," Evalle reminded her. "In your case, payback can be a bitch."

Adrianna's smile broke out from behind her clouded expression. "Ah, there's the Evalle that Storm needs."

"What's that supposed to mean?"

That wiped the smile from Adrianna's face. "Where you're going, you have to be ready for any threat, because a realm where a witch doctor of Nadina's power would have taken him will very likely be far worse than anything you've ever witnessed in this world. Do not fight the spirits as they guide you, and don't try to interfere in the realm you visit, because you can't physically influence anything that is going on."

Evalle caught her meaning when Adrianna paused. The witch was warning her that Evalle had to use restraint even if she thought Storm needed protecting. "I understand. What else?"

With a nod, Adrianna continued. "Any abrupt action on your part may cause the spirits to break the connection. Otherwise, you can return when you're ready by thinking about this spot, but I warn you now that we can only do this once. Just opening this passage will alert spirits better left undisturbed. Understood?"

"Got it."

"One more thing. Making an educated guess at the type of place he may be, for you to pass through from the mortal world to a realm of darkness uninvited often requires a sacrifice."

Was she serious? Evalle suggested, "Can we use a chicken?"

Adrianna stared at her a minute, lips twisted with disapproval. "I *don't* sacrifice animals!" Adrianna looked away, blew out a breath and looked back at Evalle. "This would be something you sacrifice *personally*."

Evalle was still processing the angry "*I don't sacrifice animals*" statement. Her whole view of Sterling witches just tilted. When this was over, she intended to become far more knowledgeable on the Sterling family.

The one thing Evalle did know about dealing with anyone in the world of nonhumans was to be specific. "What exactly do you mean about something I sacrifice personally? All I brought with me are my weapons and you told me they couldn't travel with me."

"Think along the lines of what a spirit would want. It's better for you to decide what you're willing to give up so the spirits don't *choose* what to take from you."

A string of everything dear to her that she could lose crowded her mind, from Storm, Feenix, Tzader, Quinn, and the list went on and on. She would not risk any of them. "How do I declare what I'm willing to offer?"

Adrianna angled her head in acknowledgement of another correct question. "You say, 'In appreciation for allowing me to pass unharmed to my destination and back, I am willing to sacrifice ...' then you fill in the blank."

Evalle raked hair off her forehead, thinking.

"Are you ready?" Adrianna asked.

No, but that wasn't going to change any time soon. "Ready."

"I will begin chanting as I light the last three candles. As soon as the last wick flames, tell the spirits what you offer and close your mind to everything except picturing Storm. Ask the spirits to take you to him."

Adrianna's voice was crisp in the evening air. When she began chanting, it hit Evalle that Adrianna should be singing professionally. After a moment, Adrianna held her hand open and a tiny spark flamed in the center of her palm.

Okay, that was definitely new. Up to now, Adrianna had been using a long fireplace match to light the candles. Guess that made these last three special.

The flame walked across her creamy skin, not burning it at all. When the flame reached the tip of her index finger, she held it over the first candle until the wick lit, then moved on to the next one. Evalle was so mesmerized by the ceremony she almost missed her cue of the last candle firing up.

She took a breath, closed her eyes and said, "In appreciation for allowing me to pass unharmed to my destination and back, I am willing to sacrifice whatever I possess where I stand, except for my soul."

Adrianna had continued chanting, but she gasped at those words.

Evalle would not put anyone she loved at risk. If the spirits wanted to take away her powers then so be it. She would give up much more to bring Storm back.

Wait. Adrianna didn't say *when* the spirits would take delivery on that sacrifice. What if Evalle needed her powers where she was going?

Should have thought that one through better.

Evalle closed her mind to everything except Storm's face. The harder she thought on him, the more he came into focus. He had a strong profile. A proud one. He turned and his dark eyes stared back at her, telling her how much he wanted her. She'd been a fool time and again, falling into the jealousy pit and wallowing around. No more. When she got him home, she would accept that he was hers and she was his.

Maybe even mated, if Kai had been correct.

Home. She wanted to be with Storm and Feenix.

To her, anywhere with those two would be the equivalent of a picket fence life.

Noises blurred and stretched until it sounded as if she was flying through a wind tunnel. The whirring sounds weren't freaky, just wrapping around her and making her claustrophobic.

She was supposed to be talking to the spirits. "Please take me to Storm of the Ashaninka and Navajo." *There couldn't be two of those, right?* "I wish to go to Storm no matter where he is. Please—"

Icy fingers clutched at her, dragging her out of the wind tunnel. The cold digits covered her eyes and she managed not to panic. Just. Her body was drawn to the left then to the right, back and forth, weaving a drunken path.

She stiffened at being held, but Adrianna had warned her not to fight the spirits. A cold film started coating her body. She shivered hard against the chill. Where was she going? She'd envisioned Storm somewhere akin to Christian hell where fire blazed nonstop.

Not somewhere that could compete with Antarctica.

All at once, the motion slowed until she just drifted. When the spirit removed its icy fingers, Evalle blinked to clear her vision. A huge, empty room came into view that reminded her of the amphitheater under the mountain shielding VIPER headquarters. This place looked like a giant had scooped out the rock, but left it open with no stadium style seats cut into the stones.

Ledges jutted out from the walls above the dark floor ... that just moved.

Not a floor. Bodies.

As more bodies moved, she could see that there were hundreds of them lying around. Maybe thousands. Some had animal bodies covered in fur or coarse gray skin. Others with human-like bodies were covered in tattoos of strange symbols designed in black, red or both.

She didn't see anything similar to a Cressyl or Birrn Demon, but they were from different parts of the world. Still, she recognized none of these creatures as fitting into the races of demons she'd studied. The power alone wafting off this group vibrated over her skin. She shuddered at the thought of facing even a handful of these in Atlanta.

In the middle of the room, one large shape had the body of a buffalo that was shielded in swamp-green armor plates the size of her two hands. It had a mangled human-shaped head with a pig's nose and long donkey-like ears. To the left of that one, a fifteen-foot long serpent body slithered down from a ledge. Clear scales covered the internal organs. Eww. Then it raised its head that was a mutant orange-and-brown cat shape, if the cat weighed a hundred pounds and had wide jaws that dropped open to show a double row of sharp teeth.

She had to stop shivering. They didn't know about her.

Once the serpent reached the ground, there was a ripple of movement through the room. Maybe her arrival caused a disturbance, an unexpected energy wave, because all at once a third of the heads popped up, looking around, searching.

Red eyes glowed on the demons.

The red eyes made her skin crawl. Those were the worst of all demons.

Storm was stuck in here somewhere?

Her heart kick boxed inside her chest. Where was he?

How could she move around to hunt for him? Staying as calm as she could, she tried swimming motions.

That worked.

She floated forward, eyeing the demons that appeared to be settling back down into their siesta. She had night vision, but a glow coming from the left shed enough light to illuminate much of the massive space. As she made it past a ledge to look in that direction, she squinted against the light but realized it wasn't affecting her vision.

When she took a hard look, she did a double take at the being slumped on a throne. Had to be a throne since it was the only chair in the room. Where had that thing gotten the owl shape to its head? No owl was that ugly and the bony body did nothing to improve his—she guessed it was a *he* based on the genitalia–appearance. Evidently, he had a fetish for skulls since his throne had been built out of skulls stacked like Leggos.

He was clearly head honcho over these demons, but who was he?

She couldn't waste time when she needed to get to Storm who could answer her questions faster. Stretching her head to take in the entire room, including ledges draped with more sleeping demons, she still didn't see Storm.

Her gaze caught on a recessed area on the far wall at the rear of the space–if that throne was at the front. There was a half-circle, thirty-foot-round area cleared of any demon in front of the opening to that hole.

Could Storm be in there, tucked away with his back to the wall so he could fight off these demons? That would fit for someone like Storm who knew how to best position himself in a room full of predators.

Had to be one to think like one.

Going into a dark hole raised all Evalle's childhood nightmares to the surface–the ones of growing up locked in a basement–but if she couldn't influence anything in this realm then those demons shouldn't be able to touch her. Right?

She swam above the field of bodies and worked to ignore her wildly thumping heart.

When she reached the small cavern, she eased in slowly, encouraged that her natural night vision allowed her to continue seeing in the dark because there was no light in here.

She'd just glided around a corner when she found Storm.

Naked. Sitting hunched up with his knees drawn to his chest and his arms wrapped around them. His head was turned facing away from her, staring into more black space beyond where he sat.

Ugly slashes marked his arms and legs. A nasty one gouged his shoulder. He'd fought the demons and clearly survived, but why hadn't he healed?

She didn't know, but Storm appeared in decent condition to fight. All she had to do was find out where this place was and come up with a plan to help him escape.

Deep growling rumbled then he said, "Leave, Evalle."

CHAPTER 12

Evalle got over the shock of Storm trying to send her away and kept her voice soft to keep from alerting demon central even if they shouldn't be able to hear her. "I came here to find you, Storm."

His voice normally had a rich tone, but now his words were deep and gravelly. An unearthly sound that raised the hair on her arms.

"I know. That means you survived the Medb and whatever happened on Treoir. I'm glad. Now go back."

That was it? All he had to say?

Why would he send her away?

Did he think she would shy away from fighting demons? No, but Storm would suffer anything before he'd risk her life. He didn't get that choice.

Not now that he belonged to her.

Putting steel in her voice, she said, "I'm not leaving without you or some way to get you out of here." She floated closer.

"Stop." He hadn't even turned to look at her yet, but she froze where she was and waited for him to speak again.

"Ask whoever brought you here to take you back. Get out of this place before you're discovered."

"No. I don't even know where this is. Why are you here?"

He heaved a deep breath that sounded as if he'd resigned himself to answering her questions. "I underestimated Nadina."

That bitch would die, but not until Storm got his soul back and he returned home. Evalle asked, "Where is she?"

"Gone. Waiting somewhere safe until she gets word to come back."

"We'll deal with her later. How can you get out of here?"

He chuckled, the sound so empty and flat it could have come from a corpse. "I can't."

"Storm, look at me. Why are you not trying to leave? I don't understand you giving up. That's not like you."

The silence piled up and up until Evalle feared Storm had built an invisible wall between them that she wouldn't be able to pierce.

He finally said, "I never wanted you to see me like this."

Naked and looking as if he'd barely survived ten battles with demons? Did he really think she cared when he'd seen her shift into a monster born of her Alterant genes? She wanted to tell him how she was now a gryphon, but they could catch up later, once she had him out of this pit.

When he spoke again, her heart jumped with relief that he was still talking, until he said, "And now that you've seen me, I need you to leave, never come back and forget about me. Go on with your life."

Tears burned her eyes. She covered her mouth to keep from screaming at him to stand up and fight. *Don't upset the spirits.*

Nadina might have tricked him into this place, but how had she stolen his will to live? When Storm had battled back from death after Sen tried to kill him, Storm had told Evalle he'd pleaded with Kai to help him live so that he could hold Evalle one more time. She'd never known love, not the kind that happened between a man and woman, but those words had wound around her heart and held it safe.

Storm loved her. She knew this and he knew she loved him. Her Storm would never quit on them. Whether they were mated or not.

Didn't matter. In Evalle's heart, Storm *was* her mate.

That was all she needed to know. She'd find a way to get him out of here regardless of what Nadina had done to his mind. Evalle waited until she calmed down to keep from giving the spirits a reason to snatch her away.

Her words were quiet, but commanding. "You listen to me, Storm of the Navajo. I am not going back and forgetting about you because I love you."

His muscles tensed. He buried his face in his arms, shaking.

His pain wicked out and brushed her face.

She reached a hand toward him but pulled back, afraid of causing him more anguish. If only she could go to him and find a way to rally Storm to fight with her. But he'd drawn an invisible line that all her instincts were telling her not to step over, that it was important to him she not push that boundary.

The last thing she wanted to do was draw the attention of the demons who might attack Storm. Or wake up that creepy guy on the throne. She had to respect this limit until she found out what was going on with him. Had something changed once he came here to make him no longer want to be with her?

Too impossible to even consider.

She swatted away her insecurities. Storm had proven himself time and again to her. It was time to show him that she would come through for him.

He'd only said he didn't want her *here.*

What if she questioned his feelings for her? Could she strike a nerve and force him to show some life? "Are you telling me to go because you don't want me any more?"

Storm raised his head in a bold profile. Straight hair hung past his shoulders in black streaks. His eyes were closed. Thick lashes rested above proud cheeks. His lips were taut, forced together as if holding back a torrent of words. Muscles rolled and pulsed along his arms still wrapped tight around his knees.

His throat moved with a swallow.

Nothing prepared her for the guttural pain in his voice that was a harsh whisper. "I will *always* want you. I will *always* love you." A tear ran down the side of his face. "But every time I shift into my jaguar in this place, I slip further away. I barely returned to human form the last time. My Navajo heritage—my human blood that once drove me to strive for a life of honor—is losing the battle to the blood I inherited from that Ashaninka witch doctor. Nadina bore me to be a demon. She has finally won."

She was Storm's *mother*?

The hits just keep on coming.

He took a breath that racked his body. "I will never return to your world. Some things can't be changed. Please, I beg you to please go so I can find a way to live without you, because life without you is worse than death. They will never allow me to die ... or I would."

Tears were streaming down her face. How could he quit now after he'd survived to this point? There was always hope. Without him, she would die inside. She was shaking with the need to go to him.

Chilly fingers touched her arms.

No, she wasn't ready to leave this place. Not yet.

She forced her mind and voice to be peaceful while she considered all he'd said. This was too important for her to lose her grasp on it.

Storm was fighting Nadina and everything in this place. He did not want to become a demon, but Storm would rather face that than put Evalle in danger. That was the man she loved and she would go up against any power in any realm to rescue him. He might think the witch doctor's blood ruled him now that Nadina had him imprisoned, but the fact that Storm cared enough to send Evalle away proved to her that his Navajo genes still held a grip somewhere inside him.

There was no point in arguing any more.

She just had to get him out of here before he lost what was left of his humanity. Evalle needed a game plan. To create one, she needed information.

Sounding as compliant as she could, she said, "I understand, but at least tell me who that guy on the throne is and what this place is or I'll spend forever wondering."

After another long moment of silence, Storm spoke in that rough voice again. "This is Mitnal and the ruler is Hanhau. He rules demons in an underworld from the land where I was born. Nadina made a deal with him that included getting me here so he could turn me into a demon to lead his army."

Storm thought he was doomed to only one destiny.

The Storm that Evalle knew would fight giving into the dark side with his last breath. If Nadina and Hanhau weren't going to allow Storm to die, then this had potential. Evalle just needed him to not give up in the meantime.

Nothing was impossible.

"I hear all that you're saying, Storm, but think of all the power I have at my disposal back in Atlanta."

There was that dark chuckle again. "Who in their right mind in the Beladors or VIPER would stick their neck out for me besides you, Evalle? Just go." He rubbed his forehead. "I'm sorry."

He sounded so beaten. The man she loved was larger than life, greater than the gods and goddesses. She'd seen him overcome the impossible time and time again.

Frustration burned through her. If she had to leave him in this place, she wanted to make damn sure he could kill everything that dared to attack him until she could return. To do that, she needed to tap into his inner angry child.

She'd beg for his forgiveness later, but right now she wanted to see her warrior.

"How can you give up on us, Storm? You're willing to let Nadina win? Is she that much more important than me?"

His muscles tensed again and he started growling, a deep rumble of warning.

That was more like it.

She pushed again. "I gave you more credit than that. I pretty much told Macha to eat my boots when she tried to stop me from finding you. I'm here and I'm fighting, because I love you. *I* won't ever give up on you, but you're giving up on me *and* your father."

"*Get. Out!*" he snarled.

"Make me."

"Done." That ugly black chuckle rolled out of his throat then he lunged, body shifting into a jaguar the size of a bear with eyes glaring at her.

They were demon red.

Jaws opened wide enough to snap her head off.

Evalle shoved her hands up and screamed, "*No!*"

Could he touch her?

She had no kinetic power.

Howling erupted out in the demon parlor.

Icy fingers snatched her backwards before Storm's massive jaws would have slammed shut. The frigid spirit dragged Evalle through a tumbling vortex of dark swirls. Howling filled her ears then piled into every corner of her mind. She grabbed her head, screaming at the sensation of twisting and spinning through nothing.

All at once, the spinning and noise stopped.

Cold seeped deep into her bones and formed an icy layer on her skin, but it was blissfully quiet.

CHAPTER 13

Someone was slapping her face. Brina grabbed the wrists and opened her eyes, ready to kill her attacker.

Lanna's frightened face hovered over her. "Finally."

"Why are you hittin' me?"

"You would not come back. Your energy was drifting. I told you about problems with wanting to stay in dream."

Brina took the hand Lanna offered and stood up, searching her surroundings. "Where are we?"

If Lanna had looked frightened before, she sounded terrified now. "You do not remember that we are stuck in unknown realm?"

Brina reached up to her throbbing head and clutched it, which did nothing to stop the pounding. "Sort of. I remember you and ... teleporting, right?"

"Yes, but what about the dream. You went into deep sleep. Did you find someone and tell them what happened to us?"

"I can't remember." Visions of a man flickered in Brina's mind. Tzader. "I think I saw Tzader."

"Did he say anything?"

"I *don't know*, Lanna." She hadn't meant to sound so irritated, but she was struggling to figure out what was going on and Lanna kept pressing her for answers.

"Who is Tzader to you?"

Brina put both hands on her head, but the banging wouldn't stop. "He's with the Beladors."

"I meant, how important is he to *you*? Is he your lover?" Lanna asked with the sincerity of someone trying to discern an important detail.

Brina, on the other hand, didn't care for some young woman sticking her nose into Brina's private life. She stared ahead at nothing, thinking on that. Tzader was part of her private life. Oh, yes. They'd made love under a large tree, a spot they'd chosen as their secret meeting place as teens. But that was not something she was sharing with Lanna. "You're asking impertinent questions. I'll remind you that I'm ... " Brina paused, struggling to finish that sentence.

"You are Belador warrior queen."

"I know that!" Brina snapped, but her irritation was over the momentary lapse. *So I'm a queen?* No wonder Lanna was distressed. Brina's shoulders relaxed. "I was havin' a moment of confusion, but I'm fine now."

Relief poured off Lanna. "Thank goodness. I was very worried. But I still need to know if you told Tzader anything."

Brina couldn't honestly recall. She dug around in her mind, trying to pull up details and started shaking her head. "They should have found us by now. I'm a queen and you're Quinn's family, right?"

"Yes." Lanna whispered, but her eyes matched the fear in her voice when she said, "Maybe you should try to relax."

Images started flying through Brina's mind of Tzader and warriors fighting and someone throwing Noirre majik on her. Her body began shaking so hard she couldn't make it stop.

She stumbled to the side and Lanna grabbed her arm. "Lie down and I will help you sleep again."

"No!" Brina jerked away. A vision of Lanna jumping toward her while Brina was covered in Noirre bloomed in her mind. "Who are you? She backed up another step."

Lanna yelled, "I am Lanna. You know me. Come back. Do not move any more. I can hardly see you!"

Brina took another step back. "You attacked me in the castle. You're with the enemy."

"No. You are confused. Stop!" was the last thing Brina heard before the fog closed in around her.

Chapter 14

"You will awaken now!" yelled in Evalle's ear. She jumped at the threatening sound and opened her eyes to find Adrianna

glaring at her.

"What?"

"Okay, you're really back." Adrianna stood up and shoved damp strands of hair off her shoulders.

Evalle rubbed her eyes and blinked further awake but the candles were glaring. She slapped at the ground around her. "Where are my sunglasses?"

"Over there." Adrianna pointed to where the glasses sat next to the altar several feet away.

Why am I over here? Evalle pushed to her feet and noticed the sweat streaming down both sides of Adrianna's face. "Was there a problem?"

"You might say that. You dragged a spirit back here with you."

"You didn't let it in, did you?"

"No, *you* let it in."

"Me? How was that my fault?"

Adrianna could sound pissy with the best of them. "Technically, this is *all* your fault since you're the one wanting to open a path to another realm. But to answer your question, you must have upset the spirit because it was bound so tightly to your arm I couldn't break the connection. If I hadn't figured out what to do, you would have stayed with the spirit."

Evalle shuddered at that possibility. "What happened?"

"I had seconds to either break you free or explain to Tzader why there was nothing left of you but an empty vessel. I used a spell to draw the spirit away from your body long enough for you to wake up. Once that happened, the spirit lost interest."

Looking around the clearing, Evalle asked, "Where is it?"

"Have no idea."

"Ah, crap. I can't let it go roaming free."

"Are you serious?" Adrianna asked. "This city is full of spirits. What's one more floating around?"

She had a point, but things like new spirits unleashed on Atlanta always came back to bite Evalle in the ass.

"Your turn to explain what happened," Adrianna ordered.

If Evalle shared a word about Storm's red demon eyes or how beaten he was mentally, someone would try to talk her out of going after him.

Not going to happen.

She said, "That witch doctor, Nadina, tricked him and now he's captured in this place full of demons."

"Has he turned into one?"

That was direct, but, unlike Storm, Adrianna was not a walking lie detector. Evalle said, "Not yet, but they're trying. I have to go back, but not in an astral projection."

"Where is he?"

"This huge cavern looking place called Mitnal."

Adrianna stared past Evalle, thinking so hard tiny lines formed at the bridge of her nose. Then she looked up quickly at Evalle. "Storm's from South America, right?"

"Yes."

"I think Mitnal is known as land of the dead, but the one I'm thinking of is Aztec. It's the underworld and ruled by some guy Hunna or something."

"Hanhau," Evalle corrected.

Adrianna snapped her fingers. "That's him."

"Looks like a bad Halloween skeleton costume with an ugly owl's head."

"Hanhau can look like a pickle or a giant demon or anything else he wants. He's so old he's probably forgotten his original form."

"So how do I find that place again, but in my physical form?"

Adrianna scratched behind her ear, clearly stalling.

Evalle held up her hand. "Before you waste any time arguing with me, I'm going to get Storm and I need your help." She'd never begged, but there was a first time for everything. "Please."

"Argh!" Adrianna stalked around, hands in her hair agitating the blond mass. She shook her head, muttering to herself. When she finally settled down, she came back and said, "Fine. But no guarantees on either or both of you getting out. Got that?"

"Understood."

"First we have to find Nadina."

"Why?"

"Because if she managed to make a deal with Hanhau then

use herself to bait a trap for capturing Storm, she knows how to get in and out of Mitnal. Any idea where she is?"

"Only that Storm said she was not currently in Mitnal. He thinks she's hiding somewhere safe."

Holding her chin with two fingers as she thought, Adrianna said, "Kai would know if Nadina was in our world and maybe even have an idea of how to find her."

"How long will it take to reach Kai again?"

"Depends."

"On what?" Evalle demanded.

"Whether you have to talk to her yourself or if you can keep from getting cranky if I talk to her."

Tough call on that, but Evalle was finding all kinds of new personal depths when it came to saving Storm. "You can ask her. I made the rounds on the way here to meet you tonight and found my best Nightstalker. He said he hadn't seen the witch doctor or heard any word of her in days, so if she's here in our world she's hiding like Storm said."

"When we do find her," Adrianna continued as she packed up her witch supplies with the precision of someone with obsessive-compulsive disorder, "Nadina is not going to be easy to corner, and it won't be easy to convince her to take you into Mitnal."

"She does not want to piss me off any more than she has."

"That's all good and fine, badass, but we need some major juice to pull this off."

Evalle lifted an eyebrow. "Are you saying she's more powerful than a Sterling witch?"

"Normally, no, but *Hanhau* is more powerful. If Nadina has cut a deal with him, I have no idea what we're up against."

"If we capture Nadina, can you cast a spell on her to do what you say?" Evalle asked.

"Probably, but she'd have to be incapacitated so that she couldn't bespell both me and you first." Adrianna walked around, systematically picking up her candles, thinking out loud. "We need someone like Sen to–"

"No!" Now that her arms and legs would function again, Evalle shoved to her feet and twisted out the kinks from that crazy out-of-body trip. If she helped Adrianna pick up this stuff, the whole thing would go faster.

Blue eyes slashed at Evalle with irritation. "I didn't say to call in *Sen*," Adrianna stressed, then stopped to shake her head when Evalle reached for a candle. "Thanks for the help, but don't touch my things."

Evalle lifted her hands and backed away.

Content that her majik toys were safe, Adrianna continued packing herbs and candles into plastic bags. "All I'm saying is we need some major power to pin down Nadina. If not Sen, who else do we know? Doesn't a centaur own the Iron Casket nightclub?"

"Yes, that's Deek D'Alimonte, but I can't ask him for anything. I already owe him an open-ended favor."

"Oh?"

"Not talking about that," Evalle said, nipping that whole topic. Tristan had teleported her away from a Medb ambush, back to the nightclub where she'd left her bike. But he missed by about a hundred feet and she landed in Deek's office uninvited, then tossed her cookies on the centaur's pants and shoes.

Most people that unlucky or stupid didn't live to tell about it.

Adrianna named a couple more, but Evalle nixed each one as either being an agent of VIPER and/or a Belador. She couldn't bring the team into this. Macha *could* help her, but only if she'd had a lobotomy and could be convinced that Storm wasn't a demon. Quinn could probably take control of Nadina's mind, but he was in bad shape already. Evalle needed to go check on him as it was.

"Without some serious muscle, we have no plan," Adrianna declared. Then she paused and snapped her fingers. "I've got it."

Thank goodness, because they'd run through the entire registry of nonhumans that Evalle knew. "Really? What?"

"I'll find out where Nadina is and you get that guy you know who makes mega blasters. He gave you one that stunned a troll when we had the Svart troll problem. If we can stun Nadina with one of those things, I can work a spell." She paused to pull a cell phone out of her bag of tricks and hand it over.

Taking the phone, Evalle should be happy that Adrianna had an idea, but she was talking about Isak Nyght. Isak made custom weapons that killed nonhumans. He was one of the few humans in the city who even knew that VIPER agents and other preternaturals existed.

The last time Evalle saw Isak, she'd stopped him from kissing her and informed him that she and Storm were an item.

They were a lot *more* than that now if she was truly mated to Storm.

What had been Isak's reaction?

He took it as a challenge.

The minute Evalle informed Isak that Storm was trapped in another realm, Isak would hold a party to celebrate.

"What?" Adrianna asked, evidently irritated at Evalle's hesitation. "Do you or don't you want to free Storm?"

"Of course I do."

"Then why aren't you on the phone calling your black ops buddy?"

"I'm calling now."

But she had no idea how she was going to convince Isak to save the one person he wanted out of the way permanently.

TÁµr Medb, home of the Medb coven

CHAPTER 15

"How many of our coven have we released into the mortal world?" Maeve asked, hovering near the wall of precious stones, some the size of her head.

"Only a hundred," Cathbad the Druid replied, walking from the throne over to where Maeve moved her hands slowly in front of the wall. "Half of them were sent directly to the area called Atlanta."

"How is that going?" She glanced over to see that Cathbad had dressed in a black suit with a black shirt. He would have gleaned the way mortals dressed today from their warlocks who had traveled to the mortal world. His pale brown hair still had a bit of curl in it just as it had years ago, but he was wearing it shorter now. Brown eyes that had left women strewn in his wake smoldered when he caught her looking. He grinned and she knew why she'd allowed this druid to talk her into the prophecy.

"They're surprising me with just how good they are at deceiving the VIPER agents, especially the Beladors. Have ya figured out how to unlock the visions stored in that scrying wall?"

Maeve smiled, enjoying how her reflection sparkled in the water shimmering its way down the rock face and pooling at the base inside a half circle of diamonds. She could have any appearance she wanted, but she preferred her black hair, lavender eyes and full lips. "I've made some alterations to the stones and water that allowed me to observe a few visions, but nothing useful. Of all the queens allowed to rule in my absence, Flaevynn may not have been the most intelligent, but she was definitely the more cunning based on the things we've uncovered. Unfortunately, she didn't appear to have enough common sense to keep a slug alive."

"Perhaps we should have fine-tuned the prophecy to have groomed a better lot to stand in for us," he joked. "From what I've learned through interviewing warlocks and witches who survived Flaevynn's rule, she depended heavily on her daughter Kizira."

"Didn't she die during the battle?"

"I'm not entirely certain. All I've been able to confirm is that she did not return with the Medb warriors sent to attack Treoir."

Maeve turned to Cathbad. "What of this Kizira? I heard one coven member indicate Kizira was accused of being a traitor at one point and sent to the dungeon. Her father, the reigning Cathbad at the time, was rumored to be in conflict with Flaevynn, even allowing the girl a year to live where she chose before she had to accept her priestess position when she reached adulthood."

"I've heard as much in my talks around TÅµr Medb. We need better information." He stretched his fingers and grinned. "That only takes skimming into the subconscious to find hidden treasures."

She waved him off with a hand. "That is your territory. I have no desire to wallow in the minds of those far inferior to me."

"As always, I'm the one who must do the dirty work," he said in mock despair.

"Oh, please. We gravitate to that for which we are best suited." She winked at him and swung back around to the wall, waved her hand and watched as the entire surface turned into a view of mountains and a castle rising in the mist. Large creatures were flying again. "The gryphons are still loyal to Treoir. I don't understand why, when they have Medb blood as well as Belador. How could they just change allegiance like that in the middle of a battle?"

She'd listened to several reports from warlocks who had returned from the siege on Treoir Castle.

"Perhaps they're not all loyal to Macha and the Beladors,

only thinking of self-preservation for the moment."

"You have a point. That could be it." Dismissing the view, Maeve floated back to the floor and strode over to the throne with Cathbad following her. She took in the room as she walked. "This room is not fit for a camp follower."

"From what I heard, that is exactly what it was suited for if the stories of Flaevynn's sexual exploits are to be believed."

"We are fortunate the prophecy ended with her. The Medb reputation would have suffered if Flaevynn had ended up immortal as the fool had believed would happen." Maeve would have liked to have seen Flaevynn's face as the Medb queen's body warped into Maeve's reincarnated one. Maeve and Cathbad had made a blood pact two millennia past and created a prophecy, which allowed Medb queens born after Maeve's death to live six hundred and sixty-six years. Each would marry a descendant of Cathbad who carried his name.

None of the interim queens had dared challenge the prophecy until Flaevynn, but even with her meddling, the prophecy was still realized. The true rulers returned through an altered form of reincarnation.

Maeve chuckled to herself over the look on the face of Flaevynn's Cathbad mate just before the druid's body warped and he turned into Cathbad the Druid. The original one.

Cathbad suggested, "I can release another hundred witches and warlocks into that Atlanta city. I've had only one negative report on the first wave so the second group should be fairly safe."

"What happened to that one?"

"My scouts said a Belador destroyed the mind of one of ours and the warlock was run down by a large transport."

"I thought the Belador powers were weak right now?"

"This one is known as Vladimir Quinn and is said to have the ability to mind lock. A very powerful Belador."

"What are we to do about him?"

"I've already begun a plan that will deal with him."

"Does that mean you have our Scáth Force ready?" The Scáth would be an elite force gifted with abilities unlike any witches or warlocks before.

"Almost, and I think you'll be pleased with what I've done

so far." Cathbad stepped back and lifted a finger he pointed at the spot on the stone floor between him and the double doors, which were only for those who could not teleport. "I introduce you to Ossian."

The shape of a man solidified. He first nodded in acknowledgment of Cathbad, then stood very still as Maeve floated around him. She studied this person Cathbad believed capable of leading a deadly pack of Medb warriors. Short brown hair clipped neatly, hazel eyes that should be darker to fit his Mediterranean face. But the eyes gave him an exotic appeal. He was just six feet tall, but nicely built for an average body that just did manage to fill out the flimsy shirt he wore. Strange clothing.

She turned to Cathbad. "What's he wearing? Looks like a servant."

"Those are casual clothes for the masses of this era. They call the ensemble a T-shirt and jeans in the mortal world. Our Scáth must fit in to infiltrate."

Maeve gave Ossian another sweeping look, picking up nothing that would draw attention or intimidate. "Am I correct in assuming that appearances can be deceiving?"

Cathbad's lips spread with a smile of true pleasure. "Aye. Our warriors, both male and female, will receive *some* of the gifts I have bestowed on Ossian. Show your goddess another face and change of clothes, Ossian."

"Yes, my lord." Ossian merely turned to face Maeve and in an instant his hair thickened to a rich black, growing to touch below his ears. Thick lashes surrounded eyes the color of a deep sea that smoldered with the promise of sex and his skin deepened to the color of a Moor. He picked up three inches and his body filled out with plenty of muscle to gain the eye of any female.

"Much more impressive," she murmured.

"The suit he's wearing now will blend in as that of just another businessman in the mortal world, but will be deadly to the women, no doubt." Sounding proud as if Ossian were a favored son, Cathbad said, "That's nothing compared to his other gifts. Now, Ossian, let's show your goddess what ya can do in battle."

The warlock disappeared.

Maeve blinked. "Why did you send him away?"

"Did ya not tell me this morning ya did figure out how to view the pit?"

"Yes, I did." She flashed out of sight for the tiny second it took to teleport to her scrying wall. "Give me a moment." Lifting her right hand, she whispered words to the wall. Water trembled then cleared and a large room came into view with stone walls, a metal gate built of crossbars as thick as Maeve's forearm and Ossian standing in the center of the paved stone floor, looking out of place in the battle pit.

"I believe we have a glatisant in our inventory, Maeve."

"Three actually, but one can take down an army," she pointed out, having taken inventory of all the creatures she now possessed.

"If it kills Ossian, then I'll at least know what weaknesses to overcome when I create a new Scáth leader."

"Very well." She uttered a word that tasted ancient on her tongue. A rending creak announced the opening of the gate.

Loud barking erupted that sounded as if a pack of hungry dogs approached, picking up volume. A snarling monster emerged, its head and neck shaped as a muddy-brown serpent, but as it continued to enter, the rest of the body was that of a giant leopard with lion-like haunches. It stood eight feet at the shoulders and stretched twenty feet from head to the blunt tail.

Ossian calmly lifted one hand, sliding it from the top of his head, over his face and away. With that motion, he cast aside the physical appearance of a man as his body stretched and shifted until he was nine feet tall. He grew horns that stuck out from each side of his head and his body exploded with muscle. Dense fur grew between his horns and spread down along his shoulders. He stood upright on two cloven hooves, and more fur shagged along his hips and over his groin then feathered out above the hooves. A silver ring hung from his flaring nostrils.

She started laughing. "A minotaur?"

"Mostly, once ya mix it with Medb warlock. A Scáth Minotaur."

Ossian roared, and the glatisant swiveled its head and opened jaws lined with fangs as it struck at the minotaur. At the last second, before the jaws would have clamped on Ossian's throat and ripped it to pieces, Ossian swung a boulder-hard fist, knocking the head away.

Vicious barking spiraled through the pit. The glatisant lifted up on its hind legs, ready to throw its feline body down to crush the minotaur.

Ossian opened his jaws and a blast of fire shot forth, flames blanketing the glatisant, whose barking turned into dying cries. When the glatisant crashed to the ground, shuddering, Ossian held out his hand and demanded, "Glaive!"

He closed his fingers around a weapon that resembled a poleaxe except the blade was narrow, and he swung it with a fluid motion to behead the glatisant.

Lifting the bleeding serpent head with one hand, he turned and lifted his chin in Cathbad's direction even though there was no way for anyone in the pit to view the queen's room. Ossian called out, "Will that be all my lord and Goddess?"

Cathbad spoke in a normal tone, but the words boomed into the pit. "You've earned your meal. Go clean up and enjoy it."

Maeve closed the viewing port and smiled her admiration at the druid before floating over to her throne. He would follow. Men had always followed her. "Very well done, druid. Now. What about our Alterants and gryphons? How do we get them back from Macha?"

"First we determine that she actually has control of them all. I don't believe she does since the most powerful gryphon should be leading the flock. We either bring that one to our side or kill it and inform the next one in line of his or her options. It won't take long at that point to bring the flock to our side."

"That plan will work only if we can get our hands on the leader." Maeve settled into the throne that appeared carved of a dragon, an actual beast that Maeve had placed a spell upon to serve as her throne before her death. The other queens had enjoyed its ability to observe when they were out of the room, but with Maeve back in power as a goddess, she could feel the throb of its heart pulse through the structure.

And its anger stirring.

"We'll get to the leader when the time comes," Cathbad

assured her. "But for now, what are you and I to do about leaving this place?"

She considered his question, tapping her finger on the arm of her throne. "You wrote the actual prophecy. Are you *sure* we won't burst into flames if we teleport out of TÅµr Medb?"

Cathbad grabbed his chin and stared off, thinking. "The spell I placed on it was quite specific so that the consequences of breaking a rule prior to our reincarnation would only affect those we put here to rule until we arrived. We should be able to leave."

"Should."

"Yes. Spells are generally literal in execution. I have no guarantee that we will survive teleporting away, but I'm up for the ride." He grinned at her and she remembered how a druid had come to seduce a goddess.

That sense of adventure was what she enjoyed about Cathbad. He feared nothing, which made him a strong partner as long as they always had the same interest in mind.

Maeve stood and stepped away, catching the dragon's eyes on her. She told her dragon, "Don't get excited. Even if I die, you'll still be bound to spend eternity as a chair."

His eyes glowed silver.

He should never have crossed her.

Stepping over to Cathbad, she took the hand he extended and told him, "If you're wrong about this, we may explode the second we arrive in Atlanta. Our combined power could destroy the entire mortal world."

Cathbad chuckled. "Either way, we'll finally be done with the Beladors."

CHAPTER 16

Blood oozed down Storm's thigh.

He watched it with morbid fascination. The gash on his leg was trying to heal, but his body could no longer draw on his jaguar's healing powers.

Not without shifting.

Hanhau had upped his game, sending four demons the last time. Storm doubted that Hanhau had noticed Evalle's presence when she'd visited, but some of the demons had.

They stayed on edge in this fire pit coated with ice, and that made them uber-sensitive to visiting spirits. Evalle hadn't found him without calling in spirits, but how had she done that when the only spirits who could reach Mitnal were dark in nature? Storm found it hard to imagine that Evalle would ask her white witch friend Nicole to touch anything dark.

Frigid air washed over his skin.

He'd been shivering for so long now he couldn't remember when he hadn't, yet a fire raged inside him, a constant burning that he kept hoping would torch him. Anything for relief. The slightest touch on his skin sent pain spiking through every muscle.

That's why demons out in the open space had sensed Evalle. Maybe not when she first arrived and traveled slowly through that throng of monsters to reach his hidey-hole, but he'd scared her so badly she'd flown out of here.

Speaking of monsters.

I couldn't stop my jaguar from lunging at her when all my beast could understand was that I wanted her to leave. Storm cupped his head. He hadn't been prepared or he'd have kept his animal in check.

But the longer she stayed, the more agonizing it was to forget that she'd once been his.

He still wasn't sure his beast could harm her when she was not physically here, but he'd stopped the jaguar only an inch short of reaching her.

That had been too close.

Dropping his head back against the cold stone wall, he closed his eyes and pleaded for death. If he died, he could join his father and keep him company in the realm of the lost souls. On the way there, Storm would see Kai one last time, just long enough to let her know he was gone. He'd use every second with Kai to beg her to find Evalle.

Kai would do that. She'd find his mate and make sure Evalle never risked hunting for him again, even if she could find a way into Mitnal.

Knowing his hellion, she could.

He laughed, but it ended in a moan.

She'd been so angry with him, thinking he'd quit fighting. She couldn't know that he battled with every breath, refused to give up hope of being with her again even when he knew this was no place for something as fragile as hope.

Opening his eyes, he lifted his hand.

Not a hand, but a paw. Claws extended and contracted. Fur sheathed the paw and continued up his forearm, fading near his elbow.

The rest of him had shifted back the last time.

He would never give up, but neither would his jaguar, and right now the beast was winning. One more shift might be all he had left in him. He'd heal to fight again, but if he didn't shift back to human right away ... hope would die a cold death, right along with his humanity.

When that happened, he would give the demons his throat.

Not even Hanhau could save him from a pack of hungry demons that would shred his jaguar, then devour him.

CHAPTER 17

"You can't stay in here forever, Tzader."

At the sound of Macha's voice, Tzader came fully alert from where he'd nodded off again on the cushion covering the alcove in Brina's sunroom. The temperature in the castle had dropped considerably.

Or was that just due to the frosty attitude of a temperamental goddess? One who was blocking his view of Brina's hologram.

"Please move to the left or right, Macha."

"Why? So you can stare at her image as it continues to disintegrate?" Macha still wore her dark clothes from saying words over each of the fallen Belador warriors sent home for their families to bury.

"Don't test me right now," Tzader warned. Yes, using that tone of voice was unwise with a deity, but he seriously doubted that she'd risk injuring any Belador in their current weakened condition.

"If I didn't know better, I'd take that as a threat," she warned him right back, throwing off enough energy to make the castle quake.

He stood up to be on the same level with her. "I'm not threatening you, but I am tired of being yanked around with no more concern than a child playing with puppet strings. I have always done your bidding and that of the Beladors, but you kept me apart from Brina. If I'd been *inside* this castle when it was attacked, no one would have gotten near her. Definitely not a Belador too old to carry a sword."

But Horace hadn't been too old to carry a grudge—or to go after Brina in revenge—when the goddess refused his request to bring his wife and child back to life.

Macha bristled. "Are you blaming me for Brina's being gone?"

Tzader crossed his arms, too numb to think about the consequences of speaking his mind. "I'm blaming you, me and Brina. We should have found a way to take down this ward four years ago." Plus he didn't believe that Brina had suddenly decided to marry Allyn, a guard. A memory of seeing her under their favorite tree near the lake smoked through his mind. Of making love to her ... recently. No, that wasn't right. They hadn't been able to touch in four years.

Regardless, his mind and his heart were in agreement that there was something severely off about the way Brina had gone from loving him to being engaged to a guard, practically overnight.

Now he wanted the truth. "Tell me, Macha, did Brina really want to move on from our relationship or were you playing her against me while you also played me against her?"

"Careful what you accuse me of, Tzader."

"You know what? I've got nothing left to lose if I don't have Brina. If you're going to torch me then do it, but if you want me to continue being the Maistir who will stand between you and Brina against any force, then I want the truth."

Macha's face gave nothing away until she finally frowned and her hair spun into a braid then twisted into some pile on top of her head. She put her hands on her hips and cocked her head at him. "You want the truth? Then here it is. I had no way to take down the ward on this castle or to remove your immortality. Did you ever consider that I trusted you two to figure it out on your own?"

He pulled back at that. "What?"

"Think about it Tzader. For four years I watched the two of you live this way with you coming here in hologram or her going to you that way. I couldn't allow her outside this castle when she was at the height of her power inside it and there was no other Treoir alive. Would you have risked her being harmed or killed?"

"Of course not." Was Macha saying ... "You *did* want us together?"

"Please don't tell me I've gone through all of this to mate Brina to an imbecile," Macha muttered, starting to turn away then stopping.

But not moving far enough for Tzader to get a clear look at the hologram. "If you weren't against us being together, why didn't you help us?"

Macha spun around, her dark, gauzy pants spinning into a liquid shape. "I. Did. I allowed you four years to figure it out, because I foolishly believed that two people who constantly swore their undying love to each other would be motivated enough to find a way to make it happen. When you *both* settled into this state of... of... I have no idea what to call it. Basically, you were both content to live this way forever because of being immortal. Living forever doesn't give you the luxury of sitting back for the ride. We are responsible to Beladors all over the world. Not just me, but you and Brina as well. "

The light bulb moment blinded Tzader with realization. "This whole thing about you ordering Brina to move on with her life and have an heir, then telling me to allow her to move on was *your* way of solving our problem? Are you kidding me?"

"Don't take that tone with me. It was inspired thinking. Far more than you two were doing." She glared down her nose at him. "You two did *nothing* to solve the problem. Your answer was for me to break an oath I made to each of your fathers. I'm insulted you even considered that I would do such a thing."

How had she turned the tables to make him feel like a nasty slug? She'd put him and Brina through hell because that was her wacked-out idea of tough love.

Tzader argued, "You didn't even give us a chance to come up with a plan."

Light exploded around Macha. "I. Gave. You. Four. Years. To be honest, I began to question whether you really loved her."

"*I loved her enough to run through a ward that kills immortals to get to her!*" he shouted right back.

"Then you should have tried harder to find a way to be with her."

Silence whipped through the tension, slicing it up and

shoving his anger around.

Tzader locked his arms tight, because he wanted to strike out at something, but dammit. Macha was right. He didn't want to admit that her screwed up thinking had a lick of logic, but seeing the situation through her eyes put everything in a different perspective.

Tzader's father would be ashamed of him for expecting Macha to break her word. Brina's father would be disappointed in both of them, too.

They weren't teenagers any more.

That meant taking responsibility for their decisions.

Like the fact that he and Brina had chosen to be complacent for four years. Why? Had they really thought Macha would fix this for them? What had they been waiting on?

He could only blame so much on his father, Brina's father and their duties to the Beladors.

Tzader ran his hand over his face then down to the tired muscles in his neck. When he looked up at the goddess, it was with regret pouring through his heart. "I apologize for all the times I asked you to break your vow to my father. To have even requested that lacked honor on my part. Brina and I are as much at fault for this mess." He still wanted to strike out at everyone from Macha and Allyn to the Medb, but he only had to find a mirror to locate his enemy.

"I accept your apology." Macha's hair and clothes quieted along with her voice. "Now that there is no ward standing between you and Brina, it will be up to you two to move forward. The next time you come up against an obstacle in life, and you two will, figure it out. Don't wait for me or anyone else to solve your problems. You're by far the best Maistir I have and more than suitable to be Brina's husband. If she ..." Macha took a breath that made her voice catch. "*When* she returns, you two have my blessing to be together."

"Thank you. Would you mind moving aside so I can see ... her?"

Macha took a moment, then she floated out of the way.

Tzader couldn't breathe. "No, the druid said—"

"That he hoped the hologram would last four days."

Eighty percent of Brina was gone.

At the rate the image was deteriorating, would the lingering pieces of Brina's hologram last even one more day?

Breathe. Brina had not vanished yet. Tzader shouted, *"Darwyli!"*

The druid appeared, took one look at the hologram and muttered, "Worse than I thought."

Tzader hadn't needed to hear that. "How long does she have?"

Swinging his ancient gaze past Tzader to take in Macha, Darwyli lifted two white eyebrows in question.

Macha lowered her chin and pushed a narrowed-eye look at Darwyli. "You may answer his question, druid."

Darwyli harrumphed, then his expression eased with understanding when he addressed Tzader. "'Tis not long. I think we're down to less than a day."

Tzader pinched the bridge of his nose. "This can't be happening."

"We have a greater problem, Tzader."

He dropped his hands and stared at Macha in disbelief. "Do you really think that's possible?"

Her animated face and hair turned stone-cold still. "I've been called to a Tribunal meeting."

"Now? Haven't they heard what we're up against?" Tzader shouted, furious at VIPER, the Medb, Noirre majik and the world in general.

She lifted a hand to ask for silence when she could have used that same hand to lock his jaws. When she spoke, her voice was softer than he'd ever heard before. "That's why I believe they've called the meeting. We are the force behind VIPER and the coalition. We've always held the majority of control because of that power. Now that our forces have been weakened, sightings of the Medb have been reported all over the world. Our people estimate over forty witches and warlocks in Atlanta alone."

Her words hollowed out his gut. "Tell me that the Tribunal is raising a defense to help our tribe."

Her chuckle was short and grim. "Hardly. I'm fairly certain they are calling me in to ask me to withdraw my pantheon from VIPER voluntarily so they won't have to do it by force."

Energy sparked around Darwyli. "That would be an insult you could not allow."

None of that made sense to Tzader. "Why would VIPER even consider such a thing when we still have the largest army of nonhumans?"

"For that very reason," Macha explained. "VIPER does not have the resources to defend our tribe when they know every enemy we've ever had will come for us, starting with the Medb. The Medb's current lack of leadership will only add to the chaos. VIPER is pulling in all agents to protect its base of power."

"We can only assume the Medb lack leadership at this point," Darwyli said, but Macha ignored him.

Disgust stamped each of Tzader's words. "The coalition would leave us high and dry after all the Beladors have done for them?"

Macha's hair lifted up and down when she shrugged her shoulders. "Ours is not the kind of world that binds allies forever. They may simply look at this as nothing more than evolution, the survival of the fittest."

Tzader searched for something appropriate to say, but the only word that covered it was, "Fuck."

"I'm not a fan of that language, but it's not far from my initial reaction. I'm going there now and I will stretch out the meeting as long as I can. You won't be able to reach me unless you request Sen to come for me. If he does, the mere fact that my pantheon can't maintain its defense without me will draw a vote of no confidence with regard to keeping us in the coalition. You're in charge while I'm gone. We can't afford for any issue to be brought in front of a Tribunal right now. Understood?"

"Yes."

Macha lifted her hand and paused. "If Brina returns, I'll know it immediately. Or if ... she doesn't, I'll know that, too. Pull in the gryphons and all our warriors on the island to the castle if that's what it takes to hold Treoir, but it must not fall into the hands of the Medb even without Brina here."

Macha disappeared.

Silence stumbled through the room.

Darwyli sighed with the weariness of one so old. "I don't mean to add to your burden, Tzader, and I didn't want to speak of this with Macha present, but I think you should know that the hologram's disintegration may affect Brina."

"You don't think she can return?" Tzader's heavy heart rallied from too many blows to thump with panic at that possibility.

"No, I believe she can return as long as she has something that offers a path back, which is this hologram. But that projection is part of her, just as breathing is. I only want you to be prepared for the possibility that she may not return to us whole."

As Tzader turned back to the hologram, another piece of Brina's dress broke away, crystalized and twinkled out of existence.

He wanted her back no matter what.

How had his mighty tribe come to this point?

CHAPTER 18

Everything was too quiet, even in an old neighborhood at
ten in the evening. Even the balmy breeze of earlier had settled.

Where was that witch doctor?

Evalle searched the night for movement from where she and
Adrianna hunched down in a dark shadow created by a
deteriorating, single-story ranch-style house forty years old. A
modest home on what was still a nice corner in the town proper
of Stone Mountain, Georgia. This house was newer than many
in the area like the residence across the street she'd like to own.
She loved how someone had glassed in the porch on one side.
That two-story brick-and-stone structure had to be at least
seventy years old, and came with a nicely trimmed yard.

As opposed to the weeds surrounding the house she hid
beside. A fallen For Sale sign in this yard told of the tough
housing market, and two broken windows pointed at a bad
influence infiltrating the neighborhood.

The human scum that local police handled.

But dealing with demons and witch doctors like Nadina fell
under Evalle's job description.

She studied a two-story, saltbox-style colonial house also
across the street and next door to the brick home with the glass
porch. The unadorned wooden structure leaned to one side.
Understandable for a house built before the Civil War and still
settling into the Georgia clay. A security lamp on a pole just
past that house shed the only light in this area.

Evalle reached for her spelled dagger and came up empty.
She'd left it hidden in Storm's Land Rover. Adrianna had
warned her that the spell on the dagger could possibly alert

Hanhau to Evalle's presence, assuming they found a way for her to sneak into Mitnal.

Thinking out loud, Evalle whispered, "We might be staking out the wrong house."

Adrianna hadn't moved a muscle since crouching next to her when they arrived forty minutes ago. "Kai said Nadina had taken possession of a former Civil War infirmary near a bald mountain. We're within sight of Stone Mountain, the only bald-looking mountain I know of in this area, so the question is whether your friend's intel on this specific house is good."

True. Stone Mountain was a gigantic granite belch, one big smooth chunk of rock rising over sixteen hundred feet.

"I'm not questioning Isak's intel. If I pressed him, he'd tell me the dates this place was active and how many soldiers were treated here right down to their names and injuries. His information is solid. I'm just wondering why we haven't seen a sign of Nadina."

"She probably knows something or someone is hunting her. I would."

Evalle swept a look at Adrianna, who had said that in all seriousness. "Can she find us first?"

"I honestly don't know what she can do, but I wouldn't underestimate her."

As if I have to be told that after Nadina tricked Storm, who knew the witch doctor better than anyone? "What do you think Kai meant by Nadina taking possession of this house? Does she mean literally?"

"To some degree, yes. If this house was a former hospital, then it will be full of spirits. Nadina would use her majik to overpower what is generated by the spirits still present in the building." Adrianna gave a soft sigh, the only sign of any weariness. "Where's your artillery division?"

"Isak said he'd be here by ten." Evalle lifted her watch. "He's got forty-five seconds." She looked up, took in the immediate area, then gazed over her shoulder, searching every shadow down the street behind her that crossed at this intersection.

A shape emerged from a black pocket of nothing off to her right three houses away. She whispered, "Here he comes."

Adrianna stretched to look past her. "Where?"

"Give it a minute."

Isak covered sixty feet of distance without ever coming fully into focus while doing so. Adrianna didn't have Evalle's natural night vision, but even so if Evalle hadn't been familiar with the way Isak and his men operated, she wouldn't have known what to watch for.

"Oh," Adrianna murmured with a hint of feminine admiration when Isak crossed the last thirty feet to reach them. He wore a monocular that allowed him to see everything Evalle could.

Describing Isak as attractive was too limiting.

Blue eyes full of sharp intelligence, a body built for bulldozing over the first line of any defense and a sexy grin capable of leaving panties strewn in his wake.

Big, bad and black right now from head to toe, even black smudges on his face to camo his lightly tanned skin.

Judging by the usual amount of weapons both visible and assumed hidden in that vest among other places, he was armed to take down a city by himself. The rifle-like weapon he held at ready was similar to the one he'd loaned Evalle to kill Svart Trolls, a mercenary bunch of black ops nonhumans who'd invaded Atlanta earlier this month. But this new mega weapon painted in matte black appeared to be outfitted with a few extra tricks if those three switches meant anything.

He took one look at Adrianna and she moved aside, making room for him to drop down beside Evalle, which should have lowered his intimidation factor a full notch, but no. Not when a man had shoulders as wide as a refrigerator and sharp eyes loaded with threat for any danger.

Still, she'd put Storm up against him any day when it came to a badass throwdown. Like facing an entire underworld of demons.

But thinking about that would not help right now.

Evalle said, "Thanks for coming down here, Isak. You want to show me how that works?"

"Not necessary. I'm staying until I know you're clear."

Yeah, she was afraid of that.

Adrianna turned on the sex kitten voice. "So *you're* Isak?"

He finally swung his attention to address the Sterling witch, but his entire focus had been on Evalle first.

Sure, it was tacky on her part, but Evalle enjoyed a smug moment. Isak hadn't stumbled over his tongue the minute he got a load of Adrianna in her undercover getup–a tight, black cat suit designed for maximum cleavage display ala classic James Bond flick.

But, Evalle had once again committed a social faux pas by not introducing them. Hostess skills were not her strength. She said, "Isak, this is Adrianna Lafontaine, and Adrianna, this is Isak Nyght."

Adrianna pulled out a smile that could light up the entire block. "Nice to meet you."

What was with the Sterling witch? She flirted without effort around the men on the team, but Evalle had never noticed Adrianna showing a sincere interest like this. Her smiles and attention to the guys had always been more along the lines of dressing up a display case that sat behind an invisible do-not-touch barrier.

Isak didn't rush to answer Adrianna, taking a long visual sweep of her before he asked, "What are you?"

Way to kill the sex-kitten routine.

Adrianna's entire demeanor shifted subtly, but enough that Evalle felt the need to warn Isak. "Adrianna is a witch. A powerful one you don't want to piss off."

"Witch, huh? Does that make you human or nonhuman?"

Adrianna's frosty personality re-emerged. "That makes me not the least bit interested in your opinion."

Evalle had kept an eye on the frame house and caught a shadow pass by a window. "Hey, you two, I see activity."

Isak's attention zeroed in immediately. "What are we after?"

Oh, boy. This is what Evalle had avoided discussing over the phone with him. "A female witch doctor." She eyed his mega weapon again. "That's not the same blaster you brought me last time, is it?"

"No. You said you needed to contain something, but not kill it. This is a new model that has three levels of stun."

Adrianna's eyes had narrowed more when he used the word "it" to designate what they were hunting. As an Alterant,

Evalle had suffered being called an "it" more times than she wanted to count.

And now she was a gryphon, but she hadn't shared that information with Adrianna or Isak.

"There's definitely someone in there," Adrianna confirmed. "I just saw a movement on the second floor, too. It's as if she's walking around from window to window, watching the area surrounding the house."

Isak asked, "Why do we have to leave her alive?"

Adrianna kept her voice down but snapped, "You don't even know what she's done. How can you assume killing her is the right choice?"

Evalle cringed at the censure in Adrianna's voice even though the witch was correct, but saying so right now might change Isak's mind about loaning that weapon.

"She's a nonhuman," Isak replied, voice hard. "And a threat of some kind to Evalle. That's reason enough."

Any other time, Evalle might gloat over Isak's concern, but that had been before she realized Storm was the only man she would tolerate sounding possessive around her. Isak knew that, but chose to ignore it.

Adrianna leaned in, shoving all that cleavage forward so Isak had a front row view, which he didn't miss. She asked Evalle, "Does he know *why* we're doing this?"

"No, I don't," Isak replied, turning to Evalle. "Not that it matters if this woman is a problem for you, but why are we here?"

Remind me again why I asked these two to help me?

Because Adrianna had the witch juice and Isak had the firepower.

Got it.

Evalle cleared her throat, stalling, then finally explained to Isak, "That witch doctor tricked Storm into following her to the underworld, another realm. I need her to get Storm out of there, but I can't do it without Adrianna casting a spell over her to force Nadina to do what I say. That's why I need you to stun her."

When Isak didn't reply, Evalle's shoulders fell. She hadn't lied to him, but neither had she told him everything on the phone.

"Nadina is the witch doctor?"

She had a burst of hope return at hearing Isak ask about Nadina. "Yes." Evalle risked a glance at him.

Isak's jaw could be carved from rock. He stared at the house, assessing something, then he slanted his gaze at her. "Guess I have to help you."

She liked the sound of that except for one part. "What do you mean by 'have to help me'?"

"If I don't, you won't come to dinner. If I do, you owe me dinner on my terms."

Adrianna was enjoying this way too much. Her eyes literally twinkled, the witch. It wasn't as though Evalle could refuse Isak since there was a standing dinner appointment that she'd agreed to, but that had included Kit, Isak's mother who'd issued the invitation.

Dinner on his terms wasn't hard to figure out.

Isak wanted Evalle alone for one evening.

He wasn't going to help her unless she followed through on her commitment, which she had to do anyhow since she owed Isak's mother for several favors.

Why did it feel like she'd be betraying Storm to go with Isak?

How was she going to save Storm without him?

"Fine," Evalle agreed. "But I choose the date."

"Not a problem as long as it's within a week from today."

Maybe Nadina would smoke Evalle and this would all be moot. "Okay, done."

Isak grinned. "Let's go bag a witch doctor." He flipped a lever on his weapon.

Adrianna asked, "What did you just set for power?"

"Level One. It'll take down a demon."

Evalle considered the Svart Troll she'd zapped in a recent battle. The troll had been out for ten minutes. "Is the power similar to the stun setting on the weapon you loaned me for trolls?"

"No. The first level on this has twice the takedown ability."

Would that blow up a witch doctor with Nadina's powers?

CHAPTER 19

Evalle followed Isak's moves and Adrianna shadowed behind them. When they all reached the house, Isak gently tested the knob on the rear door. Locked. He reached inside his vest, but Evalle tapped his shoulder and signaled him to move aside.

She put her hand on the knob and after two soft snicks, the door opened.

Isak's uncovered eyebrow rose at seeing her kinetics in action. He'd once seen her toss a forklift using kinetics, but he still didn't know all that she was capable of. Just the fact that he'd work with a nonhuman instead of blasting one was a major step.

But he'd cooperated with nonhumans only when Evalle asked or was involved.

When this was done, she'd make good on the dinner she owed him. She'd use that time to explain once and for all that they could continue being friends, but nothing more. She'd tried once and he'd translated her involvement with Storm as a challenge.

Male psychology.

Storm had agreed not to rip Isak to pieces as long as Isak didn't touch Evalle. Explaining this IOU dinner without setting Storm off was going to take some work, but Evalle would worry about that once she had him safe at home.

She'd face anything to make that happen.

Isak moved back into the lead and entered the dark house first. They walked silently through the kitchen that was empty of anything that might represent residents of this house. No pictures or notepads. No residual smells of cooking. Just the musty smell of age that permeated the peeling wood cabinets and faded paint on the plaster walls. A rectangular pine table surrounded by four ladderback chairs sat against the wall.

Evalle scanned the entire room, sensing nothing until she felt the buzz of energy that drew her gaze to the ceiling.

Five orbs appeared up in a corner, moving erratically. That had to be some of the spirits still living in this house. Evalle had met ghosts from the Civil War in the Maze of Death under Atlanta. Some of those had been sad and lonely, but her empathic senses registered fear emanating from these orbs. These spirits were bothering no one. Seeing them huddled together, hiding from Nadina, soured her stomach.

You might as well boot a puppy as pick on a benign spirit.

Adrianna's eyes tracked up to the orbs then she nodded at Evalle, silently confirming that this fit what Kai had described.

Now came the dangerous part.

Evalle touched Isak's arm to signal that it was time to allow her to go first.

He didn't move.

His wide body blocked her from moving forward and his face had that stubborn expression from minutes before when they'd argued over this point. She'd already explained to Isak that if they spooked Nadina, she'd disappear and they might not find her again. Not in time for Brina or Storm. Plus, Evalle had argued that Nadina wouldn't harm her as long as Evalle didn't threaten the bitch.

Of course, Evalle had lied, because based on what Storm had told her, Nadina *was* a threat to Evalle.

But Storm wasn't here to call her on the lie.

The real reason Evalle wanted to go first was to protect Isak and Adrianna in case Nadina came flying out ready to attack.

Adrianna might be a pain in Evalle's side, but she'd been instrumental in locating Storm and now Nadina. She didn't deserve to face off with the witch doctor.

And Isak had come through again, even knowing this was about bringing Storm home.

If Nadina overpowered Evalle, Isak would blast the witch before she harmed Adrianna or him. The only flaw in that plan, besides dying of course, was that if Evalle didn't survive this, Storm's only hope for freedom would vanish too, because no one else would go for him except her.

She tapped Isak's arm again because he never stopped scanning his surroundings.

When he faced her, she mouthed the word, *Please.*

He gave up and moved aside.

She continued into the dining room, opening up her empathic senses for any hint of life. More orbs cluttered along the high ceiling framed with wide crown molding.

When she reached the living room, the first thing she noticed beyond the worn couch and side chairs was the lack of orbs.

The second thing was the smell of roasted licorice.

The third confirmation of Nadina was anger churning through the still air. She gave the signal to Isak and Adrianna to wait just outside the entrance.

There. Coming quickly down the stairs from the second floor.

Evalle spun, hands up, prepared to send out a blast of kinetics at the blur of movement.

"If you harm me, you will never see Storm again," a female voice warned with a Spanish accent.

Nadina.

Evalle lowered her hands. "I was only acting in self-defense. If you don't attack me. I won't attack you."

But would Nadina believe that?

Light formed in a spot between Evalle and the stairs and brightened until a woman appeared, with tanned skin so smooth it could be polished, black hair falling past her shoulders and almond eyes upturned at the corners, laughing at the world.

Arrogant eyes now glowing yellow.

Does she think her headlights will frighten me?

She was almost too beautiful, as if Evalle stared at a vision instead of a human face. What was it with witches of the dark persuasion? Did they get an automatic stamp from the cosmetic fairies?

Evalle met her smile with a feral one. "Nice touch with the

cape. But if you were going for intimidating, you should have picked black over gray."

"I should take fashion tips from a VIPER thug who wears clothes scavenged from dumpsters?"

That's what I get for trying to have a verbal sparring match with a fashionista. Evalle took in Nadina's boot tips, two red points sticking from beneath the cloak. Bet hers didn't have hidden blades. "Thug, huh? I may need therapy to survive such brutal attacks to my psyche."

"What do you want, Evalle?"

"Storm."

"He is gone forever."

"No he isn't. We both know where he is and you're going to help me bring him back."

Nadina had been stoic until then. She burst into laughter. "What do you plan to hold over me? He is mine, and I control him. I also have the power to call you to me."

Evalle froze. "What? You're lying."

"You think so? You recall wearing the Volonte bone bracelet Imogenia gave you?"

How could Evalle forget a bracelet that enhanced her moods and had caused her to act like a sex maniac until Storm spun a calming spell around her? "Yes, I remember the Volonte, but I gave it to a willing recipient and I no longer have it."

"I cast a spell on it that would bring you to me any time I desired."

She had to be lying. "If that's the case, why haven't you used it?"

"I was not ready."

"Right. Whatever. Back to getting me into Mitnal."

Surprise flashed into Nadina's eyes, but only for a second. Just long enough for Evalle to know she'd thrown the witch off balance.

Now to manipulate Nadina into position.

Moving toward the window that looked out over the front yard, Evalle said, "Here's how this works. You're going to take me into Mitnal and help me get Storm out. If you do that willingly, I'll make sure Storm doesn't kill you as long as you return his soul and his father's."

Nadina shifted around to watch Evalle, but she didn't step into the opening between the living room and dining room the way Evalle had hoped.

Nadina answered and her words sounded carefully chosen. "Storm has already made a blood vow along those lines. I can not override a blood vow with another one."

Was that true?

Adrianna had to be hearing all this, so Evalle would ask her later. Right now she was going to keep pushing Nadina for as much she could. "But you broke that vow when you tricked him into Mitnal."

"Technically, no."

Then technically, Nadina wouldn't be dead if Evalle smashed every bone in her body and put the witch into a cement body cast to heal, would she? "In that case, we'll have to discuss this with Storm, which brings me back to you and making a trip to Demon Central."

"You mean to give me permission to take you with me to Mitnal, yes?" Nadina smiled. Anything that made the witch doctor happy had to be dangerous to Evalle.

"It's not going to be that simple," Evalle said, shaking her head and taking another step. *Come on, Nadina, keep moving so that I'm always in front of you.* Evalle continued talking to shield her movements as nothing more than keeping a reasonable space between them.

"I'm going to need a more binding agreement than us chatting," she told Nadina.

"As you wish, but I still require your permission to override Storm's vow. I agreed to not go anywhere near you."

Nadina finally took a step forward, then another tiny shift.

Evalle pretended not to notice the way she was advancing and kept talking to hide any noise from Isak and Adrianna. "A minute ago, you said you hadn't called me to you because you weren't ready. Ready for what? To kill me? Others have tried and I've left a bloody trail of their attempts."

Nadina laughed, a wicked sound. "I will not have to touch you."

"Oh, you're going to use some of your South American voodoo majik?"

"You know nothing of my kind or my powers. If you do not agree to go to Mitnal under my terms, then I will wait until Storm is prepared to return here and kill you upon my command. But if you believe you can change the mind of a demon, I will take you to him."

"He is *not* a demon!"

Nadina came right back at her. "He has *always* been one. It's in his blood. He has finally accepted his destiny."

"No!" Evalle shouted, fighting the urge to shift into her beast and show Nadina just what death looked like with wings and talons. She forced herself to stand her ground and not jump this crazy woman. "Storm's Navajo blood has always fought against your tainted blood. He would never give in to be evil and empty like you." *Come on, Nadina. One more step forward and don't look at the dining room.*

"Like me? Oh, no. He will be far more powerful once his Ashaninka blood takes over completely and by now he should be almost there." Nadina tapped her chin with a long red fingernail. "In fact, he may have already reached that point."

Don't kill the witch.

Evalle caught a flicker of movement behind Nadina just as Isak came into view.

Nadina must have sensed his presence at the same moment. She spun in a blur and pointed a finger at Isak, but she would never be as fast on the draw.

Isak unloaded a burst of blue light in a stream that hit Nadina and raced across her body from head to toe. She lifted off the floor, shaking hard as a leaf in a thunderstorm and screaming.

It took all of five seconds and her body dropped hard against the wood floor.

Evalle ran over to look. Nadina's eyes rolled back in her head. "Crap. Is she dead?"

Isak was scratching his chin. "That might have been a bit much. I'm going to have to adjust this for next time. I didn't think it would–"

"*Isak!* Is. She. Dead?"

"I have no idea." He shrugged and looked around.

Adrianna walked up, took one glance at Nadina's prone

form and said, "I don't think she's dead, but I'm not sure she has any mind left after that shock. Let's get busy because there's no telling when she'll come out of that or what will happen when she does."

Ten minutes later, Isak had Nadina sitting in a chair, arms hanging straight down with her hands in special gloves Isak had produced that looked like aluminum mittens to prevent her from lifting a deadly finger. He'd also brought a cable woven of three different metals. He refused to share the origin of the metals, since it was proprietary Nyght equipment. Evalle didn't care as long as all that heavy-duty hardware Isak used to incapacitate Nadina's arms and legs would actually hold her.

By the time Nadina regained consciousness, Adrianna had set up everything she needed for a binding spell.

Thirteen black candles adorned the room.

She produced herbs and incense, laying them out on a mat she'd spread on the dining room table much like a surgeon's tools in an operating room. The mat had glyphs woven into the material. She'd cut off six inches of Nadina's hair and wrapped a leather tie around one end. A headless ponytail.

Evalle felt a wave of menace fly through the room.

O-*kay*. Nadina was still in the building.

The witch doctor raised insane eyes to her that glowed caution-light yellow. "I will not help you, Evalle Kincaid, and when I bring Storm back he will kill you just to please *me*, the master who controls him."

Isak stood off to the side, holding his blaster ready. He didn't show any reaction to the comment, but he had to have heard Evalle mention that Storm didn't have his soul, and Nadina's claim that Storm's body cycled demon blood.

Before Evalle left, she'd have to gain Isak's promise not to harm Storm, because if Evalle was successful in bringing Storm home, those two would eventually cross paths.

Even if Isak hadn't heard everything tonight, it wouldn't take long for him to learn the truth once he got a gander at Storm's demon-red eyes.

Please tell me Storm's eyes will return to brown once he comes home.

Evalle needed a minion to organize all the things she had to worry about. Might as well start with the obvious priority. First she'd come up with a plan for Storm to escape, then she'd help him fight off his demon blood and after that she'd take him to Treoir.

Did that sound realistic? No.

Did she care? No.

Project management completed, Evalle took in Adrianna who stood a step behind Nadina with her arms crossed. Evalle said, "You have the floor."

Nadina twisted to look over her shoulder. First her wild gaze landed on Adrianna with hatred burning so hot that the room should ignite.

That couldn't happen, could it?

Then Nadina noticed the table, the herbs, candles already glowing and ... her hair. She shook her head back and forth, trying to see each side of her hair as she moved. The hair now brushed her shoulders.

Nadina screeched, "No!"

Adrianna smiled at Evalle, a silent indication of *I told you so*.

The Sterling witch had said the only thing Evalle could hold over Nadina's head was the power to control Nadina, even from the grave. But Adrianna had also quickly clarified that she would not perform necromancy, no matter what.

Thankfully, the Sterling witch had placed a protection spell around the house that contained Nadina's screaming within these walls. Adrianna said the spirits had boosted everything she did once they realized that Adrianna was not Nadina's friend.

As per Adrianna's earlier instructions, Evalle backed into the living room, close enough to watch, but far enough to stay out of the witch's way.

"Listen up, Nadina," Adrianna said, walking around her and into view. "This is very simple. If you give Evalle what she wants, you will be free to go as soon as Storm and Evalle return here safely."

Nadina started spewing words that were old and evil sounding. Blue-black smoke boiled from her lips and headed for Adrianna.

This had been a mistake. That witch doctor was going to kill everyone.

CHAPTER 20

Evalle shouted, "Move," at Adrianna so she could blast the witch doctor with a kinetic hit to stop that black majik boiling out of Nadina from taking over Adrianna.

Adrianna calmly ordered, "Do not interfere."

Had Nadina taken control of Adrianna with the spell?

Isak lifted his weapon to point at Nadina's head.

The blaster flipped back up against his chest and shoved him against the wall, pinning him in place. Shock whipped across his face. He shouted enough curses to turn the air black all by himself.

Ignoring everyone, Adrianna opened her arms until she held them straight out.

If Evalle shoved her aside with kinetics, she might do more harm with distracting Adrianna, leaving her more vulnerable. "Get out of the way so I can blast that smoke."

Words flowed from the Sterling witch, soft at first then gaining power until her chanting overrode Nadina's yelling. Lowering her head as she continued speaking, Adrianna faced the blue-black smoke that took the shape of a dragon.

Not the cute looking ones Disney created that drew millions of moviegoers to theaters.

Evalle doubted this one could be trained.

The dragon shape reared up high, ready to strike.

Adrianna slashed her hand toward the dragon and her chant boomed through the room with the power of a rocket launched.

The dragon lunged forward, fangs out to attack, but the smoke beast slammed to a stop an inch from Adrianna's face, snarling and struggling to get to her.

Adrianna never flinched, holding the filmy monster at bay with her majik.

Then she closed her fingers into a tight fist.

Nadina started choking and gagging. She fought against the restraints, trying to free her hands. Her face turned red as a thermometer about to burst.

The smoke dragon backed away then slowly turned to face Nadina.

Adrianna relaxed her hand.

Nadina's eyes flared wide open. White-hot terror circled her irises as the dragon coiled its body once more, prepared to strike a new target.

The witch doctor spat out a phrase that sounded Spanish, but had the word draco in the sequence. Nadina must have ordered it to cease, because the smoke disappeared.

Isak dropped from the wall and his weapon fell loose. He caught it in his arms and flipped it around in one single move, leveled at the back of Nadina's head.

Evalle yelled, "Don't!"

His arms shook with the tension of wanting to act and holding himself back. He glared at her, debating on what to do.

"Please don't." Evalle stopped short of saying his name. Not a wise idea to ever give a name to someone like Nadina.

He finally growled and jerked it away.

Nadina stared at Adrianna, spitting out short, blunt words in Spanish that had to be some kind of creative cursing. She sucked in a breath after that verbal unloading. "Who the hell are you?"

Adrianna maintained her usual unperturbed manner, tilting her head as one would at a mischievous child. "We don't have time to bond and share witch stories. Are you ready to do what Evalle needs, or should I use your hair to gain your agreement?"

All the pretty satin-brown skin on Nadina's face turned ash white. "No."

Adrianna angled her head toward Evalle. "State exactly what you want for her agreement."

Evalle's heart was trying to fight its way out of her chest. She pushed damp hair back and took a moment to calm her breathing before stating her terms. "Nadina will agree to take me to Storm no matter where he is. Nadina will not try to harm me either through her abilities or by directing any other creatures, regardless of what they are. Nadina will aid me in helping Storm to escape, plus help me escape. She will never try to control Storm from here on out, regardless of the realm Storm is in. Then she will make good on the blood vow that she gave Storm and explain to me what it takes to return the souls she stole from him and his father. If she does not complete every step of this agreement, she will ... become my slave to direct as I wish forever."

Even Adrianna raised both eyebrows at that, but she'd been angled to face Evalle. By the time she swung back around to Nadina, her china doll face had returned to its neutral expression.

Nadina's voice held the same anger and terror as an animal caught in the jaws of a trap. "The only way I can return those two souls is by escaping alive with Storm at the same time. That is part of the oath I gave Storm. Hanhau possesses the souls, but that ownership reverts to me if we escape Mitnal at the same moment."

"Hanhau has Storm's soul?" Muscles bulged along Evalle's arms. Her beast wanted out to stomp this miserable excuse for a mother.

"Yes." Nadina glared right back at her.

Adrianna added, "You will also tell Evalle how to open the bolthole on her own."

"Why?"

The very fact that Nadina was so quick to snap at Adrianna over that meant Adrianna had just done Evalle a favor.

"I don't need a reason, Nadina. I'm here as an advisor." Adrianna sent a sad glance in Evalle's direction. "I know you believe that you will bring him back, but Hanhau is not known for losing any that are his. They tend to stay with him."

So that's why she had added the caveat about Evalle opening the bolthole on her own.

"You think I'd leave without Storm?" Evalle asked. That was not happening.

"You don't know what you'll find. I'm giving you the

chance to escape. It will be up to you to take it." Then
Adrianna turned to their captive. "Any questions, Nadina?"

"No."

That single word was the sound of a beaten witch doctor.

Adrianna said, "Once I begin the binding spell, you will
repeat exactly what Evalle has stated and give your word,
Nadina, daughter of Sinaa and witch doctor who serves
Koriošpíri, that you will do as agreed or you will become too
hideous for anyone to gaze upon without falling ill and your
body will age one hundred years in one day."

Nadina whispered, "How did you know?"

"Your name?" Tilting her head to study the witch doctor,
Adrianna admitted, "I've grown up hearing of the Koriošpíri
followers and about the daughter of the great Spiritwalker
Sinaa, child of jaguars. I made an educated guess, but I had no
confirmation that you really existed. Until now."

Nadina might not respect Adrianna, but she feared the
Sterling witch and that was good enough for Evalle.

Evalle had worried about bringing Adrianna into this. Not
any more. She had a whole new appreciation for Adrianna's
ability, and now also realized the Sterling witch would not
have wanted to show this side to anyone in VIPER.

Evalle had promised to help Storm with the debt he owed
Adrianna, but that debt just kept getting larger. What could
possibly mean enough to Adrianna that she would do this to
insure Storm returned and that Evalle would owe her without
question?

It didn't matter.

When the opportunity came to return the favor, Evalle was
in all the way. Additionally, she'd assure Adrianna that her
secrets were safe with her, plus she'd gain Isak's agreement as
well.

Adrianna had been quiet a moment in a thoughtful pose. She
interjected one more point. "You will be required to cloak
Evalle and yourself for traveling to Mitnal and back to this
world, as well as cloaking Storm for his escape."

Nadina rolled her eyes. "This is not a Christmas list. I am
not Santa to hand you all that you wish.I can cloak Evalle and
myself. I can also cloak Storm, but only if he is in human form.

If he is a full demon—"

Evalle broke in. "Storm is *not* a demon." She hoped.

Nadina managed a limited shrug. "I am only saying, that once he *is* a full demon in jaguar form, he is bonded to Hanhau. At that point, Hanhau will know exactly where Storm is as long as he is inside Mitnal. At that point, my cloaking will not hide Storm from Hanhau or any of the other demons. Do you still wish to do this?" she challenged.

"Absolutely." Evalle put her faith in Storm. He was clearly fighting to remain as human as possible the last time she saw him. That was enough for her.

The binding spell Adrianna placed on the oath given by Evalle and Nadina wasn't as impressive as what Adrianna had executed to send Evalle's body on an astral projection, but Evalle didn't doubt the power behind it. Not after witnessing what the Sterling witch could do.

As soon as Nadina was freed from her metal bindings, which took convincing Isak that Nadina would do nothing to any of them, Evalle and her witch doctor sidekick were ready to go to Mitnal.

Adrianna motioned Evalle aside. When Evalle reached her, the Sterling witch whispered, "The oath is absolutely enforceable in this world, but I'm not so sure about Mitnal. Don't don't turn your back on her there."

"I hear you." Evalle needed a weapon of some sort in this demon world. "Do you have that ponytail in your bag?"

"Yes."

"Slip it to me so that she doesn't see."

Adrianna gave a look of approval, which Evalle shrugged off as Adrianna fished out the ponytail and put it in a small black bag that she drew closed with a drawstring. Evalle stuffed the bag with its length of hair in her pocket. The ponytail had gained Nadina's compliance here, but Evalle had no idea if threatening to hand it over to Hanhau would make any difference in Mitnal or not.

Stepping back over to the center of the dining room, Adrianna was fully back in character, polite and conservative in her motions when she addressed Nadina, repeating the entire oath.

"I am no idiot," Nadina snapped. "I know to what I have agreed."

"I am stating it once more for the benefit of the spirits in this house who have granted me aid, and extended their offer of help if I ever need it again."

Nadina said nothing, but her eyes flicked up to where orbs now covered the ceiling, no longer agitated. They'd seen who was the more powerful witch tonight and knew where to place their betting chips.

"I need a moment," Evalle said to Adrianna, tipping her chin in Isak's direction.

"We'll be right here."

When Evalle walked past Isak and into the kitchen, he followed. Moonlight spilled through the window facing the backyard where nothing disturbed the peace outside.

Would she ever have a life where her world was that calm?

She turned to find him waiting for her to speak. "Thank you for coming out tonight and helping me. I'm sorry about that moment with the smoke."

Isak studied her during a couple of shallow breaths. "You shouldn't let something like her walk around free."

Did he mean Nadina or Adrianna? Probably both. "If it was left up to me, there would be no evil in the world, but I'm not the judge and jury. I'm only a guardian to protect the innocent. And I need Nadina."

Isak looked away, staring at the same window where moonlight filtered in. "This is what you do all the time, isn't it?"

"Sort of. Not necessarily dealing with witches. Give me a demon any day."

His gaze came back to her. He touched her hair, running a finger across it. "You wouldn't have to do this if you were with me. You could have a normal life where nothing would ever harm you, and since I'm human, you'd never have to pull me out of some demon hell."

She'd met Isak before Storm, but he hadn't been the one to reach inside and jumpstart her heart. If he had been, she might have that life. But Storm was her world and all that she could think of, even if it meant going into demon hell to drag him out.

"Thank you, Isak, for being my friend and for caring, but I'm committed to Storm."

He finally nodded. "Sure you'll be safe with that bitch?"

Not really, but Evalle put her best not-a-problem face on and said, "I'm good to go."

"Let me know when you're back." With that, he walked past her to the door. He opened it, then paused.

She turned to say she would call, but he got an unholy glint in his eyes and said, "Marriage is a commitment. I don't see a ring of any sort. I'll be looking for dinner in a week."

Then he was gone.

Marriage? She'd never even thought of that.

Or of being *mated*, which she apparently was, but she couldn't waste the brainpower on either one right now.

"Evalle? You ready?" Adrianna called from the other room.

Striding back to the living room, Evalle found Adrianna picking up her candles and carefully folding the cloth with the glyphs.

Adrianna glanced up and something in Evalle's face must have given her pause. "Yes?"

"Thanks. When it's time for what you need, I'll be there."

"Let's hope so," she joked, cutting her eyes in the witch doctor's direction. Then Adrianna winked and kept packing her bag.

Nadina snapped, "You must stand next to me for the cloaking spell to be set, then you can move away and remain hidden."

"Got it." Evalle walked over to stand in front of Nadina. "Can anything break this cloaking spell?"

"Not as long as I live or until we return to this world."

Once they did make it back to this world and Nadina returned the two souls, *and* freed Storm's father from whatever hellacious place he wandered through, Evalle had the task of convincing Storm to allow Nadina to walk away.

To accomplish that, Evalle would have to get past her own homicidal urges toward Nadina.

Taking her place at Nadina's side, but leaving a smidgeon of space so she didn't touch her, Evalle tried to convince herself she was ready. She would be if she could just shake off the sick feeling in her stomach that something would go wrong, such as Nadina taking control of Storm even though that possibility had been covered in the binding spell.

Had Storm agreed to travel to Mitnal confident that he would be successful? Or had he suffered the deep-down feeling Evalle was experiencing that warned her she'd missed something? Nadina was not someone to allow a loophole.

Nadina began chanting the cloaking spell.

As soon as the cloaking draped Evalle, she could see through the shield, but it was similar to looking through a filmy window.

Adrianna remained silent. The concern in her eyes told Evalle that the Sterling witch had her doubts too, but this was what they had come to do.

As soon as Nadina finished cloaking both of them, she said, "I will open the bolthole to Mitnal next. If we are discovered, the binding spell I agreed to has no influence on Hanhau. He does not allow anyone to pass through his kingdom without permission. Keep that in mind when I tell you what to do."

In other words, Evalle had to play Follow The Leader with Nadina, even if it led her over a cliff into a volcano.

CHAPTER 21

Quinn staggered toward a bench in Woodruff Park, a place where anyone in downtown Atlanta could enjoy a peaceful break.

Correction. Where humans could enjoy a break.

Most of the VIPER force was getting run ragged trying to catch demons running the streets like hungry rats on the move. He sat down hard and leaned back, groaning at the relief just sitting down gave his body. He couldn't stay awake and moving much longer.

Not while he was having episodes of blacking out.

He wasn't *exactly* blacking out so much as losing touch with reality. Dangerous for someone with his power. If his head would stop throbbing, he could actually think and figure out a way to fulfill his duty and leave Atlanta at the same time.

And that was so fucking illogical he snorted at it.

There was no way to do both.

He'd always performed his duty from the heart. Would stand and battle against any odds to protect his Belador tribe.

But right now he had no heart. He was as barren inside as a Medb.

That was not an entirely true comparison. Kizira had a heart filled with love.

But Kizira was dead.

Flaevynn, that miserable bitch who'd birthed her, had sent her daughter into a bloody battle and blocked Kizira's ability to heal herself. Flaevynn had caused her own child to commit suicide when Kizira threw herself in the way of a gryphon diving to attack Quinn.

His sweet Kizira had sacrificed her life for him.

He hadn't deserved her love.

Then there was Phoedra, a daughter he'd never known about until Kizira's dying breath. He still couldn't wrap his head around that, but Kizira had been telling the truth, frantic for him to find their child. But she'd died before she could tell him where she'd hidden Phoedra, which he had no doubt Kizira had done to protect their daughter from the Medb.

A blast of agony swept through him with the force of a tidal wave. His chest throbbed with pain, the deep kind that would never go away.

Phoedra. He'd let down both of them when he failed to protect Kizira. Had failed to realize that Kizira was as sincere as she'd tried to show him during the times she hadn't been compelled.

He grabbed his head, clamping his hands so tight his skull should crack. Kizira's face faded in and out in his mind's eye, calling to him, crying and begging him to find their daughter.

"Quinn."

He sat up at the sharp order. "Tzader. What are you doing here?"

Tzader's holographic image hovered next to the bench. Quinn knew Tzader could project himself from one location to another as a hologram, but as far as he knew, Tzader had only traveled this way to visit Brina in the castle. Tzader's black T-shirt and jeans were his normal attire, but now his skin lacked the deep luster of walnut wood. He was still powerfully built, but his face had sharp edges and his eyes were almost black from lack of food and sleep.

Quinn could relate to what Tzader was going through, but Quinn hadn't been much of a friend before leaving Treoir. *What caused me to act like such a bloody asshole when Tzader asked for my help?*

Tzader took a minute then cleared his throat. "Before I tell you why I'm here, I owe you an apology. I'm sorry about what happened on Treoir, Quinn. I don't know what got into me."

"I was just thinking how I was the one out of line," Quinn admitted. "I don't know what was up with me either."

"Are you any better?"

Quinn gave him a grim smile. "You mean do I still want to kill my best friend? That passed as soon as I left Treoir."

Tzader frowned at that. "I'm still battling with my temper. You think something on the island caused us to rip into each other?"

Sitting up and thinking on that, Quinn said, "You know what, I wasn't hostile until I went with you to see if I could do anything about Brina." He looked up at Tzader. "Has anyone else acted aggressive?"

"Not that I've noticed. No, wait. I take that back. Garwyli tried to help, then he and Macha got into a shouting match."

"Garwyli? Older-than-Moses Garwyli?" Quinn shook his head, then stopped and rolled the sequence of events leading up to their confrontation back through his mind. "The minute I touched the hologram, it was like something bled into my veins and released all this aggression. I was better outside, but I was still struggling with control."

Tzader stared off. "Sounds a lot like what happened to me."

"Has anyone else been in the room with the hologram?"

"Just me, the druid and Macha. And Evalle, but only for a few minutes."

"Did Garwyli actually touch the hologram?"

Tzader nodded as he thought. "Yes."

"But no one else, not even that guard Allyn has touched it?"

"Hell no. I won't let Allyn step beyond the doorway."

Quinn let Tzader's sharp tone pass, because he believed he had their control issue figured out. "It might be the Noirre majik clinging to the hologram. I touched it and tried to enter the hologram with my mind. It was cold and had me on defense within seconds."

Tzader's gaze drifted away from Quinn in concentration. "Damn. You may be right. I put my hands on the hologram, too, right after you walked out. Now that I think back, it was weird how when you first came into her solarium I was feeling bad about asking so much of you when you were in no shape to do anything, but I put my hands on the hologram when you walked out and I went to major pissed off in seconds. I was furious that you had quit trying to help Brina." Tzader washed a hand over his face. "That's fucked up, bud."

"Tell me about it," Quinn muttered then nudged the conversation back to Tzader's unexpected visit. "You must have a strong reason to come here in this form. What is it?"

"Something's up with the Medb."

That drew a dark chuckle from Quinn. "You don't know the half of it. We've been spotting warlocks and witches all over the city."

"Really? What're you doing about it?"

Quinn's temper boiled for a moment at the insinuation that he hadn't been performing his duty, but now that he understood where the aggression was originating, he forced himself to settle down. "You don't understand. The Medb have actually been helping out." He took in Tzader's shock and nodded. "Now you're getting an idea of what's going on. We have Medb running around at the same time that someone has dumped at least eight demons here. Those are only the *reported* demon sightings. I'm betting there are more."

"Macha was called to a major coalition meeting and she thought it was about them booting us from VIPER, but—"

That brought Quinn to his feet. "Are you serious?"

"Yeah, she thinks VIPER wants to cut the Beladors loose because we're becoming dead weight that's drawing the attention of everything evil. I'm thinking maybe it's about this Medb outbreak of witches and warlocks. She left me in charge of Treoir with orders that she did not want an issue with VIPER right now while the Beladors are in a crisis."

Quinn had bad news for Tzader, because he'd already caused an issue with VIPER. Once he shared that incident, Tzader would understand why Quinn might just be the worst choice for acting Maistir. He quipped, "If that's the case, Macha will probably go postal when she hears about Medb saving humans from demons."

"A postal goddess. Just what this clusterfuck needs. What do you mean saving humans? Did the Medb show up at the wrong place and time then the demons went after them?"

"No, I mean the Medb are actively hunting demons and making kills, clearly before a demon can touch a human."

"That makes no sense," Tzader muttered. "Got any idea who the demons belong to?"

"I can't get close enough to one to determine an origin and, from what I've heard, neither has any other Belador. The Nightstalkers are hidden, probably terrified by so much dark activity in the city. The minute a demon shows its face in public, there's no Belador close enough to deal with it, but out of the blue a Medb witch or warlock shows up, nukes the demon then disappears. They have to be using a cloaking spell because humans are not noticing, but there are always plenty of nonhuman witnesses to vouch for what happened."

"What the hell is going on?"

"I don't know, but Sen is getting testy with me."

Tzader didn't snap at him this time. His silence was more damning, because Quinn knew his friend was biting his tongue to keep from making things worse. Quinn owed him the truth. "My control is in tatters. I managed to not kill a troll that was stalking a human, but I screwed up the mind of a Medb."

"That doesn't sound like a problem."

"Depends on how you look at the final outcome. I should have killed the troll, but I was starting to wonder just how dangerous it was to leave me in your position." Quinn cast a glance at Tzader who remained motionless so Quinn continued. "I grabbed the troll before he got close to the human, did some creative therapy and sent him on his way. He shouldn't harm anything worse than a fish or frog at this point since that's what he now believes his favorite meals are, but neither will he be able to carry on a conversation with other trolls."

"Still not seeing the downside."

That was Tzader, Quinn's friend all the way to the bloody end of the world. Quinn had to make him understand just how desperate the Beladors were if they left him as acting Maistir. He explained, "I caught a Medb warlock and intended to bring him in for questioning. I was going to charge him with having knowledge of who dropped the demons in Atlanta, plus I recognized him from a raid we did in Charleston."

"The one where those filthy warlocks were using that young girl's body to cook a Noirre aphrodisiac spell?"

"Yes."

"Fuck him then. Hope you killed him."

"I did, in a way. The arrest was going fine until he started yelling that it wasn't his fault. He'd been *compelled*."

Tzader slapped a hand over his eyes. "Ah, shit."

"That pretty much covers what happened. I heard *that* word and all I could see was Kizira dying in my arms because that whore Flaevynn had compelled her daughter not to use her own healing skills. I. Lost. It. I grabbed the warlock's mind and clutched it so hard with mine his brain literally exploded inside his head."

"I'm having a hard time digging up any remorse for a warlock. Compelled or not, that prick deserved to die."

"He wandered around in a circle while I tried to pull myself back under control. I looked up just as a MARTA bus hit him."

Tzader frowned and looked around.

"It wasn't here. It was over by Centennial Park. Had to call in Sen to clean it up and deal with anyone who saw it since there was no chance of getting someone with Atlanta PD who was Belador."

"What you did was ..."

"Unacceptable," Quinn finished for him. "Sen's furious. He keeps hearing how the Medb are dealing with the demons and the Beladors are crippled power-wise. He reminded me that as acting Maistir I'm supposed to contain a situation and he threatened to take me before the Tribunal if I caused another public scene like that."

Tzader studied Quinn for several seconds. "What'd you do?"

"I didn't try to kill Sen, if that's what you mean." Quinn gave him a half-serious smile. "I was actually starting to get a grip after I released that warlock. That might be the only thing that saved one of us." With the rumor mill purporting Sen to have powers akin to a god or demi-god, Quinn had a reasonable idea of who would have won that short battle.

"Man, I hate doing this to you," Tzader admitted.

"It's okay. I'm just disappointed in not performing better."

"Give me a break, Quinn. You just lost the woman you love and you haven't even had time to grieve her." Tzader paused. "Have you decided where to bury her yet?"

"No. I took Kizira to a friend of mine who deals with our kind and told him I'd be back soon. I ... wanted a little more time before I took that last step."

"I understand. Tell me when you're ready and I'll be there."

Quinn swallowed the thick lump in his throat. He wanted to tell Tzader about Phoedra now that Quinn could carry a decent conversation, but he didn't think he could say her name without breaking down. He said, "I know you'll be there when I ask. Now, is anything else going on with Treoir?"

"First, can you continue standing in for me?"

"Yes. I'm okay for now." That tasted like a lie, but Tzader needed to hear those words.

"Thanks. I hate asking this of you, but you're the only one I trust to be Maistir in my place. I'll take over as soon as I can, which might be sooner than I expected."

Quinn stood to face Tzader. "Why? Has something happened to Brina ... or Lanna?"

The weight bearing down on Tzader's shoulders showed in his face. "Not a word on either one yet, but I'm not leaving until we get them both back or ..."

"I understand. Just tell me what you need."

"That's why I projected my hologram to reach you. I don't know what all Evalle is doing, but I couldn't risk going to her and interrupting anything she had in the works that might lead to Storm. I need her to find him like yesterday, because our oldest druids have no idea what to do. We're running short on time."

"I thought she had two days left."

"That was an estimate based on how often a piece of the hologram disappeared. But parts are starting to vanish faster."

"Bloody hell. What can I do?"

Tzader's smile was sad and tired. "You're doing it, old friend, and I will never forget this, but I need you to have Trey locate Evalle since I don't think she has a cell phone unless you gave her one."

"No, my head was too far up my ass to think about anyone else when we got back to Atlanta," Quinn muttered. "I'll call Trey right away. How do I get word back to you?"

"It's not good news if I come back to Atlanta before Evalle and Storm arrive at Treoir. Just have Sen teleport those two as soon as you can. If Sen threatens you again—"

Quinn held up his hand. "I won't allow that to happen. I'll make nice with every Medb if that's what it takes to keep peace with Sen until Brina and Lanna are safe at the castle."

"Once that happens, the Belador power will be a force to reckon with once again and anyone who has taken advantage of this vulnerable time will pay dearly." Tzader's eyebrow lifted with a thought. "You know what, part of the problem you're having with your control may be due to Brina being out of the castle."

"I had considered that. I hope you're right."

"I need to go. I've never risked projecting my body unless I was locked in my car, and it's warded. Everyone should be outside protecting the castle, but that prick Allyn keeps coming by to check on the hologram."

"Do you really think Brina was going to marry him?"

"No." Tzader shook his head and made a sound of disgust. "That was all a ploy. Macha was behind it."

"Are you kidding me?"

"It was Macha's idea of motivating us to figure it out. Tell you more later."

"Very well. I hope not to see you again until you have news of their return."

Tzader disappeared.

Quinn used his cell phone to call Trey and gave him the message to pass along to Evalle.

Trey said, "I'll let you know as soon as I hear from her. It might take a few tries, but I should be able to connect to her mind. I was able to speak to her telepathically earlier and she was able to reply. She's impacted less than full-blooded Beladors."

"Very well. Keep me informed."

Quinn had closed his phone when he caught sight of two suspicious characters a block away. They were dressed as tourists in casual clothes, but didn't move with the easy strides of humans.

He might have dismissed that until one of them glanced around, giving Quinn a chance to see the yellow eyes of a Medb.

Had the Medb released the demons?

If so, the fastest way to find out who had dumped killers into the city would be through those warlocks. Either way, catching that pair would be quite useful if Quinn could show a little restraint this time.

CHAPTER 22

Evalle's heart thumped what sounded like a frantic SOS message.

Nadina moved into an open spot in the musty-smelling living room of the haunted house she'd invaded in Stone Mountain.

Adrianna remained several steps away in the dining room.

With arms raised out to each side, Nadina's voice turned husky with a guttural chant that sounded dark and twisted. She waited for Evalle to repeat it, which she did.

Nadina moved her hands in front of her, and power exploded in a high arch between Nadina's palms. She moved her hands forward and down, allowing the blazing yellow-orange arch to slide from her fingertips to the hardwood floor.

Giving Evalle a look of challenge, Nadina said, "This is your last chance to change your mind. Once we cross through this arch, we enter Mitnal. You may return without me, but you may not enjoy the passing."

What did that mean?

"Save your scary stories for Halloween," Evalle told her and waved a hand. "Lead the way."

Nadina's eyes lit with hidden thoughts, but she vanished through the archway before Evalle could question her.

Adrianna said, "You may or may not exit that bolthole here. If you come back here, the spirits will allow you to pass. I can't say the same for Nadina so don't stand too close to her when you return."

"Got it." Evalle blew out a breath and stepped through the blazing opening and into a frosty haze that surrounded her. In the next instant, she could feel the opening suck closed behind her.

Cold struck her skin and started wrapping around and around like a bandage of ice. It dredged up memories of artic training she'd gone through at eighteen as a new Belador warrior five years ago. But this was different than suffering the sub-freezing temps that would punish any exposed skin. A freezing paint coated her skin, but her insides had turned into a roaring furnace of heat.

One sensation should alleviate the discomfort of the other, but no. It just hurt from both directions.

While she had the feeling that she would not freeze to death or combust, the opposing temperatures were irritating the hell out of her within seconds.

What was it doing to demons kept here forever?

What's it doing to Storm?

Now she understood the vision she'd had back in Storm's bedroom. He'd been blue with cold in this realm of the dead. A bitter smell stung her nose. It could be incense if someone had decided to create one from a mix of sulfur and badly burned habaneros.

The haze cleared and she froze.

Demons surrounded her. She stood in the middle of the ones she'd seen when she visited Mitnal during her earlier out-of-body visit.

She'd had no idea how much nicer that was than an in-body experience.

Hundreds of demons covered surfaces in every direction. Some curled up on the ground and others draped over ledges. Was that all they did during the day? Rest?

That and attack Storm, because as she took in this horde of demons, none appeared battered and bruised as he had.

Now that she had a chance to take in the entire place from a standing position, she tilted her head back. This place could house a four-story building that covered a city block. Dark holes appeared at different levels. Were those recessed areas similar to the den where she'd found Storm?

Was he still in the same place?

In fact, where was Nadina?

Turning her head slowly even though the demons appeared oblivious to her presence, Evalle finally spotted the witch doctor leaning against a rock wall with arms crossed. Her cloaking fell over her from head to toe like sheer red netting.

Nadina arched a taunting eyebrow at her and smiled to emphasize that she was not required to help Evalle find her way through a sea of snoozing demons.

Keep thinking you're too sexy for your skin and I'll turn a Sterling witch loose on you again.

Evalle carefully turned the palm of her hand to face the floor and pushed down to see how far her kinetics would lift her.

Not an inch.

Mental note—no kinetics available in here.

Nadina had failed to explain that, but Evalle had been just as remiss in not asking if her powers would function in Mitnal. She was still hunting a way over to Nadina when someone bellowed, "Come to your master!"

Blood froze in Evalle's veins.

Demons stood and stretched.

Snarls and rumbling filled the air from behind Evalle, sounding like they came from deep inside some deadly animal. But the entire room glowed red from all the eyes opening.

Twisting around, Evalle found the source of the voice. It belonged to the bony guy she'd seen before.

Hanhau in all his glory.

His face was not shaped like any man's she'd ever seen. He had big round eyes filled with flames, a beaked nose and tiny ears pointing up from each side of his head. Shiny white skin clung to Hanhau's emaciated body, parts of it sunken in places, to appear as a skeleton.

If Nadina could be stunning as a woman, why was Hanhau content to be a cadaver with a giant owlish head sporting a unicorn horn?

Hair sprouted straight up on his head then more fell past his shoulders in thick braids. His bone necklace jangled when he moved to stand in front of his throne of skulls.

What kind of creep had that for a chair?

One who ruled a world of the damned.

Energy literally sizzled around his body, similar to how

steam hissed off hot asphalt in Atlanta after a summer shower.

The demons herded toward their leader. More of them than she'd realized the first time.

Some still possessed a human-like shape and moved forward on two legs, while others were animals lumbering on all fours. Jackals, black wolves, one with the body of a bear and the head of a wild hog with tusks.

Her hand itched for her spelled blade that she'd had to leave behind.

None of the animals maintained any of their natural characteristics, if they'd ever had any. Oversized beasts with misshapen bodies crowded toward the throne. More poured out of the dark crevices above her and slithered along the walls or pounced to the cave floor with the agility of cats.

Time to find Storm and get him out of this place. She was not going to accept that he'd joined ranks with this bunch.

Once the demons were moving steadily, Evalle fell into step, taking every opening that appeared until she reached Nadina.

Hanhau began working himself into a froth with some crazy chanting and beating on his chest. The demons pounded the ground with their feet and paws.

A loud rattle sounded as a giant snake joined in.

All the noise covered Evalle's final steps out of the foot traffic and her words when she told Nadina, "You aren't holding your end of the deal if you disappear on me."

"I haven't gone anywhere. I waited for you. It's not my fault you made no plans for where you would enter Mitnal."

Don't kill the bitch. "Take me to Storm."

"As you wish."

Those words had sounded charming in *The Princess Bride*. Coming from Nadina they had the ring of dire threat. Hanhau's glowing speech of how he shared his power with his demons because they were his family echoed through the room, followed by rumbling noises from his rapt followers.

Hanhau kept on. "You are mine and you will see our greatness soon."

You can't have Storm, she silently answered.

Nadina flashed ahead of her, reaching a spot as far as one

could get from Hanhau on the main floor. The witch doctor seemed to have *her* powers here, and could move faster than even Evalle was capable of with her Belador powers.

Wait a minute. How had Nadina managed that?

Dismissing the showoff for now, Evalle saw that Nadina stood at the entrance of an alcove. It was the placed Evalle recalled from her earlier trip to Mitnal.

Storm had been tucked deep inside the hollowed-out area.

She followed Nadina into the dark recess, glad to find that her Alterant night vision still worked in here. Staring through the filmy veil, the rocky walls glowed blue where they hadn't before.

Did that mean the walls were hot as a blue flame or frigid enough to glue skin to them?

Nadina slowed just before walking around a wall and stuck her head as far out as her skinny neck would allow, then whispered, "There he is."

When the witch doctor continued around the curve, Evalle mentally prepared herself to face Storm and convince him that they could escape. She also reminded herself that Storm was comfortable being naked even if Evalle had a hard time with any other woman seeing him that way.

Maybe she'd blindfold Nadina now that they'd found Storm.

But as Evalle entered the area that widened into a round room large enough to hold a small car, she faced a black jaguar rising quickly to stand eye-level with her chest.

He shouldn't be able to see Evalle or Nadina.

The jaguar cocked his head at noticing a disturbance in his area. His red gaze swept from the spot where Evalle stood to Nadina then back.

Nadina gave her a you-wanted-to-do-this look and said, "He will not hear you with this cloaking in place. To reveal yourself, put your hands together then move them apart as if opening up a cloak."

Confirming what Nadina had said, Storm must not have heard a thing because his jaguar remained still, but deep throaty growls rumbled with each exhale.

The kind of sound you heard right before something vicious

attacked.

Evalle did as Nadina had instructed and opened the cloak, pushing it back to reveal herself to Storm, whose gaze speared her with the single-mindedness of a predator.

His jaws unhinged and he roared loud enough to burst human eardrums. The sound was as unearthly as it was frightening. She'd heard Storm's roar when he attacked a troll.

This was far worse.

One look at Nadina and Evalle realized why the witch doctor was so happy.

Storm didn't recognize Evalle.

He closed his jaws and put his head down then took a step toward her.

CHAPTER 23

Out of pure survival instinct, Evalle shoved one hand up, palm out, even though she had no kinetics in Mitnal.

Storm ran into the invisible wall and jumped back.

Evalle lifted her hand to look at it, shocked that her power worked, then she eye Nadina. "You knew my powers would work here?"

The witch doctor shrugged and peeled back her cloaking. "Not while you're enclosed in the cloaking. Once you broke that barrier, I suspected your kinetics might, but I doubt telepathy will reach anyone from here."

Storm evidently didn't like Nadina any better because he growled in her direction. That gave Evalle hope of gaining an edge on Nadina until the witch doctor cast an indulgent glance at Storm as she informed Evalle, "Do not think he will attack me. He can not, even if Hanhau ordered him."

"Why would I want him to attack you when you're our guide out of here?"

"You were thinking it."

Evalle scoffed at her. "You can't read my mind."

"Perhaps not, but I can read your face."

"Tell Storm that we're going to leave here together."

"No. You did not *specifically* negotiate that."

Evalle held her temper because she might not like dealing with Nadina, but bringing Hanhau and those demons down on her head would be worse. "I did negotiate that because I said you would help us escape."

"Help comes in many ways. I am most willing to guide you out of here again. That qualifies as doing my part."

Dismissing the twit, Evalle turned to Storm and kept her voice calm. "We're going to leave."

He dove at her, lips pulled back and fangs ready to crush whatever part of her body they latched onto.

Evalle flipped the kinetic field back into place at the last second and Storm smashed up against it, sending vibrations through her arm that couldn't hurt any worse if a Mack truck had rammed her defensive wall. Her shoulder ached and now she had serious concerns about getting out of this place alive.

Her skin chilled even more, but she couldn't blame it entirely on the atmosphere in Mitnal. She stared into Storm's glowing red eyes and saw no humanity there. No one at home who would recognize her. Her heart squeezed with one painful beat after another. She was losing him.

Or had already lost him.

Her head screamed at her that this was a lost cause.

Tzader and Quinn would be dragging her away if they were here.

Nadina waited in smug silence, ready to claim victory.

You can do no less for him than he would do for you, whispered through Evalle's mind. That same voice had popped in and out of her head over the last few months. The most recent time had been when Evalle lay dying while linked to Tzader.

That female voice had apologized for not being there for Evalle as she grew up locked away in a basement like a caged animal and Evalle was pretty sure the spirit had been responsible for Evalle and Tzader surviving.

Was that her mother who had died in childbirth?

She'd find out one day, but it wouldn't be today.

If he is yours then no one can take him from you, the voice said, then withdrew from Evalle's mind.

Damned straight. Evalle squared her shoulders and told Storm, "You don't belong to Nadina. You never did and you knew that your whole life until now. She tricked you, but you are mine and I am not leaving here without you if I have to drag you back through that bolthole."

"No!" Nadina shouted. "He's mine and if you try to harm me he will rip you to pieces."

Turning to her, Evalle said in a deadly quiet voice. "He won't touch me. I'm his mate and he knows it. Now it's time for you to fulfill the rest of your deal so I can take him home."

"You'll never get out of here without me."

"I don't plan to try. You made a deal. You know the consequences of crossing me and my witch friend." Nadina didn't know who Adrianna was, and Evalle wouldn't give someone this evil any kind of edge by revealing Adrianna's name now.

Nadina's face ruptured with fury. "You think you know everything. I never put all my eggs in one basket. Storm had a purpose, which he fulfilled by coming to Mitnal of his own free will. Look at him. You have lost."

"You bitch."

"Not me." Nadina laughed. "He did all this to keep *you* safe and now he doesn't even know you."

"He'll just have to learn me again, because we're leaving here with him."

"Have you forgotten the oath? I said Storm had to be in human form–and not turned fully into a demon–to cloak and take out of here. You agreed to that. Now that he has been turned he will be a demon forever."

"He will not."

"Then make him shift back into his human form," Nadina suggested.

Evalle eyed the jaguar who showed no sign of being interested in anything she had to say. "Storm? Please shift back to your human form."

"Don't you understand?" Nadina's voice was picking up confidence with every second that the jaguar remained in place. "Storm will not change back, because the blood rules him. He has embraced his destiny. You should accept it and I will take you back. He would want that."

It couldn't end this way.

But Evalle now understood what she hadn't when they'd made the oath. She speared Nadina with the fury bubbling inside her. "You were banking on Storm being stuck in jaguar form by the time we reached him, weren't you?"

Nadina shrugged. "One could only hope."

"I don't care." Evalle was past the point of wasting energy on worry. She was taking Storm home and she didn't give a flip if it was on two feet or four paws. "We're ready to go. Open the bolthole, Nadina. That seems to be all you're good for."

Nadina smiled as if she were the only one who knew the secret handshake. "I can't open the bolthole right here."

"Why?"

"Hanhau has me bound in such a way that I must always enter and leave at the same spot. Why do you think we entered in the middle of the demons? If I had alerted Hanhau I was coming to Mitnal, he would have cleared a spot. And do not accuse me of breaking my oath. I will take you back through the original bolthole, but I have no way to cloak that jaguar from Hanhau to sneak him out."

Evalle ran through the oath in her mind. This bitch had tricked Storm and now she'd outplayed Evalle and Adrianna. Unbelievable. But Adrianna had covered Evalle's ass by making Nadina tell Evalle how to open a bolthole on her own. "You know what, Nadina, fine, stay here if you want, but I have that chunk of hair you lost and I'll scatter it all over this place if you aren't going to hold up your end of the deal. I'll keep one strand for the minute you step back into the mortal world and I own you." Evalle had no idea what she'd do with the crazy woman at that point, but the threat had a nice ring to it.

Shock washed the anger from Nadina's face. Her eyes glowed with a wild stare. "You must go and leave him here. This is where Storm belongs."

"No."

"Give me that hair."

"No."

Nadina started wringing her hands and talking to herself. "Hanhau will know the minute Storm is gone. I cannot be left here without Storm. He has to stay and protect me."

Whoa. Was Evalle hearing this right? Had Nadina boxed herself into a corner? "Let me get this straight. If *I* open a bolthole and drag Storm through it—" Evalle paused at the mental image of Storm's jaws locking on that arm and ripping it off. "Hanhau shuts down Mitnal and you're stuck here with the crazy demon ruler?"

Nadina's hair shot straight out away from her head and she kept muttering. "He'll make me do ... I cannot let Hanhau ... He'll give me to all the demons... No, no..."

Evalle couldn't wish that misery on someone more deserving, but Storm still needed this witch to get his soul back. Dammit. "Look, Nadina, just work with me to get us out of here—" While Evalle was trying to figure out how to take Storm out then come back to bring Nadina out, the crazy witch flipped a gear into nuclear insanity.

Nadina's wild gaze slammed into Evalle's. "You cannot have him."

"I'm not leaving him here. He's going with me."

"Hanhau will make me pay." Nadina shouted, "If I cannot have Storm, you will not either, and you're not leaving me here to suffer Hanhau."

That threat had barely registered in Evalle's brain when Nadina turned on Storm who roared at the witch doctor, but he clearly couldn't attack his master.

Nadina didn't have that problem. She pointed at Storm and spewed a string of words that Evalle had no chance of comprehending as bloody stripes whipped across storm's skin. Evalle dug out the hair in her pocket and waved it at Nadina who looked at it for all of a second and flicked a flame from her fingertips that caught the hair on fire. The hair on Nadina's head started to flame at the same time, but Nadina swiped her hand over it to squelch the blaze.

Evalle slung the rest of the burning ponytail away.

The possibility of being left here as Hanhau's bitch had just trumped the oath Nadina had given Evalle.

Adrianna had been partly correct in thinking the penalty Nadina would pay for breaking her oath with Evalle only mattered if Nadina left this place.

What she'd missed was that Nadina had to be sane enough to realize she was breaking the oath. Evalle watched as Nadina's model-beautiful face began to age before her eyes.

Storm went up on his hind legs, falling back as as blood poured from the wounds Nadina continued to inflict.

Evalle threw a kinetic blast at Nadina, slamming the witch doctor up against the wall. Nadina turned on her, bony fingers raised with nails narrowing into sharp points. She howled and raked her spiked nails from top to bottom.

White-hot pain sliced down Evalle's chest and arms.

Storm rolled to his feet, dropped low and shoved up hard, but was he going for Evalle or Nadina?

The witch whipped a hand in Storm's direction, snapping bones in his legs. He fell to the floor in a heap, howling with pain and anger.

Evalle shoved up a wall of power to give her the sixty seconds she needed to shift her body into something that could defend him. Her jeans and vintage shirt ripped everywhere as she released her beast that grew four times her size, extending her arms that filled the room with blue-green feathers over the wings and body of a gryphon. Adrenaline rushed the change. Her head warped and twisted into the golden head of an eagle and the lower half of her body flowed into that of lion.

She rose up on her haunches, spreading her wings and curling the talons on her front feet.

Nadina's mouth gaped open in horror.

Now who was the biggest bitch in the room?

Confidence gone and only a mindless monster left in the place of Nadina, she tossed off her cloak and called out, "Storm, protect your master!"

Storm pushed up on one front leg that had already healed, then he straightened the second one. Massive muscle bunched and moved beneath the glistening black coat. He looked at Evalle's gryphon form and shook his head as if not sure what he was seeing.

But he was healing fast and ready to fight. Red burned in his eyes. He roared in reply to Nadina's call for help then swung that deadly gaze at Evalle.

Her stomach fell.

Please don't fight me, Storm. Don't make me hurt you.

If she didn't fight him, demon or not, deep down she had to believe he'd never survive killing her. Of course, that would only happen if he ever recognized her again.

When he lunged at her, she caught him with her claws,

fighting him off and getting gouged as badly as she had to be hurting him.

Her worst nightmare had come true.

Storm had turned into a demon and attacked her.

Nadina jumped into the fray, using her majik to stab Storm, driving his rage over the top. He clawed at Evalle over and over until Evalle shot a blast of fire at Nadina that singed what was left of the witch doctor's medusa-looking hair.

Storm bit down on Evalle's paw then yanked his head back with blood dripping from his lips.

His eyes still glowed, but shock widened them.

Had he recognized her blood? Did he know she was his mate?

The emerald that had done nothing in all this time, now hummed with energy in Evalle's chest and shone brightly through the gryphon feathers. Her heart thumped a crazy jig.

She tossed Storm away as carefully as she could and he landed on all fours, spinning to take in her then Nadina.

The witch doctor ordered him, "Kill her. Now!"

Storm just stood there, confused and panting.

Evalle had been so intent on Storm, watching for a sign of recognition that she had failed to keep an eye on Nadina.

Nadina shoved one hand of long, pointy nails at Evalle whose gryphon arched up, swinging back and forth with her wings flapping. Evalle clawed at the air to make whatever was stabbing her over and over stop.

Storm took one step, then another, but he was headed for Nadina with an unholy look in his jaguar eyes.

As he leaped, Nadina howled a curse at him and her other hand turned into a blade that plunged into his chest.

Evalle screamed, a loud wrenching sound that was half eagle and half woman. She flapped her wings hard, driving her down to the witch whose majik was still ripping into Evalle.

Nadina paid no attention to Evalle, focused only on killing Storm.

Evalle grabbed the witch doctor's head in her ginormous beak and ripped it off, flinging the bloody ball against a wall.

The pain in Evalle's chest eased. She landed on the cave floor and tottered to keep her balance.

A headless body flopped to the ground.

Realization of what she'd done slammed Evalle in her chest. *No, no, no!*

Even with Storm dead, he and his father still had no souls. They had no way to rest forever. Evalle wanted to kill that witch all over again.

The jaguar stirred, jerking Evalle's attention to him. *Storm?*

But he couldn't hear her telepathically.

Relief and misery battled in her heart. He was still alive, but she'd killed Nadina.

Snapping out of his daze, Storm's gaze whipped over to Nadina's head that still rocked back and forth where it had landed. The foul smell of blood filled the air instead of her nasty licorice scent.

He swung his attention back to take in Evalle standing over Nadina's lifeless body and the jaguar let loose a long sound so forlorn and painful Evalle couldn't breathe.

She'd just killed the last hope he had of ever getting his soul back and, in that moment, he might not recognize her but he understood the loss.

A chorus of howling out in the large room answered Storm.

Okay, that just screwed any odds for a clean escape.

Bad news flash number two? With Nadina dead, Evalle had no cloaking and no idea if she could definitely open a bolthole on her own. Did she have to go back out in the middle of that open area to do it?

That was not happening.

Then there was the problem of trying to get a demon jaguar out of here, one that had survived attacks for the last two days in this place and currently had his head lowered, snarling and panting viciously.

She gambled and changed back to human in a rush, which she found out quickly was not the way to do it. Her body twisted and snapped, forcing muscles to wind back into smaller, tighter shapes and bones to shorten. She fought for breath and squeezed her eyes to stop any chance of tears. She had only seconds to get through to Storm, who still eyed her with murder glaring in his eyes.

Snatching the robe off Nadina, Evalle yanked it on and tied the string as she talked. "Listen to me Storm. I'm sorry about Nadina."

The growling picked up volume and his lips lifted to expose razor-sharp fangs.

Not the best time to discuss the witch doctor.

Evalle moved ahead. "I know you're in there. Come back with me. I think I can open the bolthole. You may not like me right now, but you hate Hanhau. You can't stay here."

Howling was racing toward them.

Storm stalked her, moving slowly forward, one paw at a time.

Had killing Nadina snapped the last thread he'd held on his humanity?

"Please, Storm. Come back with me."

He took another step.

The screaming demons were close to his den. The first one raced in and launched itself. Before Evalle could raise her hand to deflect the attack, Storm shot up, meeting the threat in mid-air. They fell into a tangle of snarls and clawing. Two more demons came through the narrow passage.

She ground her teeth against the pain and forced herself into battle form that raised the cartilage along her arms and powered up her body. Lifting her hands, she was ready.

But there was no way out of here if she couldn't open that bolthole.

First she had to stop the demon running at her. He stood upright and spikes stuck out of his head like a horned Mohawk that continued down his spine. With no reason to hold back now, she unleashed her kinetics and blasted him against the wall, crushing his skull. The second demon was the bear with the wild hog head. Sharp tusks jutted out eighteen inches beyond the thing's snout.

The eyes of this thing and the demon she'd killed were brilliant red. Like mega wattage.

Had Hanhau just super-charged his herd?

Evalle caught the tusks and dropped down, hanging from them so they didn't spear her. She held on as the thing shook her back and forth. One of his clawed paws struck out at her side and gouged a wound.

She could only keep this up for so long before her strength would give out, especially after changing into a gryphon and back so fast.

Her arms were quivering.

Let go and try to use kinetics against him?

He'd stomp her first then stab her with a tusk.

Her shoulders were dropping closer to the floor. The minute she hit, the demon would know he had her.

A flash of black jumped on top of the beast's back. Jaguar jaws clamped the hog's neck and ripped once, then again. The hog beast's wild eyes rolled, searching for what attacked it. It screamed and jumped around trying to shake that black jaguar off, but Storm held on, taking the demon to the ground.

Evalle scrambled to keep from getting trampled.

Thankfully, it fell sideways or it would've crushed her. She staggered to her feet, wiping sweat out of her eyes in spite of the frosted breaths rolling off her tongue.

Where were the other demons?

Not that she was inviting them in, but why weren't they swarming?

When the hog took its last breath, Storm stood on top of it, roaring over and over, louder each time until the walls shook.

Now she got it.

They were terrified of Storm.

These three had thought they'd heard Storm being attacked and come to finish him off. What had Hanhau promised them if they were successful?

A demon treat?

Evalle looked around at the carnage. This was it. She had to convince Storm to leave now or it was never going to happen. Waiting for the most dangerous demon in Mitnal to finish warning off the rest against even thinking about attacking him, Evalle reached into the pocket of Nadina's robe and dug for anything that the witch might have held onto that would open a bolthole.

Empty pockets. No majik wand or artifact to insure an exit route.

Storm quieted and turned to her, not a flicker of emotion

anywhere in those eyes.

She'd gotten used to the yellow eyes on Storm's jaguar, because he'd always been in there behind them. No sign of the man behind the glowing red gaze.

Licking her lips, she tried to swallow against her dry throat. "I'm going to try to open the bolthole. I want you to come with me. Please."

Still no sign of acknowledgment.

Was Storm in there?

Evalle held her hands out to the side just as Nadina had and called up the words again, repeating them louder the second time. Energy sizzled and smoked then burst into an archway.

"It worked." Maybe it was wearing the witch's robe? Evalle laughed in surprise, but the sound had a hysterical edge. Much more of this and she'd need measurements for a straitjacket.

She'd just lowered her hands to drop the archway to the ground when power, serious power, exploded into the room.

Hanhau took one look at the bolthole archway and reached for Evalle.

Something hit her in the back, knocking her through the archway. She fell forward, going into a roll out of habit when fighting. A thousand tiny lightning bolts zapped her from every direction until she'd cleared the bolthole. Light flashed on black fur as Storm followed her through, and Evalle flopped on the ground, moaning.

Dark sky. Sliver of a moon peeking through tree branches. She glanced around. They'd made it. This was the Stone Mountain neighborhood. She could see the old frame house with the orbs a block away. Falling back on the ground, she drew in a breath of fresh air from her world.

Storm leaped over her and swung around, eyes full of death staring at her.

He snarled, tufts of hair rising along his neck and shoulders.

Not again.

Evalle thought about just letting him have at her. She was bleeding and tired, but when she rolled over to push up on her feet, Storm dropped onto the ground.

Thank goodness. Maybe being home would help.

A howling noise drew her around.

The bolthole was still open. She rattled off the words to slam it shut, but not before a demon leaped out.

Ears stuck out from his head and curled into short horns. His head, neck and shoulders were covered in orange scales. Long strands of gray hair hung from his waist almost to the ground, covering the bottom half of his body and not quite hiding his gender.

He looked like a demented hula dancer.

Evalle backed up a step, shoving one kinetic blast after another at the demon, but it kept coming at her.

Clearly, she was a quart low on kinetic energy.

She looked around and Storm was ... stretched out, licking his paws?

She might kill him herself. "Storm?"

He turned to her, took a long look, then went back to poking at his injuries.

That was the absolute last good nerve she had left.

She called up every ounce of power she could find and slammed the demon into an oak tree that had a broken limb sticking out like a pike. She impaled the demon on it. Red eyes dimmed until only yellow was left. His head drooped to one side, then his body ignited, burning until ashes drifted away.

Turning to Storm, she jabbed her hands to her hips and leaned down. "Thanks for nothing."

Storm stood up and walked away.

"Where do you think you're going?"

He swung that pair of red beacons at her and gave a gravelly growl.

Was that a warning not to cross him? Maybe.

She wasn't sure how much he understood right now, but she had no doubt that he would not quickly forget who had killed Nadina. Storm had hunted that witch doctor for a long time. Nadina was the reason he'd come to the states and taken a job with VIPER. Now it was all gone forever.

But Evalle couldn't talk to him in this form.

She asked nicely, "Would you please shift back to human?"

His stare never altered. He made no effort to shift. *Could* he still shift? The only positive sign was that his body appeared to be healing quickly.

Hers, not so much.

She tried to call up her beast healing powers, but nothing more than a mild energy swirled inside her. She hadn't wanted to admit that her powers were waning, but her Belador blood was losing drive. How screwed up was it that her Medb blood, the other half of her genetics, had to be keeping her on her feet right now? The longer they stood out here exposed in a city hunting demons, the worse her odds got. No way did she want to have to battle her own Belador friends to protect Storm, or the other way around.

Taking a look around, she was heartened to find she was only about a half mile from where she'd left his Land Cruiser. Maybe he'd shift once he was inside his house where things were familiar.

That was if she could get him to climb inside his vehicle and *if* he didn't kill her first.

CHAPTER 24

Brina spun in the swirling gray mist. What was happening to her? She clutched a handful of hair and pulled, trying to yank some sanity into her mind. Why was she so confused?

One minute the Medb had been attacking Treoir and in the next she'd landed in this godforsaken place.

Okay, wait ... not exactly that quickly...

She released her hair and rubbed her temple where a headache throbbed viciously. She'd been in her sunroom. Horace, the old Belador she'd have never thought could be a traitor, had tossed Noirre majik on her and Lanna...

Where was Lanna?

Panic flooded Brina with a cold chill. "Lanna? *Lanna!*"

Now she recalled yelling at Lanna and accusing the child of being the enemy. *What is wrong with me?*

A very strained sound came through the mist that sounded like "here."

Brina headed in what she hoped was the right direction. "Talk to me, Lanna. I can't find you."

"I am here," came stronger this time. "You talk too so that I know you are not going wrong way."

Brina kept up her chatter and moved through the murky gray until she saw Lanna's blond hair bright as a beacon. "There you are."

The minute Lanna's face came into view Brina's stomach fell. Lanna was terrified and Brina knew she'd put that look on her face. "I'm sorry child. I wasn't meanin' to scare you."

In that moment, Lanna showed the depth of her maturity, swiping the dampness from her cheeks and saying, "It's okay.

Just do not leave again. We may not be able to return if we don't stay right here."

"I agree and I won't be runnin' off again. I don't know what's happenin' to me. I can't keep my thoughts straight."

Lanna's fear changed swiftly to concern before she hid her worry with a patent Lanna smile. "You will be fine as soon as we return. Maybe try to relax. You found Tzader when you dreamed. He is very smart man to be Maistir and he cares for you. He will figure out way to find us."

Brina gave Lanna a hug. "You're right. Tis foolish for me to spend energy worryin' when it's of no use. I have all the faith in my Beladors and Tzader. We need to stay close for when that happens, because it won't be long before we're goin' back."

Now if Brina could only make herself believe that and not lose control again.

CHAPTER 25

The ride from Stone Mountain to midtown had been an arduous forty-five minutes, but Evalle finally parked.

According to the clock in the dash of Storm's SUV, it was just after two in the morning, so no one should be able to see a giant black jaguar climb out of the Land Cruiser that she'd tucked far up the driveway, next to his house.

Once she had the side door to the kitchen open, Evalle stood back and waited for him to go inside. He trotted past her lightly, without hesitation. Sniffing his way, he loped through the kitchen to the living room then down the hall to the bedroom.

Evalle held her breath, hoping the familiarity of being home would trigger the change from animal to man.

He'd ignored her requests to climb into the SUV until she'd gotten frustrated and flat-out ordered him to get in. Then he'd jumped into the back, flopped down on the seat and pretty much ignored her all the way home.

And that hurt more than her still-aching injuries.

She locked the door and watched him emerge from the bedroom then retrace his steps back through the hall and turn into the living room.

That's where she found him sprawled on the Navajo blanket in front of the hearth, eyes closed.

What now?

When in doubt, ask about food. Shifting into another form burned calories and drained her. Had to be the same for him. "Are you hungry?"

He lifted his jaguar head.

She looked away, unable to hold his gaze. Not those red eyes that blamed her for losing any chance to reclaim his and his father's souls.

The fact that she'd committed the unforgivable crime to save his life evidently meant little to him at this point. Was not having his soul preventing him from returning to human form?

She might never find out.

But that didn't stop her from wanting a chance to make that happen. She'd been waiting for him to stand or growl or something to tell her what he wanted. When he didn't, she swept her gaze back to him. He'd laid his head down again. His chest rose and fell with steady breaths.

He was healed. Maybe he didn't need to eat.

She could understand that he was exhausted from all the time he'd spent in Mitnal, but dammit, he could sleep once he shifted back into his human body.

After all, how much worse could she make this than she already had? Might as well find out. Squatting down, she held the cloak closed, uncomfortable with being nude in front of him now. Until *her* Storm came back, it was too much like standing exposed in front of a stranger. "I know you're in there, Storm. I'm not going to just let this go. You're free of Mitnal and ... yes, Nadina, too."

He growled and whipped his head up so quickly she had to fight to stay balanced and not tumble backwards.

He'd clearly understood those words so she pressed on. "Shift back into human form so we can talk. I don't care if you yell at me, just please come back..." Her voice broke. She'd been holding the fear of losing him inside for so long that it bubbled up and threatened to strangle her. Clearing her throat, she said, "Please try to shift. If you won't do it for me, then do it for you."

She needed a sign, anything that would prove he hadn't lost the last link to this world.

But she sat there for a full ten minutes in a stare down.

He growled once more and laid his head back on the rug.

Dismissing her.

She stood up, holding back the dam that kept threatening to burst. Isak had offered her a normal life where she'd never have to go to demon hell to find him.

Why couldn't she want that?

Because she loved the man trapped in that jaguar body.

If Storm never came back to her, she still wouldn't consider what Isak offered. She only wanted one man and that was never going to change. She knew that.

But Storm wasn't even trying.

Where was the man who had found her in a South American jungle when no one else could? Where was the man who had held her tenderly and shown her what it was to be loved? Where was the man who had vowed to kill Isak if he touched her?

Talking more to herself than to Storm, she said, "You can hate me for losing your soul, but I'm not quitting on you. The Storm I know is in there."

His tail curled toward his body. That was it for a reply.

Shaking her head, she walked down the hall. She needed rest. Just a battle nap would help her heal and rejuvenate physically. If she couldn't bring Storm back, she might never rejuvenate emotionally.

Evalle, can you hear me? Trey asked, his voice coming into her mind.

She paused in the bedroom. *Yes. Glad your telepathy still works even if your voice isn't strong.*

No kidding. Better than nothing, which is what everyone else has. It stands that of all the Beladors you're still the only one able to reach me back. In case this fails at some point, first tell me if you've found Storm?

How could she answer that? *I know where he is, but I don't have him to take with me to Treoir yet. I still have two days.*

No, you don't. Tzader thinks Brina's hologram is going to vanish completely in the next twenty-four hours. Maybe sooner.

What happened?

Tzader doesn't know. He just said the pieces are disappearing faster.

Evalle held her pounding head. *Okay, I'll step up my plan.*

What plan? Her only plan was stretched out in the living room with no way to communicate. And, oh, don't forget the demon eyes that would give him away. Macha would fry both of them the minute she got one look at Storm even if he could talk.

Did you find a phone?

She'd looked for one in Storm's house, but she hadn't searched the Land Cruiser, thinking it would be obvious if it was there, sitting on the console or plugged in charging. *No phone yet, but I might get my hands on one soon.*

Okay, just give me a shout any and every way you can. I've got a secure setup to reach Sen.

Having to face Sen with Storm in demon mode would round out this crapfest. *Got it.*

One more thing, Evalle. There's a Medb problem in the city.

I heard a about it from my Nightstalker.

Trey said, *I have news you wouldn't have heard from a ghoul, because we're keeping it quiet. Macha was called into some big powwow with the Tribunal. Tzader doesn't know when she'll be back. He said she believes VIPER is going to boot us from the coalition.*

That's insane.

Yeah, I said the same thing, but Tzader explained that with the Medb flooding into the mortal world, VIPER might be preparing for a battle and the Beladors could be the weakest link instead of their greatest power.

Wouldn't the Medb love that? A war while the Beladors were getting weaker by the hour. She asked Trey, *Don't you wonder why the Medb haven't overrun the city with warlocks and witches?*

Don't wish that.

I'm not. Just saying this makes no sense to have a handful here when they could do so much more damage with an army.

That's the crazy part. They aren't doing any damage. Sen thinks it's fine that they're here because the Medb are killing demons. It's like the world got turned upside down.

I heard about them killing demons, but I'm not sold that the Medb have turned over a new leaf.

Trey signed off and withdrew from her mind.

Evalle stood there, forcing her knees not to buckle under the weight of so much responsibility and loss.

Quinn lost Kizira in the battle after Kizira had agreed to

fight alongside Evalle for a chance at being with Quinn.

Tzader was losing Brina every second that Evalle failed to bring the Storm she believed could help them.

And I've probably already lost Storm.

What had she, Tzader and Quinn done to piss off the Fates?

She had to rest for just a minute.

Exhaustion and blood loss were taking their toll. She sank to the floor and leaned back against the wall, unable to face that bed without Storm even if she were clean enough to consider taking advantage of it.

Closing her eyes, Evalle tried calling up her beast energy to heal her wounds again. She could feel it trickle through her. Too whipped to do battle even with her own body, she floated in a mental fog.

Despair came out in a weak whisper. "I can't do this alone. I'm losing the battle to save the person I love and help my friends who need me."

Kai's voice pushed into her thoughts with sharp clarity. "What's happened? I can't call Storm to me."

Evalle stilled at the unexpected voice then opened her eyes to find herself in another realm seated across from Storm's spirit guide. Warmth hugged her tired body even though no sun floated in the sky, only puffy clouds and a soft breeze that gently ruffled leaves on nearby trees.

"I don't understand," Kai continued. "I can see his jaguar in the human world. He has always spoken to me even in animal form."

Running a hand through her hair, Evalle explained, "I brought him back from Mitnal, but I had to kill Nadina to protect Storm."

Kai covered her mouth with a delicate hand.

Yep, that's me. The person who destroyed Storm's last hope for humanity. Even if he could forgive her for losing his soul, he couldn't live with what she'd done to his father. She wasn't sure she could live with it.

Evalle swallowed regret and struggled to push words past her thick throat. "I've lost Storm's soul forever. I believe he's in there, hidden inside the jaguar, but he isn't shifting back to human form."

"You are the only one who can bring him back."

"Evidently not."

"Yes, you are his mate." Kai sounded as if she'd been a fierce protector in her time. "If the witch doctor's blood grips him, then you are the only reason he will return."

Add failing him as a mate to the list.

Evalle rubbed her eyes and told Kai, "If I am, or more correctly *was*, his mate, he's either forgotten me or now hates me for killing Nadina. I thought for sure he recognized me when he destroyed a demon who was about to kill me in Mitnal, but now I'm thinking he was just in killing mode. That's what demons do. They kill."

"If only we could talk to him," Kai said with a deep sadness, "We'd know how to help him."

Evalle had a momentary urge to reach for Kai's hands to comfort the spirit guide, but she wasn't sure touching was allowed in this realm. Storm was the one who had taught Evalle that touch could be comforting instead of painful.

She shook that off and said, "When I traveled the first time to Mitnal and found him, Storm was in human form. He told me then that once he turned into his jaguar then failed to shift right back that his demon blood from Nadina would take over. He wouldn't be able to return to his human self. That he would be gone ... forever. He's been jaguar for the past hour I know of and I have no idea how long before that."

The pain of saying those words crushed her heart.

How can I live without Storm in my world?

"If that is the case, Evalle, then you can*not* leave him this way. Storm would never want to remain a demon. You must free him."

That took a moment to sink in. "You want me to *kill* Storm?" Evalle fought against the bile climbing her throat. "I can't do that."

"Would you want to remain a demon forever? Would you rather those with VIPER or some other being found Storm and committed worse upon him?"

"What could be worse?"

"There are others more powerful than Nadina who would take control of someone with Storm's powers."

Like Adrianna, but Evalle couldn't see the Sterling witch as a threat to Storm. "I won't let that happen."

Kai's lips softened with understanding. "You must realize now that Storm most likely fought that demon for you because once you killed Nadina you took control of Storm. You became his new master."

Thanks for destroying what hope I'd clung to that his fighting the demon had been a tiny sign he still cared. Evalle couldn't even consider the idea of being anyone's master. She started thinking out loud. "I'll keep him safe. I'll take him to my underground apartment and—"

"No," Kai said, cutting her off. "That's no different than putting him in a cage and you would never be able to have anyone around him. Not even your little gargoyle."

How did Kai know about Feenix? "Storm wouldn't—"

"*Storm* would never harm that gargoyle, but the demon sleeping in Storm's house isn't the man you knew, if what you've told me is true."

Everything was falling apart.

Kill Storm? Watch the life slide out of his body?

A scream started building inside and Evalle wasn't sure if she could hold it back. She couldn't do it. Save Storm by killing him? She'd sooner harm Tzader or Quinn.

And if she couldn't save Storm then there was no hope of bringing Brina or Lanna back, which would destroy Tzader and cripple Quinn. If the warrior queen didn't return to the castle, all the Beladors faced destruction in a war with the Medb.

Casualties kept piling up around Evalle's feet, because she was failing everyone who depended on her.

Kai said, "I am sorry that I have nothing to offer you for your tribe or your Belador queen. If you cannot bring Storm back to his human body, you owe it to him to not leave him as he is."

Kai's face swirled into a blur along with the scenery, then everything faded.

Evalle sat there numb from pain overload. Tears ran down her face. Give her a legion of demons to kill and she'd face them to protect Storm, Tzader, Quinn ... all her Beladors, but she'd rather use her blade to cut out her own heart than touch

Storm with deadly intent.

The scream crawled higher up her throat.

Allowing it to escape would be admitting defeat, but she felt defeated. She covered her face and sobbed. How could she finally have found her place with the Beladors and a man who loved her only to face watching her world shatter around her?

A jaguar roared.

She clamped her hands over her ears to dull the sound of fury.

She'd always loved how beautiful Storm was in jaguar form, but right now the longer he remained as an animal just drove home the fact that her Storm was gone.

He roared again.

She jumped up and ran into the living room, screaming at him. "*Stop it! Stop being a jaguar.* You are better than this Storm." Her voice cracked and tears streamed down her face. "You are *not* a demon."

He studied her as one would a piece of furniture. No recognition in those eyes. Sitting up like a well-mannered house cat that happened to weigh as much as the sofa, he continued to watch her meltdown without any reaction.

She swiped at her tears, but the damned things kept leaking out. Would they ever end? She'd never been one to cry, but she'd never lost something as precious as Storm and his love.

She whispered in a voice too tired to hold back anything. "I'm sorry about your soul. I'm so, so sorry. I know you're in there. Why aren't you trying to come back? Just do it and I'll do anything to fix this."

You owe it to him to not leave Storm as a demon.

Kai's words scraped through Evalle's mind with the jagged edge of broken glass.

Would Storm do that for Evalle if she'd been turned into a demon?

No, he'd fight with his last breath to save her. He'd always known how to get through to her. He'd laid siege to her heart that had never had a chance against his love.

That truth drove her to stiffen her resolve. She would give him no less than he would do for her.

If only she knew how to reach him.

She needed a shower to clear her mind. She would not quit without a fight. What she wouldn't give to go back to the last time they were in the bedroom together and he'd carried her to the shower.

After he'd loved her for hours.

Storm was a sexual man who couldn't keep his hands off her once he'd broken through her emotional walls. A fierce lover.

An idea burrowed into her thoughts.

She took in Storm's jaguar face and wondered if she could force a change by dangling something he wanted in front of him.

She had no idea how to act sexy and felt stupid trying this, but if it caused him to shift back to human she'd dance naked through VIPER. She unhooked the robe and let it puddle at her feet, leaving her as naked as the day she was born.

Still no flicker of interest.

Seriously? There went what little ego she possessed.

Maybe she should try that in the middle of a room full of men. Would that get his attention?

Kai had to be shaking her head and muttering about Evalle being delusional or in denial.

His spirit guide was probably right, but Evalle was just as possessive of Storm as he was of her. He'd once made it clear that she belonged to him and that worked both ways. She could be just as stubborn as he was.

Reaching for the robe to carry to the shower, she stopped.

Storm *did* have a possessive streak a mile wide.

He hadn't liked finding her and Tristan together in the jungle one bit, but he'd been downright hostile over the idea of Isak coming around her.

Would Storm just let his *mate* walk away to be with someone else?

The idea scrambling through her mind couldn't be any more humiliating than what she'd just done. But it might get her killed.

At this point, that would be an improvement over living with Storm's indifference.

Determined more than ever to break through his thick skull,

she tried her best to deliver her lines with a flippant tone. "You know what, Storm? Fine, if that's it between us, then that's it. I accept your decision to end our relationship."

Storm stretched his neck and rolled to his side again, yawning.

Fuck! She snatched up her robe and strode out of the room, but not before she yelled over her shoulder, "Isak will sure as hell be *thrilled* you've tossed in the towel. All I have to do is call him. At least he'll *talk* to me."

She threw the robe in a corner when she reached the supersized bathroom, one of the best upgrades to the sixty-year-old house. She wrenched on the water jets inside the glass shower, stepped under the scalding heat and leaned forward against the tile, allowing the water to run down her back.

Her shoulders shook with tremors, but she would not shed another tear.

She might shed some blood, though, if that's what it took to get through to him. He'd bitten her when she'd been in gryphon form and backed off. In that one instant, she wanted to believe that he'd recognized her blood as his mate.

As someone he would not harm.

But how could she get them back to that point of recognition without attacking him? *Hard to convince someone you love him when you're drawing blood.*

"I can do this," she coached herself, because talking allowed her to avoid thinking about how to accomplish an impossible task. "I can do this. I just need a shower so I can think then I'll–"

A roar boomed inside the bathroom.

Fear skated across Evalle's naked skin.

CHAPTER 26

The shower door was wrenched open.

Evalle flipped around, her back against the tile and water coming from all directions, splattering Storm's beautiful teak-colored skin.

On Storm's *human* body.

Hallelujah!

But the celebration music shriveled in her mind when she looked up to see red demon eyes. Words clogged in her throat.

His hands hung tense at the sides of his naked body. Claws extended from his fingers then retracted.

O-*kay*. She swallowed and said, "You changed to your human form. That's a ... good sign."

"You will not go to Isak."

Foolish or not, her heart did a backflip at the threat in his voice. She'd normally get in his face to tell him that he had no say over her actions, but now was the time to keep everything as calm as possible.

She nodded. "If you say so."

"Ever," he demanded.

"Ever."

He spun away to step out of the shower.

What the hell? How was she supposed to move forward from this? "Storm, talk to me."

He paused. Muscles rippled across his beautiful back and his biceps flexed once. "Now is not a good time."

Bullshit. "Later is going to be much worse. If you're mad at me, then say so. But I've been terrified that you'd never make it back to human form. You walk in here, demand your way and walk out. If you're done with me ..." She fought to get the words out. "Done with *us*. Then say so, but–" What could she say? "Please don't do this."

Now that he'd shifted, Evalle should be thinking about going to Treoir, but she couldn't bring herself to say the Beladors needed him right now.

Storm had always done everything *for* her. He needed her right now, whether he realized it or not. She would take care of him first, then the rest.

He still didn't turn around when he ordered, "Stay away from me."

His words cut so deep she should be spewing blood. Pain and fear were a bad combination for her. It brought out her own aggression and anger, much easier emotions for her to deal with. "That's pretty fucking clear, Storm. Fine. Go. I can accept you being a demon, but you can't even talk to me. Coward."

A blur of motion was the only warning she got before Storm had her pinned with her back against the tile and her arms shoved over her head.

He leaned into her. A feral sound rumbled deep in his throat.

Those red eyes were an inch from her face, warning her.

His strength had been undeniable before, but now she could feel the explosive power he had barely tethered. She might be able to stop him from killing her, but only if she could bring herself to use deadly force.

With him growling, she hoped whatever she said or did would not push him back into shifting, but they couldn't go on like this. She lifted her chin. "You don't scare me."

The growl picked up volume.

What was he thinking? Feeling?

She wanted to stroke his head and kiss him, to show him that together they could do whatever it took to save him from being a demon forever. She repeated the only words she knew. "Come back to me, Storm. I refuse to quit on you."

"You just won't listen, will you?" Each word came out hard and biting. "I. Am. Not. Storm. Not the one you remember. I've gone all the way to demon."

She shook her head with stubborn determination. "You

might have been forced into becoming a demon, but your Navajo blood still flows through your body, strong and just as demanding as the Ashaninka blood. Use what you inherited to fight back."

"If my Navajo blood was true, my eyes would still be yellow as a jaguar and brown as a man."

He had a point, but he was talking and that had to be positive, right?

She lifted her stubborn chin at him. "Red, yellow, brown. Eyes do not dictate who you are."

"Not if you have a soul."

I should have seen that coming. She'd flinched at the bull's eye shot and might as well deal with it now. "I wish there had been another way, but Nadina was going to kill you."

"You should have let her."

Hearing the disappointment in his voice was almost as heartbreaking as his order to stay away from him. Evalle would nurse her broken heart later. "Well, I *didn't* allow you to die and if that was the wrong decision I can live with it."

"You think so?" he asked, a sarcasm she'd never heard directed at her.

"I know so."

"In that case, you're now the proud owner of a demon." He backed off and turned once more to leave.

Evalle took a step and put her hands on his shoulders. She leaned against his back, inhaling his scent.

His body shook hard once. His voice was tight and raw. "Stay away from me. Don't you get that I have no control?"

Did that mean he wanted to touch her, but was afraid of what he'd do? The fact that he'd warned her had to mean there was a glimmer of the Storm that she knew still inside.

She turned her face to kiss the wet skin on his back.

He sucked in a breath and growled. *"Evalle!"*

Hearing her name was like flipping a switch in her brain, one that pushed her to go forward without looking back. If sex was the only way she could reach him right now, she'd hand him the keys to her body.

It wasn't as though making love to Storm was a hardship.

She nipped at his shoulder then licked it.

A challenge.

Storm swung around and tension hung suspended between them for a second then he shoved his hands into her hair and yanked her to him, kissing her as he walked her back into the shower. There was no question he wanted her. Not with his desire thumping against her stomach. He ravaged her mouth, taking her lips prisoner with no sign of mercy in sight.

He'd never been this out of control with her, but she trusted Storm.

Trusted the man inside that body who had loved her with gentleness when she'd needed to be handled carefully. But that same man was the reason she didn't back away in fear right now and offered herself freely to him. Because of what he'd shown her over months of taking his time with her, his aggression now didn't terrify her.

To be honest, she was just as turned on as he was.

She knew the difference between an aggressive lover and an abusive attack, had learned the painful side of that lesson as a teen.

No man would ever harm her that way again.

She could kill a human and, if she couldn't kill a nonhuman, she could maim one enough to make him regret ever touching her.

With the confidence she owed to Storm, she let him have free rein.

He kissed her as if he waged war on her body, determined to conquer it. She'd willingly let her walls fall. She reached around and curled her fingers into his back, holding him to her and letting him know she was not afraid.

His lips moved to her neck, biting and kissing his way to her breasts. She ached, waiting on him to touch her everywhere. His mouth closed over her nipple and he stroked his tongue over the tip.

This was definitely not the Storm she remembered.

This one was off the leash and hungry.

He sucked her breast then bit her. Not hard enough to hurt, though, and he licked the same spot next.

She trembled at the feel of him. The kissing and nipping sent shock waves straight down. His mouth was everywhere and still her body begged for more, rubbing against him until his growling deepened. She scored his back with her nails. That drew a feral sound in reaction, but this time it was one that called to her.

When she reached down between them and wrapped her fingers around his length, he released her breast and slapped the walls at each side of her head, groaning a painful sound. He panted harder with every stroke she made.

His fingers fisted and he ground his teeth.

She didn't let up.

When he spoke, his voice was hoarse, angry and shaking. "Get away from me. Now. While you can."

She paused and whispered, "No."

Dropping his chin, he locked those scary eyes on her face, but she could swear a flicker of concern flashed through them.

"Order me to leave," he practically begged her in that rough demon voice.

She lifted up to kiss him then whispered, "You're mine. I will always want you. Always."

Muscles flexed in his neck. His chest moved with harsh breaths. Was this it? Would he lose touch with reality and shift into the demon jaguar again?

If he did, he would kill her. She knew it.

Releasing her hair, he stepped back out of her grasp, raised his hands to grab his head and roared. Chest muscles tight, he went on and on.

Evalle held her breath.

When he dropped his head down, his hands landed on her shoulders. His fingers clenched, but not hard enough to harm her. He faced her again, his red eyes wild. He took one shuddering breath after another then finally warned, "Last. Chance. To. Say. No."

"No."

His eyes gave him away.

He looked hurt.

She smiled. "No, I don't want a last chance. I want you ... inside me."

In the second it took him to process that, his eyes lit with a need that was honest and hungry. He dove at her, kissing her again, pushing her up against the wet wall. Water cascaded over both of them. He bent down, kissing her chest and reached an arm under each leg, lifting her as he stood up. She cupped his face. "I love you."

"Don't look at me." Had that been an order or a plea?

Leaning forward, she felt him nudge her opening. She stopped nose to nose. "I would look at you until the end of time, but if that's what you want, then you'll have to kiss me to get it."

His mouth covered hers in a savage kiss. He lowered her down until they touched and held her there. Her legs quivered, waiting for him to move. To feel him inside her again.

She broke the kiss but kept her eyes averted from his, playing by his rules as he waited for her to speak. "Don't make me beg."

He let out a noise of anguish. If he was searching her face for a tiny bit of indecision, he was not going to find it.

She reached down to grasp him, steel covered in velvet. He flinched, his biceps full and hard as he finally lowered her onto him.

With the first feel of him pushing into her, she arched and grabbed his shoulders. Then he was moving, sliding deep inside her, and she was ready for him.

He murmured words that sounded Spanish and sexy.

She clawed at his arms. Her fingers clutched him tighter with every stroke driving deeper in and out. Heat spiraled and surged in her womb, demanding release until she ached and urged him on to end this waiting.

Storm's jaw clenched.

He was holding back with ruthless control. A demon wouldn't do that.

She said, "Touch me."

His eyes flew open and it was strange to feel Storm everywhere around her and in her as she stared into glowing red orbs that didn't belong in his face.

He never slowed from pumping into her.

She met him stroke for stroke, picking up his rhythm.

Hot energy built inside her again, but this was nothing like the time before. He held her and moved faster, growling with each deep plunge inside her. Then he held her with one arm and used his other hand to touch her. The world ripped apart, or maybe she did. Everything fragmented into a million pieces.

All the worry and pain of the last few days shattered and spun away in heart-soothing relief.

Light flashed around both of them when he roared her name with his climax.

Water sluiced down over her body and between them. She hugged him closer to her, but he just kept her pressed up against the wall. Not touching her the way he had the last time they'd made love to reassure her that all was fine.

That he cared for her.

All of a sudden, the heat that had boiled through the shower dissipated and a chill settled into her bones. She kissed his neck and ran her hands over his back, encouraging him to do the same.

Still, he didn't show any sign of the affection he'd always been generous with, the constant touching that had destroyed her emotional fortress.

She held him tighter, refusing to let go and face the possibility that this was all that was left of them.

Sex. Incredible sex, but there had been so much more before.

Her eyes welled up and she squeezed them tight, fighting against the hurt.

Lifting her head, she forced herself to smile. She would not show him the pain slashing her heart to bits.

She'd expected indifference or cold dismissal, but not the fury in his face.

He snapped, "I told you to stay away from me."

"I told you I wouldn't."

He lifted her off of him, and set her aside, but she noted that he took care how he handled her. Or she was just so determined to find any sliver of decency in him that she imagined it.

Turning to the water jet, he started washing himself with an economy of motions.

Her Storm would have wanted to wash her and take his time doing it.

Her Storm. Was he in there?

When he finished washing and stepped toward the door, Evalle said, "I meant what I said. I won't give up on you."

Without turning around, he asked, "You want to know what happened to me? I want to know what happened to you. Why would you let an animal attack you like that?"

"You're not an animal."

"I'm not a human either."

He grabbed a towel on his way out of the bathroom.

Evalle finished showering and drying off. She put on a pair of warm-ups and a pullover she found in the bedroom. When she reached the living room, she found Storm pacing back and forth.

Just as a jaguar in a cage would do.

But he was in human form, wearing jeans and T-shirt from his bedroom. She'd seen those clothes before.

He lifted his nose the same way his jaguar would and turned to her, crossing his arms. "What now, master?"

Just keep cutting me to the bone, Storm. "I'm not your master."

"You killed my owner. You own me."

"I get that you're angry about me losing your soul, but I don't get this attitude."

"You really *don't* get it."

"No, I don't."

He took a minute as if gathering his thoughts. "I have only one purpose in life and it's to kill. If I don't stay shifted into my jaguar, I have to find a prey to satisfy the bloodlust. If you don't order a kill, then my jaguar will decide when and who to kill."

"That may be a problem." At some point, she had to discuss going to Treoir to save Brina.

"I'd say so since you're liable to be the closest prey." He was shouting.

"No, I mean that I need your help on Treoir."

She'd clearly shocked him. His lips parted then he closed them, looking away before he came back to her and said, "You intend to take me to Treoir with these?" He pointed at his eyes.

"Yes."

"You really do have a death wish. Macha will probably torture you before she kills you."

Evalle asked in a soft voice, "Would you care if she killed me, Storm?"

His jaws locked for a moment. "No. I'm a demon. I don't suffer emotions."

She wished she had his ability to read a lie, but that had to be the truth because the same gift would punish him if he lied, right? Of course, that lie detector ability had been one of his Navajo gifts, which were clearly dormant at the moment. Maybe he believed so deeply that he was a demon he accepted the role.

"Well, I would care if you died," Evalle countered. "I'll deal with Macha."

His steady gaze stayed fixed on her for a long moment then he seemed to shake it off. "I'm yours to do with as you please, master."

She would not let him bait her. "In that case, you and I are going to Treoir where I need you to help find Brina."

"She get lost?" he smarted back.

That's right, Storm had no idea what all had happened. "After I was teleported away from here by Kizira right after we'd made love—" Evalle paused to let that sink in. It must have had some effect because he looked away. She continued, "I ended up in TÅµr Medb again where the Alterants were sent with an army of witches and warlocks to battle against the Beladors on Treoir."

She left out the part about becoming a gryphon, but Storm had seen her shift in Mitnal. Did he remember that or had he even been cognizant to realize what she'd become?

Regardless, she would share about her new form and the ability to walk in sunshine with *her* Storm, not this one.

"You fought with the Medb?"

Had admitting she'd fought with the Belador enemies yanked his chain?

"I had to. I was compelled, but things worked out and the Beladors won the battle." That sounded way more simple than the blood bath she'd gone through and the casualties they'd suffered.

Storm jerked back around, staring at her in disbelief. His jaw moved, but he said nothing.

Come on, Storm. Show me that you know how difficult that was for me. When he said nothing, she added, "Actually, Kizira and I came up with a plan that would free her from the Medb and allow us to save Treoir."

"No way."

"Way. Unfortunately, Kizira was mortally injured and the Medb queen, Flaevynn, had compelled her to not heal herself." Evalle still hurt when she recalled the pain in Quinn's voice when he'd cursed Flaevynn for sending her own child into a bloodbath with no protection. She wished Kizira had shared that secret with Evalle when Kizira told her of Flaevynn's intention to be the first one to become immortal, but Evalle wasn't sure what she could have done to protect Kizira when they'd been on different parts of the island at the time.

Storm watched her quietly, so Evalle cleared her throat and continued. "Flaevynn wanted to be the first one to swim in the water beneath Treoir that gives immortality, or so I've heard. The witches and warlocks were driven out of Treoir, but we have no idea what happened to Flaevynn or Cathbad, who couldn't leave the tower. Supposedly, as the battle ended, Flaevynn was to reach her six-hundred-sixty-sixth birthday, when she would die if she was not turned into an immortal. And Cathbad was to die right behind her."

"So what happened to Brina?"

"Oh, that's right." Evalle ran a hand through her damp hair, noting how Storm's eyes followed her hand, but she didn't let on that she'd noticed as she conveyed the rest.

"Brina was in Treoir Castle with Lanna in a room with an old Belador named Horace who was supposed to be protecting them. When we reached that room, we found Horace throwing Noirre dust on Brina and Lanna, who were hugged up against each other. Tzader drove a sword into Horace. At that same moment, Lanna disappeared as if she'd teleported and Brina did, too, but a hologram of Brina's body remained."

Storm still said nothing, but Evalle could tell he was thinking. She added, "The hologram has started corrupting, small pieces just twinkling away. Trey called me telepathically before I showered and told me Tzader sent word that the hologram is disintegrating faster. We're running out of time to find her."

"I doubt she can return if the hologram completely vanishes," he said more to himself than her.

She made a mental note about how that had sounded like the smooth voice of her Storm, but she kept her face neutral. "That's what we're worried about. I'm hoping you can help us."

"Do what?"

And now he was back to the rough demon voice.

She tamped down her disappointment and said, "I don't know, but you have unusual abilities that are far superior to any other tracker's. You've found me when no one else could."

"Bet you regret that now," he muttered, walking across the room toward her.

"No, I don't." She stood her ground.

He leaned down toward her and said with finality, "You will."

"No, I won't."

"You're in denial. Admit that this is what it is and stop kidding yourself."

"I'm not in denial and I know this is not all there is for us."

"Why?"

She wanted to say, "Because I'm your mate," but she couldn't face what Demon Storm would say. "Because as you explained, I'm in control. We do what I say."

Hostility flared off him, but he didn't make a threatening move. Would he just shift and attack her without thought?

Stop thinking that way.

Storm moved away from her, opening a distance that felt a mile wide. "You're the master."

That quip had her grinding her back teeth, but she let up on her jaws to say, "If that's the way it is, then let's get moving. Sen will have to teleport us. You are not to attack him."

Would Macha allow Evalle a chance to explain or take one look at Storm and go all goddess on them?

CHAPTER 27

"Would you *puh-lease* talk to me, Storm?" Evalle asked, sick of sounding like a corrupted recording stuck on repeat.

She gripped the steering wheel of his Land Cruiser, doing her best not to attract the attention of any law enforcement on her way to meet with Quinn at Woodruff Park.

Demon Storm couldn't drive.

Even if he had identification on him, she doubted a police officer would get past the red glowing eyes to determine that they didn't match the brown ones indicated on his license if they were stopped.

Not a word from her stoic passenger.

If she ordered him, he'd talk and every word would come out in that demon voice.

Don't lose your patience and snap at him. Not if she had any hope of reaching the real Storm she'd heard a hint of earlier.

At least he was going with her to Treoir. She should be happy about that, but his bland compliance wasn't enough. She pulled off her glasses and handed them to him.

He smirked. "Hiding my eyes won't change anything and besides, you need them. I don't."

"You need to keep them covered so that we don't have to fight every nonhuman who sees a demon, especially the Beladors. Plus, I hear the Medb are in Atlanta hunting demons."

"The Medb?"

"Yes. Makes no sense to me either, but that's what Grady and Trey both told me, so it must be true." She waved the glasses at him.

He kept his arms crossed. "Daylight is coming soon and you normally need your special sunglasses just to deal with any bright light. In fact, how is it you're able to see with the headlights that just passed?"

"Take the damned glasses and I'll tell you." She was tired of holding them out.

He slipped them on and returned to his cross-armed, closed-off look.

She'd really wanted to wait to tell him this, but she was willing to do anything for a chance of reaching him. "When I was in TÅµr Medb, I found out the true history of Alterants. I'll tell you about it later when we have time." And hopefully when he'd actually care. "They captured the Alterants at the beast championship and put us through battles with each other and other creatures to force our final evolution and now I can be in sunlight."

Reading anything in those eyes had been tough, even without the sunglasses, but his face softened now with a thought. It just passed too quickly for Evalle to figure out what he'd been thinking before he had that hard look to his face again, hiding all emotions.

She'd been so excited to show Storm her new form as a gryphon, sure that he'd be celebrating with her, but he had yet to ask her anything about when she'd shifted in Mitnal. He might not recall anything from when he was so entrenched in his jaguar. She'd tell him about her gryphon form now, but every time he saw her as a gryphon he'd remember that she'd destroyed everything he'd fought to regain.

"Just like that, you can see and walk in the sun?" he asked.

Her joy gone, she couldn't stop the question before it was out of her mouth. "Are you asking because you care?"

He just turned to stare out the window.

Got my answer.

Parking in a multi-level deck near the park, she turned off the engine and sat there.

Would he have a real conversation with her if she ordered him as his master?

Ugh. She cut a testy look in his direction. "You could try

just a little."

Storm turned his hidden gaze on her and retorted with cold finality, "And you could stop living in a fantasy world and accept reality."

She grabbed her dagger and the cell phone he'd located for her and shoved the phone into the pocket of her jeans. They'd stopped by her apartment long enough for her to run inside alone and change clothes. She slid her dagger into a sheath hooked to her belt, all hidden by a lightweight knee-length jacket and got out, slamming the door hard enough to have shattered the glass.

Surprisingly, that didn't happen. She must be losing her touch.

He walked off without even waiting for her.

A fantasy world?

No. This was her life and he was part of it. That was reality. Hers *and* his. Did he think just because he snarled at her and acted like a jackass she'd be so easy to push away? He'd never let her push *him* away before and she'd been no picnic more than once.

She'd knocked him across the tracks in a MARTA tunnel because he'd shoved his body close to protect her from a subway train.

A human would have had his head cracked open.

Storm had dusted himself off and come right back. He was the one who taught her that love was not convenient or easy. That she'd deserved to be loved.

Well, so did he.

Willing to accept arguing over silence, she called out, "Why would you want to stay that way? What happened to the man I knew who never backed down from a challenge?"

He paused and wheeled around, coming right back and not stopping until he was in her face so close she was leaned back over the hood, elbows supporting her.

Jaw muscles flexing, he snapped, *"I don't get a choice!* I have never had a damn choice in any of this. I was born with demon blood running through my veins. I should have turned into one a long time ago, but my father told me to fight it with all I had. So I've spent every minute of my life with this internal battle. I finally lost. That's it. The. End."

Evalle's pulse thrummed with adrenaline and the beast inside her wanted to come out and battle.

What a pair they'd make if that happened. "So that's it. You just give up?"

His face twisted with fury. He snatched off the sunglasses and used them to point at his eyes. "I don't have any control over this. Not now that Nadina's blood rules me. I can't just change my mind to not be a demon any more than you can change from being an Alterant."

He backed away and crossed his arms, looking anywhere but her face.

"I did," she said quietly.

His head snapped back to face her. "What?"

"Well, technically I'm still an Alterant, but I changed. I no longer shift into a hideous beast, but I do shift ... into a gryphon."

His face lost the harsh lines and the tension in his shoulders eased. He stared at the ground then up at her. "Green with feathers and ... thought I imagined it. That was you?"

"You don't remember me coming for you?"

Storm didn't move, but she could feel his tension rise.

"In Mitnal, yes. That gryphon was me. I shifted because I couldn't stop Nadina without more power."

He reached up and clenched his forehead, rubbing it. He spoke in Storm's voice again, to himself more than her. "I remember flashes of you then Nadina and then some flying beast. There are gaps in my mind when the demon turns me berserk. The blood burns and all I can think about is ripping whatever is near me apart to make it stop."

"Why were demons coming after you in small groups?" She watched him, waiting for any small opening in that hard shell of his.

He paused, dropping his hand. "Hanhau was determined to break me so he kept sending in a few at a time, forcing my blood to heat up. I'd kill them and he'd leave me to heal then he'd do it again. Every time would push me further from ..." He paused, shaking off some thought.

"Further from your Navajo blood and your humanity?"

"Yes."

Hanhau had found the best way to torture Storm and flip him to the dark side. With all the demon venom flowing through Storm, no wonder he lashed out at everything around him.

"Stop trying to think it right, Evalle," he said in Storm's calm and understanding voice.

"I can't stop."

"Then you're destined for disappointment. I can't go back. If I could, I would have done things differently. I knew the risk when I followed Nadina. I gambled and lost. The sooner you realize that the sooner you'll accept that you can't keep me."

He might as well have struck her. She whispered, "Don't tell me what I can do and not do."

"I'm not a pet. I'm a dangerous being who is far more powerful than you can imagine. I have no brakes on my control once it slips. I might not have harmed you in the shower, even though I damn well used you, but I don't have the decency to regret it. The day will come when I either kill you or Tzader or someone else you love."

"You didn't hurt me in the shower, because I was the one who instigated that."

"You do realize we didn't use a condom, don't you?"

Honestly, no. She'd been so focused on trying to reach him, and caught up in the moment, she hadn't thought about it.

Storm hooked a hand over his neck. "I didn't think so."

"I don't regret it, Storm. I'd do it again." Even if she had to suffer the pain of him ignoring her afterwards.

"You might not regret it, but I do. That isn't happening again."

She could hear the door slamming on every entrance she came up with for a way back inside of him. "What if I order you as your ... master?"

"Would you?"

"No," she admitted.

"That's what I thought."

He dropped his arms and shoved his hands in the pockets of his jeans. Head hanging down, he said, "Kai keeps trying to reach me. I need you to give her a message if she comes to you."

"She has. She might again."

He lifted his head. "I thought as much. Ask her to please find my father and offer what she can for comfort. Can you do that?"

His voice was devoid of emotion, but the words were pulled up from somewhere hidden deep inside him.

Evalle said, "Yes."

"You should listen to her, Evalle. She won't steer you wrong. And I won't blame you."

Evalle's mouth opened. "Do you know what Kai told me to do?"

"I have a pretty good idea since I was the one who made her agree to find someone who could stop me if I ever turned all the way demon."

Words stuck in her throat. Kai had been right. Evalle shook her head, unable to speak.

Storm said, "If our situations were flipped, I would do it for you." He turned and headed for the elevator, leaving Evalle's hope stomped to pieces.

He admitted that he could take her life.

Just that easily?

She would have torn someone apart if they'd tried to convince her he could.

Her heart was shriveling with every confirmation of losing this war. But right now, she had to get Storm to Treoir without any blood being shed and him still in human form. If that meant taking control of the situation to protect him from others, and himself, she'd bite the bullet and do it.

She caught up with him as he reached out to press the elevator button. She demanded, "Do *not* do anything unless I give you an order."

He pulled his hand back and his lips parted for a second then slammed shut.

Sounding like his *master* appeared to be one way to make sure he didn't kill indiscriminately.

At least until she came up with a new option.

The look that passed over his face was filled with the kind of disgust he'd had for Nadina. That was to be expected if

Evalle had any hope of pulling off the role, but this stupid master power was the only choice he'd left her. For now.

They still had to meet Sen.

Evalle said, "Put on the sunglasses."

He smirked. "I see what you're trying to do, but it won't work."

That just pissed her off, which would make this so much easier. "Let's get something clear. I've accepted my role as master. You underestimate me if you think I'm not going to use that to protect my Beladors."

Storm studied her a minute then his demon voice said, "Part of my job as your demon is to protect you, regardless of who attacks. That includes protecting you from the sun, which is only twenty minutes from rising. You're positive it's no longer your kryptonite?"

"Yes." She enjoyed his shock and explained, "I had hoped to share my first time here in daylight with you–or I should say *my* Storm–when we were together again, but since you've made it clear that what we had was nothing significant, I might as well get some sun with my new demon."

That struck a chord. He said, "I didn't say–"

She held up a hand. "Let's not waste any more time on yesterday. You want me to deal with reality, you got it."

His voice turned as cold as his attitude. "About time." He crossed his arms, standing to the side like a hired goon.

The best she could do to hide her feelings was to nod, punch the button and step into the elevator.

She didn't look at Storm, but when she opened her empathic sense to his emotions she picked up a glimmer of something she'd have to call regret. But was that just regret in general or that he would not be sharing something special with her?

Out on the street, predawn light had yet to brighten enough to shut off photocells on street lamps. Atlanta moved with a gentle bustle as the city came alive.

She had just seen a handful of workers heading for a diner on the street she and Storm had just crossed. She turned the corner and caught sight of a demon sneaking down the street to her right. He must have some cloaking spell because the humans who had just passed him paid no attention to his blue-black skin and seven-foot-tall body shaped like a praying mantis. All except his head. That was closer to a human's, with a mouth full of fangs where the mandible would be, a long bulbous nose and two bulging yellow eyes. The front legs had three straight claws on each one.

He was moving away from her destination in Woodruff Park, which was to her left, but she couldn't leave a demon walking around loose.

Well, all except the one under my control.

She whispered, "Did you see it?"

"Yes. I can take care of that one with little fuss."

"We'll go together."

Storm made a disparaging sound in his throat. "You're not getting a handle on this master thing, are you?"

That almost sounded like the old Storm who'd enjoyed poking at her, but every time she lowered her guard around *this* Storm, she suffered a backlash from the demon. She cocked her eyebrow at him. "You don't get to criticize my choices or refuse my orders, right?"

"Right." He ground out that word.

"In that case, I think I've got it down. Let's go."

She almost chuckled at his growl in response.

It took them a block of walking and avoiding several humans they met before Evalle saw a place where she could confront the demon. She fingered her spelled dagger that hung at her hip, but VIPER needed to find out where these demons had come from before she decapitated any.

"Why bloody your clothes when you have your own personal demon weapon?" Storm asked, keeping stride with her.

"Because first of all, I don't want to just kill him. I need to find out where he came from."

"I can capture him faster in my jaguar form."

"No!"

Storm's sigh said as much as his words. "I'll shift eventually whether you want me to or not. If you prevent me from killing or shifting, the time will come when I can't stop myself from either. If you wait until then, I may not recognize you as my master."

Was there nothing positive he could say to her? He just kept shutting down every idea she came up with and forcing her into a corner where the only way out was through his death. "I'll deal with that if and when it happens."

"There is no if."

CHAPTER 28

Evalle was so intent on Storm's threat that she didn't realize the demon they were tracking through downtown Atlanta had stopped moving.

Storm put his hand up to stall her forward progress and pointed toward where the demon stood next to a three-level building under construction.

"What's he doing, looking for a place to set up an office near Five Points?" she whispered.

"Stranger things have happened in this town."

True, but that demon seemed to be searching specifically for something. Or someone.

When the creature stepped through a dark opening, Storm dropped his hand from in front of her and took off to catch up with the demon.

Evalle was right beside him when he entered the bottom floor of the building. She gave her eyes a second to adjust, just in time to see the demon's legs moving up scaffolding to the second floor.

Waving Storm behind her to follow, which brought out another growl, Evalle climbed quietly up the scaffold, poking her head through the opening to the next floor to check out the area.

The demon was walking around the support walls that would probably house the elevator. He seemed to still be searching for someone.

Had he expected to find workers up here?

She checked her watch. Sunrise hit about ten minutes to eight this time of year. He was here ahead of the crew showing up.

Climbing the rest of the way until she could step off the scaffolding, she pulled out her dagger. Storm was right behind her, silent as a shadow when he stepped close.

She put up a hand for him to let her go first.

Walking out into the open space, she sniffed at the smell of fresh concrete.

And something else. Her next whiff came loaded with a rotted stench.

And the demon must have sensed her. He turned his scrawny body and angled his head, staring at her as if he tried to determine whether he knew her. The bulging eyes beamed bright yellow.

Evalle asked, "What are you doing in Atlanta?"

"Pay up. My master waits."

"Who is your master?" Storm asked, stepping up next to Evalle.

When the demon continued to stare, Evalle whispered to Storm, "Can you tell what that stinky smell is?"

"It's not one scent. It's a mash of more then ten scents. Someone is trying to mask the true odor."

"Pay. Me. Now." the demon ordered, which sounded weird coming out of something that had no pockets for money.

Evalle said, "What do you think I owe you?"

"Body."

"What's your flavor? Male or female?" she asked.

The demon cocked his head in a perfect confused dog look. "Master calls. Give me body."

"Whose body?"

Opening his mouth to answer, the demon arched and twisted, lifting off the ground. It began spinning in a circle, faster and faster until the blue-black turned into a purple blur.

The human tornado made a pop sound and burst into purple ashes that blew away.

A creak sounded to the right as a new smell hit Evalle that she did recognize.

Evalle and Storm swung around to where two men stood next to the scaffolding. One was short with a buzz cut on the sides of his head, a fuzzy patch of hair on top and wearing a poorly made brown suit. The other one was tall with curly red hair, ruddy skin to match and a bright orange jogging suit.

They stank of burned limes.

Medb warlocks.

Storm's fingers lengthened into claws and his face started to change shape.

"*Do not shift!*" Evalle ordered.

He swung jaws at her that were already widening for the fangs and snarled.

"No. Stop it."

He slipped back into his human form, shook his shoulders and twisted his neck, muttering, "Your death."

Maybe, but that was her choice.

The warlocks advanced, showing no signs of threat, yet. The taller one said, "You will report to your VIPER that we have rescued yet another agent from a dangerous demon."

Good thing Storm had her sunglasses on or these two self-appointed demon catchers might want to add Storm to their list.

Evalle asked the warlocks, "What are you doing here? The Medb are not allowed in VIPER territory."

"We are now."

She laughed. "I should just believe you?"

The tall one shrugged. "Matters not. We have Sen's permission."Did they expect her to trust their word that Sen would go against a Tribunal ruling, one that had stood for centuries?

Why not ask the resident lie detector?

She turned to Storm who said, "They speak the truth."

Now what?

Storm asked the pair, "Why are you killing demons?"

"We are following orders," the short one said.

"From whom?"

"We do not have to answer that."

Evalle picked up Storm's line of question. "Did someone in the Medb send you?"

"We don't have to answer that."

She looked around. "Must be an echo in this place. Let's try this again." She speared the tall one with her next question. "Did the Medb release demons into Atlanta?"

Their joint hesitation was answer enough.

And with Evalle figuring that out, the rules of engagement changed in a heartbeat.

Whipping his arm across his chest, the tall Medb released a blast of energy.

Evalle and Storm dove away from each other, leaving the spot vacant. She threw up a wall of kinetic energy, driving the tall one back, but had to hold up from harming Storm who had moved as a blur toward the second Medb.

When Storm came back into focus, he and his Medb were wrapped up battling. Sharp spikes had shot out of that Medb's head like a human porcupine before Storm could get a chance to rip his head off. The Medb released a purple smoke that began wrapping Storm in a cocoon.

Had there been a sale on black majik smoke lately?

The Medb Evalle held off with her kinetics struck her energy field with one blast after another of energy that rolled off his hands in fiery bursts.

She was starting to feel the heat come through.

Her Alterant power was stronger than a pure Belador's, but the weakness from the Belador blood had been manifesting itself since she left Treoir.

She tried calling out telepathically. *Trey! Can you hear me?*

Silence answered her.

Storm hadn't shifted but his claw-tipped hands were slashing away the cocoon and advancing on the Medb he fought at the same time. That little warlock was spewing smoke for all he was worth, which meant the minute he ran out, Storm would have him.

Evalle started backing up, but at some point the concrete floor would run out. She could defeat this warlock as a gryphon, but Tzader had warned her not to shift in the mortal world until the Tribunal had ruled on guidelines for such a thing.

She was going to get torched by a crazy warlock because of red tape.

Evidently this warlock had a limited supply of fireballs, because he tossed one that fizzled before it hit her kinetic wall. Good thing too, because the ball broke through and rolled to a stop near her boot.

She stomped her boots, releasing blades and pulled her dagger up from where she'd dropped it back into its sheath to use her kinetics.

Something crashed on the other side of the empty elevator tower. She hoped that wasn't Storm losing because she'd denied him the ability to shift.

Should I let him?

Not without a guarantee he could come back to his human form.

"You will be a gift to our queen," the tall Medb said, laughing as he raised his arms.

Evalle laughed at him. "You have no queen. Flaevynn is dead."

His yellow eyes glistened, smug with a secret. "She was not the true queen. We are now the power to be reckoned with."

She didn't need Storm to know this warlock was speaking the truth. His words were pure boast and confident at that. Dread climbed up her spine. She needed to capture him to find out what the Medb were up to, because whoever was in charge had cut a deal with someone, but whom?

Sen would only allow them to stay if the Tribunal authorized it. Trey hadn't said a word about anything of the kind. As far as Evalle was concerned, these Medb were here without permission.

Evalle and the warlock she fought circled each other, two fighters watching for any weakness.

A loud growl and scream jerked Evalle's attention for a second, giving her opponent an opening to attack.

The warlock rushed her.

She shoved up a kinetic field that he broke through, arms stretched straight out with sharp fingernails that extended two inches long before he gouged her abdomen, driving her to the ground.

Her stomach was on fire.

She whipped her dagger across his throat.

He yanked a hand away from her to grab at the clean slice where nasty Medb blood gushed from his neck.

A boot kicked him aside.

Storm grabbed her dagger and finished cutting the warlock's head off, then he dropped down beside her and leaned over her with his hands covering the ten holes in her belly. "Why didn't you let me kill him?"

It hurt to breathe. She squeezed out, "Wanted to interrogate ... him."

"For VIPER? Why don't you just jump off a cliff if you're that determined to die?"

"I'm not suicidal."

"Could have fooled me. Why aren't you healing yourself or can't you use your new gryphon power? That would be just like you to go along with whatever orders Macha issued *just for you*."

"That's not why. The Belador side of my blood is weak with Brina not in the castle. I ... can't call up my beast to heal myself."

He cursed and pressed on the wounds then started murmuring words. After a moment the words took on a life, sounding like a chant. Something old that Evalle had heard before.

It was Navajo.

The pain eased until she could breathe again.

When he quieted and moved his hands, he studied the wounds that had sealed. A muscle jumped in his jaw. "It's not healed. You have to fix it internally. I can't do that."

He could have at one time, but she wouldn't push him beyond what he'd done. She reached up and pulled the glasses away.

"Did you think that little chant would get rid of my red eyes?" he asked.

Yes, but she wasn't going to admit that. "Just curious." She put the glasses back on Storm and pushed up to a sitting position. She grimaced against the needle-sharp pain attacking her stomach and grunted out, "I'm good."

"No, you're not," he argued. "I told you I couldn't heal you internally."

"Got it. No Navajo juju available." She ignored his hand offering to pull her up and gritted her teeth as she reached her feet. Then wobbled sideways.

He muttered a scathing curse and caught her to him.

She leaned in, smelling his scent. Demon or not, he smelled like Storm.

Her abdomen ached, but there was no way she could heal it until she got to Treoir where her powers would get a boost. But to do that, she risked walking Storm into a potential trap with Sen. If the Tribunal had agreed to allow the Medb to hunt demons, then Evalle had no idea if she could trust Sen meeting Storm.

She took a step back out of his arms. "I have to ask you something."

"No, you don't. You have the power to order me."

Don't yell at him for acting like a demon asswipe. "Then I'm going to order you to choose whether you want to go to Treoir or not."

"Why would you do that?"

"Because you said nothing has ever been your choice. Saving Brina and the Beladors is my choice, but I'm not going to force you to do it. First we'd have to get past Sen who might be playing ball with the Medb. Don't ask me why, but it's possible, which means he might figure out your demon status."

Storm listened, no expression of concern.

Evalle continued, "Then, if he teleports us to Treoir, Macha is an unpredictable force. She would not allow the druids to bring in anyone with dark arts to remove the Noirre threads on Brina's hologram. I can only imagine her reaction if she realizes you're a demon."

"You're the master. I go where you go."

"If that's the case, I'll take you to my underground apartment and leave you there while I go to Treoir."

Storm became very still, working through his answer. "If you show up empty-handed, Macha will hold you responsible."

A very real possibility. Evalle lifted her shoulders. "You're a demon. That shouldn't matter to you."

His lips flattened into a line. "It doesn't. All the word games in the world won't change the fact that I'm dead inside. I'm only assessing a threat to you, because that's what my job is. I would have had to do the same for Nadina."

She snapped, "Don't ever put me in the same category as

her."

"I didn't. You did when you took possession of me. But to get back to the point, the answer is yes. I'll go to Treoir with you."

His easy agreement should have thrilled her, not raised warning flags. It wasn't that he'd agreed so readily, but he'd sounded as if he *wanted* to go.

She hated not knowing this Storm and why he would or would not do something, but she couldn't waste any more minutes figuring it out right now.

"Just as long as you're doing it of your own free will." She grimaced at another wave of pain through her middle. She clutched her stomach with her hand.

That drew his eyes to her abdomen. His mouth twisted with a bitter thought. "You got what you wanted. I *choose* to do this. If we're going then let's get moving."

One tiny concession, but she'd take that over none at all. "What about these warlocks?"

Storm glanced around. "Tell Sen two of his Medb buddies cornered a demon over here and they need his help."

Had that been a touch of Storm's wry humor?

"Workers will show up as soon as daylight hits."

Storm huffed out a sigh, his gaze taking in the building. "I don't have time to ward this place but I can put a spell on it that will make a worker not recognize it as the building he's looking for. That'll last about fifteen minutes."

"That should do it." She was only a one-minute walk from Woodruff Park. Once they were back on the sidewalk and Storm had put a spell on the ground floor concrete, she used Storm's cellphone to call Trey. He confirmed that he was still able to reach Sen by telepathy.

Before she hung up, Evalle added, "Would you ask Sen to bring my Gixxer back with him?"

"I'll ask, but do you really expect Sen to do anything for you?"

"Good point. Tell him Tzader wants my Gixxer returned. I'm sure I can get that backed up."

Trey chuckled. "I like the way you're thinking." Then his voice turned gruff. "Good luck with Brina. We're all pulling for you and Storm."

She glanced over at Storm and hoped she wasn't putting Storm and all the Beladors at risk. In the end, she just said, "Thanks."

Trey said he'd send Sen to meet her in five minutes and he'd try to find Quinn, who had been in the area earlier.

By the time she reached the park, her stomach felt as if scorpions were chewing their way out. Sweat ran down the sides of her face. Storm kept glancing over, but offered no more help, which told her he had used whatever Navajo healing powers he could call up.

She squinted against the brightness. She hadn't needed eye protection on the drive over or the last time she was in the sun, but even humans needed sunglasses. She'd get another pair to wear when she came back from Treoir.

Tiny rays of sunlight were stabbing the park and sidewalk. She'd covered this same area on foot so many times close to daybreak that she knew exactly where sunlight would strike all throughout the year. She could dodge the pattern between here and the next intersection of Five Points with the agility of a jewel thief weaving through security lasers.

Like that spot just ahead of her on the sidewalk where two cracks intersected that she'd reach in ten more steps. The sun would make a laser thin strike any moment now.

Right on time, a bright finger of light touched the sidewalk.

No different than people walking past a "wet paint" sign who felt the need to test it, Evalle just had to swipe a finger through the sunbeam and prove the dark no longer owned her.

Burning pain ripped across her finger.

She shrieked and snatched her hand protectively to her stomach. Tears stung her eyes.

Storm spun around, searching for a threat. "What's wrong?"

Evalle uncurled her hand to find the skin burned to the bone on her finger. She shivered. "I thought ..." She looked up at him. "I ... the sun burned me."

"You said that wasn't a problem any more."

"It shouldn't be. It wasn't when ..." She caught herself. The last time she'd been in sunlight was right before Adrianna had sent Evalle in astral projection to find Storm.

Adrianna had warned her that the trip would come at a price.

Evalle had offered anything from her as she stood there, thinking she might lose her powers. They'd taken her ability to walk in the sun. The freedom to live like anyone else.

"What happened?" Storm asked.

"Nothing. I was wrong."

"That's a lie. What. Happened?"

She jerked at his cold tone, in too much pain to guard her words. "You want the truth? I had to make a sacrifice to travel to Mitnal the first time to find you. Looks like the spirits who played tour guide to the underworld finally figured out what they wanted in payment."

"Evalle, I–" "Don't care," she finished for him. "So let's just drop it."

"But–"

His words were cut off by energy sweeping briskly around them, stirring leaves and loose sand.

Sen had arrived.

The six-foot-seven bane of her existence. His hair that sometimes grew several feet overnight was now a half-inch long. All that did was accentuate the square jaw and blue eyes that didn't belong in his Asian-influenced face.

He ruled VIPER headquarters located in a mountain in North Georgia, where no sign of it was obvious from the outside, because Sen could literally move a mountain if he chose. One day she would find out where he came from, or more importantly, who held the hammer over Sen's head to make him play liaison between VIPER agents and Tribunals.

Evalle had to calm down or she'd never reach Treoir. One wrong word to Sen and he'd find a reason to drag her to a Tribunal court.

If the goddess was still at a Tribunal meeting, Evalle getting dragged in during the middle of it would only make things worse.

Before Evalle turned to Sen, she shoved her hand into her pocket, biting her lip against the pain of anything touching her ravaged finger. She was in no mood to get into a verbal throwdown with Sen or to give him time to figure out that

Storm had changed into a demon.

She managed to sound calm. "We're ready to go to Treoir."

Sen gave her a look reserved for small, ugly insects. "I didn't ask."

Storm made a slight move toward him and even though Evalle appreciated the show of protection it was nothing more than Storm defending his master, which she didn't need or want right now.

Two dead warlocks had to be dealt with and Evalle had more to worry about than Sen being his usual jockstrap self. "By the way, I left two of your Medb friends in the building being constructed a block that way." She pointed behind her.

"I don't have friends."

"True, but you have a mess those warlocks created on the second floor. They specifically said they were performing duties sanctioned by you."

Sen's face tightened with threat. "I've been cleaning up Belador crap all day. What the hell did you do now?"

"Me? The way I see it, I did you a favor by keeping that little issue away from the public," she quipped then looked around for her motorcycle. "By the way, where's my Gixxer?"

Sen lifted a thumb he pointed over his shoulder. "Up there."

She took in the area behind him and the roof of a two-story building that sat on a triangle piece of property right at the intersection of five roads. Thus the reason for the area named Five Points. A huge Coca-Cola sign with scrolling neon and flashing lights rose fifty feet above the roof.

She could just see the tops of her motorcycle handlebars. Her Gixxer had been deposited inside the parapet wall of the roof.

You jerk. "Did you have to put it on top of a building?"

"The way I see it, you're lucky I brought it at all." He wasn't smiling.

Just toss in the shovel and stop giving Sen more opportunities to screw with me. "I'd love to stay and chat, but we're getting later by the minute and I'd hate to tell Macha that you held us up."

Sen flipped his hand at her and Storm, spinning her world with gut-twisting speed. Her stomach was already miserable from the burning pain and now she held her charred finger tucked close to her body.

She closed her eyes against the sudden vertigo.

Her stomach lurched at realizing she hadn't specified where to send her and Storm on Treoir.

CHAPTER 29

Maeve materialized in the queen's chamber of TÅµr Medb and waited for Cathbad to arrive next to her before she noted, "It appears we can teleport in and out of the tower any time we choose."

Devilment sparkled in Cathbad's brown eyes. "Oh, aye. That was a productive trip for our first time back in the mortal world."

"Absolutely." She rubbed her hands together. "I haven't enjoyed myself this much in, oh, a couple of thousand years." She laughed at her personal joke, and the way she was assimilating the modern use of language, then swung around to take in the chamber. "I really hate what Flaevynn, or maybe her predecessors, did with this room."

"Don't tell me you'll be spending your time redecorating."

She smiled. "All in good time. First, I have to break the warding on that scrying wall." With a blink, she crossed the room to float in front of the wall built of rare gems. "From what I heard today, Flaevynn wasn't stupid, but neither was she an intellectual giant. This can't be that difficult to figure out."

Cathbad joined her, but remained on the ground. "Come down here, Maeve."

She dropped slowly until she stood beside him. "Did you find something?"

"Not exactly." He turned his head to one side and back to the other. "I do believe this might have been warded by one of *my* descendants instead of Flaevynn."

Maeve had hesitated once to join forces with this druid, but he'd proven his ability to be shrewd and powerful when dealing with entities. Just as he had today. "Do you think you can break it?"

"No, I would not do that."

"Why?"

"Because that might destroy the wall." He leaned forward, placing a hand over one specific stone, and runic inscriptions appeared, etched into a ruby the size of a loaf of bread. "If we damage the wall, we have no way to find out what happened before we arrived in this tower."

Yet again, he earned his place with her.

She held the power of an entire pantheon, but every ruler needed a right-hand man. She asked, "Can you take control?"

"I'm doin' it as we speak."

The wall of stones came alive. Scenes were drifting in and out. Maeve caught a flash of mountains that rose from a mist, then a battle being waged with gryphons.

Her gryphons.

Just as the Alterants were hers. There had to be more Alterants to change into gryphons and she would find those as well.

Cathbad waved his hands quickly above several stones. Each time his palms passed over a stone, the runic inscriptions would glow.

He slowed his hands, staring up at the virtual screen as the images emerged one at a time, following the speed of his hand movement.

A woman and a man came into view. Maeve said, "There! Stop on that scene."

"Just a moment," Cathbad murmured, maneuvering the images with the skill of a captain piloting a ship in calm seas. "That one?"

Maeve studied the scene where a man held a young woman in his arms. He was crying. And he was clearly a Belador based on the aura surrounding him.

She looked closer and said, "That woman ... would that be Kizira? I saw her father for a moment just before you returned to take his place, and this young woman favors him."

Cathbad gave it a long review. "I do believe it is her." He leaned in, squinting at Kizira dying next to a Belador. "Strange pair, those two. Why would a Belador be holdin' her as if she were precious to him?"

Good question. Maeve said, "Go back to see if you can find the gryphon attack that happened just before Flaevynn died."

He did. They watched what Flaevynn must have seen once she released her gryphons to attack Treoir. First there had been a squadron of ten gryphons flying toward an opening in the Belador defenses on the island. That had to be the work of the Belador traitor she'd been informed of, who'd died that day. The woman riding one of the gryphons was the same one that had been dying in the arms of a Belador.

Cathbad scrunched up his face in a frown. "Why did Kizira die? A priestess can heal herself."

"True, but the bigger question is, why did Kizira throw herself in front of a gryphon attacking a Belador and protect him?" Maeve pondered that and asked, "Can you give us sounds?"

"Not yet, but soon." The images were flying faster again then stopped abruptly. "That's as far as Flaevynn's scrying went. Probably stopped at her death."

That had been enough to show Maeve that some of the gryphons had continued to fight until they were ordered to stand down. Who had that power once Kizira had died? She had clearly controlled her attack team until then.

The last scene included that Belador carrying Kizira's body toward the castle.

Maeve had never been one to wait for an opportunity to come to her. She believed in grasping it by the balls any chance she could. "We need sound for those scrying images, but in the meantime I want that Belador warrior found." She started toward her throne and turned back. "In fact, where is Kizira's body?"

"That's another good question we can't answer until we either have sound, or him."

"The images stop too soon to find out where he took her. We need to find him and her body. I'll get answers from one of them."

Cathbad scratched his chin. "We should be able to gain one answer now." He turned toward the open area near Maeve's throne and lifted his hand, moving his fingers quickly.

Ossian appeared, this time as a warlock in a robe. His head was smooth now, covered only with the tattoo of a snake. The diamond eyes and snout of the snake stopped above the bridge of his nose. "Yes, Lord Cathbad and Goddess?"

Maeve gave Cathbad a nod.

The druid held out his hand. A three-dimensional image appeared in his palm. It was the Belador last seen with Kizira on the scrying wall. Cathbad asked, "Can you identify this Belador?"

"I can. He's known as Vladimir Quinn who possesses the most powerful mind lock ability. He is the one who crushed the mind of our warlock in Atlanta."

"What else can you tell us?" Maeve asked.

"This Belador is close friends with the Maistir of North America and one of the Alterants."

Cathbad perked up at that. "Was it an Alterant captured by Flaevynn?"

"Yes, my lord. She's known as Evalle and one of the five who had a golden head when shifted into a gryphon."

"What happened to her?"

"She flew to Treoir with the others. That's all I know."

Scratching his chin, Cathbad nodded. "You'll find out more when we need it."

"Of course, my lord."

Maeve was having a great day. She turned to Cathbad. "Have him pull together a team capable of capturing this Vladimir Quinn."

"Consider it done. When do you want to send them?"

"With the next wave of witches and warlocks going to Atlanta." She added, "And I will reward the first person to bring me this Quinn, regardless of who it is, but they must be able to capture him without drawing the attention of the Tribunal."

Now Cathbad rubbed his hands together. "Ah, just like the old times. This will be fun. Oh, and I have also Ossian's Medb scent."

Maeve smiled in response and took another glance at the screen where Vladimir Quinn carried Kizira's body. That was genuine pain that came from caring for someone. This Quinn warrior was not in agony over just any Medb protecting him, and that pain was not just because she was female.

Unraveling a mystery such as that one would be far more than fun. The Beladors had another weakness that she intended to exploit.

CHAPTER 30

Tzader circled Brina's hologram, trying to will her back. Why couldn't he have that ability instead of immortality? No physical torture could ever equal living forever without Brina in his world.

He'd lost track of how many times he'd walked around what was left of her image, searching for any glimmer of life.

Any reason to hope.

Energy sifted into the room from over by the door.

He turned, prepared to send Allyn on his way again, and found Macha. He'd never seen her when she hadn't carried a cockiness that came with being at the top of the power food chain.

But the Celtic goddess over all Beladors stared back from eyes wracked with despair. Her lively hair that normally moved of its own accord and changed colors from blond to auburn to coal black with her shifting moods, now fell over her shoulders in limp strands of dull brunette.

Macha studied the hologram. "Has it shown any improvement?"

"No."

Her throat moved with a thick swallow. "We need to warn the entire tribe."

"But they know about Brina," Tzader said, surprised that he had to remind the goddess.

Shaking herself out of whatever had held her attention prisoner, she walked deeper into the room when she would normally float around or zip in and out of view by teleporting. Her eyes locked on the hologram with so much intensity that

Tzader expected the filmy image to respond in some way.

Macha once again tore her gaze from the pieces left of Brina's face and neck. She told Tzader, "We need to warn the tribe about the Medb."

"Every Maistir has been put on alert. Quinn is keeping check on our forces in Atlanta and—"

She raised her hand in a silent order to stop speaking. "I've been in meetings nonstop at the Tribunal. I stretched them out as long as I could, but in the end I lost my argument against the Medb joining VIPER."

"They *what*? How could VIPER allow them to join the coalition when the Medb have not been allowed in our territories for centuries? The original Tribunal passed that decree. Now the Medb are not only allowed to enter the mortal world unchecked, but we have to stand beside them as part of the coalition?" He stopped himself when he realized something was missing in all this. "Wait? Who's in charge if Flaevynn died? Did Cathbad live?"

Macha's lips twisted with bitterness. "Oh, they both vanished. In their place, the goddess Maeve and the original Cathbad the Druid were reincarnated. Maeve and her druid faced the Tribunal and argued that she should not be held responsible for anything the coven did in her absence. That she had not been controlling the Medb warlocks and witches over all this time."

Tzader couldn't wrap his head around this. "The Tribunal agreed?"

"Not at first, especially when I argued that the Medb coven had attacked us as part of the prophecy Maeve and Cathbad could not deny instigating in the first place. But Maeve had Cathbad read the prophecy word by word. It never specifically said to attack Treoir or Brina. Those two claimed that Flaevynn strayed from the vision they'd left of a peaceful coexistence between our groups."

"Oh, sure. Maeve and Cathbad never planned to extinguish the entire Belador tribe," Tzader muttered, clenching his fists. "I'm sorely disappointed in the Tribunal allowing that flimsy argument to sway them."

Macha floated around this time, following the same path

that Tzader had been walking. "That wasn't the deciding point. By coalition rules, voting to accept a new member into the VIPER alliance requires the entire group of deities."

There had not been a gathering of every deity in one place that Tzader knew of in his time. "How'd they manage that many shoved together in one spot without a confrontation?"Macha gave him a wry glance. "It was testy at times, but I think they behaved only because they were all more curious to see what would transpire between my pantheon and Maeve's. It was the perfect setting for her. Maeve challenged each deity to admit that if he or she had died as Maeve and Cathbad had, would any of them agree, upon being reincarnated, to be held responsible for actions of their pantheons." Macha stopped moving and faced Tzader. "There is no precedent for this, so even I would not agree to that."

He reached up and ran a hand over his smooth head, trying to figure out what to do next. "Does this mean the Medb coven is going to be allowed to infiltrate the mortal world at will?"

"No."

He blew out a breath, feeling some relief until Macha finished her statement.

"It's far worse than that. Maeve's warlocks and witches have been behaving like model citizens, killing demons before our Beladors have a chance to step in. The Tribunal knows my entire pantheon is in critical condition with Brina gone. From their point of view, this alliance couldn't have happened at a better time."

"Pretty fucking opportune, I'd say," Tzader bit out. "Can't those deities see a setup? Clearly Maeve turned the demons loose *and* has her coven killing them just to make our warriors look inferior."

"I raised that possibility, though they had to all realize Maeve's game, but she denounced any criticism I raised as being expected from someone who had carried a grudge for two millennia. Maeve quickly assured the entire assembly that she and Cathbad had already begun making changes that would bring about peace between our pantheons ... as long as our people did not attack hers."

Tzader chuckled and not with any humor. "What a brilliant

strategic move and none of us saw it coming."

"Why should we?" Macha raked her fingers through her hair, muttering with disgust. "So much for all our tribe has sacrificed as the iron fist of VIPER. I was hoping you had news on Brina. Bringing her back is the only hope for our people. By now, Maeve has returned to TÅµr Medb to begin releasing her coven in waves of a hundred at a time. That was the only concession I gained, to limit the influx weekly. The first group goes directly to Atlanta."

Tzader didn't want to acknowledge what this meant, but he had a duty to everyone. He would have to let go of Brina and return to Atlanta to stand with Quinn, Evalle and the other Beladors. "Can the gryphons go to Atlanta?"

"No. Maeve and Cathbad are opposing my claim to the gryphons."

"How?"

"Because the gryphons carry Belador and Medb blood. Once my petition for being a recognized race is decided, the gryphons can choose which pantheon to join. Until then, if they leave the protection of Treoir they'll be fair game to be captured as lost property."

"What about Evalle?"

"That's a difficult subject. I was asked if she'd fought for the Medb at any time, which she had so I had no choice but to tell the truth. However, I explained that Evalle claimed she'd been compelled, as well as the others, and as soon as Kizira died that she was free to choose. At that point, Evalle chose to remain a Belador."

"Damn right she did."

"Maeve is claiming that I'm compelling the gryphons and Evalle now, which is why the Tribunal will not recognize any of them swearing fealty to me in the meantime."

Brina's neck disappeared, then her mouth and cheeks, leaving only her eyes and forehead in a ghostly mask.

Tzader had never felt so damned helpless in his life. He squeezed his eyes closed to stem the misery wanting to flood out of them and looked away. "I'll go back to Atlanta, but there's only ten, maybe twelve minutes left, based on what I've noticed." Yes, he'd been keeping count by the minute, analyzing by the square inch just how quickly Brina's hologram was disappearing. "I want to stay until ... she's gone."

When he glanced back at Macha, she was reaching over to touch the dark green strings woven around where Brina's body had been.

Tzader shouted, "Don't touch her!"

Macha's eyes narrowed with threat. "Who do you think you're ordering?"

"You don't understand. Quinn and I both touched the Noirre before he went back to Atlanta. He was searching with his mind for any connection. I just felt the need to be close to her and put my hands on the shape. Two minutes later we were at each other's throats. If Evalle hadn't interrupted, blood would have been shed."

Horror reached Macha's eyes as she realized what he was saying. She snatched her hand back.

He nodded. "Exactly. You might destroy everything in sight before you realized what was affecting you."

"Where are Evalle and that Skinwalker?" The room trembled with Macha's agitated voice.

"I don't know–"

A guard appeared at the door to the hallway. "Excuse me, Goddess. The Maistir asked to be notified when your guests arrived."

Tzader's heart took off galloping. "Where are they?"

"They just appeared on the lawn."

Macha lifted her hands in a move that Tzader knew would end with Evalle teleported. He rushed toward the door and called out, "Please don't, Macha. It makes Evalle sick and Storm won't focus on Brina if Evalle is harmed."

"He will if I order him to do so."

Tzader had reached the door and paused long enough to say, "I'm not sure even you can stand between him and Evalle. Testing him will only waste time we can't afford."

With that, Tzader raced to the front of the castle. He had to get to Evalle and Storm first so he could warn Storm about the Noirre majik. But surely a Navajo with his shaman background was far enough removed from any dark majik that Storm would be safe from the affect of the Noirre threads if he touched them.

CHAPTER 31

Oddly, halfway through the teleporting, Evalle had felt a soothing warmth blanket her. When she opened her eyes to find she'd arrived on the Isle of Treoir, Storm was standing right in front of her and she had her hands on his arms.

She didn't cling to anyone.

Snatching her hands away, she stepped back. "Did you do something to me during the teleporting?"

"No." He crossed his arms and lifted his head in a way that seemed as though he was gazing over her shoulder.

Lie or truth? He wasn't twisted in pain, so that had to be the truth.

She hated those sunglasses that prevented her from seeing his eyes. Even if his gaze still blazed red, which she didn't doubt, she'd have an inkling of what he was thinking. Dealing with that barrier between them gave her a new appreciation for everyone who'd had to deal with her wearing sunglasses all the time.

That wasn't changing at this point.

Guess she'd need them again when she returned to Atlanta unless she wanted to test her eyesight on the sun the way she'd tested her finger.

"Going to Mitnal was a bad move on your part," Storm criticized.

With her finger seared and ten spots of Noirre poison ripping up her stomach, Evalle was almost inclined to agree. But not quite. "That was my choice and one you clearly wouldn't understand, so I'm not wasting my breath trying to explain it."

He heaved a breath and started to speak again.

She gave him a sharp look. "Stop. I don't want to hear anything else from *Demon* Storm unless I ask you for it."

An eyebrow quirked above his sunglasses. "Demon Storm?"

"That's how I think of you right now to separate the two of you. You may think you're all demon, but *my* Storm–the one who would understand why I offered any of my powers in exchange to find you–if that Storm wants to speak to me he's welcome to at any time, but Demon Storm needs to hold his tongue."

Showing up here with her own control slipping away and delivering this stubborn version of Storm might be the height of insanity. She could blame the rage threatening to break loose inside her on the pain her body still refused to heal, or she could be honest and admit that the longer she spent with Demon Storm the more she stared at defeat.

"Here they come," Storm murmured in a bitter tone.

Evalle turned as ten royal guards converged on them.

Thankfully, she recognized the guy she'd seen inside the castle protecting Brina in the past. "Hi, Allyn."

The head of the royal guard gave an order to stand down and every sword pulled back. Allyn addressed Evalle. "It's good to see you, but you're cutting it close."

She didn't react to his words. He wasn't chastising her so much as giving voice to the frustration everyone felt. What she took away from that statement was that Brina still had time. "I know. We'd have come sooner if it was possible."

Allyn nodded and waved his hand that opened a path to the castle as he turned and strode ahead of them.

Storm fell into step next to Evalle, whispering, "Thought you were stronger here. What about healing?"

Her stupid heart thumped at any sign of concern on his part, but she was learning not to read what she wanted into his words or actions. "I'm working on it."

She tried to call up her beast again, but no energy surged through her as a sign of rising to heal her. It felt like nothing more than her beast being jostled from slumber. She drew hard again. Little by little, power seeped into her body. She sent the first healing arc to her stomach and could feel every little repair being performed at a tedious pace.

By the time she reached the castle steps, her abdomen no longer ached viciously. Not entirely healed, but it felt free of poison. She could breathe more easily. Now, if she could only repair her finger that throbbed like crazy from the bone still being exposed. But that was all the help she could ask of her beast for now.

Storm reached the top step and turned to block Evalle's way. "Why can't you heal?"

How had he figured out she couldn't do it all? Was he tapping his empathic senses? "I've repaired my stomach. My hand will have to wait for another wave of energy."

"Let me see your finger."

"No."

"Why not?"

Allyn called, "Evalle, are you coming?"

She folded her arms, hiding her finger. "I need you to use every ounce of whatever you can call up to help Brina. If that doesn't work, losing my finger will be the least of my worries."

"*Evalle!*"

She stepped past Storm into the foyer to find Tzader rushing toward her. The foyer had been repaired to the point there was no sign of the battle that had been fought between two gryphons in here just days ago.

Evalle had been one and she'd faced Boomer, the largest of the gryphons when they'd all left the Medb tower to attack Treoir. The moment Kizira died, Boomer became the most powerful gryphon of the flock, which meant no one held control over him. Boomer had been determined to reach the river of immortality beneath the castle.

Evalle hadn't gone along with that plan, and Boomer's bid for living eternally had fallen victim to having his head cut off.

Then Tzader had broken through a ward that killed immortals. He'd survived when Evalle linked with him, but he wasn't fully recovered yet.

He'd never looked so awful. His eyes were sunken from lack of sleep and he was losing body mass. He ignored Allyn and ordered the guards at the door to return to duty before Tzader told Evalle, "We're down to minutes."

"I'm sorry. Getting here was complicated."

Tzader waved her apology off. "Don't worry about it, but first, I–" He looked over his shoulder until that guard Allyn walked away. Once Tzader was alone with Evalle and Storm, he continued in a hurry. "Brina's hologram is almost completely gone. The only thing left is her eyes, nose and forehead."

Evalle's skin tingled with fear. She looked at Storm. "Can you work with that?"

"Is there anything else left to indicate where her body stood besides that part of her face?" he asked Tzader.

"Yes, but that's why I came to talk to you first. The Noirre majik thrown on her turned into threads that wrapped the hologram. Now it's just her partial face and those threads shaped like her body."Storm nodded, letting Tzader continue.

"There's a problem with the Noirre threads. When Quinn and I each touched them we became aggressive and had control issues."

Evalle interjected, "You mean right before I left when it looked like you two were going to tear each other apart?"

"Exactly. The Noirre caused Garwyli to react so badly he was yelling at Macha."

Storm asked, "Who's Garwyli?"

Evalle answered, "The oldest druid of the Beladors. Of all our druids, he's the most formidable but he would normally never lose his composure around Macha."

"Right," Tzader said, still talking faster than the Maistir she'd known for years. "The Noirre affected all of us adversely. If I hadn't stopped Macha from touching it, we might be tiny bits floating in the universe by now."

Tzader paused only long enough for his throat to roll with a hard swallow. "Standing in the room with Brina's hologram is fine, but touching it causes a combustible reaction. I know Storm has used his Navajo powers to soothe you and I'm hoping he has enough of that juice to prevent the Noirre from triggering aggression in him."

At the abrupt silence that followed, Tzader frowned over at Storm. "Why are you wearing sunglasses?"

Oh, hell. Evalle couldn't dodge the truth. "Storm, would

you please take off your glasses?"

He lifted them off his face.

"What the fuck?"

That's pretty much what Evalle had expected Tzader to say.

Evalle said, "I'll explain it later, but Storm was tricked into going to Mitnal where this happened. He's still our only hope."

"Are you kidding me?" Tzader bellowed.

"Might as well let me try," Storm offered.

Evalle assessed the situation and came up with a new disaster. She asked Storm, "What if the Noirre harms you?"

Storm snorted. "I might not be able to break the spell, but Noirre can't break me either."

That sounded encouraging.

Tzader covered his eyes for a second then dropped his hand. "Yeah, but Macha might kill you on the spot even if I try to stop her."

"I know," Storm answered with too much confidence.

That's when Evalle realized why Storm had been willing to come here without an argument. No, he'd actually *wanted* to come here. She turned on him. "You expect her to kill you."

Storm's burning gaze met hers. "You can't do it."

Before Evalle could respond, Macha's voice boomed through the castle. *"Get. In. Here. Now!"*

Tzader took off toward the solarium at a dead run.

Evalle did her best to reach Brina's sunroom before Storm, but he still managed to step in ahead of her and position himself between Evalle and Macha's back.

The goddess faced the hologram, blocking their view.

Evalle circled Storm to stand next to Macha. When the goddess turned to Evalle, she said, "We need Brina now more than we ever have."

Licking her dry lips, Evalle said, "I understand. I'm going to ask you to trust me."

"Why?" Macha started to turn.

"Wait. Please." Once Macha stilled, Evalle explained, "I need you to trust that I'm always going to work in the best interest of the Beladors. Brina is probably a minute from slipping out of our reach. I brought someone who's willing to put his life at risk to help us, but I want your promise you won't harm him while he's helping us with Brina."

"*Evalle!*" Storm warned.

"*Silence!*" Evalle shouted right back.

He pressed his lips tight.

This master thing had its upside.

"Done," Macha said. "Now hurry up and do something."

A swirl of light appeared on the other side of the hologram. Garwyli had joined them. "My apologies for my earlier lack of respect, Goddess."

Macha waved it off. "I've been informed of how the Noirre influenced you. Apology accepted. No more discussion from anyone until we deal with Brina."

Garwyli must have bad hearing. He spoke up again. "I am glad to see you took my advice, no matter how inappropriately it was offered." His gaze tracked past Macha.

The goddess turned, following the direction of Garwyli's gaze, and got a good look at the Demon Storm.

Evalle rushed to intervene. "If everyone will step back as far as you can, Storm can get started." Doing what, she had no idea, but hoped he was feeling inspired.

Macha's hair had been calm, but now it flew wildly around her head, the colors radiating from vivid reds to glaring blond. She literally shook with leashed power and turned a glare on Evalle that should have singed her eyelashes. "Just to be clear on our agreement. I won't touch him until Brina is back or gone for good."

Crap. Evalle should have had a chance to phone a friend whenever she made deals with Macha.

Tzader shouted, "*Do something!* Brina just lost half her forehead."

Everyone went into position as if choreographed.

Storm stepped up to the twisted green threads and opened his arms, curving them to wrap around the hologram, but he paused before touching it.

Evalle chewed on her lip to the point of tasting blood. That took her mind off of her throbbing finger.

With his hands still hovering near the Noirre, but not touching, Storm's lips moved silently. Was he talking to someone or having a debate with himself? Finally, he closed his eyes for a moment, gave a little nod of some sort and started speaking in a deep tone.

That was Demon Storm talking.

His body glowed. Was that what auras looked like to other people? Evalle never saw them, but Storm had a purplish glow. His guttural voice raised the hair on her arms. She cut her gaze over to Tzader who she hoped was too confused by Storm's appearance to realize he was not hearing the voice of a Navajo shaman descendant.

Storm's words were twisted and undecipherable.

He clenched his jaw, but kept ripping the words out as though he had to claw each one from his throat. His extended arms yanked forward and clamped the hologram, his hands gripping the form shaped of Noirre threads. The black majik came alive. Green filaments twisted and sizzled with energy. An acidic smell that was ancient and nasty filled the room.

Storm's voice went deeper then turned hoarse and halting, each word a battle to drag out. His fingers curled tight, clenching the electric threads.

The purple glow began to dim as the threads in turn began glowing brighter every second.

Was the Noirre dragging power out of Storm?

Evalle lunged around the opposite side of the hologram and reached for his hands, gripping them tightly.

Storm yelled, "*No!*"

"Yes. Do it. I believe in you."

"Let go. My blood is at war."

Did he mean his demon blood wouldn't allow him to call up his Navajo powers? Or were both bloods fighting for dominance inside him? The green threads turned a brilliant hot flame blue and burned through her clothes to her skin, branding her everywhere they touched.

She could smell her body being seared. Her mind screamed to let go.

If she did, she'd lose him.

CHAPTER 32

Pain seared deep into her chest from where it pressed against the threads wrapping the hologram. Evalle shook off the battle to keep from passing out, but her body begged for relief. If that happened, she'd lose her grip on Storm's hands and the black majik locked in his blood would destroy him.

She knew it with a certainty that had to come from being his mate.

If the black majik didn't kill Storm, Macha would finish off whatever the Noirre left of him.

Please don't take Storm from me.

Evalle was staying with him all the way, even if he died, but her grip was slipping. The agony of being burned all over kept dragging her away, pulling her towards relief and darkness. She shook her head and fought to stay conscious.

"Let. Go." Storm ground out the words.

"You can do this, Storm, please," she pleaded in a hollow voice. How could she help him reach deep enough? What would make him try?

Only for his mate will he come back, whispered through Evalle's mind.

Her body trembled, going into shock from being branded. She whispered, "I hurt so bad, Storm. I can't heal. I need you to do this. I need you ..."

His body shook so hard it shook the entire hologram and he growled.

Evalle chanced a look at Brina's hologram ... just as the last piece of the warrior queen's face vanished.

Storm's fingers flipped around, latching onto Evalle's in a

death grip. She gasped at him squeezing her index finger that was still raw to the bone.

The blasted threads glowed white hot.

Sweat ran into her eyes and down her cheeks. She fought to keep her face away from the threads, but her lips cracked and bled from the scorching heat.

"Stay with me, Storm," she kept repeating. They faced all or none. He couldn't quit now.

Somewhere far away, Tzader shouted and the room rocked back and forth. This was it. The castle was going to explode.

Then all at once, she heard Storm's voice.

Her Storm.

He was chanting and the air filled with words that sounded familiar. She recognized some of the words from his Navajo chants.

The Noirre majik began to lose intensity. She took a labored breath and her body still hurt as if someone had shoved a hot branding iron all the way through her chest, but the threads lost their glow, turned back to green and stopped sizzling.

She could see Storm through the other side of where the translucent hologram had been. His lips continued moving and his eyes were closed.

His hands held hers.

She wiggled her index finger. It didn't hurt.

He used one of his fingers to tuck it back in place inside his gentle grasp. Words spoken in his beautiful voice wrapped around her, soothing her burned skin.

Now cooled completely, the threads shattered, floating away from the form to suspend in the air. They poofed into dust and rained down on the stone floor.

Evalle smiled at Storm, but his face began to fog and blur until she couldn't see him.

What was happening? "Storm? Storm?"

"I'm here."

"I can't see you."

He chuckled. "That's because Brina and Lanna are in your way."

She pulled back a few inches to see Lanna's blond curls tipped in black, then Brina's face above Lanna's head. Brina's eyes were closed. Was she asleep?

Storm released Evalle's right hand and carefully drew her away by pulling on her other hand. He said, "Their bodies are back, but I'm not sure about where Brina or Lanna's minds are, or whether their spirits are present."

Tzader appeared next to Evalle and Macha next to Storm.

Relief and panic flowed from Tzader in a frenzied mess.

Macha was uncharacteristically quiet, which might not last for long. Evalle whispered, "What should we do? How do we wake them?"

Storm murmured, "We will all do more for the people we love than anyone else."

Evalle asked, "What do you mean?"

"I don't know," Storm said with honesty. "That came to me out of nowhere, but it felt like Navajo, so I'm thinking it means that it may take them wanting to come back for someone they care about."

Like dragging you back from Mitnal and being with you even when you were a demon, Evalle wanted to say but kept her thoughts to herself.

Evalle had an idea, but she decided to test it on Lanna first. "Lanna? Quinn is worried about you."

When that did nothing, Evalle added, "Quinn is not doing well, Lanna. He needs you."

Slow as a morning flower unfolding, Lanna's eyelids fluttered open and she looked around. She saw Evalle first and lunged into her arms. Evalle hugged the girl close, thankful that she could bring someone back to Quinn.

"Brina?" Tzader called softly, his heart exposed and hurting. He took a step closer and said, "Brina, come back to us."

When nothing happened, Tzader turned around, demanding, "What about Brina?"

Lanna pushed away from Evalle and took in the group, then she said, "The majik has not been good to Brina. I tried to keep her calm, but she struggled with problems the whole time we were gone. When my body start pulling, I thought maybe I was coming back. But Brina was not moving. I grabbed her to bring back with me."

That didn't sound encouraging.

Evalle reached for Storm's hand, surprised when he folded his around hers. He said he couldn't read minds, but when he spoke it sounded as if he'd just read hers.

Storm turned his attention to Tzader. "If I'm not mistaken, this woman means a great deal to you."

"She means more than my life," Tzader said without hesitation. "Why don't you tell *her* that?"

Tzader turned around and lifted a trembling hand to Brina's face, but stopped as if he feared the wrong move would lose her again. Pain lashed through his expression. "Brina of Treoir, the woman I have loved since the first time I set eyes on you, come back to me or take me with you, because I can't live without you."

At one time, Evalle would have been upset with Tzader for such a statement, but she now knew what those words meant. The only place they could come from was the very core of the heart, because a mind can't fathom the depth of that kind of love.

Brina stayed motionless as a statue for what seemed like an eternity, though it had only been thirty seconds when her eyes twitched and her lips parted a tiny amount.

Evalle was breathing for Tzader, who hadn't moved a muscle.

Suddenly, Brina gasped, drew a deep lung full of air and clutched her throat, stepping back. Eyes wild, she looked at her hands and arms then her gaze swept around the room.

Macha uttered, "Thank the gods."

Someone shouted then it sounded as if the entire castle was cheering. Power flashed through Evalle, which meant all the warriors had just received a burst of energy that told them Brina was back and alive.

Evalle wheeled around and hugged Storm, enjoying the sound of happiness all around her. The next thing she knew, he was kissing her.

Not the Demon Storm, but *her* Storm. She knew this man. He was worth whatever it took to keep him.

When he broke the kiss, she was staring up into reddish brown eyes that simmered with heat.

"Your eyes aren't glowing Storm."

He sighed heavily. "But they're still red, aren't they?"

She couldn't lie, not to the human lie detector. "A little."

"A little is the same as yes." He hadn't snapped at her, just letting her know that he was still a demon even if she wanted to believe otherwise.

Macha called the room to order. "This is truly a day to celebrate."

Garwyli grinned and ran his fingers down his white beard.

Storm tucked Evalle into his side.

She didn't know where they went from here, but she was determined that it was together. Lanna stood close to Evalle, but watched Brina with confusion on her face. Evalle noticed Allyn, the guard, had entered the room and was also staring at Brina, but as if she were *his* long lost love.

That was weird.

Tzader shot a glare at Allyn, then he took a step toward Brina, who backed away.

Tzader stopped and his eyebrows lifted in bewilderment. "Brina?"

"Yes?"

"What's wrong?"

"Nothing as long as you're not oversteppin' your boundaries."

"What?"

"I'm barely back from wherever I went and you're comin' all up in my face. I am still the Belador warrior queen, correct?"

"Yes, and I'm still the Maistir of the North American Beladors. Now that we have our titles out of the way, aren't you glad to see me?"

Brina gave him a long look then her gaze slid sideways to Allyn before coming back to Tzader. "I'm a bit foggy on everything at the moment, but I distinctly recall that I'm engaged to him." She pointed at Allyn, who brightened like a Christmas bulb.

"You are *not* engaged to him," Tzader snarled.

"Why not?"

"Because you love *me*, dammit."

Brina stared at him for a long assessment then shook her

head and told Tzader, "No. I also recall that you and I had
some sort of history."

"Some sort of?" Tzader sounded as if he were strangling.

Brina ignored that and continued, "But we ended that
arrangement. You and I were in agreement, as I recall. Is that
not true?"

Tzader turned to Macha. "Are you going to straighten this
out?"

Brina said, "You expect the goddess to deal with trivial
issues such as who I choose to be marryin'?"

Lanna's mouth gaped open. Evalle was no better off.

"Macha?" Tzader boomed.

"Tzader Burke!" Brina snapped then thought a minute. "It is
Burke, right? That sounds correct."

Macha's face had never carried the confusion it was toting
right now. "Perhaps we should let Brina settle in a bit and rest,
Tzader."

He stood there as indecision warred in his face, then he
smoothed out the anger lines creasing his forehead before
turning to Brina. "You've had a difficult time. Why don't you
and I take a walk and talk about it?"

Brina huffed. "What kind of honor do you have to be
suggestin' anythin' of the sort in front of my fiancé?"

Allyn broke out a full body smile and started toward Brina
who turned to him and asked, "What *is* your name?"

"Allyn McDonahue, your p-personal guard, your highness."

"You can't be serious."

"Uh, yes, I am."

Brina glared at Macha. "What has been going on about this
place? Why would I agree to marry my guard? When did that
happen?"

For the first time since Evalle had met Macha, the goddess
was at a loss.

Brina stretched her neck and yawned. "I've had enough of
this. None of you are makin' sense. I'm going to my chambers
and I don't want to be disturbed." She waved an arm and
disappeared.

Lanna said, "She must teach me that."

Nobody moved for a moment until Tzader shoved a fierce

glare at Macha who gave him a what-do-you-want-me-to-do lift of her shoulders.

Tzader growled something acidic then walked over to Allyn and warned, "I'm going back to do my duty as Maistir, but I'll return and I had better not find out that you've laid so much as a finger on her. Dis-*missed*."

Allyn had enough sense to walk away.

Macha finally spoke. "This is going to take some time to sort through."

"You think?" Tzader grumbled.

Evalle went over to Tzader and whispered, "Brina is clearly confused. That might be a residual of the Noirre majik. Just give her a little time to rest. Maybe that's all she needs to bring her memory back entirely."

"I guess." That was the weary sound of a man whose heart had taken one blow too many. Tzader called over to Lanna. "Come with me and I'll take you back to Atlanta. Quinn deserves some good news."

In the next instant, Macha teleported Tzader and Lanna away, then she turned to Evalle and Storm.

Storm had the sunglasses perched on top of his head. Yes, his eyes were apple red, but nothing like the Demon Storm glow.

Evalle ventured, "Storm did bring Brina back."

Macha nodded as she moved toward them, stopping just ten feet away.

"And," Evalle added, "he isn't really a demon. You can tell that, right?"

Macha asked Storm, "Are you a demon?"

"Yes."

Evalle groaned. "That's not the exact truth. He was born with mixed blood, part of which came from a witch doctor who wanted a demon child and part of it was from his father who was a Navajo shaman. Storm can control his blood."

"But he's still a demon," Macha pointed out. "You should be asking me to allow him to leave here alive."

After all this, the goddess was going to hold him to that rule of measurement?

"But don't you feel it's only fair to reward someone for

returning Brina?"

Garwyli interjected, "That's a reasonable request."

Storm reached for Evalle's hand, specifically the index finger that had been burned by sunlight and warned, "Evalle, any reward you ask for had better be for you."

She smiled at him rather than say anything that would start an argument and watched his face relax, because he'd taken that as her agreement. She turned to Macha. "Please return Storm and his father's souls."

Storm shouted, "No, give Evalle back the ability to be in the sun."

"Who has their souls?" Macha asked.

Evalle quickly supplied, "The witch doctor called Nadina stole them first then made a deal with Hanhau of Mitnal."

"Just *stop*, Evalle," Storm ordered.

"Hanhau?" Macha gasped. "Nobody deals with that slimy entity."

Storm was making growling sounds.

Evalle said, "He *is* a really nasty guy."

Garwyli pointed out, "That was technically two requests."

Evalle played innocent. "I don't think so. If you use the word *and* in the correct placement in a sentence, it's really only one request," she bluffed.

Storm shouted, "I don't care if it was six requests, you're not doing this."

Garwyli's wrinkled eyes widened, but he said nothing.

Macha and Evalle turned to him, but Macha's words scorched the air first. "Do you think to tell *me* what I *can't* do?"

Now might be a good time to take Macha up on that request to leave here alive. Evalle held in her next breath, hoping Storm did not make this any worse.

Storm calmed down and said, "I wouldn't dream of daring to tell you what to do. I'm only saying that any reward should be for Evalle, not me."

Evalle caught his chin the way he did when he wanted her attention. "This *is* for me. I can spend my life in the dark, but I can't live without you in the light."

The red receded a little more from his eyes and he touched

her cheek. "Don't sacrifice any more for me, sweetheart."

Tears stung the corners of her eyes. Evalle didn't want to humiliate herself in front of Macha, but Storm had said *sweetheart*. Her Storm.

She'd thought she'd never hear that again.

"Please, no more nauseating speeches," Macha ordered. "In one respect, Evalle is correct in that *she* should choose."

Storm opened his mouth to protest again, but Macha cut off any further discussion by declaring, "Upon my commitment to the coalition, I am required to order all demons killed upon sight. You did bring back Brina, so to show my deep appreciation I will spare your life and send you back to your world." Macha flicked a finger at Storm who disappeared, then she swept her ire in Evalle's direction. "You brought a demon into this castle!"

Evalle was still trying to catch her breath over Storm being teleported away. "What did you do with him?"

"Do I need to use smaller words? I said I was sparing his life and sending him away from Treoir."

"But did you send him to Atlanta? They're hunting demons there."

"I thought you just said he wasn't a demon."

You're such a–

Both of Macha's eyebrows lifted. "A what?"

She heard my thought? Or did I project that out for anyone to hear?

Evalle rubbed her head, still running hard on adrenaline from moments ago. Blowing out a breath, she knew better than to try talking her way around almost calling Macha a name that she'd regret. Instead, she focused on what some might consider an impossible task–to guilt Macha into using her goddess connections.

Clearing her throat, Evalle softened her tone. "Bringing Brina and Lanna back was huge for the Beladors and for Quinn. Storm managed to do what your druid couldn't." Evalle turned to Garwyli and apologized. "That wasn't meant to sound like a dig at you."

"No insult taken." He smiled in a contented way. "Carry on."

She nodded and returned to Macha whose lips twisted as if she sucked on a lemon. Evalle had never considered herself a smooth negotiator and found the blunt truth much simpler, so she said, "All I'm saying is that establishing the last Treoir descendant in the castle again has to be worth a boon, right?"

Cocking her head to study Evalle, Macha tapped a finger on her crossed arms. "So now you want to benefit from the attack on Brina?"

"Of course not, but I did find Storm and he did do what we asked even at the risk of the Noirre attacking him. Isn't that worth something?"

"Modest are we?" Macha said in a dour tone.

Garwyli spoke up. "The girl has a point, Goddess. We'd have offered a fortune for Brina's return, if money had been all we needed to accomplish that, but we had no one to call. She speaks the truth. I failed to retrieve her and we ran out of time."

The girl? Evalle let that pass.

Sounding more put upon than accepting, Macha said, "Very well. What do you want?"

"Storm has a grip on his humanity, but I'm asking for his soul to be returned."

Macha's eyes filled with compassion that gave Evalle hope until the goddess replied, "I don't have any way of giving him his soul back. That takes someone with different gifts."

Disappointment swamped Evalle, but she hadn't expected this to be as easy as asking a genie for a wish. "In that case, I have a second request."

CHAPTER 33

Storm shook out the blanket that had belonged to his father and laid it on the grass covering the back yard of his house. Macha had dumped him near his Land Cruiser, which surprised him.

He'd really thought the goddess had been teleporting him to the Amazon jungle where she'd once kept an Alterant in an invisible cage bound by majik.

But she'd teleported him to Atlanta instead. That had been ten hours ago and it was closing in on eight at night.

No sign of Evalle.

What had transpired after he left? *Tell me Evalle didn't get herself in more trouble with Macha.*

Or had Macha sent Evalle home with orders to stay away from any demon unless she intended to kill it?

Settling down beneath a clear, starry night, he sat cross-legged and closed his mind to everything except finding his spirit guide. He still had not fully conquered his Ashaninka blood, but he'd held onto the energy flowing from his Navajo side since returning to the city.

With a little luck, he'd be able to connect to Kai.

He searched inside himself for the peace that his Navajo ancestry had brought him over the years when the battle to walk the line between human and demon had potholes threatening to suck him down to the dark.

"Storm!" Kai's voice burst into his mind with so much happiness he found a smile for her by the time he opened his eyes.

Her hands were clasped under her chin and her face held an

adolescent excitement that warmed him. "You are safe."

Was he? Maybe he would be, if he was somewhere other than Atlanta.

Without Evalle, he had no reason to stay. But he also had no desire to be far away from her. That was too conflicted for him to figure out tonight.

"Storm?"

"Sorry, my mind is wandering. I'm glad to see you. Thank you for watching over me."

She gave a nod. "However, there were others who came to your aid."

"I know Evalle did, but who else?"

"Your friend the Sterling witch showed up at your house when Evalle was trying to contact me."

He cupped his eyes. "I can only imagine how those two got along."

"They worked together."

Lowering his hand, Storm started to question if Kai was telling the unvarnished truth, but Kai would only have known as much as she perceived from conversations with Evalle or Adrianna.

He would expect both of them to treat Kai with respect, which would have hidden the fact that Evalle hated Adrianna. Hate was too strong a word for a simple case of jealousy though, and Storm enjoyed Evalle's streak of possessiveness.

Or, he had until now. Macha had very likely put an end to Evalle ever seeing him again, and Storm couldn't blame the goddess. Why allow Evalle to see someone who would be a hunted man once word got around?

"Why are you sad, Storm? Is Evalle in danger?"

"No, she's safe and she'll remain that way as long as she stays away from me."

Kai's frown was comical, as if she couldn't decide if he was joking or not. "You do know that is not going to happen."

His throat tightened, but he managed to say, "I'm fairly certain the Belador goddess will forbid Evalle from any further association with me."

Leaning forward with her hands on her knees, Kai shook her head at him. "Evalle traveled to another realm first to find you then she returned to bring you back. That was no easy task."

"And it cost her something she'd never had until the last couple of days. She *gave up* the ability to walk in the sunlight," he said with more force than he'd intended.

Oddly, no thunderstorm boomed overhead, the usual sign of Kai's displeasure with him when he raised his voice. She said, "That was Evalle's choice."

He kept his words calmer. "It doesn't change the fact that she made a huge personal sacrifice."

"That in itself should be enough to tell you Evalle will not stay away from you regardless of who orders her."

Not unless Macha threatened Storm's life, but he wouldn't debate this further with Kai. He changed the subject. "Would you please go to my father and see if you can offer him any peace where he is? I have no way to free him."

"I will be happy to go as soon as our time ends, but I am not certain I can do much." Her brown eyes filled with sadness.

"I understand. Just do what you can and tell him I love him." Storm had no one to blame but himself for allowing Nadina to get the upper hand. Evalle thought she was responsible for losing his father's soul as well as his, but she had only done what Storm would have in her shoes.

"Stay in peace, Storm. We will visit again later." Then Kai faded as Storm closed his eyes and slowly flowed back into his body where it still sat on the blanket.

He stretched back with his head pillowed against his arms.

Energy swept toward him from the side of the house.

He recognized the source and didn't move. "Did Macha finally do something for *you*, Evalle?"

"Yes." Her footsteps were light, but his jaguar hearing picked up the slightest sound.

He let out the breath he'd been holding, worried that she'd come after dark because she had not regained her ability to be exposed to the sun. "I'm glad. That's how it should be."

Three more soft steps and she stood at the side of the blanket, looking down. Black hair spilled over the shoulders of a vintage BDU shirt that had seen its share of time on a working soldier in the past. Jeans hugged legs that were impossibly long from this vantage point and ended at the worn boots that hid razor sharp blades.

Five foot ten of badass female.

Sexy badass female who propped her hands on her hips.

He lifted his gaze back to her face. "Should you be here?"

"I don't know. Should I?"

He tried to take his eyes off her beautiful green ones, but he was drinking her in with deep gulps, needing to save this view of her for his future when he'd be all alone. "No, you shouldn't be here. This won't be a safe location once word gets around that I'm in Atlanta again."

"I would have thought you learned your lesson today, Storm. You failed to shove me away then. You can't do it now."

He growled and finally sat up, then pushed up to his feet to face her. Now, if he could just keep his hands off of her. "It's not that I don't appreciate all that you did for me. There are no words to express how much you amaze me over and over again, but VIPER is hunting demons. You're expected to hunt them. Being with me is going to put you in conflict at the very least and in danger at the worst. I'm not shoving you away. I'm trying to keep you safe. I *need* you to be safe."

He gave himself credit for not grabbing Evalle and running as far as he could to keep her with him, but that would take her from all that she held dear.

Clearly disinclined to help him out, she stepped up and looped her arms around his waist and laid her head next to his heart. "If anyone shows up we'll deal with them together, but right now VIPER and the Beladors have their hands full with the Medb infiltrating the city. Tzader is reinstated as Maistir and Lanna is safely back with Quinn. Quinn's another worry, but one that will wait for tomorrow." She lifted her face to him. "I'm tired of battles. Don't make me fight to stay with you, because I will."

His body longed for her touch and he had no discipline left when it came to her. He wrapped his arms around her and his world paused in that moment. The feel of her in his arms could only be described as coming home.

Except for regaining his father's soul and his own, all Storm had ever wanted was right here with her.

Someone made a harrumph noise.

Within a second, Storm flipped around to face the threat and had Evalle behind him.

The old druid from Treoir stood ten feet away with his hands behind his back, and appeared to be patiently waiting.

Evalle shoved up beside Storm, muttering, "We're going to have to talk about you doing that." Then she exclaimed, "Garwyli!"

"Good to see ya, girl. Did ya tell him?"

"Not yet. He was too intent on sending me away."

Garwyli must have thought that was absurd. At least that's what the expression on his face showed. He told Storm, "I hadn't considered that you might be addle-brained."

"I'm not," Storm ground out.

"Then you should be thankin' this young woman for puttin' your father at peace."

"What?" Storm turned to Evalle. "What did you do?"

She scratched her head. "Macha said she couldn't return your father's soul so I asked if she had someone who could help him cross over to his final resting place. Macha was going to tell me no again, but Garwyli offered to do it. She said she didn't care who did what as long as I was done irritating her."

The old druid cackled. "The goddess can be a bit tryin' some days."

"Some days?" Evalle asked with a smile that lacked humor.

Getting past his shock, Storm asked, "My father is really at peace?"

"According to Garwyli," Evalle confirmed. "It took a while and he did a bunch of things that I couldn't begin to explain since it was in something that sounded like Gaelic."

"'Tis a bit older language than that," the druid said, smiling slyly. "I was able to reach the spirits that could guide your father to his final resting place. It was much simpler than tryin' to return his soul."

"I appreciate you doing that, but you could have put in a word with Macha before you left me stranded for eight hours," Evalle said with good-natured prodding.

"It's not as though you could return to Atlanta until darkness fell."

Everything skidded to a stop in Storm's brain. "What? Didn't Macha fix your reaction to the sun?"

Evalle shrugged. "I didn't ask for it."

Garwyli added, "To be honest, Macha would not have been able to change that part of your organic makeup without knowing specifically who took the ability from you."

"I didn't realize that. Thanks for explaining." Evalle acted too casual, but Storm knew that ability had to be a devastating loss to her. One he had no way to fix, which was going to make him crazy. She lifted her chin to the druid, humor lighting her voice when she said, "I'm glad to see you, but what are you doing here with us mere mortals?"

Garwyli sobered. "I listened to your pleas to Macha and witnessed what Storm did in Treoir even at risk of what might happen with him going there as a demon."

Evalle flinched at that term, but Storm had been trying to tell her that some things just couldn't be fixed. Storm leaned over and kissed her forehead then her lips. "I wish there was a way I could thank you for my father."

She lifted up and held his face. "I wish there was a way to give back your soul."

The druid made a testy sound of clearing his throat. "And I wish for a way that you two would be quiet for a moment."

Properly chastised by the old goat, Storm gave in to the need to hold Evalle close and put his arm around her. "Sorry. You were saying?"

"After watching the selfless way that you two were willing to sacrifice for each other, I decided to visit someone I hadn't seen in over a thousand years. He owed me a favor that I thought it time to call due."

Who held onto IOUs for a thousand years? Storm kept his question to himself, allowing Garwyli to continue.

"I told this old friend that his son had been misbehavin' and had taken somethin' I wanted returned." Garwyli lifted his hand, palm out and a bright glow bounced on his palm with the enthusiasm of a two-month-old puppy. "Hanhau's father ordered him to return your soul and I have the honor of delivering it to you."

Storm stared at Garwyli's hand, not sure he could believe

what he saw.

Evalle touched his arm with trembling fingers.

He met her gaze that floated in liquid happiness.

His eyes were no drier. Heart thundering in his chest, Storm looked to the druid. "What do I do?"

"Call it home to you. Just reach out and open your heart to it."

Evalle stepped away and turned to watch him with encouragement shining in her eyes.

Storm extended his hand that he had to admit was trembling as well. The second his fingertip touched the glow, energy flowed into him like a gentle river, filling him from head to toe as his soul flooded through him to become one with the rest of his body.

There was no way to describe the sensation of having a soul returned to someone who had never lost one.

He bowed his head to Garwyli, humbled by what this druid had done.

Evalle said in a hushed voice, "You're glowing, Storm."

Lifting his hands, he could see the hum of light she was talking about. It was pale green, as natural as the forest. Then the glow dimmed until he stared at his human hands.

"Your eyes are brown," Evalle cried out and launched herself into his arms. He caught her, pulling her to him and swinging her around and around, listening to the beautiful sound of her happiness.

When he finally eased her back to the ground, he hugged her back against his side and turned to Garwyli. Swallowing hard, Storm said, "Thank you. I wish I had more than mere words to give you."

"It wasn't my doin' entirely. You had a champion. I knew Hanhau when he was a boy destined for ruin. Had he found someone who fought for him the way your champion has for you, he might have been saved."

Storm knew Garwyli's words were the truth.

No one would ever be equal to his Evalle.

"Let an old man go home," Garwyli said, scratching his chin. "I'll inform Macha that Storm's soul was returned and it would be a blow to the Belador reputation should someone not inform VIPER of such to prevent any mishaps."

That meant even Sen would not be able to take a shot at Storm out in the open. The liaison for VIPER had already tried to crush Storm's jaguar once when there'd been no witnesses present.

But that was because Sen hated Evalle and Storm had stepped between them. It was bound to happen again, but this time Storm would be ready for Sen.

"Good night to ya." Garwyli shimmered with blue sparkles, then vanished.

With the old guy gone, Storm drew Evalle around to face him. "I owe you an apology. Several, in fact."

She looked away, but not before the hurt slid through her gaze. "It's okay. I know you said a lot of things you didn't mean as a demon."

Touching her chin to turn her face to him, Storm searched for a way to repair the damage he'd done. He would never be able to make up for what she'd gone through and what she'd sacrificed, but he could give her the honesty she deserved.

"I wasn't telling you the truth when I said I couldn't feel anything and that I wanted you to go away. Even while my Ashaninka blood ruled me, you kept breaking through the cold emptiness inside me with your relentless determination. I said that I would have killed you if you had turned into a demon. That was a lie, too."

Her eyes widened then squinted in suspicion. "How did you lie without it harming you?"

"I felt twinges, but with my demon blood ascending, my body had no problem with me lying so the consequences were minor compared to what it was like before and would be again now." He stroked his hand over her hair. "I will forever regret the pain I caused you regardless of thinking I was doing my best by you when I tried to make you leave me. I also need to apologize because I failed to tell you that we're ... mated. I shouldn't have–"

Grabbing the collar of his shirt, she pulled his mouth to hers for a kiss that burned with hunger. *Holy mother of ...*

When their lips parted, she licked hers and said, "Of course we're mated and I'm not the least bit unhappy about that even though I'm not sure exactly what it means. You'll explain it to me. I forgive you all the rest if you promise to never do it again."

"I promise and, as for being mated, it means you're mine. Forever." Storm scooped Evalle into his arms.

"And you're mine." She chuckled when she'd normally be barking at him for acting like a caveman. "Decided to finally go back in the house?"

"No." He laid her down on the blanket and straddled her hips, sitting on his knees.

"Uh, Storm." She laughed, green eyes glowing in the dark night. "I know it's hard for humans to see in pitch dark, but what about everything else that rambles around at night?"

He had her shirt off and reached for the zipper on her jeans. "No one will see us as long as we stay on the blanket. I put a spell over it when I planned to sleep out here." He paused, thinking of their last time together. "I *was* out of control ... in the shower. That won't happen again. I'm going to love you the way you deserve."

He'd majik up a condom from the house and hope nothing came of that one time they hadn't used protection. Not that he had anything against children, especially with Evalle, but she had a lot of life to live first.

"Is the demon gone from your blood?"

He stilled and let the red glow roll over his eyes then returned his gaze to its natural state. "I will always carry both bloods in my body, but I regained control after locking my power with yours to bring back Brina. I am now fully in control instead of the other way around, even more so with my soul returned."

"So no replay of what happened in the shower?"

"No. I won't ever lose control like that again with you."

Evalle reached up and ran her fingers through his hair that had tumbled free from the leather thong. Her lips twitched with a saucy smile that turned into a sexy pout he'd never seen on her before. "See, I don't remember our shower as you being out of control. I think of it as finally getting a look at just what I've been missing with you being so careful around me." She lifted an eyebrow of pure challenge. "But if that was too much for you or you don't think you can handle another round of–"

"Ever the hellion." He leaned down to kiss those sexy lips while he got busy unclipping her bra and baring her breasts to his eager fingers. "Mercy. How did I end up with the most beautiful woman in the world?"

She smiled, a gift he'd never take for granted.

He touched her tightly budded nipples and dragged a moan of pleasure from her. He pulled away from her mouth just long enough to warn, "Don't expect to walk for a week."

"Talk, talk, talk. Is that all you can do with that mouth?" She ran her hands over his chest.

He reached down and slipped his hand inside her jeans, fingering her damp heat until she lifted off the blanket.

When she sucked in enough air to come back to earth, Evalle started unbuckling his belt with impressive speed, but then she *was* a Belador. Her eyes flicked up at the sky for a moment, then back to her task.

He assured her, "I'll have you home before daylight even if it kills me to leave this blanket."

"What's with the blanket outside? You have a bout of camping fever?"

"Not even. The house smells of the witch doctor whose name we will not speak tonight." He pushed Evalle's shirt off her shoulders. "I'm not spending another minute in that place with her taint floating in the air. I'm sure as hell not taking you around it again."

She sat back on her elbows, some important debate going on behind those bright green eyes. "How do you feel about living in an underground apartment with a small gargoyle?"

He bent down and kissed her, just because he could when he'd never expected to be able to again. When he broke the kiss, he studied the face he was sure he'd need a lifetime to memorize. "I can live anywhere with you, I just can't live without you. I'll spend the rest of my life trying to show you how much you mean to me."

She smiled with contentment. "Just do me a favor and don't worry about me not being able to go outside in sunlight, okay?"

"Okay." He hadn't actually lied to her. He wasn't going to waste time worrying when he could do so much more.

There was plenty of time tomorrow to start working on what he had in mind.

For now, he'd show her what it was like to make love for hours under the stars.

WITCHLOCK

Belador book 6 (June 2015)

After finally earning her place among the Beladors, Evalle is navigating the ups and downs of her new life with Storm when she's sucked into a power play between her Belador tribe and the Meb coven. Both groups claim possession of the Alterants-turned-gryphons, especially Evalle, as an influx of demons and dark witches into Atlanta threatens to unleash a war between covens, pitting allies and friends against each other. A legendary majik known as Witchlock escalates the conflict while driving powerful beings mad, forcing Evalle to put her own sanity at risk to save her loved ones, or Atlanta will fall.

DEADLY FIXATION

"I adore the city of Savannah. . .but this story reveals a side of it I've never explored! With incredible imagery, Love has created not just another Savannah, but another world." ~~ Sandra Brown

Devon Fortier eased forward through pitch-black passages where death waited for foolish humans in Savannah, Georgia's forgotten underground.

He was neither foolish nor human.

Deep voices growled up ahead in what had once been a rum cellar. The argument echoed off the packed-dirt walls that seeped water. Dank odors of rot, urine and unearthly creatures clogged every breath Devon inhaled.

Creeping closer, he made out three shapes hunched around something on the ground that cast an orange glow across the trio of predators. Two were ten feet tall. One had scaly skin and the other had pointed ears that curled up to his bald head.

Trolls.

Devon's informant looked to be spot on about some black market deal going down with trolls in this coastal city.

The third figure appeared to be a human male of average height. But he was probably a glamour-concealed troll.

Whatever those three had pinned down snarled, "Let me go you stinkin' vermin!"

Devon sighed, recognizing the voice. He ought to let the trolls continue.

A fourth-generation leprechaun and pawnbroker, Coldfinger had just enough majik to be dangerous. A sick piece of work the world wouldn't miss if the trolls wanted to finish him off.

But Devon's oath as a Belador meant he had to protect everyone—even a slimy bastard with the integrity of a jackal—if those trolls decided to chow down on orange fast food.

He moved closer for a better view.

Curly-ears held his prey in place with a four-toed foot as wide as a briefcase. He shook his head at Coldfinger. "You think faerie dust is gonna cut it? Think you can screw us?"

Trading faerie dust was illegal, but a petty infraction of VIPER laws. Not enough for Devon to risk his skin arresting three carnivorous beings. He couldn't spend much energy on this bunch when nothing here fit the profile of a major operation.

Beladors served as one of the enforcement arms for VIPER, an international league of warriors that protected the world from supernatural predators...like trolls.

And deadly leprechauns.

"How dare you accuse me of scamming," Coldfinger whined in a voice bloated with insult.

Devon rolled his eyes. How could someone with no conscience be insulted?

All the trolls started yelling, threatening to dismember Goldfinger.

Baldy bared his fangs. "We got you the scrying dish. Where's the spell?"

"You lying 'chaun."

Devon used the cover of their voices to close the thirty feet that had separated him from the argument.

Coldfinger's voice tiptoed up an octave with fear. "Calm down, I got it. I got the Noirre Fixit spell."

Oh, hell, no. Noirre majik *definitely* fit the profile of his black market investigation. Devon had no choice but to take all of them to headquarters now...*if* they didn't kill him.

Trolls were a nasty bunch who ate their opponents, which left no evidence and made it hard to try them in a Tribunal court. Devon could attempt to call in Belador reinforcements, but he had faulty telepathic ability at best, especially underground. No worries. He might have gotten shorted in the telepathy department, but his other gifts were just fine.

Besides, lowering his personal shields to call Beladors would blow his element of surprise.

Murdering trolls had no business getting their hands on Noirre majik, especially a fixation spell that could freeze a person long enough to do harm. As the deadliest of black majik, Noirre carried a high penalty for dealing, even death.

Human law enforcement didn't know VIPER or supernatural beings existed. Handling trolls, leprechauns and Noirre fell to agents like Devon.

He paused. Most trolls wouldn't touch Noirre since few of them were powerful enough to control it.

Ah, hell. Could these be Svart Trolls?

Only if the gods really wanted to piss on Devon's day.

The Swedish term for black, *Svart* trolls were preternatural black ops mercenaries.

Reaching over his shoulder, Devon slid his short sword from the leather sheath attached to his back.

Bullets only annoyed Svarts.

"Did you think I wouldn't find you, Lambert?" a throaty female voice called out from the other side of the trolls.

Devon stilled. No way.

He leaned right to see past the criminals. One look confirmed he had the worst luck ever handed out in this world.

Joleen Mac, a pain-in-his-ass bounty hunter whose four-inch heels on black lace-up boots boosted her height to just under six feet. Viper-tongue-red lipstick accented lips that could sink a man to his knees when she smiled—or issue a deadly spell. Black hair flashed past her shoulders, two long braids slicing down the side of her face. Scary as she was gorgeous, Jo worked for Dakkar, a rogue mage who ran a bounty hunter operation. VIPER allowed Dakkar freedom of movement as long as Dakkar's hunters didn't interfere with official missions.

Like this one.

Devon's recon mission just turned official with Noirre being traded and Svart Trolls congregating. But he needed backup on this and he had no way to reach anyone from down here.

Lambert, the troll in human glamour, grinned. "Jo, baby. Good to see ya. We got business?"

"You could say that." Joleen stepped close to the group. A tangerine glow washed across her loose-hanging rawhide coat, saddle-brown leather vest and jean shorts. She held a compact weapon with a short, squat barrel built to shoot two-inch-thick rounds that could kill a demon.

Devon had seen that weapon once before.

She pointed the muzzle at Lambert. "You're coming with me."

The two big trolls stared at her with bright yellow eyes and green saliva dripping from their lips. They growled low with menace.

"No, he's not going with you," Devon said, stepping from the shadows. He dropped his personal shields, allowing his power to radiate. Call it male arrogance, but he wanted the first shot at intimidating the trolls...and he liked the way Jo's cheeks flared with color when his power brushed across her skin.

"Stay out of this, Devon," she warned in a voice spiced with French influence.

"*Alll*-right, now we're talkin'," Coldfinger said, enthusiasm bubbling. "What say we all go topside, grab a brew and discuss this like sociable folks."

Joleen kept her weapon trained on her quarry, but ignored Coldfinger's bravado, pinning her gaze on Devon. "Lambert's behind a contract killing of a Connecticut witch."

Coldfinger howled. "You trolls tradin' stolen goods?"

Lambert said, "No, she's lying." He sneered at Jo. "I ain't goin' with ya."

"Yes, you are," she said without a hint of concern.

Devon sighed. "No, he's going with me."

Jo shifted the weapon toward Devon. "We're having a communication breakdown. That could be dangerous."

"You don't want to threaten *me*, Jo," Devon warned. "I caught them dealing Noirre. Makes this VIPER business. Lambert's got to face a Tribunal. That's the law."

All the trolls swung around to look at Devon.

Coldfinger howled again and glowed bright as a warning beacon. "You idiots. He's Belador. Heard everything you said. Stinkin' morons."

Jo asked Devon, "How can this be a sanctioned operation?" Her gaze shifted, scanning quickly before a smile teased her lips. "Where's your team? VIPER doesn't send their people in without backup. Doesn't want them *hurt*."

She was goading Devon over how she'd used that same weapon to kill a demon hanging on his back the last time they'd met.

He owed her and she was calling in the debt.

But he couldn't pay up right now. "I have orders to pick him up." Big lie. "Let's work together this time. You cover them and I'll call in backup."

Her eyebrow arched sharply in a saucy smirk. "What gave you the idea we were negotiating, Dev? Lambert's mine. You can have the other two and the orange toad."

"You can't prove nothin' without Lambert," Coldfinger yelled.

Not technically true, but if Lambert was running a Svart Troll op Devon needed him most of all.

Lambert inched a step away.

Jo swung her weapon back at him. "Let's go."

Hellfire. Devon could use her help, but he'd just have to contain them without her. "Sorry, Jo, but VIPER laws take precedence over bounty orders. I'm taking them all in." He turned to Lambert and bluffed about using telepathy. "I've already sent word to VIPER for backup. Resisting will only make it worse when you face the Tribunal. You three, face down on the ground next to Coldfinger."

Intelligence gleamed in Lambert's eyes. He shrugged and turned to his two giant sidekicks. "Sorry guys, I know I said this would be a quick job. Guess there's nothing to do but...*kill them!*" He ducked and the huge trolls roared.

One giant rushed Devon and the other one dove at Jo.

A flash of green light burst through the room. Some kind of stun grenade? That wouldn't stop a Svart.

Devon swung his sword in a high arc. The blade sang with sentient power, but a second flash of light from Jo caused a strobe effect that threw off his timing. He slashed across the troll's arm and dodged the snap of fangs so close to his neck that his hair stood on end. Losing an arm didn't slow the bellowing monster, whose armhole spewed murky-colored blood that smelled like sewage.

These ornery things were hard to kill, which was why Devon couldn't miss again. With the next swing of his Belador sword, he severed baldy's head. It bounced away...the only sound in a sudden brittle silence.

Not good.

Devon walked over to where chunks of troll lay scattered around Jo. So the flash had been a high-bandwidth laser? He glanced at a slender barrel camelbacked onto the demon blaster, then at the ground were Coldfinger had been. *Had* being the operative word.

Glowing yellow-orange embers sizzled on the dirt floor.

"Any chance that means you got him, Jo?"

"No. That's residue from Coldfinger's body being held still too long. He escaped with Lambert." She stood ten feet away with her blaster hanging from a shoulder sling and hands propped on her hips. "They'll have made it to where the tunnel dumps into the river by now. What a krikin' mess you made of this."

"Me? You're the one who wouldn't keep this simple." He turned on her and moved forward with each word.

"Stop right there."

Not a chance. Nothing intimidated this woman.

He couldn't decide between wringing her stubborn neck and kissing her. Like that adrenaline-pumped kiss they'd shared the last time they'd survived a bloody battle. Was she thinking about that kiss? "With a little cooperation, we'd have hauled in all four and gotten you a nice fee for helping."

"I don't work for chump change...or VIPER." She raised her weapon and shoved it into his chest. "And if you get in my way again, there won't be enough of you left to feed a gnat."

That'd be a "no" on her thinking fondly of their last kiss.

This woman had unusual hunting skills. And based on what he'd seen, a little majik. She could be a witch. When you moved in a world where a broad spectrum of majik was the norm, identities were tough to nail down without information.

Jo might find Lambert faster than Devon could pull together a team. He had to cut a deal for any hope of stopping Svart trolls from accessing that Noirre spell. "I get that Lambert was your bounty, but—"

#

"Not *was*. Is my bounty," Joleen said, setting Devon straight. Which goddess of fate had the twisted sense of humor to stick Devon Fortier in her path again? Blonde strands fell loose from where he wore his shoulder-length hair tied back. Those dark hazel eyes were flecked with gold and seemed to maintain a perpetual anytime-is-playtime look.

A look that could make a woman do asinine things.

And make tactical errors. Like kissing Devon after their last unplanned meeting. She should shoot the cocky Belador just for interfering again.

"We can work out the money on this, Jo."

"It's not about the money or I'd charge you double and be done with this. I have quotas. I'm behind and need to hand in Lambert by tomorrow afternoon or Dakkar will cut me loose." That could not happen. Dakkar was the sole person who could keep her identity secret. And he would. For a price. She couldn't lose this gig or allow Devon to ruin it for her.

"What's the big deal on this troll, Jo?"

"He's not just a troll. Lambert is the bastard son of a Svart Troll and a black witch. He's slippery. I've been tracking him for days." She glanced past him. "Where's your team?"

He gave a half-assed look over his shoulder. "Should be here soon."

Liar. "You didn't call anyone." She let her weapon swing down and under her coat. "I got a bounty to pick up."

Sliding his sword into the sheath on his back, Devon said, "Then we better get rolling."

"Don't make me tie you up, Dev."

His grin ignited with lust. "We don't have time for that, but I like the way you're thinking."

One round from her demon blaster and he'd be little Devon pieces. Tempting. "I'm not joking."

His sigh accused her of being as much fun as rain at a picnic. Tough. She *had* been fun at one time in her life, but someone had stolen that life.

Devon scratched his whisker-darkened jaw—as unshaven as the last time she'd seen him. Did he never shave? He sighed and his voice shifted from teasing to serious. "Here's the thing. Based on what you said about Lambert, he'll use that Noirre spell if we don't stop him."

"Don't see how theft is my problem." She beat down her surge of conscience. Nobody would waste that level of a black majik spell for simple robbery.

"Theft? That's a Noirre Fixit spell. Most fixation spells just freeze a human for a minute, but Noirre could be much worse."

Could be? He didn't know for sure what that spell was capable of? Damn him. She couldn't let this Belador go off thinking that. "If it's Noirre, it's not *just* a fixation spell that freezes someone long enough to rob them."

Devon crossed his arms, waiting.

She cursed herself. Why couldn't she be like Dakkar's other bounty hunters who put their own needs first? "Using Noirre Fixit will freeze everyone within twenty feet of a single person hit by the spell. The freeze will last approximately two minutes, but when it dissipates, the memories of every person affected or watching the spellbound area will be wiped clean. They'll continue living as if nothing had happened, but without their memories up to that point."

Devon's words came out slow and tight. "I can't share all my intel, but it's looking like Lambert has a team here for a specific hit. Based on what I know about his ability and now about now this spell can affect large masses, I'm betting his target involves the St. Patrick's Day Parade tomorrow."

"Trolls wouldn't risk exposure in a crowd that big," she argued. "VIPER would send death squads after them."

"But as you just pointed out, this spell comes with a memory wipe. If Lambert pulls this off, VIPER will have nothing to use as evidence."

She considered that, not liking how logical it sounded, but she couldn't risk her entire future on a maybe. "Why this parade?"

Scratching his head, Devon stared off, thinking. "My informant thought the trolls were here to glamour their way through the crowd to steal gold, but I ran all possible scenarios and cross referenced with any notable celebrities attending this event. I found out an Ansgar descendant is studying art here. She's in the parade. Six members of her family are joining her tomorrow, including the matriarch who goes nowhere without wearing her solid gold Celtic choker—"

"—that holds the power to their entire Fae family." Joleen got it.

"Right. I blew off the possibility of a troll making that, because the Ansgars always travel with security. But now that Svart Trolls are involved, I'm thinking they're after the choker and/or the family members for someone else, because they don't put their people at risk unless they feel confident they can succeed and the price is right. I'd like to know who's behind this. My bet is an enemy of the Ansgars, but that doesn't narrow the field. If that family *is* Lambert's target and he pulls this off while wiping the minds of any witnesses, war will erupt between powerful adversaries once the finger pointing starts. The human world won't be a safe place for anyone."

Dakkar would be furious if Joleen had any perceived part in that happening, since shielding nonhuman existence from humans was part of Dakkar's agreement with VIPER.

Pushing hair off her face, she hissed out a steam of air. How had one simple bounty gotten this convoluted? "How many people show up for this parade?"

"Close to half a million." Devon hit her with a hard look. "And with the memory wipe, nothing would stop those trolls from snacking on a child, who would then end up on a milk carton."

Playing hero was Devon's job, not hers, but she'd never allowed innocent people to be hurt when she could prevent it. That would mean zip to Dakkar if she didn't bring back her bounty. "Here's my deal. I help you get the spell and you give me Lambert."

Hesitation played through Devon's face. "I'll do what I can, Jo, but I don't make promises I can't keep. I'll give you Lambert if I can and *if* he doesn't die in the process."

A dead Lambert was of no use to her. She either gambled on throwing in with Devon or locked him in a rum cask while she hunted Lambert alone. But if she lost Lambert, she'd have to

live with the guilt for any devastation he caused *and* face
Dakkar empty handed. "I'm in, but no promises from me either
on what happens once we find Lambert."

She expected Devon to agree or argue, but he just lifted the
hood of his fleece jacket over his head, covering the sword
handle, and led the way out.

After backtracking with him to the exit point beneath the
Pirate's House restaurant, they emerged on Broad Street. A
balmy March sun had daffodils blooming and tourists crowding
cobblestone streets along the historic district, clueless about
nonhumans moving among them. She fell into step with Devon
who said nothing over the next half hour as he led the way to
Coldfinger's pawnshop on the outskirts of Savannah. Once
they'd left the dense pedestrian traffic in the city behind, he'd
picked up the pace.

Joleen stayed with him step for step. She stayed in top
running condition, because exiting quickly often made the
difference in living to fight another day or not. The area had
been abused by age. Spider webs covered steel-barred windows
on shabby buildings and the homeless loitered on the
sidewalks.

She mused, "Would have expected Coldfinger to be in a
finer part of town."

"Not with a clientele that shies away from crowds and
humans to do business."

Devon lifted his hand and signaled for silence as he slowed
to enter a wooden shack-of-a building through a doorless
opening.

She followed him in, allowing her eyes to adjust to the
sudden darkness. Sunlight filtered through holes in the walls
and ceiling, offering a dingy view of musty piles of clothes and
a smelly mattress.

Did Devon know where he was going?

He paused six feet from a door at the back of the room, then
crept forward.

She drew her weapon, though she'd prefer to use the wand
she kept hidden along with her mage identity.

Devon eased over to stand at one side of the door where
light sifted out from the bottom. He tested the knob. Locked.

Before she could suggest finding another entrance, Devon moved around in front of the door, put his boot up and kicked.

Rotten wood shattered.

Joleen shook her head, muttering, "What is it about boys and kicking in doors?"

The smell hit her first, warning that the view wouldn't be much better.

#

Devon stepped through the remnants of the door and took in the hideous scene against one wall of the pawnshop. Coldfinger was dead, frozen with his remaining arm up in defense and his face contorted with a scream of fear. Devon wrinkled his nose at the scorched sherbet ice cream stench.

Jo pointed at a pile of half-chewed orange glob that might be Coldfinger's upchucked arm, and smirked. "Looks like Lambert tested the spell on Coldfinger. Trolls have a weak stomach for leprechaun, eh?"

Devon let the rare humor in her voice pass without comment. He had to contact Tzader. As the Belador Maistir over North America, Tzader directed a large portion of VIPER's force.

Jo must have picked up the track of his thoughts. "If you're thinking of calling in backup at this point, you better reconsider unless you want Lambert to use the spell on VIPER agents as well."

She had a point, but he knew that wasn't her real concern. "You're just worried VIPER will pick up Lambert before you do."

"True, but what if you call in agents, and he unleashes the spell? Svart trolls got any old scores to settle with Beladors?"

Mostly in Europe, but Devon doubted a Svart would pass an opportunity for payback regardless of where they found a Belador. "I've thought about that," Devon admitted. "But even with my intel I can't just assume it's only a hit squad and that Lambert is only after the Ansgar family. We have to cover more area than that. *And* we're not sure how long the spell will last now that Lambert is using it."

She hissed something that sounded like a curse. There was that look on Jo's face again, like the one she'd had right before she clued Devon in on exactly what a truly powerful fixation spell could do.

Devon needed whatever she could tell him about the spell and she needed a nudge, so he said, "What?"

When glaring at him had no effect, she finally said, "A Noirre fixation spell of that type, which can be used in volume, has a short shelf life. The spell must be contained in a way that allows Lambert to release it as needed, but he wouldn't have wasted activating it unless he planned on using the spell again within twenty-four hours. Even if you call in VIPER, you still can't prove Lambert took the Noirre spell from Coldfinger *and* you put your teams at risk."

Hellfire, she was right and Devon believed she knew her stuff with spells. He'd love to find out exactly what Joleen *was* and not just because she held an encyclopedic knowledge of black majik details. Nothing about her fit the gutter profile of Dakkar's usual bounty hunters.

Devon snapped his fingers. "That confirms my timeline for the parade tomorrow."

She nodded then pointed at Coldfinger. "That was a message for anyone who tries to cross Lambert. The spell's probably been working about twenty minutes because we've been here half that, and Coldfinger's blood has started congealing."

Devon glanced over his shoulder. "Got what he deserved for dealing Noirre with a troll." He swung his gaze back to her. "Any ideas on how to find Lambert?"

She pondered her answer too long, as if debating once again on how much to share. "He'll likely position himself in a safe place to use the spell. Knowing Lambert, he won't risk being with the other trolls in case something goes wrong or VIPER rolls in."

Devon had to contact Tzader, but without Jo knowing or she might disappear. And beyond needing her help, dammit, he didn't want her to vanish. "Our best use of time is figuring out the most advantageous place for Lambert to release the spell tomorrow morning."

Anyone watching Jo would think she might just be staring off as she processed information, but Devon could feel energy building that had to be coming from her. Energy she worked to keep contained.

What was she? Besides hot and dangerous?

Her lavender-blue eyes fluttered back to life, and that oddly interesting gaze met his. "You know the parade route for tomorrow?"

He lifted his smart phone up for view. "I can pull up everything we need. It starts on Abercorn Street near Forsyth Park."

"Then that's where we start." She walked off and Devon let her lead the way.

What man wouldn't want to follow something that fine?

He also took the opportunity to text Tzader a message. Not much for typing to begin with, Devon just punched in two words. **Call me.**

As one of the stronger telepaths among the Beladors, Tzader could reach across two hundred and fifty miles from Atlanta. His rumbling voice entered Devon's mind. *What's up, Dev?*

Devon didn't have that level of ability, but once Tzader initiated the contact, Devon could respond. *Have a situation we need to handle carefully. A troll got his hands on a Noirre fixation spell.*

How'd that happen?

Devon explained about his investigation to this point. He finished by saying, *Lambert got the spell from Coldfinger.*

You bag the leprechaun?

No. Lambert tested the spell on him.

Joleen glanced back at Devon with a questioning look about his lagging behind. He smiled and held the phone sideways as if busy working on the parade route that he already knew.

She shook her head and kept walking.

Tzader said, *Call me when you contain Lambert. I'll send a team to transport him.*

If only it was that easy. Devon added, *One problem. I'm pretty sure Lambert plans to use the spell during the St. Patrick's Day Parade.*

Why?

Devon went through how the spell functioned, adding, *Got some help from a bounty hunter. She knows her stuff.*

She?

Hellfire. Tzader wouldn't like this. Devon said, *Joleen Mac. What's she doing there?*

This is where things got tricky. Devon wasn't sure how any of this would play out, but he still owed Jo big time and didn't want her marked as a VIPER target for interfering. *Jo was hunting one of the trolls. We intercepted the deal in progress at the same time. She's agreed to help.*

After a brief silence, Tzader said, *I'll bring in every available agent by tomorrow morning.*

That could be risky without knowing where Lambert plans to release the spell. If the team is too close they could be compromised.

We'll stay a hundred yards away. You find Lambert.

The connection died just as Devon reached Abercorn Street.

Jo waited for him on the sidewalk. "Lambert wouldn't be down here on the streets even with a Svart team. He'd be up there." She pointed to the rooftops.

"Then that's where we're headed."

By the time Devon had walked Jo across every rooftop on the parade route, twice, Jo finally agreed with Devon on the best place to expect Lambert to show. They'd passed that spot the last time a mile ago.

The plan was to hunker down on roof of a building next to the one where they expected Lambert.

On the way back, Devon picked up a succulent meal from the Sapphire Grill. Who knew when he'd see the sexy Joleen Mac again? Looked like a good spot for a rooftop picnic. He'd like to also squeeze some information out of her, but pulling gold out of a troll's fist would be easier. And she sounded exhausted from tracking Lambert for two days.

Plus, too many questions might snap the thin commitment of this short-term alliance.

When she finished eating, Jo frowned. "Lambert won't arrive until he's ready to unleash the spell...unless he comes by early to scope the location."

"Sounds right to me." Devon got up and stretched, taking in the city lights coming to life beneath a blanket of darkness. A yellow glow hovered over River Street where tourists and locals would soon be enjoying Savannah's nightlife.

"You got first watch," she ordered and leaned back, closing her eyes, not waiting for his agreement.

He considered settling down beside her to keep watch, but that might end with her waking up in his arms. Which could end in one of two ways—with him finishing that kiss they'd started the last time, or getting his head handed to him.

If he didn't have to watch for a murdering troll, he might just risk it to taste that mouth again.

#

Seven hours later, crowds packed the sidewalks on each side of the parade walk below. For six of those hours, Devon had debated on how he could keep Jo out of danger's way. If he so much as suggested it, she'd laugh in his face.

But that didn't stop the bad feeling creeping up his spine.

Jo stepped up beside Devon, who leaned forward against a chest-high parapet. She looked over the edge to the lower roof of the next building. "You sure about this?"

"Sure about the location or making that thirty-foot leap the minute Lambert shows his ugly mug?"

"The jump." She straightened and faced him. "Or aren't you concerned about breaking both of your legs?"

Did that mean *she* was worried about *him*? He shouldn't be enjoying this, but he liked the possibility that Jo wouldn't like to see him hurt. That'd mean he was right to think she'd enjoyed their kiss as much as he had, but he'd like a refresher kiss to add to his collection of Jo memories.

Since she was waiting on a reply, Devon shrugged. "I can handle that jump."

She must have read something in his face, because she scowled at him. "Is making a death-defying leap another boy thing like kicking in doors?"

Devon lifted his hand slowly and rubbed his knuckles along her cheek. "I won't let you get hurt."

She cocked an eyebrow at him. "I'm not the one in danger of ending up crippled."

"So you can fly?" Would he finally get to see just what kind of power she had?

Ignoring him, she shifted her gaze toward the direction of the approaching crowds.

Marching band music and crowds cheering surged from a distance. The thick of the parade would be right below them in another couple minutes.

"Where's Lambert?" Jo wondered out loud.

"Right here, Jo baby," Lambert said from behind them.

Dammit. Right idea, wrong rooftop.

Devon noted how Jo still leaned her arms on the short wall in front of them, but moved her fingers inside her jacket and slid out a short stick she kept hidden before turning around.

She gave Lambert a disgusted look and warned, "You'd be making a big mistake to use that spell on us."

"That's what Goldfinger said." The glamoured troll produced a glowing pocket watch in one hand, thumb resting against the clasp, ready to pop the cover.

Devon considered their options. Would a field of kinetic power shoved at Lambert do anything against the Noirre majik controlled by that watch? Only one way to find out. He started to lift his hands.

Jo sighed and whispered, "Don't."

Did she have a better tactic? One that would stop the troll from freezing them? Or was this part of her plan to snake her bounty out from under Devon?

Decision time. He wasn't sure he could stop Lambert on his own and his gut said to trust her. He whispered, "Okay. I'll back you up."

Lambert asked, "Any last words, Jo?"

She smiled. "Never assume all opponents are equal."

"They are when I hold this. Admit it. I beat you." Lambert lifted the pocket watch higher.

Devon tensed, fighting the urge to use his kinetics.

Jo moved so quickly Devon barely caught the motion. In the microsecond that Lambert's thumb moved to the clasp release, Jo pointed a pencil-sized length of carved wood at him. It lengthened as she rattled off a chant.

Power met power halfway between Lambert and Jo.

The backlash of energy hit Jo and Devon. He caught her arm just before she'd have flipped over the wall and used his kinetics to shove them forward.

When the power cleared, Lambert stood frozen with a mask of shock.

What the hell? Devon stared at Jo. Wizard? Mage?

Jo walked over to Lambert. "He didn't get a direct hit of the Fixit spell when it backlashed. Might not hold him long."

She pulled a titanium shackle from inside her jacket and snapped it around Lambert's neck.

He roused, muttering, "Bitch."

Devon clubbed the troll with his elbow, knocking the slimy bastard to the ground. Once he clamped a pair of titanium cuffs on Lambert's wrists, Devon smiled, ready to offer Jo a celebration meal.

Then lost his grin.

She held the closed pocket watch that was still loaded with the Noirre spell.

Ah hell. "Don't, Jo. If you freeze me long enough to snatch Lambert, I'll have to report you...oh. Guess I won't remember."

"No, you wouldn't."

With powers like hers, what was a woman like Jo even doing with Dakkar? The answer hit Devon between the eyes. She didn't need money, but she did have to deliver a quota to keep Dakkar happy, which meant Dakkar represented a safe zone.

Jo was hiding from something or someone.

She walked over to Devon, hand extended, offering the watch. "I would never use the dark arts. Just wanted you to know I *could* have."

His chest eased with relief. He took the watch from her and shoved it in his jacket pocket. "Fair enough. Lambert's yours."

Her voice lit with suspicion. "What about VIPER?"

"I contacted Tzader last night."

That narrowed her eyes. "Figures."

He shrugged. "My duty to protect comes first. I'm telling Tzader that you single-handedly got the Noirre spell back and once I had that in hand, your bounty took precedence."

Surprise brightened her exotic gaze. "Why would you...?"

"Not bring in VIPER? Because then I'd have to tell them about your powers." He smiled. "Your secret's safe with me."

Appreciation relaxed the delicate muscles in her face until she paused. "So you're going to let me just walk away with Lambert?"

"Not exactly." Devon stepped closer and slipped his fingers into her hair. He gave her a chance to back off as he lowered his head, but she lifted up and met him half way with a kiss of pure torment. His mouth fit hers as if there were only two in the world that matched.

The longer her kissed her, the more he wanted, but he had to let this one walk away. For now.

His body wouldn't let him forget *that* kiss any time soon.

He plunged in for one last tormenting taste.

Sinfully sweet and without a chance of satisfaction.

She nipped his lip before stepping back, eyes sparking with challenge. "You think giving me Lambert pays off saving your hide from that demon."

"I know better." He didn't want to wipe out that debt too quickly or he might not see her again. "There's always next time."

# # #

The Beladors are part of a powerful coalition of nonhumans who protect humans across the world from supernatural predators, even though humans don't know they exist. You'll meet Devon again in THE CURSE (book 3) and Joleen in future books, but the series is based on the lives of Belador best friends Evalle, Tzader and Quinn.

Currently, there are five books in this *New York Times* bestselling urban fantasy series with more coming in 2015. DEMON STORM (book 5) continues where we left off in RISE OF THE GRYPHON with a major step for Evalle (an Alterant) and Storm (a Skinwalker/Shaman who shifts into a jaguar) that turns out like neither expects, and the Treoir Castle reeling from a brutal attack.

With this being an ongoing story line, it's advisable to read the Belador Series in order:

Blood Trinity
Alterant
The Curse
Rise Of The Gryphon
Demon Storm
***More coming in 2015**

For more on NYT bestseller Dianna Love and the Beladors visit **www.AuthorDiannaLove.com**

AUTHOR NOTE

Thank you for reading the Belador series. I hope you enjoyed DEMON STORM and you'll see more of Evalle, Storm and the Beladors in WITCHLOCK (June 2015). If you did enjoy this book, one of the best things you can do for me and other authors is to leave a review at the online bookstore where you bought it or anywhere else you choose. I really appreciate it any review short or long!

I'd also like to invite you to join my Dianna Love Street Team (Facebook group) where I visit with readers and please sign up for my quarterly newsletter to catch the latest news and be first to know when my next book is being released.

Kindle Readers – You can sign up at "Stay Up To Date" to be informed as soon as I have new release.

Thanks again for reading my books.
Dianna

MORE BOOKS FROM DIANNA LOVE

Belador urban fantasy Series
Blood Trinity
Alterant
The Curse
Rise Of The Gryphon
Demon Storm
Witchlock (June 2015)

Slye Temp romantic thriller Series
Last Chance To Run
Nowhere Safe
Honeymoon To Die For
Kiss The Enemy
Deceptive Treasures
Stolen Vengeance (February 2015)

Micah Caida young adult Trilogy
Time Trap
Time Return
Time Lock

INVISIBLE MAGIC

CHAPTER 1

First demon you summon, it's kind of scary. After a few hundred, it becomes just another job. Unfortunately I hadn't reached that point.

My name's Alex Noziak and I'm one of the five sorry-assed members of a team called the Invisible Recruits that are supposed to stand between the world's humans and the rising population of non-human bad guys. One of the team was here voluntarily, and it wasn't me. But that wasn't my biggest problem right this minute.

Wrestling with an echo-demon that looked mostly like green slime and a smattering of the living dead was.

I'm part shaman, part witch, not a card-carrying Wiccan but a blood-born witch, and one of my abilities was to summon others to me, both human and non-human, but only within a limited range. Sounds useful, but how many times do you really want to invite a Were, or vamp, or foul-mouthed dark angel to a party? Exactly, which was why that particular summoning spell was a little rusty. Okay, a truck that sits on the back forty for twenty years is rusty. I was in the what-the-hell-am-I-doing category.

Embracing magic was not a piece of cake, because it came at a cost. Always. My last summoning here at the IR (I for Invisible and R for Recruits) compound was coming back to bite me now. Sort of like an athlete who was a star performer one day but a dud the next. So now I was more witch-wanna-be who had to produce something, and fast, to keep my spot on the team.

A thought one of my team members actually voiced just about then. "You going to make this demon appear sometime in this millennium, Noziak?" Mandy Reyes snapped, standing kitty-corner from me across the training gym at our Maryland facility.

Mandy had hot Latin blood, a mouth like a stevedore, the patience of a gnat, and was one of the four non-voluntary members of the team. I wasn't sure what was being held over her head to work this gig, but I knew it couldn't be pleasant. I also knew her talent-she was a spirit walker. Which meant she could walk between the spirit world and the real world. Again, sounds cool, but the price for that specific ability was to be soulless. Which meant when you were on the spirit side, or when spirits crossed over or remained on our side, you were an empty vessel with a neon For Rent sign flashing. Any spirit looking for a new home, she was the perfect candidate.

Right now though roving spirits weren't our issue; a missing echo-demon was as four of us maneuvered in a gym that looked like an average high school holding cell. Nothing fancy for our group. Mandy and fellow team members Jaylene Smart and Kelly McAllister formed a triangle around an X-marked-the-spot circle. A circle that was outlined in salt for protection once I called forth the demon as training for taking one down in real life.

Our instructor, M.T. Stone, and our team leader, Vaughn Monroe, the only one of us not coerced into being an IR agent as far as we could tell, were watching this exercise from a room near the rafters. Smart people.

Not that an echo-demon was all that threatening; they were nuisances more than deadly as they had earned their names based on their willingness to make a lot of high-volume screams that could scare the willies out of people and echo in a person's mind long after the demon had departed. At least when the demons traveled alone they were manageable. In packs, they could turn really nasty, really quick.

The intention of this little training session was to make sure I knew what the hell I was doing, which I didn't. Get some practice in whipping demon butt before we left the safety of the compound. And learn to work as a team.

That last was the biggest challenge. None of the five IR members were even trained to fight *human* bad guys yet. We were just humans who had a little extra-extra to our genetic make-up which would make us freaks among humans, *if* the humans knew what we were. The four of us had spent most of our twenty-some years hiding our talents unless we really needed them, like I had when a rogue Were was about to kill my brother.

I had used a summoning spell. That was my first mistake. Second was summoning a death demon who made such a mess of the Were that I faced life in prison for murder. Try telling a lawyer or judge there were extenuating circumstances, like the victim was a Were and my brother was a shifter who was caught turning, which meant he was too vulnerable to defend himself. I was damned lucky I hadn't killed my brother along with the Were.

Yeah, so that's why I was here, sweat pouring down my face, my arms shaking from holding them straight before me for the last thirty minutes and my throat getting hoarse from repeating a summoning spell that wasn't working.

Instead of telling can't-you-do-more Mandy where to shove her comment, I was saved by Kelly. "Leave her be, Mandy. You can tell she's trying."

That was Kelly all over. Raised in the flat farm country of Iowa and a former kindergarten teacher, Kelly could make muggers melt with kindness. She was our team placater, the rah-rah cheerleader and the let's-all-play-nice playground monitor. She'd never said what had landed her here, but it was probably because she had sweet-talked someone to death. Nothing else made sense.

Kelly's ability was to disappear. Which sounds uber cool, but that too came with a price. She could remain truly invisible for only a few minutes at a time and when she reappeared she was blind for twice as long for every minute of invisibility. Which made her really vulnerable to attack if all the bad things were not vanquished. Another downside to her ability was that she wasn't very good with it, so that when she was frightened she could wink out of sight unintentionally.

But then who was I to talk about being proficient?

Kelly stood braced just to my right, and though I couldn't see her except out of the corner of my eye, I could feel her gripping a sword with a white-knuckle death grip. Echo-demons hated metal, as did a lot of the non-humans, so this late afternoon's session was steel vs. demon blood.

If I ever called the freaking monster forth.

I glanced at the observation room window and caught M.T. Stone eyeing his watch. But what did he expect? We were barely three weeks into our regular training and only just started flexing our other abilities earlier this week. That was after one of our fellow recruits tried to kill me and wasn't too picky who else she took out at the same time. About the time, I wondered if prison might not have been the safer option.

Then we'd gone on one official mission, but that was mostly a babysitting session when Vaughn went up against the son of a Russian mob lord-a guy she had known in her previous life as a debutante. It wasn't a picnic, but it wasn't demon baiting either.

Talk about neophytes. Most of us rarely, if ever, voluntarily used our gifts in the world we came from and some, like Jaylene and Mandy, had skills that didn't directly translate into taking down anyone. Jaylene was a psychic, or had visions. A fat lot of good it did to hang out with visions when monsters were out for blood. Human blood. Even I could guess at what the future held in that situation.

M.T. Stone's voice broke over the loudspeaker making all of us jump. "This is a no show. We'll call it a night. Try again tomorrow."

"No," I shouted back. I'd been raised with four older brothers; I could hear M.T.'s tone if not his thoughts. Wimp. Lightweight. Poser. No one called a Noziak a loser and got away with it, even if it was my own inner voice. "Give me one more minute. Let me take this up a notch."

"You sure that's a good idea?" Jaylene asked.

"Yeah." Though I wasn't really.

I heard Mandy and Jaylene groan, which only helped me go deeper. I could do this. I would do this.

Here in this place and before the eyes of the unbelievers, come forth.

I call the creatures of the elements. The seekers of release who wish to walk amongst the humans.

I bid you to destroy the binds holding you in thrall.

Come. Prove yourselves.

Salty sweat seeped into my eyes. I bit my lip till I could taste blood.

Of course! There was no human blood. What an idiot I was. That was the missing piece.

"Jaylene, cut your finger and squeeze a few blood drops into the inner circle," I shouted, holding my pose. This was blood magic, second cousin to black magic, but just a smidge might help. White magic sure wasn't doing squat.

"No way am I cutting myself," came the bullet-fired retort. Jaylene might be six feet tall and built like an Amazon, with looks that could earn her a fortune as a model, but growing up alone on Chicago's south side had made her very wary of sticking her neck or a bloody finger out for anybody.

"I'll do it," Kelly offered and stepped forward.

"No." She'd probably cut a vein with her sword and then disappear on us before we could stop the bleeding. "I'll do it myself."

I dropped my arms, swiping one bare arm across my forehead to wipe the sweat as I reached with the other toward Kelly. "Put your sword out here."

She did as I asked even though the blade shook. It was wicked sharp, the better for demon killing, but instead of a paper cut I dug a pretty deep slash into my right finger. "Ouch."

I swear I could hear Mandy snicker so I shot her a glare, cupping my right hand with my left to make sure I didn't leave a trail of blood for the demon to escape the inner containment circle. Just in case my teammates were not quick enough, or skilled enough to kill him.

That was one of the sucky parts of being the one doing the summoning. I couldn't be holding a weapon of any kind, no matter how deadly the non-human being called. If this echo-demon found a way past the containment area, I was sorry out of luck. Except for my anathema dagger I had stashed against the nearest wall. Noziaks came to a rumble prepared to fight, but witches couldn't carry other weapons when using magic. Which made us very vulnerable.

Using magic with a physical weapon in hand—a gun, knife, staff—meant the magic was not being honored and it could back fire on the user.

It took a few steps to reach the crudely salted circle where the demon should appear, and only seconds to have a nice snack of fresh human blood drops scattered on the floor.

Man, a sliced finger could hurt. Sucking it as I returned to my spot I realized I was focusing on the minor pain to avoid the bigger issue. If the blood did its thing then I was about to break a promise made to my father years ago. He was a full-blooded shaman, a shifter, and a wise man in his own right. Plus he loved me to the depths of his soul. He rarely punished his children, especially me, the baby, but when he did it was serious.

"Great gifts are not given lightly, Alex," he'd said. "They come with great responsibility and consequences. Do you understand?"

I nodded my head like any fifteen-year-old who wanted to get out of immediate trouble for doing something wrong.

"Then you must promise never to use your abilities for harm of anyone or anything."

More head shaking on my part. Right then I'd have agreed to anything he'd asked. That's how much trouble I was in.

"Promise me as a Noziak."

My head had started to bob faster when he'd raised one calloused hand. "And the love you have for me."

That wasn't playing fair. Especially since, after my mother had left us when I was five, my dad had been my whole world.

"Will you promise this, Alex?"

What could I say? I nodded and meant it.

I sucked in my breath, ignoring the throbbing in my finger which I pressed tight against my thumb to make sure the blood flow was stopped. It was harder to push aside the tenseness in my gut, wondering if calling a demon to its death meant I was harming another? Or if my dad would forgive me if he ever found out, because I felt a shift in the air and I wasn't giving up now for anything.

INVISIBLE MAGIC, book 1 of Invisible Recruit series
www.MaryBuckham.com

TIME TRAP

Red Moon Trilogy book 1

Rayen's memory is blank. Her future's in question. Her power is dangerous.

I awoke in an unknown desert landscape that seemed familiar, yet I had no real memory of this place or...who I am. A strange ghost told me my name is Rayen and that I'm seventeen, but he disappeared just as I could have used some help. I was captured along with others my age who said the land was called Albuquerque, then I was dropped at a private school where at times things seem as familiar as the nearby mountain range and as alien as the image of my face. Everyone thinks I'm a Native American runaway, whatever that is, but the school has offered me a place until they learn my true identity, or my memory returns. As if things weren't confusing enough, I end up stuck working with a smart-mouthed computer savvy boy then meet a strange, but gifted, oddball girl, and the three of us discover a secret that threatens the existence of this world - and the future. In the middle of all that, I'm drawn to a seventeen-year-old boy who is as deadly as he is attractive ... and thinks I'm the enemy.

Time Trap – Book 1
Time Return – Book 2
Time Lock – Book 3

Dianna Love and Mary Buckham coauthor as USA Today bestseller Micah Caida, author of the Red Moon sci-fi/fantasy young adult trilogy.

www.MicahCaida.com and **www.RedMoonTrilogy.com**

AUTHOR'S BIO

New York Times bestseller Dianna Love once dangled over a hundred feet in the air to create unusual marketing projects for Fortune 500 companies. She now writes high-octane romantic thrillers, young adult and urban fantasy. Fans of the bestselling Belador urban fantasy series will be thrilled to know Demon Storm (book 5) was released Oct 2014 and Witchlock (book 6) will be available June 2015. Dianna's Slye Temp romantic thriller series launched to rave reviews with five books so far and more coming in 2015. Look for her books in print, e-book and audio. On the rare occasions Dianna is out of her writing cave, she tours the country on her BMW motorcycle searching for new story locations. Dianna lives in the Atlanta, GA area with her husband who is a motorcycle instructor and with a tank full of unruly saltwater critters.

http://www.AuthorDiannaLove.com or Join her Dianna Love Street Team on Facebook and get in on the fun!